THE nascent bloom

BOOK 1

caught

Books by Evie Kelley

My Bicentennial
A Mostly True Tale of the Far-Out '70s

The Nascent Bloom
A Young Adult Science fiction Suspense Series
The Nascent Bloom Book 1: Caught
The Nascent Bloom Book 2: Running
The Nascent Bloom Book 3: Home

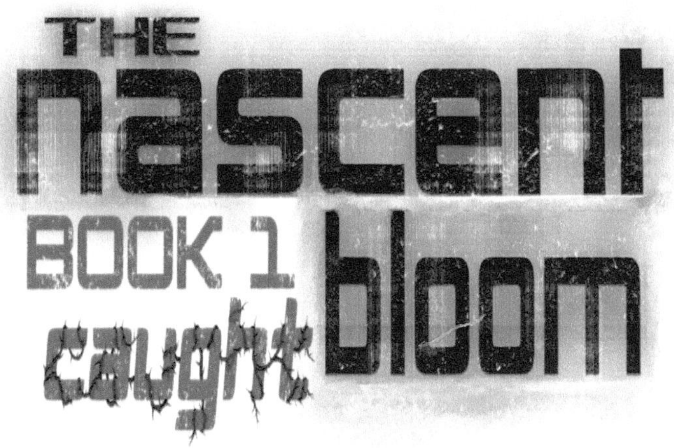

EVIE KELLEY

Great Brook Publishing

ISBN 978-1-968928-04-9 (Paperback)

ISBN 978-1-968928-05-6 (E-book)

Cover design and interior illustrations by Hannah Hill

THE NASCENT BLOOM Book 1 Caught Awards:

Young Adult Romance Writers of America *Rosemary Award* Winner

Killer Nashville *Claymore Award* Finalist and Top Pick

Romance Writers of America *Golden Heart* Award Finalist

Dedication

To Jenny Applegate, who believed in this book long before I did

Chapter 1

Kai

"Hsst, Kai," Hesk calls from the corner where he's on lookout. "Hurry lad, there's lawkeepers a block away."

I slap paint onto the door, smearing it over *Habeni Corporate Council Headquarters* in the rough shape of a flower petal. It looks more like a purple-yellow blob than a nascent bloom surrounded by thorns, but it'll do. I've got to go, or my first time tagging Habeni property for the resistance will be my last.

Hesk tears past me into the night. I toss the brush and take off after him, accidentally kicking over a paint can. Bright yellow splatters across the sidewalk. I wince. No way is any smug Habeni going to clean up the mess. They'll force a Matalan, one of my people, to do it. While their so-called betters howl at them to hurry the job.

No time for regrets. I run harder.

"Having fun, my boy?" Hesk yells back over his shoulder.

A glance behind me and I see three Habeni lawkeepers in armored black uniforms racing up the sidewalk, getting closer. Light glints off their helmets and their long-barreled silver weapons.

Yeah. *Fun.*

I pour on the speed, desperate to get out of range. The lawkeepers shout for us to stop. I wonder if that command ever works.

We reach the Osch River. The waterway slices the city in half as cleanly as a knife, the posh Habeni estates and businesses on this side, the shanties and stench of the Matalan sector—my home—on the other. A crisp spring wind whips off the water, which reflects the violet glow of the rising moons. Overhead, low-grav transports whoosh by buildings that poke up into the sky like uneven teeth. Surface vehicles wind along the river road.

Hesk gives me a nod and we separate. My hobnail boots pound the pavement as I run east toward the Condati City Spaceport. Two lawkeepers follow Hesk, only one comes after me. I thank the gods for my luck.

I round a corner and dive into a dimly lit alley between two brick buildings. A tick later, my pursuer dashes past the alley opening. I've got to hurry. There's not much time before he figures out where I went and comes back.

Struggling to slow my breathing and my thundering heart, I peel off my gloves and hooded black coveralls. Now I'm in the gear they make all Matalan males wear, rough wool tan tunic and trousers. I lift the lid of one of the refuse bins lining the alley, releasing a host of garbage smells, and stuff the coveralls and gloves deep down inside.

I wipe my sweaty forehead with my sleeve and flatten my mop of red hair the best I can then snatch up a small wooden crate I'd stashed by the bins earlier in case I needed it. Clutching the crate, I walk toward the other end of the alley as the lawkeeper returns.

"You there. Halt!" he shouts.

I do.

"Turn around and face me. Slowly."

I do that too.

He steps close enough for me to catch the scent of something spicy he ate for dinner, not so close I can get hold of him. Not that I would, though I'm much bigger and likely stronger than this scrawny fellow. Younger too. I'm eighteen, he's old, maybe forty. I could take him. I'm itching to drop the crate and prove it, but that would be suicide. I have to comply with whatever he demands without a peep.

It's the law.

My gaze drops to the magshot he clutches in his hand. And if I should forget the law, he has the right to use that weapon to remind me. The magshot looks delicate, with its long, thin barrel and narrow grip, but its sting is deadly. Its burst of juice will fry a body's guts from the inside out. Too many Matalans have found that out the hard way.

That's why I took up with the resistance. Why I volunteered to paint a nascent bloom, our symbol of defiance, on the front door of the most powerful Habeni in the land.

To fight that weapon. And the authority behind it.

The lawkeeper unclips a torch from his utility belt with his free hand and thumbs a switch. Light blares into my eyes. I pray there's no paint specks on my face.

"Where you headed, Mucker?" he demands, spitting the Habeni slur for my people like a curse.

"Spaceport, sir." Careful not to move too fast, I swivel slightly and jerk my chin toward the opening at the alley's other end, and the towering building beyond, across the street. Its metal façade gleams in the moonslight.

His bushy, straw-colored eyebrows scrunch in suspicion. "What for?"

"They run out of pickled clewfish at the launch party. Sent me out to fetch more. Velten Academy's senior class is flying out tonight on a trip to Aine, you know, and they're having a big send-off." I add that as if it's the most important fact in the history of facts.

He snorts. "I didn't ask for your life story."

He skims his light over me, lingering on my hands, looking for paint I figure. He shifts and directs the beam up the alley, flashing over the refuse bins. It's cool here between the buildings but I'm drenched with sweat. If he looks inside the barrels and finds my paint-splattered coveralls and gloves, I'm cooked.

After what seems like days, his light comes back to me and centers on the crate I'm holding. "Open it."

I lift the lid. His grip tightens on his magshot as he leans closer and cranes his neck to peer into the box. The clewfish is two days old and smells like it, but it still cost plenty to get my hands on a batch. The stuff turns my stomach, even without the rancid stink, but the Habeni upper crust loves it.

The lawkeeper pushes several of the curly-tailed silver fish aside with his torch, hunting for I don't know what, but finding only more clewfish underneath.

He grunts and clicks off the light. "All right, beat it," he orders. Then he's gone.

I don't relax as I hustle down the alley. I half lied to the lawkeeper. I'm headed to the spaceport, but not to serve this foul fish at the launch party for Velten Academy's senior class trip. I'll be going on that trip. *If* I can evade the law long enough to board the school's spaceship with the rest of my classmates.

Classmates.

That's a laugh. I'm nowhere near equal to them. Matalans are only allowed to attend Velten if we agree to work in exchange for lessons. It's been ten times more work than lessons for me for four years now, but the lessons they do allow I gobble down whole.

More work for me and the other servants on this trip, too, but at least the journey will take me off planet long enough for what Hesk and I did to die down. Or the resistance's next defiant act catches the law's attention.

And there's one thing to look forward to. The only Habeni I can tolerate, a certain feisty redhead, will be there. Perhaps we'll have the chance to talk. Or be alone together.

An unwelcome warmth shoots through me at the thought. I suppress it.

Meili Bengough is one of *them*. The people who've lorded it over mine for generations, the people who've forgotten we were once akin. The people who see the small differences, the color of our hair and eyes, as proof of their superiority. Meili may have taken a shot at Habeni pride with her recent—and surprising—act of defiance, but that doesn't mean she's thrown in with the Matalan cause. She's still one of them.

She's still my enemy.

The sooner I remember that, the better.

I reach the end of the alley and pause at the opening to do a recon. The spaceport building, thirty-eight stories of gleaming steel, takes up nearly the whole block. Lights flash outside the launch bay doors that ring the top floor. Launch Bay Six is my destination.

The street I have to cross is broad, clogged with surface vehicles rumbling along the pavement. Pedestrians throng the sidewalk.

So do lawkeepers.

"Dageth's balls."

A pack of those peigus converge on the corner, near the service entrance. Maybe they're on the hunt for a resistance tagger on the run, maybe just looking for Matalans to rough up. No matter, I don't have much time. I've got to get over there.

I grip the crate tighter and dodge traffic as I cross the street then move slowly but steadily down the sidewalk toward the corner. I adopt a cool expression but my insides roil as I near the lawkeepers. I'm so close I hear the low roll of their voices and smell the electricity spitting from the barrels of their idle magshots.

"Hold up," one of them says as I try to sidle around them.

My gut turns to lead. I'm desperate to keep moving but I know I can't. Disobeying a lawkeeper's order is asking for trouble. I stop and brace for arrest, or worse. Sometimes obeying an order is asking for trouble, too.

He steps closer. His body odor is rank and I force myself not to flinch. His keen, yellow-gold eyes bore into me. My heart thunders and I clutch the crate so tight I'm sure the wood will splinter.

"Is that a box of shit?" He points with his weapon and sniffs theatrically. "Or is that your Mucker stench I smell?"

He laughs. A long, self-satisfied guffaw. I yearn to pummel him. The others laugh too, and, though it kills me inside, so do I. I grin and nod like a slupa then bolt around the corner before things can turn ugly.

At the service entrance, I toss the crate. My hands shake and I have trouble gripping the door handle. Dread rushes up my spine. I fear the lawkeepers are creeping up behind me but don't risk looking back to find out for sure. I somehow manage to get the door open and dart into the building. No one follows.

I snatch up my travel satchel from a corner where I stowed it earlier and stab the button for the freight elevator. It's the only elevator a Matalan's allowed to take, unless I want to walk a thousand steps up to the top floor. I hit the button again and again until finally the elevator arrives and the doors *shuff* open.

I step inside. My heartbeat slows, returning to normal. I allow myself a grin at my success. But it's only when the doors close and the elevator lurches upward that I'm able to breathe again.

Chapter 2

Meili

"Tell me you're joking." My shocked gaze bounces between my mother and father. "Tell me you are *not* serious."

"We are serious," Mother chides. "You're to join with Ullr Notal this summer. Your father and Ullr's father agreed on the contract terms last night. Isn't that right, Lex?" She looks at Father expectantly.

He clears his throat. A delaying tactic he always employs before delivering bad news. "You'll need to sign the contract, of course, but the details, your dowry, Ullr's family's rise in status after you two are joined, and other incentives have already been worked out."

Anger and hurt clog my throat. One detail Father forgot—to tell me. "But I barely know Ullr. We haven't spoken more than twice at school."

Mother dismisses that with a wave. "I didn't know your father when our alliance was struck. You'll get to know him. Your trip will last a week, that's plenty of time."

I search for Ullr and find him standing with his parents near our school's interplanetary transport. The *Whittal* bobs in its dock, chuffing out oily-smelling exhaust as the spaceship powers up for our journey. Ullr has straight, yellow hair and pale amber eyes, as do most Habeni, and he's dressed in his Velten Academy uniform like the rest of our class. The only thing that sets him apart from the other lads is his spiky mustache.

I shiver. If I sign that contract, we'll be joined. I'll be his. Forever. "What if I discover I don't like him?"

Mother releases a gusty sigh and looks to Father again.

"You'll *learn* to like him, Meili," he says. Weakly. If he can't convince himself, how does he expect to convince me? "I know it's a lot to take in, but you'll understand in time and accept the match. You'll see."

"But... don't I have *any* say in the matter?"

"Lower your voice," Mother says.

Her gaze sweeps the room, but I doubt any of my classmates or their family members here for the launch party heard. They're too busy chatting, sipping champagne and nibbling on buckleberries, pickled clewfish, and other Habeni delicacies to pay attention to our family drama.

"Consider yourself lucky the Notals will have you at all," Mother continues in an angry half-whisper. "We would've preferred an alliance with a top-status family, but they won't have anything to do with you, after what you did."

I lift my chin. She acts like I've committed a crime, when all I did was stop bleaching my hair. I have red hair, and everyone knows it. Why turn my hair to straw trying to be as fair-haired as all the other Habeni, when people already know I'm different? I'll be teased and mocked, no matter what. Three weeks ago I decided I'd had enough. I found a hair dye close to my natural color and dyed every last strand a silky, pinkish red.

"Ullr's your only chance, Meili." Mother shifts her tone to coaxing. "Unless you prefer to live a life unjoined?"

This is her main line of attack. An effective one. There's no worse fate for a Habeni woman. Unjoined means without status. Unloved. Unjoined ladies are never seen in society, not at balls or parties or in the shops. Is that the future I want? Stuck at home forever, with only my parents and our servants for company?

"Majj, leave her be," Father says, stern now. "It's done. The deal is struck. Give her time to adjust."

She sniffs but doesn't argue. That'll come tonight, when they're alone. I've heard the angry words through the walls. Mother blaming Father's ancestors for the inferior gene that made me sprout hair as red as a Matalan's, Father denying it over and over. An alliance between a Matalan and a Habeni is illegal. A child born of that union is a *neb*, shunned even more than an unjoined woman. Father has always insisted my hair color is a fluke. No one in our family has *ever* broken the law, he says, and I've believed him.

Until now, when even he seems to think my hair matters, the way he's pushing me into this alliance.

Our chaperone, Mr. Kirl, bounds up the *Whittal's* carpeted ramp to the front hatch. "Are you enjoying yourselves?" he calls and a muted cheer rings out. "It's time to set out on our journey." Another cheer, heartier this time. "Line up, students, and we'll get this ship in the air."

An excited buzz fills the room as everyone says their farewells. I look toward Ullr again. He hugs his mother goodbye, but his eyes are on me. He seems a fine fellow, but what if he's not? What if he's the type to go on about how lucky I am he agreed to join with me, as Mother does with Father? What if Ullr and I become them?

Mother's lips brush my cheek in goodbye. Father draws me into a hug that nearly suffocates me. "Be careful," he says, a pleading note in his voice. "And don't worry."

That makes me worry more, and so does his hug. He never displays such brazen affection, even when we're alone. I watch him and Mother join the other guests heading toward the commuter craft docking bay, my emotions in a knot.

A petite Matalan woman appears at my elbow. Taryn, my minna, a sort of nanny and governess rolled into one compact package. Silvery strands lace through her dark red hair and the sweet scent of a fresh nascent bloom clings to her ankle-length blue gown.

"Taryn, what should I do?" I know she's heard everything. She's been with me my whole life and is always at my side.

"You know what you must do." Her voice is small, like a songbird's, masking the steel beneath. "I know you don't like it. I don't like it either, but you must do as your father wishes. It's your duty." She touches my hand, the barest squeeze. "Sometimes we can't do what we want. We must do as we're told."

I gaze into her emerald-green eyes. When I was young, I thought she knew everything. Thought she had all the answers too. This is one answer I don't want to hear.

"I guess," I mutter. "But I don't have to like it."

A fond smile touches her lips. "You've always kicked, love. I don't expect you to change." She hands me my rucksack. "Go get in line. Try to enjoy yourself and try not to fret."

I shuffle toward the ship, determined to fret the whole way to Aine and back again. I'm in such a daze I nearly collide with Kai, one of the Matalans allowed to work at our school in exchange for lessons. A fair bargain, Mother says, since most Matalans don't enjoy their own schools and quit to find work at a young age.

I assume he wants my bag, but he doesn't reach for it. He just… scowls.

"Yes? Is something wrong?" I ask, rattled. He stares at me as if there's a large insect crawling across my face and he's desperate to swat it. "You may speak."

He does. With a ferocity that takes my breath away. "If I was you, I'd tell them where to stuff that joining contract."

I blink in surprise. I don't know what shocks me more, Kai's brashness or that he openly admits to eavesdropping.

No. What shocks me is the way my belly flip-flops as he steps closer. Close enough to catch his scent, musky and a bit like clewfish. He's tall and broad, with thick, tangled, copper-red hair that brushes his collar, and a face as solid and defiant as his expression—square jaw thrust out, wide nose stuck firmly in my business, and eyes as bright and green as a forest glimmering in the morning sun.

Annoyance, that's what this flustered feeling must be, what's making my pulse race and heat tickle my skin. I *should* be annoyed. Kai's a senior, like me, and has been at school for years, but I've had little contact with him. Now here he is, so near, gazing at me in such an unsettling way.

"You don't understand," I snap. "I've got to do my duty. I must do what's expected of someone in my position."

"No, you don't." His voice rumbles with urgency. "You don't have to do what they tell you. You have a choice. You can say no."

I must get away. I don't like the way those piercing eyes make me feel. I don't like the ideas he's trying to push into my head, either. "Well, that's your opinion, for whatever that's worth. Is there anything else you'd like to give me advice about before we leave?"

Kai's gaze shifts to my hair. I don't see scorn or derision in his expression as I do when a Habeni looks at me. I see disappointment. I don't know why that should bother me, but it does.

"You're right, my lady." His voice turns mocking, almost angry. "My opinion's not worth a ha'penny to someone in *your* position. Just thought you might stand up and not let them push you around."

My cheeks burn. Is he calling me a coward? Suddenly I'm glad I've never had much contact with Kai at school. He's the most impertinent Matalan I've ever met.

I shove my rucksack at him and dart to the ship. I take my place in line, in the middle as befits my status. He scowls at me as I inch up the ramp. I scowl back.

Changing my hair seems a small act of defiance compared to willfully scuttling an alliance. To intentionally choose to be unjoined. Surely Father would be furious if I refuse to sign the contract. His anger would pale in comparison to Mother's. Even Taryn thinks I should agree to the match. Everyone thinks so.

Everyone except one bold Matalan with more opinions than sense.

And me.

Chattering voices and the smell of warm bodies and circulated air greet me as I enter the ship. I follow my friend Gwynn down the broad aisle, past plush seats facing each other the length of the cabin. Gwynn scoots into her seat at the middle of the transport and pats the cushion for me to join her. As if I'd sit anywhere else. Our seats are assigned according to status, males and females on opposite sides.

I flop down with zero elegance. Ullr glances at me as he passes on his way to his seat at the rear of the ship. I firmly ignore him and buckle my safety straps, prepping for liftoff when all I really want to do is find an airlock to shoot myself out of.

We soon level off and enter the channel, the travel stream between the planets in this sector. We'll fly all night and reach the resort moon of Aine late tomorrow morning. A bell dings and we're free to get up. A Matalan who's about seventeen and has long, ginger hair tied back by a black bow, begins to move up the aisle, bringing us our rucksacks. Gwynn thanks her with a shy smile.

"That's Ayva. She's Kai's sister," she says after Ayva passes, as if this is news. The resemblance is obvious, minus the scowling. Gwynn turns back to me and her eyebrows lift in curiosity. "And speaking of Kai, what in the worlds were you two arguing about back at the spaceport?"

I cringe to think of the spectacle I must have made of myself, but I tell her everything. She's less shocked about Kai's eavesdropping than the dubious good news of my impending joining.

As soon as the Matalan servants finish loading our gear and board, our chaperone Mr. Kirl seals the hatches and sets the auto-flight controls. The hiss of pressurization fills the cabin and my ears pop. The engines under our feet pulse as the *Whittal* shimmies forward out of its dock. A moment of hesitation follows, as if the ship is deciding whether to stay or go, then it rockets upward with a roar. My belly falls out of my body. Feels like it, anyway. I doubt I'll ever get used to spaceflight.

"Ullr? He's nice, but dull. You don't seem suited. You're too lively for him. Are you going to accept the offer?"

I lift a shoulder.

"But you don't love him."

"Does that matter?"

Gwynn's gaze darts to the back of the ship and pink circles dot her cheeks. "Meili, that's the *only* thing that matters."

Fondness surges in my breast. Gwynn's the model of Habeni perfection, tall, slim, sweet disposition, and sunshine-gold hair that falls to her waist. She's already rejected four offers. She'll have more suitors. Her alliance will be based on love. Not because someone agrees to sign a contract.

I sag in defeat. "Mother says Ullr's my only chance."

Gwynn seems about to argue the point, then switches topics and we talk of trivial things—our new designer boots, the sweeping vistas we'll see on Aine, and the gem caves we'll explore searching for a souvenir diamond or ruby.

Soon, she yawns, nestles back against the cushion and nods off. Most of the others sleep too, including Mr. Kirl. He slumps in the plushest of plush seats up front with my top-status classmates, Agron and Varina.

I pick up my com-pad and try to read but I can't concentrate, not with Ullr down there in the seat next to last. He's twiddling his mustache, staring at nothing. I can't imagine being joined to him. Touching him, kissing him or... anything else. My cheeks heat with discomfort.

I feel someone's eyes on me. It's Kai, sitting on a bench beyond Ullr, next to the lav.

We lock gazes and my face burns ten times hotter. My belly flutters and tingles dance along my spine. I've never encountered anyone whose very presence could make me feel so... annoyed. Why won't he mind his own business and go to sleep like the other servants squeezed beside him on their bench?

I shoot him a withering look Mother taught me and go back to my com-pad, determined this time to concentrate.

A few ticks later, a game of cuttleball breaks out. Most of my male classmates spill into the aisle. Even snooty Agron Osch deigns to join in. Shouts ring out and boots thump along the carpet as the players race up and down the ship's aisle, tossing the ball. The noise wakes Gwynn, the Matalans, and everyone else, except Mr. Kirl.

Agron dashes to the back of the ship and reaches to catch the ball, but he trips over one of the servants and splats onto his bottom. Agron is number one in status, so nobody dares laugh at him, but I hide a smile behind my hand.

Agron jumps to his feet and glares at the person he tripped over. "Watch your big feet, Mucker."

The offender, a boy with feet no bigger than a bobnut, jerks them up as if he's afraid Agron's going to cut them off.

"What's wrong with you?" Agron snarls. "Look at me when I speak to you."

"Leave him alone."

I gape but shouldn't be surprised to hear Kai speak up.

Agron turns his glare on Kai. "*What* did you say to me?"

Kai stands. They're both the same age, eighteen, but Kai's a full head taller. He stares down at Agron, who flinches but holds his ground. Everyone swings their attention to the back of the ship.

"I said leave the lad alone. Pick on someone your own size."

A gasp ripples through the ship, me included. Kai mouthing off to a mid-status Habeni like me is one thing, butting up against someone as important and well-connected as Agron is another.

Agron eyes Kai like he's an insect he longs to squash, then his gaze hits on something on the floor. Gwynn and I stand up for a better view, and I see Agron kick a battered leather satchel by Kai's feet.

"What's this?" Agron asks.

Kai tries to push the bag under the bench with his boot heel, but Agron snatches it up and rips it open. He yanks out three old-fashioned printed books with worn bindings. One has a nascent bloom etched onto the cover. I recognize the flower's distinctive violet and yellow petals. Another book has *Poetry* written in faded letters on the spine.

"A Mucker who can read?" Agron flings the books to the floor with such force the poetry book's binding splits. "I don't believe it. You don't have the brains to know your own name."

Varina Meade hurries down the aisle to stand next to Gwynn and me. She's the top-status female in class and also the shortest. She has to hike up to tiptoes to get a clear look at Agron, who she's been contracted to join with for more than a year.

"Agron's goading him," she says, chewing a fingernail, her eyes glittering in anticipation. Varina wants a fight. I look around. Everyone does, except me. I want Kai to ignore Agron and sit down. What little I know of this bold Matalan, I doubt he will.

Agron's gaze skims the other servants cringing on the bench. Rost, a beefy lad of sixteen, a boy and girl of about ten, twins, I think, and then he fixes his attention on Kai's sister Ayva.

"Who are you, lovely thing?" His voice is like silk.

Ayva shrinks as if trying to disappear. Kai straightens. A small move, but he seems even taller, more menacing. Agron smirks, knowing he's hit his target.

"By the gods, you're the tastiest morsel I've ever clapped eyes on." Agron reaches for an auburn curl nestled against Ayva's neck.

A flash and Kai's hand locks around Agron's wrist. The air seems to go out of the cabin. No one speaks. No sound, except for the engines' hum and Mr. Kirl's snores. Agron and Kai are whisper close. The other males close ranks around them. My heart thuds. Surely Kai knows the stakes if he strikes a Habeni. He'll go to jail for a long time. It's the law.

"Let go." Agron's voice is ice cold.

Kai does, with a shove. "You best walk away." His voice holds a dark threat. His tunic clings to arms and chest made solid through hard work. I fear he'll follow his threat with real violence.

Agron snorts. He's strong, trained in the defensive arts as we all are, though my skills are so poor everyone laughs at me, even our instructor. "Certainly I'll walk away." He reaches for Ayva. "With this pretty bit—"

Kai punches Agron in the face. A crack of knuckles full on, and Agron's nose snaps. A satisfying sound, I'm ashamed to admit.

Blood spurts, speckling Agron's uniform shirt. He drags the back of his hand across his mouth and stares at the blood, dumbfounded.

I flash to Mr. Kirl. He hasn't stirred, not one muscle.

"Kill the Mucker," Dipro roars. The others echo his cry, pressing in. Ullr too. My heart squeezes at the feral way he looks at Kai. Agron, rigid with fury, clenches his fists. The Matalans on the bench tremble. Ayva sobs. Kai braces, his breathing ragged.

This is *madness*. The lawkeepers will arrest Kai as soon as we return. His family will lose privileges and he'll go to jail. Penalty enough for breaking the law. He doesn't deserve a bloody beating too, simply for trying to protect his sister.

And what do I do? Nothing. I just stand there and watch like everyone else. Too scared to speak up, too frightened to move. Kai was right.

I am a coward.

Suddenly, the ship lurches. I teeter, trying to keep my balance. People shout in alarm, the fight instantly forgotten.

The ship rocks again. Harder, as if it's a toy shaken in a hound's mouth. Everyone not buckled in whips about. Varina falls. Agron, Kai, Ullr and the others topple like trees in a forest felled all at once. I bang to the floor. My palms scrape the carpet. The acrid smell of fuel oil and exhaust stings my nose.

A muffled boom sounds from above. Everyone freezes where they fell. Hushed. Listening.

The cabin lights flicker. Something thumps against the hull. Four hydraulic clicks, followed by *tick, tick, tick* from the cockpit auto-flight controls in the nose cone. The ship jerks left, as if yanked into some sort of hold. The engines sputter. The lights flicker again. The engines grind to a stop. The ship lists drunkenly, floating adrift.

Then, silence, except for Mr. Kirl's steady, unnatural snores.

A warning light up front pops on. *Hull Breech.* Alarms bleat. Screams and terrified shrieks break the silence, filling the cabin.

Gwynn helps me off the floor. "We're cooked," she cries.

I drop into my seat, quaking in terror. "It's a glitch. Someone will fix it." I focus on Kai. He's back on the bench, one arm around his sister, the other reaching for the twins. He'll fix it. He fixes things at school. Surely he'll know how.

Metal scrapes metal. A *whirr* scratches against the front hatch. Gwynn's fingers dig into my arm. An angry hiss comes from the door. Panic grips me. Our oxygen's escaping into space. No, wait. It's the cabin depressurizing. The whirr is from a drill, loosening the hatch's rivets one by one.

Not very reassuring. Who's out there?

Blix scuttles down the ladder from the observation deck above, where he's been studying the stars since we set out. He falls into his seat across the aisle, trembling as much as I am. He gapes at me.

"What is it, Blix? What did you see?" I shout to be heard over the chaos in the cabin.

He whips his head to look toward the front. "They must be operating remotely. That's how they stopped the engines." His voice wobbles in fear. "They did it from their ship as they came alongside. How did they get the access codes?"

His fear doubles my own. My teeth chatter. "Who? What're you talking about?"

The whirr at the hatch becomes a whine. The stench of hot metal burns my throat. The hiss grows louder as the atmo seal slackens. The hatch will open in two ticks.

"Them." Blix looks back at me, horrified. "*Pirates.*"

The lights flicker a third time, then go out.

CHAPTER 3

Meili

PIRATES.

The word spreads through the dark cabin in fearful whispers. Everything I've ever heard about the Adsullatan pirates chases all rational thought from my mind. Horrific tales of space travelers waylaid, beaten, robbed. Other travelers snatched off their ships and funneled into bound servitude in the troci markets. Sent to toil in the most ghastly conditions. Never to be seen again.

The emergency lights pop on.

Varina scrambles up off the floor. "It *can't* be pirates. There's a treaty in place. They're not allowed to catch any Habeni." Her voice squeaks in terror. I'm just as frightened. Maybe more.

The buzz of the drill digging into metal intensifies. The hatch gives way and the atmo seal breaks with a final, sad hiss. I watch the door swing open, barely able to breathe. Four burly figures in black coveralls stomp into the ship. They wear colorful head scarves, their faces grotesque. A scream bubbles in my throat. Then I realize they're wearing masks painted with angry scars and sharp fangs designed to terrorize. More than effective. I fear I'll wet my frillies.

"Stay where you are," one of them hollers.

For a moment, everyone does. We freeze in... Fear is too light a word. Petrified is more like it. Wide-eyed with terror and too scared to move. Then something snaps and there's a stampede for the back of the ship.

I join the shrieking mob stumbling over scattered com-pads and rucksacks. The servants are plucked off their bench and squeezed like paste from a tube, propelled in the opposite direction to make room for us at the rear hatch. Several people hurl themselves against the door, desperate to break the seal and force it open.

Z-z-zap.

My scalp tingles and heat sizzles over my head as a pirate blasts a hole in the lav wall. Bits of scorched plastic flutter down like black snow. We instantly halt and our panicked screams hush. The pirate who fired the shot steps forward.

"Where do you peigus think you're going?" The mask muffles his voice, but I'm shocked to hear him speak Habeni. "Sit down." No one moves. He brandishes a thin, silver weapon with a long barrel. His hand curls around the grip, his finger twitches over the trigger button. "Don't test me. If I fire again, it won't be at the wall. You all know what a magshot can do."

A frightened murmur of recognition bubbles through the ship. Magshots are weapons used by our lawkeepers to protect us. They work on some kind of current that burns a person's insides.

"I see you get my meaning." The pirate lowers the weapon. "Now, sit down."

A gruesome game of musical chairs ensues as we jostle for a seat. I'm shoved forward, ending up with Gwynn next to Mr. Kirl at the front. How can he still be asleep?

"Thank you," the pirate says when we're seated, polite and sarcastic at the same time. "I'm Captain Tura of the *Kestral*. I regret to inform you that your ship has strayed into Adsullatan space. This violates the treaty of Malkin, settled between the planets of this sector two-score years ago."

Blix, on my right, stiffens. "We're nowhere near Adsullatan territory," he whispers. "The autopilot was on the programmed course. I examined the charts three times since we left Condati City."

I don't encourage him to debate this point with the pirate.

"According to the treaty's terms, you must pay a forfeit for your crime." Captain Tura jerks his head and the other pirates begin to walk up and down the aisle.

Voices raise in alarm and indignation. Down the aisle and across from me, Varina is clinging to Agron. She loosens her grip to clap a hand over her array of necklaces. "You're not taking my sparklers," she cries.

The pirates don't grab jewels or baubles, they simply look. At us. A foul-smelling pirate stops in front of me. The mask's not as scary up close, but I shudder when I look into his eyes. Not real eyes. Mesh circles that softly whirr as a mechanical iris opens and closes, as if cataloguing me. He studies Gwynn then pokes Mr. Kirl with his magshot. Mr. Kirl doesn't twitch. The pirate snickers and moves on.

"Meili, look." Gwynn lifts our chaperone's arm. It flops to his lap when she lets go.

My belly tightens. Has he been drugged? What are the pirates looking for? The foul-smelling one approaches the Matalans. They huddle together, sinking into luxurious cushions. Kai's on one end, Rost the other, like bookends shielding Ayva and the twins between them.

The pirate stops in front of Kai. "Get up," he says in accented Habeni.

Kai straightens and thrusts out his chest. "I will not."

Gods and goddesses he's brave. Not exactly smart, but brave.

The pirate growls, clearly not used to being disobeyed. He yanks Kai up by his tunic's collar. They're nose to mask. "Anyt'ing to say now, scum?"

"Yeah." Kai brushes off Ayva, who tugs at his trouser leg in frantic warning. "You smell like a dead hoacta."

I shrivel. Kai's going to die.

"Let him go, Wilf." Captain Tura boots a rucksack out of his path and strides up to them. Wilf does as ordered and the captain studies Kai, his mask's mechanical eyes whirring. "Kai ObDen. Residing at 26 Pickett Lane, Matalan district, Condati City." He recites as if he's reading data from a file. "This is you, boy?"

Kai finally has enough sense to keep his mouth shut and simply nods. Tura straightens Kai's collar then runs a gloved hand over his tunic, speckled with Agron's blood. Tura says something in Matalan. I know only a snippet of the ancient language, but I think he says *you have a fierce heart*. The captain sounds as if he's smiling under the mask.

"You'll bring me a goodly sum at the troci market," he continues in Habeni, then steps back and nods to the pirate he called Wilf. "Take him. Take all the Matalans."

Kai bolts. Or tries to.

Wilf grabs him. Kai kicks and the pirate gets a hobnail boot dangerously close to his groin. Wilf bellows for help. The other pirates race over and seize Kai's arms and legs, lifting him. He twists and strains to break free. They lose their grip and Kai bangs to the floor. Wilf yanks his weapon out of its sling. Ayva wails and I want to echo her cries. A sickening crack of metal on bone bursts through the cabin as Wilf cuffs Kai's face with the magshot's barrel. I wince, though strangely relieved Wilf didn't scorch him with the weapon.

Barely weakened from the blow, Kai cusses and struggles as the pirates drag him down the aisle. His tunic sleeves ride up, revealing an ink design etched on his upper left arm. A nascent bloom, like on Kai's book, five broad, hearty petals the color of an angry purple sky, streaked with yellow. The flower seems to burst out of a bed of thorns. It's illegal for a Matalan to sport body ink, but I'm not surprised Kai has such a thing carved into his skin. He seems to thrive on defiance.

He spears me with a desperate look as he's hauled past, as if pleading for my help. I don't move. I can't move. I don't possess even a whisper of his courage. All I can do is watch, frozen in fear, as the pirates and Kai disappear into the apparatus that joins the two ships.

"Good riddance, Mucker filth," rings out the moment they're gone.

The captain cocks his head then steps toward the speaker. "Agron Osch," he says, after studying him a tick. "Son of Noel Osch, head of the Habeni World Council and chief of Osch Industries. Manufacturer of military transports, armor, and this beautiful weapon."

Tura holds up the magshot, sounding as if he'd like to kiss it. Maybe he would if he wasn't wearing that mask.

Agron returns a haughty glare that's less than effective with his bruised, blood-caked nose. "Correct on all counts but one, pirate." The scared wobble in his voice undercuts his disdain. "Father also owns the security fleet that patrols the channel, so you better run before you're caught."

Tura laughs. "Oh, I doubt that." He taps the magshot to the tip of Agron's swollen nose, making him wince. "How'd you get this cracked snout? That Matalan do it?" He sounds pleased. "Yes, I think he did. You're an opinionated Habbie, and that's no soap. Probably deserved it."

He laughs again then turns back to the remaining servants. He gestures with his weapon toward the hatch. After a moment's hesitation, Ayva turns to the girl next to her, takes her hand, and they march down the aisle. The girl's twin and Rost follow, with the last pirate trailing them. Only Captain Tura remains.

"That wasn't so bad, was it?" he says, ambling up the aisle. "Ladies and gentlemales, I thank you for your time. You're free to go on your way."

Relief floods me. The pirates only want the Matalans. A few people titter nervously. Others talk in excited whispers. At the front of the ship, Tura opens the cockpit control panel and taps several buttons. Resetting our course, I think. Then he steps to the hatch.

He stops. Turns back. Conversation falters. Fear blooms anew in my chest.

"Oh, there *is* one more thing." His voice is no longer kind. It's a sly purr that causes my belly to cramp. "I need to send your people a warning not to stray into our space again."

His creepy mechanical eyes hum as he strolls up the aisle, scanning us. I cringe as his scrutiny on me lingers for what seems like days before he moves on and stops in front of Agron.

Tura leans down close to his ear and says in a stage whisper, "Tell me, Agron Osch, which one of you quivering Habeni is Newell Creig?"

All eyes turn to Newell, next to Ullr on the Matalan's bench. Tura would have no problem finding him, even if Agron didn't immediately point and squeak, "There. In the back."

The captain looks toward Newell. "Come here, son," he says, like a patient father. Newell doesn't move. Tura taps his weapon against his thigh. His tone hardens. "Come. *Now.*"

Newell stands and inches forward. He faces the captain but stares down at his feet. The mechanical eyes in Tura's mask whine.

"You're Newell Creig." It isn't a question. Newell gives a curt nod. Tura slips the weapon's barrel under Newell's trembling chin, forcing his head up. "Speak up. I can't hear you."

"Yes," he chokes out. "I'm Newell Creig."

"Then I'm sorry for you, son. But you Habeni must learn to abide by the treaty and stay out of Adsullatan territory." He points the magshot at Newell's forehead.

Newell gasps. "No. No, please."

My throat closes. This can't be happening.

"Remember this, you spoiled, spineless twits." Tura raises his voice. "When you return to your comforts, tell your fathers we've taken your servants in payment for violating the treaty. And we took the life of one of your own as a warning to stay out of our sector."

His finger touches the weapon's trigger. Tears stream down Newell's face. Helpless, I chew my bottom lip but can't look away. Newell's family is the lowest in status of anyone I know. He's a nice fellow. Kind. He doesn't deserve this. A wet spot blossoms and spreads across his trousers as his bladder lets go. Agron snickers and I want to pummel him.

Tura jerks toward Agron. "You don't know when to be silent, do you? It kills me that a kutama like you will live, when this one, who never hurt nobody, will die."

Tura puts the weapon to Newell's forehead again. Newell quivers, his eyes wild with fear. Silence hangs, the atmosphere in the cabin brittle. I can't breathe. We all watch. Waiting.

The weapon explodes. Screams rip the air. Newell hits the floor. I bite into my lip and taste blood.

Wait. Newell's on his back, wide-eyed, as if stunned he's still alive. I'm stunned too. I look up. The lav wall's taken another hit. Smoke coils out of a hole bigger than my fist.

"Chuny!" the captain bellows.

A tick later, a wiry pirate in wrinkly coveralls pops through the hatch. "What?" He speaks Habeni, like Tura, and sounds aggravated. "Can it wait? I got a situation. That Matalan lad's a handful."

"No, it can't wait. Get the others back here. Prep the ship for the rest of this lot." He looks down at Newell. "Except him. We done enough to this poor slupa. Leave him here with the chaperone. Take the rest."

"Boss?" Chuny asks.

"We're taking them all," Tura says, to horrified, outraged cries. My blood turns to ice.

"What? All of 'em? Boss, you can't do that. That ain't the deal."

"Deal's off." Captain Tura swings toward Agron. "I never liked the terms anyway."

Chapter 4

Kai

The smelly pirate bounces Ayva into a seat across the aisle. I'm trussed up like a Gods' Day roasting pig, belted, bound, and hobbled by ropes and leather straps. I can barely move.

That's a good thing for the pirate. If I was free, I'd crack his skull wide open for roughing up my sister. Bad thing for me. I'm caught, *we're* caught, with no way out.

The ship's a pit, reeking of metal, rotting food, and male stink. Cold as a tomb. But a high sight better than where I'm sure we're headed. I watch the pirate key in a code, making Ayva's safety belts lock over her chest. He moves on to Lil and her twin brother Pyrr, then to Rost. My gut burns. I'd rather rot in a Habbie prison than to see my sister look so scared. Rather walk into the fire pits than to watch poor Lil tremble like a sapling in an earthshake.

I bite back my anger and fear the best as I can. "It's gonna be okay," I say to them. "I promise."

Ayva spins an eye roll, not buying it, but Lil, who's nearly swallowed up by her safety straps, brightens.

Thumps sound from the tube between the ships and I swivel to see several Habeni shoved through the hatch. They wail and beg to be let go.

By Dageth and all the gods, these pirates are bold. A handful of Matalans to offer at the troci market won't make them much coin, but a shipload of Habeni? They're looking at a handsome payday. And possibly war with the Habeni government.

Meili's pushed into the ship and I sit up as much as I can with these klacking bonds choking me. The short, thin pirate who helped tie me up throws her down next to me. Her head spanks the wall. I growl and silently vow to kill every last one of these stinking kutamas if I can get free.

I don't listen to the word *if* banging at my brain.

The thin pirate, whose name is Chuny, secures Meili's belts then moves down the aisle, locking in the rest of the Habeni. I'm too aware of her, so close to me. Her silky red hair spills down her back and over her shoulders. Her scent circles me, buckleberries and losys flower and a hint of sweat. Who knew Habeni gells could sweat? I feel her body's warmth. It ignites a fire in me I don't want lit.

Her gaze hits me for a hot tick. Her eyes are wild and filled with fear. She looks away and searches the cabin, settling on Ullr, further down, on the right. I snort, remembering the gooey-eyed way she gazed at him on the ship. Does she think he can save her? He's as caught as she is. As we all are.

"They're all secured, boss," Chuny says to the captain, dragging my attention up front. "Ready to go when you are."

Tura taps on a com-pad he's holding. His head tilts up then moves like he's scanning us. "Good," he says. "Tell Zeb to put some ginger into sealing that hatch. Then you and Wilf get those translation buds in."

The pirate hops into action. A few ticks later, the Habeni cry out as Chuny and the smelly pirate move down the aisle. They reach the tall one, Gwynn, on Meili's other side. They bend over her and she bleats in pain. My gut cinches. What're they doing?

I find out fast. Smelly and Chuny come at Meili. I will her to fight, but she barely whimpers as Smelly grabs her head with his huge paws and holds her still as Chuny jabs a hypo into her neck. She screeches. I glare at the angry red spot with a ding of silver at the center under her ear.

I'm next. Smelly closes in, wrapping me in his stench like a putrid blanket. He shoves my head to one side, nearly snapping my neck. Chuny stabs the needle into my skin and I wince. Dageth's balls, it hurts.

"What in pakao did you do?" I demand.

"Stuck a translator in your scrawny neck," Smelly says. "So's you can understand your new bosses. And so ya hear me good next time I tell ya to do something."

I spit, nailing him between the eyes. He backhands me across the jaw, a stinging slap, then wipes off the spittle and moves on to his next victim. My temple still hurts from that magshot blow earlier. Now both sides of my face throb in pain.

"Why do you persist in fighting?" Meili says. "Are you so intent on getting bruised?"

"I'm no quivering Habeni. I fight back."

"I see that, but there's a fine line between brave and foolish."

Anger flares. The Habeni scoff and call me names all the time. I shake it off like tepid water. But it frosts my blood to have her, someone who knows the sting of scorn, calling me a fool. I suppose I *am* a fool, to think she'd be any different from the rest of them. To think she'd listen to me when I dared speak my mind at the launch bay. No Habeni, not even a redheaded one, will listen to a Matalan's opinion about anything.

I'm unable to hold my tongue. "At least I got a spine. I don't let them push me around, like you do. I stand up for myself."

She stiffens. "And look where it's got you, my lord of the fearless, captured by pirates like the rest of us. Bruised and bloody, to boot."

I get it, they caught me. She doesn't have to rub my nose in it. "If I'd known they'd stick me next to a stuck-up, gutless shrill, I would've fought to the death."

She gapes at me and her red lips pull into a surprised O. Her teeth are like two perfect rows of pearls, her eyes the color of honey sparkling in the sun. I've worked at her school for years, but this is the first time I think she sees me, really sees me. I don't think she likes what she sees. Not sure if I like it either.

"Watch your mouth, Mucker. You're talking to a lady."

That comes from Lord Swollen Nose, across the aisle, down past Rost. Despite my anger and the chaos around us, I can't help but smirk at the proper mess I made of Agron's face.

"You stay out of this," Meili snaps at him. "You don't care about me. You just want to make trouble. I'll fight my own battles."

Now I can't hold back a grin. Maybe there's a Matalan fighter in her after all.

She swings on me. "Why are you laughing? There's nothing funny about any of this."

A yelp pulls my gaze toward Ayva. The pirates descend on her and stab her with the hypo. They go at Lil next. I strain against my bonds again. No, there's nothing funny about this, and all I can do is watch.

The pirates complete their tasks soon after. One of them bumps a cart filled with rucksacks, luggage, and all manner of other loot into the ship. Another pirate in an orange head scarf follows, carrying a tool pouch. They all climb a ladder to the deck above and snap shut the hatch behind them.

Only the captain is left. He taps on a portable control pad. The ship shudders, followed by clanking as the apparatus connecting the two vessels decouples and retracts. The hatch seals with a grinding *thunk*.

"Ladies and gentlemales," Tura says. "We're about to set out. Please sit back and have a long, relaxing sleep. It's a lengthy journey to Adsullata."

He presses a button and the lights dim. Another button and a narrow door up front pops open, revealing an old-style cockpit and controls for manual flight. The captain slips inside, and the door silently slides shut.

The hum of the cabin pressurizing slowly fades and all is quiet. Then a *whoosh* as mist spurts from the air ducts above. Cool, bitter-smelling liquid sprinkles my face. My gut squeezes. What is this? Poison gas?

Terrified wails fill the cabin. Ayva looks to me in desperation. I grind my teeth. I can't help her, can't even comfort her. I glance at Meili. She's linked arms with her friend. Can't help her either, though I doubt she'd let me anyway.

I try not to inhale, but that's impossible. My nostrils tingle. A tick later my face goes numb. I start to droop. Ayva tips forward. Her breathing turns rhythmic. Lil and the others sag. By Dageth, it's not poison. It's sleeping gas. Meili blinks rapidly, struggling, but soon, she's asleep. Everyone's asleep.

I fight it as long as I can but I give in too. My arms feel like bags of wet sand, impossible to lift. My head becomes as heavy as a boulder. My fear eases. My thoughts turn peaceful.

I close my eyes.

Chapter 5

Meili

I wake to the hum of the engines and the murmur of voices. Something rough tickles my forehead. I open my eyes. It's the stubble on Kai's chin. My mind's so fuzzy it takes a tick to realize my head's resting on his shoulder. I struggle to sit up. Kai looks at me with half-open, glassy eyes. I hope he's asleep enough to think my shocking lack of propriety is a dream.

Someone steps into view. I can tell by his tall, slim build that it's Captain Tura. He's removed his mask.

"You're Matalan," I say, or try to say. My lips feel as thick as rain-bloated teakslugs.

I guess he understands because he nods, his green eyes bright with awareness and more than a little mischief. My gaze drifts toward Kai.

"No worry, my lady. He sleeps. Your secret is safe with me." Tura leans close. I try to muster fear, but the sleeping mist has me as placid as a lamb. His warm, sweet-scented breath gusts against my ear as he whispers, "I won't tell a soul I caught you sleeping with a Matalan."

He straightens, chuckling softly, then slips his hand into my hair. I don't have the strength to lift my arm and push him away.

"Lovely." He lets the thick tresses slide through his fingers. "You put the goddess Rossa in the shade."

The sun goddess Rossa put in the shade by anyone strikes me as funny. A smile touches my lips. I blink, and Captain Tura's gone. I drift off again, wondering if I dreamed the whole thing.

I snort awake many ticks later. The mist must be wearing off. I'm still weak but feel less loopy. My throat is dry, my limbs stiff. I stretch and gaze around. Ullr, Gwynn, Varina and most of the others are still asleep, but Kai is awake, staring at me. Heat rises on my cheeks. I hope he can't remember me snuggling against him while we slept.

"They've taken off their masks," he says.

Oh. He's not looking at me. He directs his gaze at the pirates up the aisle. They're yanking sparklers, timekeepers and boots off my sleeping classmates and pitching the loot into a big bucket. Unlike their captain, these pirates are Adsullatan, or at least what I gather an Adsullatan looks like from the few digipix I've seen. Long face, grayish skin, dishwater hair, and mud-colored eyes.

"Guess they're not afraid to show their faces now." Kai's voice is slightly slurred, the only outward effect of the sleeping drug. "We're caught good and sure and those curs know it."

I'm miffed at his chattiness. He's downright friendly after the way he grumped at me and hurled insults last night. "Do you think that means we're nearing Adsullata?"

"That's my best guess." He directs a murderous gleam at the pirate who's bent over his sister, pulling off her boots. "They've done this before. Seized a ship, stole what they could sell, then shipped the passengers off to the troci market for even more profit."

My teeth should chatter at that, but I'm oddly calm, thanks to the drug still in my blood.

The pirate in the orange head scarf, whose name is Zeb, reaches me, bringing with him the scent of something sweet and tangy that makes my empty stomach growl.

"Don't move," he says. If I had any doubt that translator tingling in my neck would work, I believe it now. He speaks Habeni, but his lips move discordantly, as if I'm watching a holovid in Matalan that's been dubbed into Habeni.

Zeb needn't warn me to be still. My limbs feel as if they have no bones. I'm helpless as he slides the ring Father gave me for my seventeenth birthday from my finger. He squats, yanks off my new boots, and flings them into the bucket. A sob catches in my throat.

"Are you crying over a pair of boots?" Kai asks, back to his crabby, scornful self.

"I am *not* crying." Mother says real tears are a sign of weakness. To shed them in front of a Matalan is probably doubly so. I blink them away. "It's dust, nothing more."

He snorts. "I'll never ken gells, Habeni or Matalan."

Zeb steps over to remove Kai's boots. He glares as the pirate struggles to find the correct knot to untie among the many knots holding the worn and broken bootlaces together.

"Don't you dare kick him," I whisper, reading Kai's intentions. His legs are bound but not secured to the seat. "You might get shot."

"Your concern is touching."

That stings, though why should his disdain bother me? "Don't be flattered." I look to the weapon on Zeb's belt. "I might be in the line of fire."

Kai snorts again. He seems to enjoy making that sound.

Zeb growls in frustration. He can't get Kai's bootlace knots to loosen one whit.

"Forget the Matalan's boots," the small pirate, Chuny, calls. He stands outside the cockpit door, as if guarding his captain, who's still within. "Those hobnails don't fetch a ha'penney a bushel anyway."

Zeb grunts and moves on. I wiggle my toes, exposed to the cabin's frigid air, jealous Kai gets to keep his crappy boots with their broken laces.

Soon, the ship begins to decelerate. My ears pop as we descend. The change in pressure wakes everyone, and a frightened buzz of voices rises, with a goodly number demanding to know where their boots and sparklers have gone. Beside me, Gwynn blinks in sleepy confusion.

The last wisp of calm evaporates from my brain and I clench with renewed dread as the ship drops further then slows to a crawl. A tick later, it bumps against docking clamps.

"They've timed the trip perfectly," Kai says, sounding impressed. He jerks his chin at the rank-smelling pirate, who stands nearby, picking his teeth with a small knife. "They knock us out so we'll be no trouble most of the flight. Wake us up before we dock. They're professionals at this."

"Good to know. I was worried a gang of amateur pirates had caught us." I expect him to snap at me like before. Instead, a grim smile tugs at his lips.

"And these Adsullatans are the ugliest bunch of amateurs I ever—"

Kai stiffens from head to hobnail boots as Captain Tura comes out of the cockpit. A chorus of gasps and cusses erupts in the cabin. I hadn't been dreaming earlier. The pirate eyeing us with a smug grin is a Matalan. We've been captured by ruffians led by someone my people consider inferior in all ways.

Pirated by a Mucker.

"Son of a spunhound," Kai breathes. He fixes his eyes like daggers on the captain, who's making his way down the aisle, unlocking our restraining straps.

Tura reaches me and gives me a wicked grin as he unlatches my belt. "I trust you slept well, my lady?"

My cheeks roast with embarrassment. *Take hold of yourself, Meili.* Feeling mortified about a silly thing I did while asleep *and* drugged is the least of my problems now.

Kai watches stonily as Tura unties him. Free, Kai stretches his arms and flexes his fists. His knuckles crack.

The captain eyes him coldly. "Are we gonna have more trouble with you, brother?"

"You're no brother of mine. A Matalan would never sell his own people for a bit of coin."

Tura shrugs. "You would if you want to eat."

Kai stands, his expression as angry as a thunderclap. He and the captain are akin in height and build. I'm reminded of Kai facing Agron what seems like moons ago, but now his opponent is armed.

"Kutama," Kai spits. "You're a stain on the memory of your ancestors. A traitor to every Matalan who's ever fought to throw off the Habeni boot. You should burn in pakao for eternity."

The captain lets out a harsh laugh. "Feel better now you've said your piece?" He moves closer to Kai and touches the grip of the magshot hung on his belt. "Brother, when I give the command, you're gonna move. Quickly and quietly. Give me trouble, or even a hint of trouble, and I'll fry your sister's brains to dust. Got me?"

Beside me, Gwynn gasps. Ayva, her frightened gaze pinned on her brother, claps a hand over her mouth. I do too.

A long, heated tick passes before Kai steps back. "You win. For now. But mark me. I swear I'll get free. I'll find you. When next we meet, I *will* kill you. Brother."

Tura studies him. He seems composed, but his expression is tight, making me think Kai's gotten to him. Then he grins. "I look forward to that day, Kai ObDen."

He strides away. Kai sinks into his seat and slowly lets out his breath. His hands are shaking.

At the back of the cabin, the captain presses a button. The cargo door creaks as it descends into the ship's belly, letting in a blast of humid air. Two silhouetted figures outside roll a steel ramp up to the opening. Sunlight bounces off the metal, spilling into the ship. I shield my eyes. Any wisp of serenity is gone. I'm more afraid than I've ever been.

Captain Tura turns, sweeps his gaze over us and gestures toward the open hatch.

"Ladies and gentlemales," he says, as genial as a flight steward. "Welcome to your new home."

Chapter 6

Kai

THESE PIRATES ARE EFFICIENT. In two ticks, we're off the ship and pushed forward, shunted along a dirt tarmac toward a row of rickety-looking vans. Nearby, Captain Tura counts a stack of coins an Adsullatan in a patchwork coat hands him. His payment for us.

I burn with fury. I cannot ken how a Matalan could sink so low as to not only throw in with these pirate ruffians but end up leading the whole treacherous bunch. Tura shoots me a smug grin as a watcher hustles Ayva and me past and I burn even more. There's going to be a big pile of bodies to clean up when I get out of this mess, with that mother-humper at the top.

I doubt I'll get my revenge anytime soon. We're surrounded by watchers swinging silver sticks that look like cattle prods from back home. Electricity sparks from the tip. My goal now has to be Ayva. Protect her, and the little ones. How, I don't know. We're deep in the Adsullatan shit and I don't have any idea how to get out.

I see Meili ahead with Gwynn, walking next to that top status priss, Varina Meade. Varina hangs on Lord Agron. He's calm, compared to the rest of the Habbies. While the others sob and wail and beg to be set free, he demands it, and even offers the guards exorbitant bribes, with little success. A bold few test the watchers and try to bolt. They get a jolt from that stinging weapon for their trouble.

I'm not slupa enough to try that means of escape. Yet.

We reach the end of the tarmac and the row of vans. The watchers steer us up a ramp into one of the transports. It's icy cold inside, the stench so foul I can almost taste it. Ayva groans in disgust and looks down. Her feet are bare, and the floor is coated with slime and the gods only know what else. I don't get a chance to strip off my boots to give to her. The doors clang shut and the van herks into motion.

Meili bangs into me, and we're face to face, with my nose buried in her hair. The van and its fetid smells fade away. All I see is her. All I feel is *her*. Her warmth, her curves, the gentle pressure of her firm breasts against my chest.

I hold her upper arms to steady her. She tips up her head. Our gazes connect. Light slips in through the van's slatted windows at the top of the walls. A glimmer brushes her face. She's not sobbing or cussing and threatening like the others around us, but I know she's scared. It's in her eyes, terror so naked it stops my breath.

That desperate fire ignites in me again. I want to hold her, protect her. Save her.

I grind my teeth. No. I've got my own to think about. I can't be responsible for someone else. Especially someone who despises me, who thinks I'm the dimmest slupa on all the worlds.

I tighten my hold on her arms and ease her away.

Her face blushes as red as the sunset. "I beg your pardon," she says as if we're at a garden party. Then she turns away as much as she can in this tight space.

The van propels forward at a steady clip, its engine humming. People bleat frantic questions. *Where are we going? How can this happen to us? How could the pirates break the treaty? Where did they get those magshots?* Others cuss out the pirate's Mucker captain and turn accusing eyes on me, as if I had conspired with him.

I ignore them and search my brain for an idea, some way to escape, but nothing comes.

A long time later, the van pitches hard right and jolts to a stop. The door bursts open. Two burly watchers join the guards who herded us from Tura's ship and they stand on either side of the ramp, waving their scorching weapons and shouting at us to move.

Once we're out of the van, the watchers close around us and hurry us toward a white clay building surrounded by a tall fence. We move too fast to talk, too fast to make a break. The soil's gritty, littered with sharp stones. I feel bad for Ayva's bare feet, even worse for the Habbies. They spend more coin pampering their feet than they do feeding their servants. Their soles must be raw and bleeding by the time we reach our destination.

Ayva's sweaty hand holds mine. Her grip tightens as a huge metal door rumbles to the side and a blast of cool air rolls out. We're funneled inside a dimly lit, high-ceilinged corridor with a frigid, concrete floor. My eyes adjust to see several more watchers swarming toward us.

One of them gestures and we're pushed toward smaller rooms on either side of the corridor. I try to keep Ayva with me but a watcher jabs an electric prod in my face. The tip sizzles and I can smell the electricity waiting to shoot out and burn my skin off. I let my sister go with an angry growl. The watcher sweeps her away and she vanishes into one of the rooms with Lil and the other gells. The door thumps shut behind them.

No time to think. I'm shoved into what looks like a dressing room and told to change into troci uniforms, long-sleeved wool tunic and drawstring trousers. They make me give up my boots in exchange for cheap shoes made of synthetic material that pinches my feet, but I get a chance to drink some water and take a piss, so I guess I come out even.

Then we're back in the corridor, lined up again. Ayva scuttles next to me. She's dressed like the other gells, in a knee-length wool dress the color of blah and an equally bland scarf covering her hair. I take her hand. Lil's hand too. Meili's in front, hovering near Ullr, as if he'll protect her. She puts her faith in the wrong person. He's shaking like a leaf in a hard wind.

Get over yourself, Kai. I'm just as terrified.

Gears grind, chains clank, and a metal door groans open. Sunlight streaks in. My empty stomach heaves. No escape now. We march forward, into the light.

Into the troci market.

CHAPTER 7

Meili

We've been standing in this pen for hours. The sun beats down, blistering my always carefully shielded skin. My wool dress itches from the sweat rolling down my back. My throat's parched, my belly hollow with hunger. The ground is as dry as bones, except a corner of the pen that smells like piss. A dozen of these pens ring the yard, each with a chest-high slatted fence topped with barbed points.

Behind me, my classmate Ithell is bawling. She's been scorched three times and told to hush, but she still sobs. She's sweet, with never an unkind word to me, but at this point, I want to grab one of the watchers' stingers and scorch her too.

The other pens hold only two or three unfortunates. Ours is jammed with twenty-six of us waiting for... what? I don't know and am too terrified to think about it. I can only silently beg the gods to please let me wake up from this nightmare.

I'm up front. Gwynn's behind me, speaking with Ayva. Kai stands stony-faced next to them. Varina clings to Agron. I don't have anyone to cling to. Ullr, the best catch a redhead like me could hope to snare, shook me off as soon as we walked into the pen. He's hiding at the back fence, terrified. I hoped he might protect me. He can't even protect himself.

Yorath and Halia speak with the two fellows in the next pen. I edge closer to listen to the story of how they were caught. They were on a small medical transport from the planet Dryas when the pirates attacked.

"Bold of the pirates to prey on a large ship like yours," one of them says. "They usually stay away from the big fish. Must be desperate for new troci to snatch so many folk at once."

"Habeni, too," the other one adds. "They're supposed to leave Habeni trading ships alone. Strange they'd violate the treaty after all this time. Stranger still to let your ship go. Ours was towed for scrap."

Perhaps not so strange. Captain Tura was about to leave with just the Matalans when Agron mouthed off and the pirate changed his mind and took everyone. I direct a withering look at Agron. It's *his* fault we're in this mess. If he didn't anger Tura, the pirates would've gone and I'd be home now, soaking my throbbing feet in a hot bath Taryn would draw for me.

Please, please let me wake up.

At last, something happens. A metallic moan and the broad doors of the main gate open. People stream into the yard. The Matalan girl, Lil, who hovers near me, begins to sob. I curse these Adsullatans and all their forbears for making this tiny thing cry. I touch her thin shoulder. She gazes up at me.

"I know you're scared Lil," I say gently. "To tell you the truth, so am I."

Lil drags grubby knuckles over her teary eyes. "*You*, my lady?"

It's the first time I've heard her speak. Her voice is deep for a girl, especially one so small.

"I am. But let's not let them see our fear." My dry lips crack as I smile down at her. "Let's stand as tall as the god Valasin facing the beasts of the underworld. We'll look those culbanas right in the eye."

A bold declaration, bolstering words meant as much for myself as for Lil. She laces her fingers through mine. I've never held a Matalan's hand, except for Taryn's, and this girl's thin, work-callused hand is worlds away from my minna's smooth touch.

"You alright Lil?" Kai asks, sidling up beside us. He speaks to the girl but his eyes are on me.

I shift from foot to foot under his hard stare. With all this madness around me, why am I so aware of him? Like those moments in the van, the two of us pressed together in an intimacy that at home would require me to swoon and would get Kai arrested. He'd steadied me as the van rocked and though I trembled in terror, all I could think of was the heat of his body against mine, his firm but gentle hold on my arms, and *him*, so strong, so safe.

Until he'd pushed me away, as if my fear was contagious.

I squeeze Lil's hand and lift my chin, eyeing him coolly. "She's as well as can be expected in such a predicament."

His gaze roams over my face. "And you, my lady? Are you well?"

Does he truly care or is he mocking me? I don't get a chance to find out. The mob of Adsullatans that have entered the yard reach our pen and a watcher with greasy hair and a huge wart on his nose clangs his stinging stick on the fence.

"Git to the front," he shouts. "Hands out. Yaps shut."

I have to release Lil's hand as we step to the fence and squeeze next to one another. I stick my arms between the fence's cool metal slats, hands palms up. The crowd files past, looking us over. Most are male, older, around fifty, my parents' age. One of the few women, a matron wearing a swirled-pattern shawl, stops and pokes a fat thumb into my mouth. I taste an unfamiliar spice. She inspects my teeth. I'm tempted to bite her to prove they work.

"Hmph," she says and moves on. I spit out the spice taste. A watcher jabs me with his stinger but doesn't scorch me. A warning, I guess. No spitting allowed.

An Adsullatan with a belly so swollen he looks nine months gone clucks when he sees Ithell's hands, singed from several fiery jolts.

"This one's insolent, I gather?" he asks.

"She's feisty but strong, my lord." Wart Nose indicates Ithell's solid arms and build. Her wracking sobs intensify, belying his assurances.

The parade of spectators continues, inspecting us, ogling, reaching through the fence to squeeze arms and thighs. Two younger women fondle Kai's biceps. They giggle. His jaw works, but he stares straight ahead. The men stare lewdly, as if undressing us. My dress is prim, with long sleeves and down to my knees, but still I feel naked.

I'm reminded of an early morning visit to the Condati City marketplace years ago with Taryn, to pick up seedlings for our herb garden. Dozens of Matalans were lined up as we are, being inspected by some Habeni.

"Unskilled laborers," Taryn said when I asked who they were. "They come here looking for day work. Any work they can find to feed their families. It's bychen."

Bychen, a Matalan word I never understood until now. It means humiliating. Degrading. Making me feel as less than nothing.

"Bychen," I murmur.

Beside me, Kai shifts, his expression curious, but he says nothing.

A trim woman in a silken red robe stops at our pen. She signals to Wart Nose. They speak, then the latch clicks and the gate squawks open. Everyone recoils and jumps back as one entity, chattering. The Adsullatans stop to watch. A transaction, I gather. My stomach clenches. Which of us has been chosen?

Wart Nose swishes his stinger like an insect swatter to shoo us out of the way. He aims for me and I seize up. Then he clamps a meaty hand on Lil's arm. He looks to the lady in the red robe and she nods.

"Come, puss," he says, reaching for her. "You and the little mister have found a new home."

Lil clutches my hand and presses to my side as if trying to melt into me. Wart Nose eyes me and spits something brown and vile between my feet. Warm, sticky slime spatters my ankles.

"Let go," he growls. He stabs the stinging stick into my belly. "Let go or I'll fry yer gut."

He punctuates that threat with a zap that sizzles my insides. A taste of what's to come if I don't comply. Lil gazes up at me, her huge eyes begging me to help her. I want to. But I don't. Instead, I do something awful. *The* most shameful thing. A cowardly thing.

I drop Lil's hand like a burning coal.

"Now that's seeing sense." Wart Nose holsters his weapon and takes Lil by the arm. Two steps and he grabs her brother too. Pyrr kicks his shin. Lil bites his wrist. The crowd laughs. Grunting, he scoops Lil up under one arm, tucks Pyrr under the other and puffs toward the gate.

Suddenly, Kai leaps on his back. He locks his arm around Wart Nose's neck and grabs for the stinger with his free hand. The watcher spins, as if the force of motion will rip Kai off his back. The little ones under his arms fly out like they're on a grisly carnival ride. The onlookers cheer. Ithell's sobs become wails. I bite my knuckle, trying not to scream. Ayva *is* screaming.

Another watcher trots up. He digs his weapon into Kai's side and squeezes the trigger. Kai's body convulses and spasms. His eyes roll back into his head and his grip slackens. The watcher peels Kai off Wart Nose's back like a piece of sticky paper. Kai thuds to the dusty ground, still twitching.

"Anyone else eager to get juiced?" the watcher shouts, earning applause from the spectators and a fair number of glares from us.

Wart Nose carries Lil and Pyrr to the woman in the red robe and she leads the twins away. Lil swivels and pins her accusing gaze on me before she disappears into the crowd.

Burning with shame, I hustle over to where Kai sprawls in the dirt. Ayva's on her knees beside him, weeping. Gwynn's hand hovers over Ayva's shoulder, as if she wishes to comfort her but doesn't know how.

Ayva shakes Kai. Her tears drip onto his tunic. "Brother, wake up."

I glance at Gwynn then squat beside Ayva. The acrid scent of singed flesh hangs in the air. Kai's new tunic bunches up, exposing a nasty patch of charred, bubbled skin across his muscled abdomen. His body is stiff and still, but his chest rises and falls.

"He lives," I say. "Don't fret, Ayva. He lives."

She sniffles, looking at me with a frantic expression. "Oh, thank you, my lady."

"You're allowed to call me Meili." I don't know why I say it that way, formal permission to address me by my first name. Habit, I suppose. "Please, call me Meili," I add hastily.

Ayva nods but I don't think she hears me. She brushes back her brother's thick hair.

Agron comes over, looks down, and spits. A feeble stream after so many hours without liquid. "Stupid Mucker," he says.

I disagree. Kai's not stupid. Far from it. He's the bravest person I've ever seen, Habeni or Matalan. But he's rash. He couldn't stop the watchers from taking Lil and Pyrr any more than I could. I was wise not to risk trying.

At least, that's what I tell myself.

An excited chatter breaks out. I get to my feet and see the Adsullatans drift away from the pens and gather at a grassy area surrounded by towering trees at the center of the compound. The main gate doors yawn open once more. A tall figure in an ugly pink robe strides in through the main gate to respectful applause. Nav Panjour, I hear people murmur, awestruck and a little bit frightened. He's the ghoul in charge of this whole gruesome spectacle, I gather.

He beckons and the watchers snap into action. They pull the Dryans from their pen and shove them toward the crowd at the center.

"Let us begin our offerings today with these lads from the planet Dryas," Nav Panjour calls out, his voice strong, commanding. "Two healthy lads with medical skills, an asset to any industry or business. Who will show me their interest?"

Many hands shoot up. The bidding's competitive and the price rises. Nav Panjour preens. The number climbs and climbs until a satisfying sum is agreed upon. A tick later, the Dryans are led away, their expressions grim, bound for a future I cannot even begin to imagine or comprehend.

When it's my turn, will hands raise? What do I have to offer? A pampered Habeni, skilled at dancing and flirting and spending copious amounts of coin and not much else. Raised solely to make a match with a male equally as spoiled and with as little to offer as me.

What's going to happen to me?

I really, really wish I would wake up.

Chapter 8

Meili

They finally get around to us.

Our pen's gate swings open and Wart Nose steps in. He chooses seven of us. I let out a *whoosh* because one of them isn't me. Temporary relief, I know, but there it is in all its selfish glory.

Yorath is one of the seven. Halia shrieks and reaches for him through the fence. He skims his fingers along hers, a final touch before a watcher prods him to move. Her shrieks turn to heartrending sobs. Tears poke my eyes. To be separated from her love like this, someone Halia's been contracted to since grade school, must hurt like a knife to the heart.

I turn away from her pain to watch the drama at the center of the yard. Yorath, five others, and the Matalan servant Rost cluster together, standing straight, trying to be brave. I hope I can be equally brave when it's my turn.

Nav Panjour begins his patter. He talks up my classmates' strengths like an oily salesmale eager to seal the deal.

"Here's a prime one," he calls, circling Rost. He's shorter than Kai, but his build is akin, muscular and strong. "He can push a plow or swing a pickaxe all day, I'll wager."

Excitement hums through the crowd and Nav Panjour moves on to the still weeping Ithell. "How about this gell? Mayhap you can use her to water your garden."

The onlookers hoot and laugh and Ithell sobs even more as the bidding begins. Nav Panjour jabbers. Hands pop up. The bids climb. Nav Panjour talks even faster until the pregnant belly Adsullatan is the victor.

Whispers spread across the pens as a white van cuts through the crowd and the watchers thrust my classmates inside. They're being transported to a quarry operation on the outskirts of Plim. I have no idea where Plim is, since we're taught so little about Adsullata or any of the other nearby planets in school. The white van swings around and hums by us toward the main gate. Halia watches it pass with hollow eyes.

The gate to our pen opens again. Six are selected, Butay, Blix, Dipro, Loyd, Agron. And me. Gwynn lets out a mournful moan. Quaking, I join the others at the gate.

"You first, my lady," Agron says, with a mocking bow.

I flash him a sour look. This is the only time I've heard him address me this way and even now he can't release his disdain.

The sun beats down and waves of heat shimmer over me. My legs wobble like they're made of rubber. I fear I'll be sick. But, somehow, I move forward, leading the way out of the pen.

I don't look back.

In a moment we reach our morbid destination. Four trees with thick scaly trunks and large, round, bright orange leaves tower over us. It's cooler here in their shade. That does little to ease my terror.

Wart Nose arranges us in a line, with the bidders and the spectators gathered to watch surrounding us. They talk and laugh. Some have brought baskets of food and drink and have spread out blankets to sit on. I catch the savory scent of braised boar. I don't have a drop of liquid left in me, yet my mouth waters.

Nav Panjour clears his throat and the crowd snaps to attention. Tall and slender, he has white scars that run like rivers down his gray face. A wide belt with a gold buckle in the shape of a snarling beast cinches his pink robe at the waist.

"My lords and ladies today's your lucky day," he begins. "It's been a long time since we've had so many healthy Habeni to offer for your consideration." He sweeps an arm toward us. The buzz from the crowd builds. "They're strong, young. Each a valuable addition to your farm or industry."

Whistles, whoops, and shouts of "Let the bidding begin," ring out.

Nav Panjour grins and raises his hand over Blix's head. "Here's a compact model for your consideration. Can sweep chimneys or shimmy into tight spaces."

Laughter and jeers for Velten Academy's top student.

He moves to Agron. "How about this brawny lad?" He squeezes Agron's arm, getting a glower in return. "I'm certain he can carry twice his weight."

More whoops and applause. In the pen, my classmates gather at the fence to watch. Even Kai, who's recovered enough to stand with Ayva's help. I'm too far to see their faces clearly. What does Varina think of Agron being catalogued this way?

Nav Panjour reaches me. He raises his hand above my head. His armpits stink and sweat dots his forehead. "Well, well, my precious Aunt Fanny, isn't this one a beauty?"

A roar of agreement shoots through the crowd. Before I can duck, Nav Panjour snatches the scarf off my head. The crowd *oohs* as my hair tumbles free.

"A *redhead*," he cries in a vulgar tone that makes my skin crawl. "You know what they say about redheads. My brethren, which of you will spend the coin to find out if the stories are true?"

He reaches to stroke my hair. My teeth snap. He wrenches his hand away before I can bite him. He laughs, his expression amused, but his eyes are cold, empty. As bleak and barren and unfeeling as I imagine his heart to be.

"Ah, the stories *are* true," he crows. "Think what this fiery one can do for your... staff."

Guffaws and thunderous applause. *Bychen.* Humiliation times ten. I want to sink right into the concrete. I lift my chin and stare straight out, imagining I'm far away as the bidding begins.

"One hundred, a hundred ten, do I hear a hundred twenty?" Nav Panjour cries. His voice echoes off the buildings and hands shoot up like arrows into the sky. "How about one fifty? There it is. Do I hear two hundred?"

The bids rise. A fellow in a topcoat and crisp bowtie runs over and pushes to the front of the throng, out of breath. He raises his hand and the price climbs further. Fewer hands go up as the price soars to an amount that would make even someone as wealthy as Varina dizzy. Nav Panjour's voice squeaks in excitement and soon it's between the man in the bowtie and one in a powder blue suit.

Dread coils in my belly. One of these people, doesn't matter which, will win, and then I'll be his troci—bound servant. Caught and trapped in a nightmare I can neither comprehend nor believe is happening.

"An agreement has been reached," Nav Panjour shouts. "The gentlemale from Mollystone Manor wins the day." He gestures to Bowtie, who grins and mops his brow with a silky-looking handkerchief.

Mollystone Manor. Sounds pleasant, but I have a solid feeling it's anything but.

Things happen fast after that. Nav Panjour tosses me my scarf. I tuck my hair away and follow the others over to Wart Nose, who's speaking to Bowtie. He calls him "Sir" in the most toadying manner then hands us off to a guard I don't recognize. His body odor makes my head spin and I wonder if poor hygiene is a requirement for employment as a watcher.

The watcher prods us toward the main gate. I drag at the end of the group, not daring to think what comes next on this horrific journey.

I risk a glance back at what's left of our class. Wart Nose is hustling the rest of my classmates out of the pen, including Ullr, who covers his face with his hands as if that will make him invisible. Kai's out front, moving stiffly from his injury, leaning on Ayva for support. He looks toward me. I can't see his face clearly but I think he's scowling.

My belly burns like I swallowed a bucket of hot embers. I'll never see any of them again. I'll never see my home again, or Mother or Father. Or Taryn. I'm about to blubber worse than Ithell when the watcher slaps his stick across my back, like he's correcting a disobedient hound.

"Eyes front, slag. Move."

I wipe my eyes and pad behind the others out onto a busy boulevard in a sprawling city. Illchyd, someone called this gloomy place. People rush along the sidewalks and gleaming silver surface vehicles hum down narrow streets. All around, tall buildings reach into the sky, shrouded in haze. Smells both putrid and pleasant hit me, making me dizzy.

The sun is setting and the oppressive heat begins to wane. Two young females make a wide berth around us as if we have a disease. Their shoes clack on the sidewalk. An older female in a gray dress trots behind them, struggling with a pile of packages. An orange ring of smooth plastic circles her neck.

She's a troci. *Their* troci. What I am now.

"Meili. Wait!"

I spin to see Gwynn rushing at me. Has she escaped? The others are with her, running. Have they all busted out? No. Wart Nose is behind them, pushing them forward.

Gwynn reaches me, out of breath. "There's been a deal. We're to all be troci together."

She sounds way too excited by this gloomy fact but my heart jumps anyway. We hug. I hug Varina too. I would hug everyone, even Kai, if Wart Nose didn't demand that we keep moving.

We enter a lot filled with air transports of all shapes and sizes. A watcher aims us toward a low-grav airbus hovering at the curb, its engines powering up. Bowtie stands near the open door. He speaks with another man I think is the pilot.

"A low-grav," Gwynn says. "Must be a far journey. Do you know where we're going?"

I shake my head. "Some place called Mollystone Manor."

"Might as well be Dageth's realm," Varina grumps.

"Stop yabbering and git over there." Wart Nose gestures and we form a line next to the airbus. I peer through the windows at the interior to see two long rows of seats with circular headrests.

"My name's Mr. Deke," Bowtie calls out, pacing in front of us. He has the same white streaks on his face as Nav Panjour, but in a different pattern. "You're now bound to Lord and Lady Forseti of Mollystone Manor. You'll be assigned to mine Mollystone on the ridge or to work on the farm that supports the mining operation. You'll find my lord and lady are fairer than most employers. As long as you work hard and do as you're told, you'll be clothed, fed, and your aches and pains tended. You'll have a good life."

"If the Molly fever don't get you," Wart Nose says.

"And the rachee don't eat you," the other watcher adds, then they laugh, a cold, cruel guffaw that sends a shiver up my spine.

We begin to board. I gaze dejectedly at what's left of the merry band that set out to Aine not long ago. We're just seventeen now, five females, twelve males. Status no longer matters. Ullr boards first and needs a push. No one fights, not even Kai, though he looks as if he'd love to take a swing at anyone in arm's reach.

I'm at the end. I stare at the lettering on the side of the airbus as I move forward. It's a jumble I can make no sense of, like everything that's happened to us since we set out toward Aine.

At the low-grav's door, Mr. Deke holds out his hand to help me up the steps. Tears prick my eyes, my legs threaten to buckle, and fear tries to consume me. I won't let it. I square my shoulders and straighten my back. I *won't* let these Adsullatan goons see me tremble. I *won't* bawl my brains out like Ithell. I won't give them the satisfaction. I'll face whatever the gods have in store for me clear-eyed and strong.

It takes every bit of will I have, but I do it.

I climb the steps.

Chapter 9

Kai

WE'RE IN THE AIR a while before our captors toss the next torment into our path. A *swish* at the back of the ship and a refreshment bay window slides open. The aroma of spiced meats and fresh fruit rolls out.

Food, and not a lot of it. Guaranteeing a stampede.

I hurl myself into the mob. Ayva's behind me. Elbows jab and Habbies claw and shove like feral animals. Mild-tempered Blix heaves people aside, his eyes glittering. Varina shrieks and scrapes her fingernails like a hurdybird's talons gouging its prey. Meili pushes in but she's shut out by Agron and his minions Dipro and Loyd, who swoop in and snatch up the goods.

I'm no better than them, despite the stinging burn in my gut. Agron gets a clip across the jaw, Dipro a punch to the throat as I fight my way through. I get what I'm after, bread, meat and cheese, and two water flasks before every last crumb is gone.

People stumble back to their seats. Some grumble over the paucity of their haul. Agron ignores Varina. She's empty-handed and begs him to share his bounty.

Meili pauses at Ullr's seat. He didn't move during the scramble for food. He stares at nothing, like he's gone feeble-minded. She's managed to grab a chunk of bread and some cheese. She breaks off a piece of both and offers them to him. He takes it, his movements listless and wan.

I glower. At *her*. She's got a soft heart. She's got to toughen up or she'll be eaten alive when we get wherever we're going.

After she moves on, Jervis, sitting next to Ullr, makes a move on Ullr's food. I shove up to him and curl a fist until my knuckles crack. "Don't even think about it," I warn. Jervis shrinks away but Ullr better eat fast. I doubt I've put off that hungry Habbie for long.

Ayva tries to give me a larger share of our goods but I insist we split evenly. I don't know when we'll eat again. I chew on a string of beef that's not half bad and gaze across the aisle. Meili gives away even more of her food, sharing with Gwynn, who peels an oval-shaped, yellowish fruit and offers half of it in return. Meili nibbles on a piece. Juice drips down her chin. She makes a face. The fruit must be sour.

"What's so interesting over there?" Ayva asks.

I jerk back to her. Dageth's balls. She's caught me staring. "They have fruit," I say, as if that's important.

"Oh, do they?" Ayva's eyes twinkle. They're as green as jade, just like Ma's were. "You know, if you spoke to her like a real person instead of glaring at her all the time, she might be more friendly."

"The Habeni aren't our friends. They're the enemy."

"Still?" She bites into a piece of cheese. "Seems we need every friend we can get now. You, especially."

I snort. "I don't need any candy-livered Habbie to get in my way." No matter how beautiful. "And didn't Ma always say not to talk with your mouth full?"

"Ma also said she wished we could travel and see the worlds." She swallows then gulps down some water. "I don't think this is what she had in mind."

Bitter humor. The ObDen family trait. The way we get through bleak times. And the rare good times, too.

Ayva polishes off her bread then presses her forehead to the window glass, gazing down. "Where do you think we're going?"

I lean over and look out. We've left the city behind. Below, a river snakes through the countryside, reflecting the glow of the setting sun. We're heading southwest, fast, further from where we were sold by the tick. Further from escape. I flop back against the seat and drain the last drop of my water. I take Ayva's hand, having no answer.

The lights dim. The cabin falls silent as everyone nods off. Ayva sits back and soon she's asleep. I hope she dreams of home.

I should sleep too. I'm exhausted. My stomach's full, or at least full enough to ease the hungry ache. Water spreads through my veins, uncoiling my tight muscles. But I can't relax. Our chance for escape has all but slipped away. The gaping darkness of what's to come gnaws at me, keeping me awake.

What's to come for Ayva nicks at me most. She looks like Ma in one of the few digipix we have of her as a girl, a beauty sure to catch many lecherous eyes. She shivers, as if she kens the dark direction of my thoughts. I touch her cold arm. There's no blanket of course. Why make it comfortable for us? I curse our captors for the hundredth time today.

My gaze drifts to Meili across the aisle. Her companion Gwynn is curled up, fast asleep, but Meili is awake, fidgeting. She pulls off her scarf, uncoils her hair and runs her fingers through the tangles. A soft overhead light shines down on her. I can barely breathe, looking at her. I want to bring her into my arms. Want to hold her close and...

By all the gods, I've lost my mind. Snared like a hunted spunhound with no way out, and all I can think of is nuzzling a snooty Habbie who barely knew I was alive before today.

She catches me staring and her eyebrows rise. I have to get away. I unbuckle my safety belt and stand. I feel her gaze on my back as I head for the lav. There's only one, no separate lav for us as there would be on a Habeni ship. I guess we're all equal now.

Later, I move back up the aisle all the way to the front, a plan in my mind. I slide my hands along the front panel. Deke and the pilot are in the cockpit on the other side. They chat amiably, their voices murmuring through the door.

"We outnumber them," Meili says in an excited whisper. She sits up straight, watching me with eager eyes. "There're only two of them, and that Mr. Deke looks sickly."

I'm impressed by her newfound grit but can't help a snort. Could've used that bloodlust when they took Lil. Now that little one and her brother are alone, likely terrified, far from all who know them. Meili's brightness dims, as if she knows what I'm thinking.

"It won't work." Blix pokes his head over the back of her seat. "The door's surely locked on their side. And they have weapons. They've done this before. They won't risk getting jumped."

Meili's expression turns dejected. Mine too, though it was a mad plan. Who among us can fly an airbus?

I pace to the exit hatch and Blix weighs in again. "Open that door at this altitude, you'll be sucked into oblivion. Along with anyone else not belted in."

My gaze lands on Agron, sleeping with his mouth slagged open, his safety strap unbuckled. "Tempting." I look back to the door. "What about when we land?"

Blix considers for a few ticks. "Still pretty dangerous. We'll be moving at a speedy clip. Your only chance is to throw the door open before we touch down. Risky jump, but you might survive. You going to try it?"

He sounds gleeful, as if a Matalan hurling himself out of a speeding airbus is his idea of fun. He and the rest of those kutamas would press their snouts to the window to watch me fall, no doubt. I shift to Meili. Her saucer eyes are still on me. Would she? Would she care if I got splatted on the ground, as flat as a jocake? And why do I care if she cares?

I grunt my answer. Blix clucks his disappointment and goes back to sleep. I abandon my fool ideas and return to my seat.

Ayva moved when I got up and she's now sprawled across both cushions, softly snoring. I don't want to disturb her, so I hunker down in the aisle with my back against the side of the seat. I pull up my legs, resting my arms across my knees. One of my shoes brushes Meili's. Her foot twitches and I quickly shift my own foot away.

The burn on my side throbs, so I reach back for my water flask. I lift my tunic, exposing the charred skin where I got zapped. I slosh the last drips of water in the flask on the wound and wince.

"Does it hurt?" Meili whispers.

Not as bad as the juice that burned me. Felt like the stinging rays of a hundred suns pumping into my gut. I don't want to admit that to her so I shrug. That makes the burn sting more, bringing on another wince.

"Of course it hurts." Her hair slips over her shoulders as she leans toward me to study the wound. She doesn't flinch in disgust at the scored flesh, as I would expect a gell to do. "Some spencer's boot will lessen the sting and also leach infection."

"I'll run right out and pick some." Thirst and fatigue have deepened my voice. I sound more scolding than I intend to be. "How does a Habbie like you know about healing herbs?"

She huffs. "I know more than you give me credit for."

I nod and pull my tunic down, covering the wound. Why must I forever act like I'm trying to score a point in some game?

She clears her throat, a prim sound. "That was brave, what you did. Trying to help Lil."

I shrug again. It was stupid but typical for me. I never think before I act.

Meili leans back and sighs. "How did this happen? How's it allowed for the Adsullatans to force people into servitude? For them to snatch folk off their ships and sell them like a piece of furniture?"

Not sure she wants an answer, but I give her one anyway. "Because no one's stopped them. Too much coin on the line. There's profit in the troci trade. A *lot* of profit. Enough to encourage governments on several worlds to turn a blind eye. Especially our own."

"Well, it's sickening. No one should be treated in such a vile manner. As if we are nothing."

"Hunh. I'm sure you've said the same whenever us Matalans are abused at home."

She meets my gaze and her brow furrows. "At home? What do you mean? The Habeni don't treat Matalans like troci. You're free to come and go where you please."

"I'm not free. No Matalan is. You Habbies make sure of that with your rules and laws we got no choice but to obey. And even when we do obey, we still risk punishment. Might as well be troci for how so-called free we are. We gotta pay for it. too. Your people got your hands out wherever we go. Like the tolls we have to pay each time we cross a bridge to the Habeni sector."

"Tolls? What're you talking about?"

"Are you so sheltered in that palace you live in you don't know?" Someone in the back mutters for us to hush. I lean toward her and lower my voice. "When a Matalan goes to your side of the river, the Habbie manning the tollbooth demands a fee. One credit to cross the bridge, sometimes two or three if the gatekeeper's in a mood. And where are the jobs? Where is the school you allow me to work in? Where are the meds we need when we sicken? Across the bridges in your sector. A sad joke on us, isn't it?"

"I didn't know." She sounds shocked. "I've seen your people from the window of Mother's low-grav when she takes me to school. Lined up at Sklon Bridge, waiting to cross." A hard pause. "I suppose there's a good reason for the tolls. Safety or some such."

"Yeah, it's called greed." I stare at her, softening a whit. "You don't know any of this, do you? I suppose if they taught history in school, true history, you might know something about us Matalans. You might know how we were once, if not the same, then akin. Balanced. People like your father changed that."

She gasps. "My father?"

"Your father, your father's father, all those bandits who've been running things for centuries. They itched for more, scratched away at any strengths we had. Pulled us down and controlled us with low pay and no opportunity 'til they got us where they wanted. Desperate for any scrap we can get."

"My father gives your people jobs." Her voice hikes up in anger and there's more grumbling from the back.

"*Jobs*? Servitude's more like it. My uncle Jaff worked in your father's engine factory. He got sick but had to go to work all the same. There's no excuse for not showing up, you know. They expected him to punch rivets dawn to dusk. He had to sit 'cuz he didn't have strength to stand anymore. They fired him on the spot."

A host of emotions dance across her face. "That *can't* be true. I *cannot* believe it. You're lying. You must be. My father wouldn't do that. He gives his workers decent pay for a day's work. He treats his workers fairly."

"Fair?" I snort. "Your father and all those Habbies blow a lot of hot air about being fair, while doing everything they can to push us down. They want every Matalan under their heavy boot."

"And you Muckers always want stuff from us. You can't blame the Habeni for your failures and weaknesses. You have representatives in the councils. Why haven't they stood up for your people?"

"A handful of Matalans corrupted by heaps of Habeni coin? Yeah, they can be expected to stand up for our demands."

"My stars, you're opinionated. It's a wonder I never heard you speak so bold at home."

"What? Speak and have Lord Agron beat me bloody for my insolence? Or get my tongue cut out for sassing some high status culbana?" I give her a hard stare. "Or offend a naïve Habbie by telling her the truth about her father?"

"Stop calling me a Habbie. It's ugly."

"I will when you stop calling me Mucker."

She swivels to face me, her expression livid. "You *are* a Mucker. You lie like one and you're a hothead, like all the others who'd rather fight than work. I hope you get more than a hole in your belly next time. I hope they scorch you twice as good, you... you Rowlanite!"

If she thinks to insult me by lumping me in with the Rowlanite resistance fighters branded as terrorists by the Habeni Council, she's wrong. I'm proud to share their name. "Ye gods, what a spiteful priss you are."

"And you're annoying. I see why Agron popped you."

"You forget, I popped *him*. I'll pop anyone who threatens Ayva or any of my people. I protect my own. That's more than I can say for you and yours. Where's your lover? The one you were so eager to shackle yourself to? He should be protecting you, yet he trembles and hides, leaving you to the wolves. T'were me, I'd be by your side."

My anger fizzles and I curl my fists in frustration. Now I've done it. Let my feelings free.

Meili sputters. "I wasn't eager to shackle... He's not my lover. He's... he's nothing." She shoves her hair under her scarf and ties the strings with vicious motions. "In any case, don't get your Mucker frillies in a twist worrying about me, Kai ObDen. I can fight my own battles."

Can she? I thought she had guts to let her hair go red, but she buckled under when her parents demanded she agree to that alliance. She barely fought those reeking pirates as they shoved her around. I saw the way that auctioneer drooled over her. Noticed every lewd smirk tossed at her and Ayva by the watchers and the Adsullatans who'd oozed past our pen.

The nauseating thoughts I've been battling to keep away since those pirates caught us spill into my brain. Images of what's to come for them, for us all.

Can Meili stand up for herself now that the stakes are as high as the sky?

"You'll need to fight, my lady. Unless we find a way to escape, this nightmare's only gonna get worse. You'll need—" I almost say she'll need the grit and ferocity of the Matalan ancestor responsible for her red hair, but I bite it back. "You'll need to toughen up that soft heart. You'll need a spine of steel to stand up to what's coming."

For a flash of a moment, she meets my gaze, looking young, vulnerable. Frightened. Guilt flashes through me and part of me is tempted to reach for her, to ease the distress of my harsh words, not that my attention would be welcome. The other part is glad she's scared. Pa says fear is like a tonic. Nothing like a touch of terror to rouse a person to fight.

Then, without another word, she breaks off her gaze and turns, putting her back to me. She nestles her head against her seat cushion, chasing sleep.

I sit back and do the same, though I doubt sleep will come for a long, long time.

CHAPTER 10

Meili

THE SUN IS IN the west before the low-grav begins its descent. There's no water and the food is long gone. My belly gurgles, beyond empty. Gwynn is napping. Or trying to. Her stomach gripes louder than mine.

"We're coming up on what looks to be the Mollystone mines," Blix says from behind me.

Listless, I lean over Gwynn and look out the window. The low-grav's shadow ripples over rocky, brown hills that snake along for miles, like never ending ravines of chocolate. People dressed like us haul carts filled with blue-gray stones out of gaping mouths in the hills. The carts wobble over uneven ground toward yellow bins, where more people toss the stones in.

"What *is* Mollystone?" Gwynn asks, her voice no more than a dry croak.

I peep at Blix between the seatbacks, curious to know too. Most everyone else watches him, waiting for the answer.

"Mollystone's a mineral used as fuel. It's a lubricant for greasing things, too, like engines." Blix sounds pleased to have an audience interested in his facts for once. "It's rare on Hephas, rarer still on the near planets our Matalans are sent to mine. But these hills look to be full of it. Mining's brutal work. That must be why they use troci."

He snaps his mouth shut on that last word. That's what the Adsullatans want *us* for. To toil for them in those creepy looking mines until our backs are as bent as the people I see below.

"Surely *I* won't be expected to shovel Mollystone," Varina says. "That's Mucker work."

Kai flashes to me, as if to say, *See? The high and mighty Habeni, expecting the world to cater to her.* I want to tell him that Varina and I are as different as night is from day, but there's no way I'm speaking to him, not after our fight last night. I'm still furious with him.

Or... perhaps I'm angry with myself. For letting him get to me. For letting those snapping green eyes unsettle me so. And for saying I hope the watchers burn him again. Kai hasn't exactly been nice to me. His blather about Father being unfair to his workers can't possibly be true, but that doesn't excuse wishing him physical harm. That was unkind and something a lady should never do.

I lift my chin and look out the window. Not that I'd ever apologize for my rash words. A Habeni *never* apologizes to a Matalan. It just isn't done.

The low-grav glides over a sprawling electrical power grid next. The complex of transformers and relay stations has a towering brick smokestack at the center, puffing thick smoke into the air. We fly over a village with cobblestone streets next, then a forest of trees with spiny needles.

Several ticks later, our airbus descends further. Everyone sits up, alert. The forest gives way to an expanse of open land. A sprawling stone manor house atop a gently sloping hill looms ahead. Three stories high, with long, one-story wings on either side, the house looks like a blocky bird about to take flight. A paved drive flanked by stubby trees leads from a gated entrance up to the wide, paneled front doors.

My heart races. Mollystone Manor, our destination.

The low-grav swings to the rear of the property and passes over a row of thatched-roof cottages lined up alongside two massive farm fields. Green shoots push out of black soil in one field. In the other, troci operate mechanized devices that turn the soil, readying it for planting.

We hover over a meadow filled with what appear to be cattle grazing on blue-green grass. The creatures are large, with thick hides, furry tails, and a pointed horn on top of their heads. The landing gear thumps and we drop. The cattle barely flinch as the wind from the underbelly turbines flattens the grass around them.

We land with a soft thump and the engines stop. All is silent. Several ticks go by. Suddenly, the door *whooshes* open and I nearly jump out of my skin. Halia shrieks.

Mr. Deke pokes his head in. "Come. Your employers want to inspect you."

We shuffle off the bus. No one speaks, no one fights, not even Kai. Even he's given up hope of escape. I put on a brave face, but my legs quiver like jelly.

Mr. Deke's outside with the pilot and two watchers. The watchers grab each of us as we step off. One pins my arms while the other clips an orange plastic ring around my neck. He bumps a control wand against it and the choker tightens. A hum pulses through it, vibrating against my throat.

I claw at the ring. "What does this do?" I ask, though I already know. I saw the troci outside the marketplace wearing a choker like this. It's a restraining device.

"Try walking that-a-way," a mean-looking watcher says. He's massively large, with rough skin like a galaxy of small pebbles dotting his face. "You'll see what it does."

His companion chortles. His breath is sour, his grin full of gaps where teeth used to be.

They hustle us toward the manor house. The silky grass tickles my ankles. We pass a weather-beaten barn, other outbuildings, and an orchard of stubby trees weighed down with the yellowish fruit Gwynn and I ate on the bus. My mouth waters, remembering its tangy taste. Even mixed with the cattle stink, the smell of the fruit makes my stomach wail with hunger.

Mr. Deke tells us to stop and line up, females in front, males in back. A breeze kicks up. The green stalks in the nearby field sway with a lush, musical swish. The workers tending the crops pause to look us over. I can't tell their ages. Old as time I'd guess, from their leathery skin and stooping backs but I have a feeling I'm wrong.

The watchers snap to attention as two males and two females come out of the house onto what I think is a raised stone balcony that runs a goodly length along the west wing. The quartet move along the balcony to a flight of stone steps at the end. They descend and walk across the lawn toward us. The male leading the way limps as if his leg gives him much pain.

"Lord and Lady Forseti," Mr. Deke says when the group reaches us. "I am right pleased to see you again. You as well Sir Juning. And Lady Netti." He ends this toadying speech with a bow that scrapes the ground.

An odd crew of nobles stands before us. His lordship is gray-haired and tall, but frail-looking and nearly twice his lady's age. Lady Forseti is half his size, thin and delicate, wearing an unflattering flowered gown. Their daughter, who's about fifteen and plumper than her mother, looks like a Gods' Day gift package in a gold gown, a gold ribbon twined through dark braids, and several layers of face paint slathered on a roundish face. Sir Juning, who's around twenty, is decked out in hose, breeches and a red-gold tunic more garish than his sister's gown.

"Come, Deke," Lady Forseti says. Her voice is high-pitched and strained, as if struggling to find its way out of her slender throat. "Let us see what you've spent so much of our coin on."

"Certainly, my lady." Mr. Deke's nose is in the dirt again and he gestures frantically for us to do the same.

"What fine manners," her ladyship says almost with surprise at our deep and perfectly executed curtseys. I rise and lift my chin. Of course our manners are fine. Habeni are trained in the gracious arts as soon as we can walk.

Deke is in danger of nodding his head off his body. "Oh, indeed, your ladyship. And they're a healthy lot. Soon's I heard some young Habeni had been caught, I hied right to the troci market. The price was climbing steep, but I says to myself, her ladyship has dire need of more workers, especially in the mines, so I took the liberty to bid—"

"Yes, yes." Lady Forseti cuts him off with a wave. "You spent an extravagant amount but got the pick of the market. I hope they aren't as weak as the last bunch. Let us proceed with the assignments."

"Of course." Deke sweeps his gaze over us. "Listen now, you're to answer all questions honestly and with respect. And be quick about it," he adds, as if we're the ones who've been dawdling and not him with all his fawning and bowing.

Deke and the mean watcher with the pebbled face, whose name is Hup, begin to toss questions at the fellows lined up behind me. *What skills do you have? Can you plant and reap? Can you wield a sledge?* I can't imagine what any of them can answer to such questions. The front line is shorter, only five of us. Her ladyship, with Lord Forseti trailing, approaches a hollow-eyed Halia first.

"You appear hale and fit," she says. "Can you stitch, girl?"

Halia gapes in response, as if her translator has broken and she can't understand a word.

Lady Forseti clucks impatiently. "I bet you can pluck sissy fruit or dig taters. Tell Deke to assign you to the farm."

"There's a good girl." His lordship pats Halia on the head as if she's a pet that's performed a delightful trick.

"I get it," Gwynn whispers, tipping her head toward me. "They're seeking specific skills."

"Which none of us have," I say glumly, picturing myself digging taters with Halia.

Gwynn nudges me. "So what? When it's your turn, lie your head off."

Lying seems to be working behind us. After Deke deems several of my classmates fit for the mines, thanks to the Habeni obsession with physical training, Agron and Dipro catch on. When it's their turn, they claim to know all about farming. Blix goes on so long about robotic hoes and advances in the science of pest control, I think Deke marks him for farm work just to shut him up.

And Ullr? He stares into the distance and doesn't even blink when he's asked the same question three times. My heart sinks to see him brought so low.

"No mines for this one, Hup," Deke says, with a hint of genuine concern. "He'll hobble himself with a sledge the first day. Best keep him here under close watch."

My attention's brought back to the front line by Varina's raised voice. "I certainly *do not* sew."

I cringe at her haughty tone. A Habeni would rather die than admit she possesses any lowly Matalan skills but now is not the time for such pride.

"I see." Lady Forseti purses her lips. "Perhaps we have another task that would befit your exalted station." She looks at her spouse. "My lord, do you think crushing Mollystones in the mines would suit this Habeni princess?"

Though Lord Forseti nods, his expression is as vacant as Ullr's and I don't think he understands. Could this limping lord be hobbled in the head as well?

"Out of the question," Varina huffs. "I would *never* do such demeaning work."

Lady Forseti's eyes narrow to slits. "No, I suppose you wouldn't. Well then, gell, since you are so special, I shall give you a choice."

Varina turns hopeful. Clearly she's missed the archness in her ladyship's voice.

"You may choose scullery work, or you may swing a sledge in my mines. What'll it be?"

Varina chokes. Her cheeks blaze fiery red. I feel for her. I really do. What Habeni lady of any status has ever scrubbed a dish or mopped a floor? But the choice is obvious.

"I'll take the scullery," she says between clenched teeth.

"I thought as much." Lady Forseti's thin lips twitch in a victorious smile then she moves to Ayva and asks her favorite question, getting an eager nod in response.

"I can sew, my lady. I can also hem, embroider, darn, and wield a flatiron." Ayva punctuates this amazing list with a curtsey.

"Worthy skills." She inspects Ayva's hands then strokes her face. The multiple rings on her fingers sparkle in the sunlight. "How beautiful you are." Her forehead crinkles. "You are *all* so very lovely."

She casts a troubled look toward her son. I suspect why. Sir Juning's gaze has prowled over each of us since he got here. A hungry look that makes me wish I had a burlap sack covering me head to toe. Kai may accuse me of being naïve, but I'm not so thick that I don't get Sir Juning could be trouble. And I sense Lady Forseti thinks this too.

She turns back to Ayva with a sigh. "Very well. I have need of a lady's maid. I hope you aren't afraid of hard work. There's much mending and needlework to do. No time to dawdle."

"Yes, my lady. Thank you, my lady." Ayva drops another curtsey.

"Are you deef, son?" I hear behind me. I glance back. Kai's so focused on his sister's fate he barely notices that Deke has reached him. "Tell me quick what you can do or you're off to the Molly mines. We could use your broad back on the sledge gang."

Kai's agony is clear on his face. If he goes to the mines, he'll be far from Ayva. He looks around, as if scrambling for an idea. Suddenly, his expression transforms. His forehead crinkles and his shoulders droop. He looks as confused and lost as Lord Forseti.

Kai stabs a finger to his chest. "You talkin' to me?"

"Yeah, turd," Hup snaps. "Answer or I'll juice ya. Can you swing a sledge?"

"Dunno. What's a sledge?"

Hup growls. "It's a hammer, you slupa. Ya hit rocks wit it."

"Uh, sure," Kai says, as slow as a teakslug. "I s'pose. Uh, what I gotta do again?"

I bite back a gasp as Hup reaches for his weapon. Deke stops him.

"Don't. This one's as frail brained as..." Deke's eyes flick to Lord Forseti. "He'll take a week to do a day's job." He raises his voice, as if volume will improve Kai's understanding. "See here, Matalan, what *can* you do?"

Kai scratches his head, as hammy as an actor in a penny holodrama. "Dunno." He points toward the barn and the horned cattle grazing nearby. "I can shovel shit."

Deke laughs. "You're dim, but honest. I'll give you to Stitch, to help with the cattle. You can shovel shit to your heart's content."

I don't hear the rest of it because the lord and lady have moved on to Gwynn.

"I can dust and do laundry and make beds too," she blurts before a question is even asked. "Anything you require, my lady."

"What I require is a chambermaid, gell. You seem tidy and biddable. You'll do."

Then they're in front of me. "I can dust too," I lie. Weakly.

"Mother," Lady Netti calls.

Her ladyship winces in annoyance. "Not sure I need any more help in the house," she says to me. "Deke may need you on his mining crew, though you hardly look like you can pick up a sledge. Mayhap you can thresh?"

Thresh? What in Rossa's pocketbook is that?

"Mother!" Lady Netti again.

Her ladyship swings toward her daughter and scowls. "What *is* it, Netti?"

"Can we hurry?" She fans her face with a hand bedecked with as many jewels as her mother's. "It's so terribly hot. You know how much I detest these inspections."

"And you know how important it is to undertake an inspection yourself. It's a critical part of managing a household. You'll thank me someday."

I hear my own mother in what she says, always lecturing me on the importance of learning to be a great lady. I'm shocked to think they're alike in any way.

"But I *really* need to leave," Netti whines.

"To do what, Netti? To go to that reading room again? I told you I don't want you there."

Netti's looks stricken, as if her mother's caught her fibbing. "Of course not. I promised Cayla I'd go to the dress shop with her post-noon. That was *ages* ago."

"Be still, we're almost done." Her ladyship turns back to me and waves a hand. "Report to Deke's mine gang, gell. Come my lord, we're finished here."

She takes his arm and they turn to leave. A crater seems to open beneath my feet, threatening to swallow me up. I bite back a sob.

I'm going to the mines.

You'll need a spine stronger than steel.

That was Kai's warning to me on the airbus last night. An unwelcome criticism then, a rallying cry now. I squeeze my hands into fists. He's right. I can't just give in. Can't let this imperious Adsullatan send me to those mines. I have to stiffen my spine. I must fight.

"Wait. Your ladyship, *wait*."

She swivels, eyeing me. "Yes?" She draws the word out to many syllables.

I need to think of something, and fast. I look around, as frantic for an idea as Kai was moments ago. I spot a sprawling, overgrown garden between the fields and the east wing of the house. Clearly, no one has tended that sad patch of weeds for a long time.

"My lady, I'm quite skilled with herbs and flora *and* coaxing them to grow." A lie. Though I spent many hours with Taryn in my family's herb garden, my experience is limited to snipping flowers to arrange in a vase and plucking the occasional weed. "Your garden's in deplorable shape. It needs tending to flourish. I'll put it right, if you give me a chance."

"M-o-t-h-e-r-r-r," Lady Netti howls. "Let's go."

Her ladyship's gaze flicks to her, back to me. I fidget, struggling to hold her attention.

"I'll work hard, my lady, I promise. I'll grow a variety of herbs and other tasties your cook will use to make the most exquisite and savory meals. Guests will rave about what you serve at table. You'll be *the* most envied hostess in the land." I toss that in, hoping she's as vain as Mother when it comes to what her guests think of her hospitality.

She tilts her head, considering. My heart thuds violently. Finally, after an eternity when I see myself swinging a sledge in the mines or doing whatever job a thresh is used for, she nods.

"Perhaps you *can* be useful."

Useful. A word I've never heard directed toward me. Toward any Habeni female, for that matter. It lights me up inside.

"You'll assist the parlor maid with household chores," she says. "When you're done, you may tend my garden. Tell my housekeeper you're allowed garden access. I expect results, gell." Her dark-eyed gaze digs into me. "I *do not* like being lied to. It makes me unhappy. And if I'm unhappy, so will you be. I promise."

Threat received, I drop the deepest, most subservient curtsey of my life, sighing in relief.

She steps back then sweeps her gaze over us. "Listen well. You've been blessed to come under the care and consideration of my lord Gugg Forseti." She nods at her husband, who's occupied studying the birds flittering about overhead. "You'll find he treats his troci well. You'll be clothed and fed, and your medical needs treated. In exchange, his lordship expects you to work to your best ability." Her genial tone hardens. "If you shirk your duties, or disrupt the smooth operation of our enterprise, you *will* be punished. No excuses."

Deke and the other watchers pat the weapons holstered on their belts for emphasis.

"Finally, when we take on new troci, there are some who reject our generosity and endeavor to run." Her gaze settles on me and I gulp. "Let me assure you, any attempt to flee will *not* be successful. The perimeter is secured by an electrified barrier tied to your security collars. Should you attempt to breech the barrier... well, when the zati and a current collide, the end will be quick, but not pleasant." She pauses to let that sink in. "Am I clear?"

No. Nothing's been clear since those pirates boarded our ship. I don't understand any of what's happening, but I mutter, "Yes, my lady," along with everyone else.

"Well then," she says. "Welcome to Mollystone Manor."

A moment of gloomy silence, then Deke and the watchers break into a round of polite applause. She turns and strides away beside her lord. Lady Netti quickly follows, and after strafing those of us in the front line with one last leer, so does Sir Juning.

The moment they're out of sight, the watchers descend. They attach a small box to the zati collars of my classmates assigned to the mines, for travel I think, and hustle them into a surface transport. Deke and a watcher get into the van's control pit, and the vehicle bumps across the grass toward the drive at the front of the house.

"Move it," Hup barks to those that remain, gesturing to the cottages beyond the fields.

Halia and the others do as ordered. Ullr straggles at the end. Kai reaches for Ayva, but a watcher yanks her away and points her toward the house. I'm close by and Kai seizes my gaze. His expression takes me aback. Not scorn or anger.

For the first time since this ordeal began, he looks scared.

A lump fills my throat, our fight on the low-grav forgotten. I don't have any siblings, as it's not the fashion for Habeni to have more than one or two children, but if I was so cruelly separated from my family members, I'd be frightened too.

"Don't be troubled, Kai. I'll watch out for Ayva." The words tumble from my mouth before I can consider what I'm saying. Though I assured Kai otherwise, I don't know if I have the ability to watch out for myself, never mind Ayva. "And for Rossa's sake, don't get yourself killed."

Before he can answer, Hup looms up and gives him a shove. As he joins the others stumbling toward their new home, he glances back at me and smiles. Fleeting, like a starburst, but somehow that makes me feel better.

I smile back, but he's already turned away.

CHAPTER 11

Meili

"Halloo, missies," the housekeeper says as the watchers deposit us into her care. "You're a fine sight for these sore eyes. I'm Bridgie."

I gape in surprise and Varina's eyes pop. "You're Matalan," she cries.

There's no doubt about that. Roughly forty, Bridgie's as tall and as solidly built as most Matalans, with pale green eyes and dark red hair streaked with gray. She's handsome too, but, like so many others we've encountered here, white scars mar her skin, spurting across her face, forearms, and throat like ice cracks in a frozen pond.

"I was once Matalan, love. Now I'm a troci, like you." Bridgie taps the ring circling her neck. She's worn it a long time, given how her skin has grown around the faded plastic. I touch my own zati, suddenly unable to swallow. "I'm housekeeper, cook, and head of the house. You'll answer to me."

Varina bristles. I feel strange too, though I don't know why. Our world's been upended. To take offense that a Matalan is to be our superior is absurd.

Bridgie leads us along the trimmed lawn of the east wing toward a door to what she calls "our quarters." I get a good look at the garden as we pass. It's in no better condition up close, all tangled weeds and broken fence that would challenge even my minna Taryn's considerable skills. A strange sort of spiny vine grows throughout, choking the life out of any respectable plant trying to sprout there.

"Her ladyship's kindly allowed you the rest of the day to settle before beginning your duties." Bridgie steps up onto a stone stoop and punches a series of numbers into a keypad next to the door. Her fingers move too fast for me to see the code. "I wager you missies are hungry after your long journey. There's food and drink inside."

The word food puts the keycode and all other thoughts from my mind. The door whooshes open then snaps shut behind us with the ominous clunk of a deadbolt shunting into place. We're locked in.

"This is the kitchen," Bridgie says.

"Kitchen?" Gwynn whispers. "More like a palace."

She exaggerates, but only a little. The room is spacious, with a high ceiling, two large cookers, and a center island longer and wider than I am tall. The double-tub sink has a looped faucet. Several ladderback chairs and a small dining table cluster around a temperature control element. An open door to the left gives a peek into a well-stocked pantry.

The whole place is twice the size of our kitchen at home, and I suspect even larger than Varina's by the way she goggles.

Bridgie opens cupboard doors to show us the crockery, tea service, dishes and plates stowed within. I'm less interested in conducting an inventory than I am in the smells—braised beef, I think, and gravy, definitely gravy. My belly makes a *gimme* growl.

A door to our right opens and an Adsullatan girl with a mop of black hair and big brown eyes emerges. Her gown is tattered and stained. She's maybe sixteen, though as small as a child, and she reminds me of Lil so much my heart squeezes.

"This is Ellse, parlor maid, kitchen maid, and about all other chores since the others—" Bridgie swallows the rest. Since the others *what*?

Ellse creeps up to Varina, sniffs her, then frowns. "Bad egg."

Varina snorts. Ellse gives Ayva and Gwynn a gap-toothed grin and studies me with open curiosity.

"Good gells," she says.

"Leave them be, Ellse." Bridgie waves her off. "Get the stew off the cooker so's the missies can eat. Do you gells want to sit down?"

She doesn't have to ask us twice. Chairs scrape the tiles as we sit. All except Ayva. She stands awkwardly nearby. Gwynn and I exchange glances.

"Sit down, Ayva," Gwynn says and I push out a chair with my foot. "Matalans and Habeni can sit at table together without the worlds coming to an end."

Ayva sinks into the seat with a grateful smile. Varina scoots her chair away.

Ellse serves us heaping portions of a stew thick with chunks of beef, taters, carrots, and other vegetables I can't identify. We dine, by which I mean we toss table manners aside, open our mouths and shovel the stew in, followed by bread and that yellow, oval-shaped fruit Bridgie calls sissy fruit.

Bridgie watches us a tick, then insists we tell her the duties we're assigned to. She beams with approval when Ayva mentions her stitching talents.

"You'll be welcome above stairs. The last lady's maid couldn't stitch a whit. Pricked her fingers and bled on Lady Netti's underthings more often than not. I pray you know how to remove stains. My lady can be... sloppy sometimes."

She clears her throat, as if realizing she's spoken too freely. I wonder if our servants back home say such spiteful things about

Mother. Or me. And then I get sad, because… Home. I vow to banish the word from my mental vocabulary.

Bridgie turns to me. "What about you, my lady?"

How strange she uses that title. All these years away from Hephas and she still hasn't shaken our formal ways.

"I'm to help Ellse," I say, completely forgetting Mother's warnings about speaking with my mouth full. "And tend the garden, too. I have knowledge of herbs and weeding and such."

Hoo, what a load of manure, but Bridgie buys it. She coos excitedly, as if I've announced I've cured the Matalan flu.

"My lady must be pleased to have an herbalist for her garden again. Wynnie could coax the most delicate leaf to grow from nothing. My cooking ain't been the same since poor, dear Wynnie…"

She falters and stares off with a mournful frown, looking so distressed I don't dare ask what happened to poor, dear Wynnie. Besides, I'm not sure I want the answer.

"Bridgie, how did a Matalan end up here?" Gwynn asks, tearing off a piece of bread.

"Got caught on a mucking ship comin' home from Aine, my lady." She sips from a small glass filled with a lavender-hued liquor she calls dromé. "T'were a half dozen of us. I'm the only one left. Must a been near on twenty seasons ago."

I drop my fork with a clatter. *Twenty* seasons. That's an entire lifetime.

"Now then, what's all this ruckus?" a lanky male in a black tailcoat says as he ducks under an arched opening between the kitchen and a hallway I think connects to the main part of the manor.

"Ah, there you are, Hervey." The lines framing Bridgie's eyes crinkle. "Come meet our new troci. Ain't they a fine, healthy-looking group? Gells, Mr. Hervey's our butler. He came to us from Dryas, when was it? Last year?"

He shrugs off his coat and hangs it on a rack. His shirt's snowy white, the collar points pressed and starched. "You're slipping, Missy Bridgie. I was caught two years ago." He scans us with eyes the color of a bobnut. "My stars, I've never seen a more homely looking crew in all my days."

His voice is so full of mischief I don't take offense. In fact, I like him immediately. That he's from the forest planet Dryas seems appropriate. He's as tall as a tree, with long arms like branches and knobby, twig-like fingers.

He settles into a rocking chair close to the temperature control element. "Just the lord and lady home for supper tonight, Missy Bridgie. The young miss is out with a friend and Sir Juning's off to town." Bridgie stiffens and the butler hastily adds, "Don't fret. Jinks is with him. He'll keep the lad out of trouble. That's his job, isn't it?"

Bridgie lets out a heavy sigh and downs the rest of her dromé.

Mr. Hervey slides a pipe from his trousers pocket and tamps a sweet-smelling tobacco into the bowl. "Now, let's get down to business. Where are you missies from? How were you caught? How many in your group? I must hear the entire story."

He lights his pipe, listening as we recount the details of our capture. Before I realize it, my dish is scraped clean and so is the stew pot.

"You're fortunate you weren't sent to the mines," Hervey says. "It's dangerous work, with constant threat of a fall-in trapping one deep in the earth with no air or light." Ellse, curled up at his feet, watches in fascination as he puffs smoke from his pipe and it rises in lazy circles. "Then there's the rachee. They roam the hills and forest at night, looking for troci to munch on. And of course there's the fever."

"The fever? Molly fever?" I ask, alarmed. "I heard about that. The watchers said it's really bad."

"No denying that." Mr. Hervey ignores Bridgie's frown and goes on. "It comes from the mines and no one is spared. It's a fiendish thing to go through. Or so I hear tell."

He looks at Bridgie and it clicks. The streaks on her skin, Lord Forseti's scars, the white marks on so many other Adsullatans I've seen. They're from Molly fever.

"Ain't as bad as that." Bridgie touches her cheek, almost protectively. "The watchers like to tell stories to scare the new troci. No worry, loves. You're healthy. That's why you was chosen. Besides, there ain't been a outbreak of the fever for almost a full year."

That's not very reassuring. A heavy pall falls over the kitchen. Is that what happened to the other troci? Did the fever sweep through and... I can hardly think it. Did the Molly fever *kill* the ones who were here before us?

Several ticks later, Bridgie breaks the silence with a falsely cheerful, "Well, now. You missies look like well-fed housecats. I'm sure you're exhausted from your travels and want to clean up and rest. Ellse will help Hervey with the family's needs this evening."

Mr. Hervey says good night and Bridgie follows us into the room Ellse popped out of earlier, a narrow space with cots lined up in a row. At the end of our sleeping quarters is a lav with, I'm happy to see, a showering stall. Bridgie directs us to take linens out of a dresser in the corner and make up a cot. We also find clothes in there, a wool nightdress for each of us, clean dresses, and several pairs of frillies.

"Sleep now, gells. Tomorrow you'll be up at dawn to begin your chores, so don't dally. Don't pout, love." She directs this to Varina, who eyes her with something more than a pout. "You'll learn to like it here and will take pride in serving the family as I do. Afore you know it, you'll forget all that came before and call Mollystone Manor home."

She beams a motherly smile then disappears through the doorway.

"She's loopy, or drunk," Varina snaps and I think she may be right.

We take turns washing up, luxuriating in, if not hot, then a warm shower. Varina goes first. We each select a cot. Varina takes the one closest to the temperature control element.

I don fresh frillies—they're so big they need to be double laced—then pull the nightdress over my head and settle on a cot as hard as a slab of granite and not half as comfortable. Gwynn switches off the lamp. I see through the sole barred window that it's only sunset, but storm clouds are rolling in and they darken our room as if it's night.

In the kitchen, something sizzles on the cooker. Plates and silver rattle. Bridgie speaks to Mr. Hervey. Her voice is too low to make out but his reply is clear, "They should know about it now, rather than later."

Raindrops begin to patter the roof. I let out my breath. I'm full and clean and feel somewhat human again. I can almost think things aren't as bad as all that. Except for the word *troci* weighing me down. Except for the fever that's so deadly nobody wants to talk about it. Except for being stuck in this house, behind locked doors, with this awful plastic thing around my neck.

Outside, a beast howls. A blood-stilling sound of despair and fury, like a mother whose child is ripped from her arms. Promising revenge. I shudder under the thin blanket.

Except for *that*—the rachee.

Gwynn lets out a watery sigh. "How long has it been since we left home?"

That word stings my heart. "Two days, three?" I honestly don't know.

"Surely something's being done," she says. "The Adsullatans have broken the treaty. The Habeni Councils must be addressing that.

They must be negotiating a ransom or making a rescue plan. Right?"

"They better be." Varina flops around on her cot. "The very idea of me, scrubbing dishes. The Councils had better send a ship to get me *now*."

Ayva pulls the blanket over her face and begins to sob.

"Oh, Ayva, please don't cry," Gwynn urges, struggling to hold back tears of her own.

The blanket moves as Ayva nods underneath, sniffling harder.

Varina growls in annoyance. "Gods. Will you just shut up, Mucker?"

Gwynn gasps and I stiffen. "Her name is Ayva," I snap. "*Ayva.* If you address her again, you'd better use it. Or better yet, why don't *you* shut up?"

Varina turns her glare on me. She's always been at the top of the status heap. I doubt anyone's ever dared speak to her like this, but I'm past caring. I told Kai I'd watch out for his sister, and that's exactly what I'm going to do.

"I will *not* shut up. We're locked up like criminals and that Matalan sleeps beside us and I'm to w-wash d-dishes—" Varina's voice catches. "And you tell me to sh-shut up. I *will not!*"

But then she does because she's crying so hard she can't speak anymore. Gwynn and Ayva join in with great, big, gut-wrenching sobs, weeping freely.

And so do I.

I've been fighting tears since those pirates bumped into our ship. I can't fight any longer.

I shut my eyes and imagine I'm home, in my bed. My soft pillow and my silken sheets. The honey scent of the freshly picked losys flower Taryn places by my bedside each night. Taryn herself, switching off the light. Mother and Father's voices, sometimes gentle, sometimes harsh, drifting up from downstairs as I fall asleep.

Warm, safe. Free. Home.

The drum of the rain picks up, until a torrent beats against the roof.

I bawl like a baby.

Chapter 12

Kai

"I SEEN A RACHEE sniffing around the perimeter earlier," Stitch says when I get to the barn. "I sneaked up on the bloater and chased him off."

I dump a bucket of water into my barrow and slosh it around, loosing bits of dung stuck to the wood. Sneaked? That's a hopeful word for Stitch. He's a big, lumbering Adsullatan who couldn't sneak up on a kettle at full boil without it noticing.

Stitch leans against the wall of the barn, chewing on a piece of hay, watching me work. "Prey must be thin in the forest this summer for a rachee to come out in the open like that." He spits. "Keep a close eye on the cattle when you're shoveling shit, boy, in case that beast comes back."

I keep an eye on the cattle anyway, since they're prone to stomping on my feet, but I nod and grunt like the slupa I'm pretending to be and dump the water from the barrow. Brown liquid makes strange patterns in the blue green grass before seeping into the soil below. I don't know why I have to clean the barrow. It still reeks and I'll fill it many times over again tomorrow, as I have for the three weeks I've been locked up here. But that's what Stitch wants and who am I, a lowly troci, to argue?

"Watch out for yerself too," he adds with less urgency. "The rachee like cattle but won't turn up their snouts at a taste of people meat."

I follow Stitch into the barn and help him secure the cattle pens for the night. Not that he'll be far away if there's a problem. He bunks in a corner of the loft and never leaves the property.

Can't figure him out. There's no zati choking his neck, so he's not a troci. But he's not a watcher either. At least, he doesn't strut around, fondling a juicer as if it's a favored part of his anatomy like the guards do. He reminds me of Pa, in some ways. A bit dense but dedicated to his family. His four-legged family, in Stitch's case.

I slip the rope over the gate, securing the last pen. Stitch pushes me toward the door. "Better get along now, boy. I know you got a big supper waiting."

He never says my name. Not sure he remembers it. And I'm not sure if he's funning. My supper isn't big, not by a long shot. And the chances of it waiting if I'm late are slim to none. Food's more precious than gold in the troci camp and hoarding is rampant. I go to bed hungry more often than not, just like back home. I've traded one life of drudgery for another.

I nudge my zati. With this necklace as a grim addition.

Back outside the barn, I stow my barrow and the stout wooden shovel I use in my chores. I peel off my tunic, fill a bucket from one of the rain barrels and plunge my head into the cold water. I scrape dung off my face and out of my hair, then I scrub my hands and arms. I'd climb into a rain barrel every evening if Stitch would let me, just to be free of shit for a blessed tick.

It's twilight. The dark clouds that bring the nightly rain are gathering as I pass the orchard then cross between the fields and the house. I glare at the east wing and the metal door Ayva disappeared through three weeks ago. I haven't seen a peep of her since.

Can't help thinking Pa's heart must've cracked in two with Ayva gone. Especially after losing Ma not long ago. I miss Pa, that stubborn old gump. I miss the little tykes, too, always running around our shanty, getting their grubby fingers into everything. My chest hurts I miss them all so much.

I scratch my neck—the collar chafes and sweat makes it itch twice as bad—digging in with all the frustration boiling inside me. It does me no good. My skin still itches. It'll do me no good to turn myself purple with grief missing home, either. I need to focus on getting Ayva out of there. Meili too, though I don't know why I should risk my neck for her.

How to free them is the question.

There's no way into the house, Stitch says. It's locked up and electrified. Even the thick, concrete wall that leads between the east wing and the watchers' cottage is electrified. Stitch says there's a courtyard inside there. Where the indoor servants hang linens to dry and grab a rest when they have a minute to themselves.

Getting Ayva and Meili out of that house is one problem. The barrier is another, a bigger one. There's no busting through that invisible wall of electricity around the ranch.

There's no escape from this dirt hole.

My mood's as gloomy as the darkening sky by the time I reach home sweet home. They've crammed fifty of us into four pin-sized hovels lined up near the northeast perimeter. The white-washed clapboard is cracked and dry as dust, the roofs patched and double patched, flimsy protection from the nightly rain and morning heat.

Still, these dumps are better than bunking down in tents at the mines, as Stitch says, wondering what's going to get you first, a mother-humping rachee or that Molly fever everyone whispers about.

I squeeze down a cool, narrow alley space between two of the buildings to the cookfire. It's full dark now. The security floodlights that ring the property have popped on. Most everyone's here.

Some sit on the ground, some stand, some are lucky enough to have grabbed space on one of the wooden benches.

Agron eyes me from a bench as I cross to the cookfire. A lanky Dryan female serves him a bowl of stew, like he's still a top status goon and she's his personal servant. That kutama's been pushing the other troci around since the first day we got here, and they let him.

I ignore his smug grin and grab a tin bowl from a stack on the table next to the cauldron hanging over the cook fire. The gell on kitchen duty this week slops a ladleful of thin stew into my bowl. I grab a hunk of bread then sit cross-legged on the ground and slip my spoon out of my pocket. Bowls are plentiful, spoons are not.

The stew's a mix of limp greenies and old taters and smells like greasy swamp water. The cook's tossed some sort of spongy leaf into it to give it a kick. Before long, my bowl's scraped clean and my stomach shuts up.

For now. It's a long time before sunrise and breakfast.

I sit back and scan my fellow troci. They talk in small groups. Agron's Dryan companion sinks onto his lap. Her translator's busted, but she understands what Agron wants. All the gells do, and some of the males, too. As soon as we stepped into camp, the others began to buzz around us, sizing us up, offering themselves in exchange for protection. I glare at Agron, openly fondling the Dryan. He's been more than willing to take advantage of the offer.

I'm not interested. I don't need anyone else to worry about. Ayva's enough. And Meili, I guess.

I turn my gaze to Blix. He's hunkered down by the fire, reading a book he's managed to scrounge. Probably had to trade a week of bread rations to get it. I miss reading and the bread's mealy and as hard as a rock, but unless that book is a how-to on escaping this place, I wouldn't give up a single morsel for it.

"How was the shit today, Kai?" Petra says, plopping down next to me. An Adsullatan with big, brown eyes and sleek black hair, she's pretty, even with the fever's white streaks dug like claw marks into her cheeks.

"Shitty, as usual," I say, studying her a tick. She claims not to want a protector. Says she's been here three years and has looked out for herself all that time. If that's so, what does she want with me? I put my empty bowl on the ground between us. "And how was threshing?"

"Ugh. Those greenie stalks are as thick as my auntie's ankles. Can't even cut 'em with a rachee-tooth saw."

Petra digs into her meal. Her spoon is old and bent and *tings* against her bowl. There's a bump on the underside of her wrist, from a contraceptive disk just beneath her skin. A *stopper*, she calls it, inserted the day she came to this paradise. Not out of consideration for her or the other gells, but to keep them at work and prevent time lost to birthing and childrearing. For the best, Petra says, as the fever preys on children and females carrying a babe most.

I sit back and idly pick at the latch sealing my zati with the dull tip of my spoon handle.

"What did I tell you about doing that?" Petra says. "That thing will explode if you disturb the latch."

I grunt. So she says. So does everyone else. But is it true?

She mutters angrily, as if she knows what I'm thinking. "Why do you doubt me? Fellow I worked a thresher with was as doubtful as you. A twip by the name of Elgin. He swiped a bit of metal from the toolshed. A nail, I think. He picked at the zati's seal until... Well, he murdered himself quite brutally." She eyes me a long time. "I seen it, Kai. Blew his head right off."

I swallow. The choker squeezing my throat bobs up and down.

"You wanna escape? Take to the black leaf, like half the fools here have." She tips her head toward Ullr, over by Blix. He sits on the ground with his shoulders slumped, eating listlessly, his gaze vacant. "Like that lad. The black leaf's an easy way out."

She means abyssa, a plant with blackish leaves that grows in the mountains. The only item more precious in the troci camp than a spoon. Smoked or eaten, black leaf sends the user to happy land. Ullr's been as high as the noonday sun on the stuff since we got here, his eyes so glassy I can practically see my reflection in them.

"What about you?" I ask. "You get looped?"

"Not me. It gets in your blood so's you want more and more of it, and you'll do almost anything to get it." She scrapes up the last of her stew then licks the bowl. "You should warn him to bug off the stuff before he gets zapped again. Or chops off his leg with the thresher."

I raise an eyebrow. "What's it to me what happens to him?"

Petra's dark eyebrows pop up in surprise. "He's your friend, ain't he? Come in with your lot. Thought you might want to warn him to watch out."

"He's no friend of mine. None of them are. I watch out only for me."

She laughs. "You're a hard son of a cur, Kai."

I flinch. Maybe so but hearing it knocks me down a bit.

"No disrespect," she adds, laughing again. "Hard is smart. You might have a chance to survive here."

I don't want to survive here. I want to escape.

Petra stiffens at the sound of a vehicle in the distance, drawing closer. I stiffen too. It's Sir Juning, puttering toward us astride a two-wheeled metal rev cycle with steering controls up front. He's come around a few times since I've been here, always at supper. He circles our group on his cycle, eyeing the females, licking his lips and leering, then he rides away.

Tonight is different. He drives his revver around and around the camp but he doesn't leave. Petra does. The moment Juning stops the vehicle and gets off, she disappears. The long-time troci jump to their feet. His haughty gaze moves over all of us, challenging us, until we're all standing. I get up, real slow, adopting my slupa expression.

"That's better," he says, a smirk in his voice. "You new troci need to learn proper manners, I see."

He strolls casually through our group. We stand still as the grave, barely breathing. He passes me. He's wearing a golden coat that shimmers in the floodlights' glare. He smells like an ale house.

Finally, he stops in front of Halia and rakes her with his hungry gaze. I remember Agron toying with Ayva on the *Whittal* all those weeks ago and I ball my fists. Juning trails the back of his hand down Halia's face. She trembles from head to toe, and not from delight.

"Don't be afraid, gell. I don't bite," he purrs. "Not unless you want me to."

His lips curl into a lewd grin and bile rises in my throat. He looks down at Halia's bowl, shaking in her hands. A bit of greasy stew slops out.

"Is that your supper? How pitiful. Would you like something nice to eat? I've got just the thing. A meal fit for a lady as lovely as you." He moves back to his rev cycle. "All you need do is get aboard." He tips his head and cocks his eyebrow, like the slick predator he is.

Halia hesitates. Her gaze flicks around, looking for help. No one moves, no one speaks. Dageth's grubby fingernails. A female choosing to cozy up to someone for protection is one thing, but to be forced to give in by this goon is vile. And low.

A sharp object suddenly digs into my side, nearly piercing my kidney. A bleat of pain escapes my mouth before I can hold it back. Behind me, Agron snickers softly. That kutama's sneaked up and stuck me with a sharpened stick or something. He gets what he wanted.

Juning's attention—on me.

The creep's neck cracks as he swivels to stare at me. Halia eyes me too, her expression hopeful.

"Have you anything to say, troci?" Juning says. The cookfire's light flickers over his eager face. "Come now, I give you permission to speak." His hand rests on the holster holding his juicing weapon, giving lie to his words.

He reminds me of Old Tuck from down the block, who set elaborate traps for mice and other rodents to blunder into. I hear Ayva's voice in my head, warning me not to blunder into Juning's trap. I hear Meili too. *Don't get yourself killed.* My gut still stings from that juicing in the troci market. And I took that punishment for Lil. Why should I risk a zap for a Habbie, especially when none of her own people will stand up for her?

If that makes me a hard son of a cur, so be it.

I shake my head. Juning's face falls, disappointed. Halia's shoulders slump and she drags over to the cycle. Juning cups her bottom and helps her to mount the leather seat. In a tick, the cycle purrs into the night.

I swing on Agron, murder on my mind. "Time to crack your nose again."

He flinches and I allow myself a flash of satisfaction. He's afraid of me.

"You won't dare lay hands on me, Mucker." He jerks his chin toward his minions standing nearby. Dipro and a couple of Adsullatans wait for his signal to pounce.

Agron I could take. A gang would do real damage. But Dageth's balls, I won't show any of them fear. "I'll do worse if you ever touch me again. Now get out of my way."

I stomp down one of the alleys, feeling powerless and without hope, but mostly angry.

Later when I come out of the privy after prepping for bed, I see Halia stumble toward her quarters. She hunches from the rain, a bowl clutched to her breast. It's heaped to overflowing with taters and chunks of bread and what looks like beef. Her reward for services rendered.

I return to my hovel and step around the cots to my space near the wall, crawling into bed. Not really a bed, just two wool blankets sewn together and stuffed with greenie husks. I stare at the wall for a long time, dark thoughts beating at my brain.

If Juning openly plays his lewd games in camp, what must go on in that house, behind closed doors? The thought of my sister and Meili and the others at the mercy of that Adsullatan pimple in people clothes triples my anger. Triples my resolve to break out of this place.

Escape *can't* be impossible, no matter what anyone says. I'll find a way to get the gells out of that house, find a way out of this stink hole for all of us. No matter how many alarms and barred windows and walls and electrified fences are between us and freedom, I'll find a way.

I'll find a way.

Chapter 13

Meili

"Begone, pests."

I roust the last of the dust balls clustered in the temperature control element's core and flip the switch. The cooling fans power up, battling the humid air with a determined *thup-thup*. I sit back on my heels and look up at Ellse.

"How'd I do?"

She emits a wordless gurgle, which I take as high praise. Have to admit, I'm impressed too. Who knew Meili Bengough, high born Habeni, could learn how to dust?

I pick up my work bucket and follow Ellse from the ballroom. A gaudy gold carpet runs along the hallway from the front entrance to the library at the other end. A dozen framed portraits hang on walls papered with even busier patterns, stripes and swirls that make me dizzy. Lord Forseti and his lady pose stiffly in one digipix, another depicts Lady Netti, nearly swallowed by shadows. The rest are digipix of Sir Juning.

A swish from above draws my attention upward. Gwynn dashes down the grand staircase, clutching a bundle of sheets. The reason she's fleeing this way instead of using the servants' hidden passageway leans over the upper rail—Sir Juning. He's up oddly early. He usually stays abed until well past noonday.

"Hello, Red," he calls down to me, with a sly grin.

I return a frown and skitter away, popping into the library behind Ellse and locking the door in case he gets the notion to follow. That hasn't happened yet, but the way he lurks, watching us as a raptor eyes its prey, it's only a matter time before he swoops in for the kill. The only question is when.

I put him out of my mind and get to work sweeping the floor with the electric broom. Ellse runs a cloth across his lordship's desk, polishing it to a shine. Until we came along, she had to do all the house cleaning, as well as washing bed linens, tending to the ladies and their wardrobes, and scrubbing dishes, a job that seems to never end.

Bridgie says Ellse has been here four years, bound to the Forseti family by her coin-strapped family when she was twelve. Four years of mind-numbing, back-aching drudgery. I don't know how she can stand it. After only a month, I'm ready to buckle.

And I'm more than ready to get outside to the garden.

Bridgie won't let me go until she's satisfied I can properly complete my house duties first. How long will that be? Lady Forseti didn't give me a deadline to set the garden right, but surely she'll want to see some progress soon. How can I do that if I can't get to it?

We finish cleaning the library and move on. I get to the door first. I flip the lock and push it open when... *thump*. A solid thump. The sound of the door smacking something. I crane my neck to see and my heart shrivels. Not something. Some*one*.

Lady Netti.

It's my first real look at her. She's plain, and her shapeless gown does her no favors, hiding what I think might be a nice figure. Her gold makeup is as thick as a plaster mask. It almost hides the ravine-deep scars the fever has cut into her face.

"My lady." I drop a curtsey, not one of my best, "I beg your pardon. I didn't know you were coming into the library."

She bristles. "I wasn't going into the library."

Then what's she doing hovering in front of the door? Of course I don't say that. I know she carries one of those stinging weapons in her gown's pocket. All the Forsetis and even Bridgie carry the juicing guns, as if they're a must-have accessory and not an instrument of punishment.

I curtsey and beg Lady Netti's pardon once more.

"Very well." She rubs her injured nose, putting several cracks in her makeup. "Just don't do it again. Go on, both of you. Get out of my sight."

We gladly oblige, scurrying along the hallway to the servants' stairs. In the kitchen, Bridgie's standing at the center island. Her scarred hands sink into a mound of dough she's kneading. She calls Ellse over. Gwynn's at the table and Varina's at the sink, up to her elbows in sudsy water.

I stow my work bucket on its shelf and fall into a chair. I'm almost too exhausted to peel the sissy fruit Gwynn hands me. I'd better eat it though. I need to grab my meals when I can since I'll be back to work in two ticks.

Ayva rushes in a moment later. Gwynn sits up, alarmed.

"What's wrong?" I ask. "Is Sir Juning after you?"

Ayva crams the ball of fabric she's carrying into the soak sink. "I gave him the slip." She turns on the water. "It's this. Her ladyship's morning gown. She spilt gingerberry jam on it. Ordered me to scrub it before the stain sets in."

Or she'll get a juicing. That's the part of her ladyship's orders Ayva doesn't have to share. We all know it.

Gwynn sighs and drops a sugar lump into her tea, stirring lethargically. "Poor Ayva. Run, jump, hop for her ladyship." She looks at me. "Were we such demanding ladies?"

"You? Never. Me? Maybe. Varina, definitely."

"I heard that," Varina calls from the sink.

Gwynn sips her tea. "What do you suppose they're doing at home now?"

I wish she wouldn't say that word. "Father's at work, of course. Mother has physical training at midday, so her trainer's yelling for her to move her lard bottom."

"You know what I mean."

I do. Are they mounting a rescue? Lodging formal complaints? We ask those questions every moment of the day. I bite into the fruit. It's so tangy it tickles my throat. I wish I could say I'm sure our fathers are doing everything possible to free us, but I'm beginning to have my doubts.

"Truth, Gwynn? I don't know. I keep thinking about when we were captured. The pirates were only going to take the servants, remember? Captain Tura changed his mind, said something about the deal changing. Do you wonder what that means?"

She ponders a tick. "Maybe he thought he could get more money for all of us."

"Maybe. But maybe someone wanted to get rid of Kai and Ayva and the other Matalans and made a deal with Tura to do it."

Her brow furrows. "But why?"

"No idea. Any more than I know why he'd want to kill Newell. Well, threaten to kill him." I hadn't forgotten that, not for a heartbeat. The pirate's weapon pressed to Newell's head, about to fry the poor lad's brains to mush. Then he didn't. "Remember him saying we'd violated Adsullatan airspace? Blix said we were nowhere near their territory. We were on course."

"Maybe he was wrong."

"Blix wrong? I doubt it. There's something off about the whole thing. Why pick Newell? Why say the deal was off? Who was the deal with? I can't puzzle it out no matter how I try."

Not that I've had time for that mystery. Too focused on more pressing things. Like wondering when we'll get out of here. And keeping out of Sir Juning's way. And work.

Mr. Hervey comes in from serving in the morning room upstairs and nods to me and Ellse. I gulp the last piece of sissy fruit and head back upstairs, to retrieve the breakfast dishes from the sideboard where he left them.

Several days later, I enter the kitchen and Bridgie turns to me with a grin. "Well, Missy. Think yer ready to tackle that garden?"

I nearly drop the tea tray I'm carrying. "Yes, more than ready." I place the tray next to Varina at the sink, unable to restrain my excitement. I'd almost given up hope of ever seeing the garden.

"Come along then." She puts aside the taters she's chopping, wipes her hands on her apron, and bustles to the door. I follow eagerly. She quickly taps out the keypad code. Giddiness flood my veins at the *clunk* of the bolt retracting. I feel Varina's jealous gaze on me as I dart out into the light.

Standing on the stone step outside, I hug myself. *I'm free.*

After nearly a month as a prisoner in that house, I'm free. I tip my head back and breathe in the sticky, sissy fruit-scented air. The hot sun warms my face. Then I remember the zati squeezing my neck and I crash.

I'm *not* free. Never free until this thing is off and I'm on a fast ship back home.

I head for the garden, taking in the hum of activity beyond. Dipro and several others toil in the newly turned field, tilling long rows of young plants pushing through the dark soil. The green stalks in the other field have grown tall enough to harvest. Agron wields a mechanical device that slices the stalk at its base. Blix follows with a tube-shaped vacuum that sucks up the entire plant and spits it into a barrow a troci I don't recognize pushes after them.

Watchers keep an eye on them, and also on the troci swarming the orchard, feeding sissy fruit into the hungry jaws of the fruit press. Halia totes a basket full of the yellow fruit. Sir Juning, seated on a two-wheeled metal vehicle that gleams in the sun, rides slowly by her side. He chatters at her the whole way across the orchard.

At the garden, I scan my new kingdom with flagging spirits. The fence slats have disintegrated. The weather-beaten fenceposts and wooden gate still stand, sagging like old ladies. The gate's rusted hinges squawk as I open it, and I face the mess of weeds and prickly vine spread out before me.

How can I nurse this sad patch back to health when I don't know where to start? Or *how* to start.

Begin at the beginning, Taryn would say.

I suppose the beginning begins with tools. I wish I had Agron and Blix's wondrous electric devices, but there's nothing even remotely resembling them around. I don't want to ask for help, preferring not to get within spitting distance of any of the watchers, so I go on the hunt on my own.

I find a moss-caked wooden storage box near the courtyard wall. My heart sinks as I peer inside to see an ancient wooden rake missing most of its teeth and a spade so dull it wouldn't cut through soft butter. Still, they're tools, and I bring them to the garden, ready to work.

A conversation I overheard between my parents long ago comes to mind.

"I don't want her toiling in that garden with Taryn," Mother said. "That's Muckers' work."

"Where's the harm in her digging in the dirt a little each day?" Father had argued.

"She'll get calluses. She'll develop a stoop and grow a hump on her back. Her joining prospects are already limited. Who'll want her then? A low-status farmer from one of the hill towns? Is that what you wish?"

"I *wish* her to be happy, Majj," he'd said, and that was the end of it.

I kneel down, inhaling a pungent mix of wet soil and rotting vegetation. If they could see me now, about to do much more than dig in the dirt a little and likely grow calluses over my entire body.

I tackle the weeding first. Dirt showers from twisted roots as I yank the greenery from the ground then toss each clump into a pile.

As I work, I wonder about the troci who once tended this garden. Poor, dear Wynnie, Bridgie called her. Was she caught by pirates, like us? How many seasons had she toiled here? Did she die of Molly fever? *Did* she die? Bridgie had appeared stricken at the mention of Wynnie's name but wouldn't elaborate on her fate. If the fever didn't get her, what happened to her? Was she eaten by the rachee whose roar we hear through the rain that falls every night?

I look up anxiously, half expecting to see a horde of rachee stampeding across the compound. Nothing so dramatic, just Kai, heading for the fields, pushing a wooden barrow with a squeaky wheel. I don't know why, but my heart kicks up, seeing him again. He arcs toward the garden, rapidly moving closer.

I stand and pick my way through the weeds and brambles to the garden's back fence. I get close enough to Kai to catch a whiff of his barrow's contents. Close enough for me to get a good look at him too. He looks tired, his hair's grown scraggly and his beard is filling in the color of a copper coin. He's torn off his tunic sleeves.

The vibrant purple and yellow of the nascent bloom carved below his left shoulder stands out on his muscled upper arm.

He centers his gaze on me, his expression serious. "Meili."

Hearing him call my name tickles my belly, as if a host of flappermoths are dancing a delighted jig in there.

"Meili, I want—"

"You. Git back to work," a threatening voice shouts. It's the mean watcher, Hup, waving his juicing gun.

Kai grimaces angrily, as if he wants to dismember Hup piece by piece, but, with a last, desperate glance at me, he swings the barrow and quickly moves on.

Unsettled and still fluttering inside, I watch him disappear into the greenie stalks. Surely he wanted to ask me about his sister Ayva. He wouldn't risk punishment to inquire about my health. I catch Hup eyeing me and bend over my work again before he turns that punisher on me.

I make little progress. The spade is useless on the thick vines choking the few plants struggling to grow. I name them snakevines for the way they slither and twist across the garden. Their thorns contain a venom that burns then numbs the skin. I find that out the hard way. Several times. It's now painfully clear why Taryn always insisted I wear gloves in the garden.

Sweat pools under my arms and drips down my back, soaking my wool dress and making my skin itch. I stop to rest and stretch my back some ticks later and scan the property again. Where is that invisible barrier that locks us in? How far can I go across the fields or into the meadow where the cattle graze before hitting that wall of electicity?

I spot Ullr. He's drifted away from the field, walking toward the orchard, putting one foot in front of the other as if he's one of the mechanized workers in Father's factory. My belly clenches. He's come down so far in such a short time. A watcher chases after him and orders him back to work. Ullr gazes at him dumbly and I look away, fearing he's about to get punished.

Back at work, I yank weeds and hack at snakevines as if I'm attacking the watchers' thick necks until the sun begins to set and I'm needed inside to help prep dinner. Every part of me aches as I creep toward the east wing. I'm filthy, too, and will need to wash and change into a clean gown and apron.

I reach the door and climb onto the stoop. Then, as bold as any Habeni could be, I reach for the doorlatch. A current bursts from my zati, as if I've touched a live wire. Electricity stings my throat and flashes through my veins, burning me from head to toe. I wrench my arm away and the current instantly halts.

Frickle! The security system works both ways. Locking us inside the manor, keeping everyone else out.

I step back and ring the bell. Cautiously. Bridgie's there in a flash and the door slides open. She hustles me inside, the door snaps shut, and I'm locked inside once more.

The next few weeks are draining. Each morning Ellse and I dust and clean, I grab some lunch, and if Bridgie's satisfied my chores are complete, she releases me to the garden. I work until sunset, when, aching and exhausted, I ring the bell to go in.

For weeks I wrestle with stubborn weeds and chop snakevines, pausing only to mop my brow and catch my breath. Kai passes several times a day with his barrow and our gazes connect, but the watchers are about so he doesn't stop.

After copious weeding, I find half a dozen plants struggling to grow. To my surprise, I discover flora found on my home planet—losys, spencer's boot, and even some dorette, which, when ground into a paste, makes a soothing balm. I pluck some dorette leaves to use on my blistered fingers.

I finally reach the garden's end post near the fields and crow in delight to see what appears to be scucca plants poking out of the soil. Taryn says scucca are the hardiest of all the root plants and quite versatile, their flowers fragrant, their leaves edible, and the roots medicinal. I push bits of rotting wood aside, liberating an army of insects, and brush dirt and grass away from the scucca's buds.

Then I sit back and admire that precious bit of green.

Chapter 14

Meili

"MY DRESSMAKER'S DESIGNING THE most delectable gown for me to wear at my ball." Lady Forseti snaps her napkin open and spreads it across her lap. "She knows the ball will be *the* social event of the season. A prime opportunity to advertise her skills."

She beams, but gets no response from her family, gathered around a long dining table with legs as thick as the pinum tree it's made from. Lady Netti stares down at her plate. His lordship stares at nothing. Sir Juning, at the head of the table, stares into his drink—when he's not staring at me.

It's my first time serving dinner. Unnerving enough to have Mr. Hervey watching me as if I'm his child taking her first steps, I don't need Sir Juning's leers to add to my jitters.

I serve her ladyship first, chasing a butter-drenched greenie stalk around the platter with a pair of tongs. I've been on the opposite end of this ritual my whole life, but I never knew how stressful a job it is. I finally capture the greenie. Careful not to get too close to Lady Forseti and risk dripping on her orange and gold checkered gown, I plop the greenie onto her plate. The splatter is minimal and I *whoosh* in relief.

"Another." Her ladyship taps the plate with a red fingernail filed as sharp as a raptor's talon.

I oblige. Another finger tap, and I oblige again and again, until I'm certain I'll run out of greenies. How odd. At home, we just ask a servant for more, not bang on the plate like a famished farmhand. A smile flickers on my lips. Mother would take to her swooning sofa and never get up if she witnessed such a spectacle.

"You find something amusing, gell?"

Lady Forseti's brittle tone freezes me in place. How many times do I have to remind myself to school my face to blandness, to hide my feelings and take great care of what I say or do? Or think.

She looks me up and down with a sniff. "Wait. Aren't you the bold troci who claimed to be a skilled horticulturist?"

My wariness turns to terror, remembering her threats if she caught me lying about my skill. "Yes, my lady."

"Well, what do you have to say for yourself? I haven't tasted a single herb in my meals in weeks. What have you been doing in my garden all this time?"

Really? My arms ache from weeding and my fingers are blistered and cracked. What does she think I've been doing?

"My lady, you shall see the results of my work in a tick. The beef's been tenderized with lutea, which I picked fresh today. It's the first herb to flourish under my hand, but certainly not the last."

I speak in a rush and direct a nervous nod toward Mr. Hervey, who approaches her and piles two thick slices of beef onto her plate. She cuts into the meat and shoves a piece into her mouth. Her eyes widen.

"Hmph. Seems Bridgie can work magic with any old leaf," she says, but I can tell she's impressed. She dismisses me with a wave. "You may carry on now."

I curtsey and carry my platter to Lord Forseti, hiding my smile this time.

"Why, hello." His lordship gazes at me in surprise, as if I've appeared out of thin air. "You have red hair. I knew a gell with red hair once. Suelena was her name. An uncommon beauty." His voice thickens with emotion. "We were to wed. But the fever took her, the summer of the dark moon."

Sir Juning whinnies a cruel laugh and Lady Forseti shoots her spouse a loathing look. "Be still, Gugg. No one wants to hear your sob stories."

I move on to Lady Netti, appalled. My family isn't exactly happy times and gushing sentiment, but this crew is a low-grav of malfunction.

"I have news, Junie." Lady Forseti tilts to gaze at her son around the electrified candelabra flickering at the table's center. "Cistella Crowell and three of her cousins have sent word they're attending my ball."

"Cistella?" Juning twists his goblet stem between his fingers, studying the swirling liquid inside. "I remember her. Fat and ugly as a rachee."

"Now, Junie, don't be difficult." Her ladyship sighs. "You *must* find a mate. You're of age and it's time to settle down. Cistella Crowell is a fine catch. She's healthy *and* wealthy. She'd be the perfect match for you."

"Anything with breasts is the perfect match as far as he's concerned," Lady Netti mutters, turning the page in the book I notice she has open on her lap. She hasn't been staring at her plate and ignoring the dinner table conversation. She's reading.

Juning shoots daggers at his sister. "Says the gell who'd prefer a book in her bed than the wealthiest lord on the Ridge."

"Netti, stop teasing your brother. And put away that cursed book, before I have Hervey take a flame to it." Her ladyship's voices shifts from severe to gooey as she looks from one child to the other. "Nothing's settled, my love. If you don't care for Cistella's looks, mayhap you will find one of her cousins more pleasing."

"Yes, more pleasing," he muses, turning an eager gaze on me as I reach him.

I drop a greenie on his plate and suddenly, his hand is on my bottom. He pinches me through my skirt. I jerk away so fast the last greenie shoots off the platter onto the table. I gape in horror at the greasy stain spreading on the snowy white tablecloth.

Lady Forseti gasps. "Clumsy gell, you've ruined my linen."

Juning jumps in before I can blink. "My fault, Mother. Don't hold the troci to something I caused. I jostled the gell. Didn't I?"

He looks at me expectantly. His nostrils are as wide as canyons. I long to shove a greenie into each one. *He's* the mope who caused the spill. He *should* take the blame. But I can't point that out. I've already aggravated her high-and-mighty ladyship enough. He offers a way out of trouble and I can only swallow my fury and accept it.

"Yes, Sir Juning."

Lady Forseti's annoyance evaporates. "Do be more careful, Junie. Gell, I expect that stain to be gone next time I see this linen."

I bob another curtsey, scrape up the mess and flee to the sideboard. I stack the platter with the other dirty dishes, my hands shaking. Mr. Hervey comes over and covers my hand with his own to still my trembling. His skin's as rough and scaly as tree bark.

"Relax, child." He plucks the cover off the greenie tureen, spears several stalks, and shakes them off the fork onto a clean platter. "I dropped a tray of honeydots my first time out. What a mess that was."

"How do you stand it?" I whisper between gritted teeth. "I think I'll go mad."

"You will if you let it get to you. My advice? Put your mind somewhere else. A place you feel happy and safe. Me, I'm with my wife, my son Jarl. We're chopping wood to put up for winter." He hands me the full platter and replaces the tureen's cover. "I'm not here and never will be."

"Hervey, stop dawdling," Lady Forseti calls. "Bring more beef."

He returns to the table and refills her ladyship's plate. His expression softens, his gaze turns vague, and I think he's taken his own advice.

I follow him around the table, serving each Forseti in turn, weighing his words. Where am I most happy? Once I might've said shopping in the marketplace or playing chess with Father or sitting in the sun on the terrace while Taryn brushes my hair.

Now, my thoughts whisk to the garden.

The time I spend there is the closest thing to happiness I feel here. The challenge, the satisfaction of defeating those weeds. I've found more scucca and dorette and other plants I can't begin to identify but am eager to try. A fence. I'll need a real fence to protect my growing greenery and not that decaying pile of sticks. Perhaps I can put those snakevines to good use.

Somewhere far away I hear, "Knew a gell with red hair once. Long ago. In the summer of the dark moon."

After dinner, Mr. Hervey follows me downstairs. My arms are loaded with dishes, the soiled tablecloth on top.

I'm pleased to see Jinks, Sir Juning's valet, seated at the kitchen table, at home for once. A short, stocky Adsullatan of about thirty, he wears a special zati that lets him pass through the front gate. Which he does with frequency as he accompanies Juning into the village.

"A demon lives in them mines," Jinks says to the others gathered around the table, listening with rapt attention. "Lurking, waiting. When an unsuspecting troci comes along, his blood so fresh and tasty, that old demon... *pounces*." Gwynn squeaks in fright and clutches Ayva's arm. "The poor lad's dead afore he knows what hit him."

Glasses clink as Mr. Hervey sets the tray he's carrying next to the sink. "Don't be dramatic, Jinks. The fever's no demon." He hangs up his coat and settles in his rocker. "What the disease does may be evil, but it's nothing but a germ, plain and simple."

Bridgie pours two glasses of dromé and hands one to Mr. Hervey. She eyes Varina and jerks her head toward the sink. "Move along, gell, you got work to do."

Varina groans but goes. She shoves the stopper into the drain and crashes dishes and platters into the rapidly filling sink. I stuff the tablecloth into the soak sink and pour a liberal helping of soap on the stain, fingers crossed the suds will loosen the grease. Leaving the cloth to soak, I take Varina's seat at the table and pour myself a cup of spiced tea.

"How do you know you've got the fever?" Gwynn asks.

"Oh, you'll know," Jinks says. "You shiver so hard you think you'll shake your skin off. That ain't the worst of it. You disappear into a dreamland so savage it makes a rachee attack look like a pillow fight. If the fever breaks, *if* you live, then you're left with these."

He rolls up his sleeves and I stare with a queasy stomach at the puckered white scars on his arms. But his neck and his face are unscathed. The fever seems strangely arbitrary in where it leaves its mark.

"Not to worry, loves." Bridgie sips her drink. "Mayhap you won't get it. Not everyone does."

"Like Sir Juning," Mr. Hervey says. "The fever's passed him by each time it comes round."

"Not the little puss, though." Jinks sounds almost affectionate. "Poor Netti got it bad and almost died. Might a wished she had, the way they blame her."

"Hush now." Bridgie scowls. "That's none of our business."

"Does the fever addle the mind?" Ayva asks. "His lordship, I mean. He don't appear to be quite... there."

Jinks laughs. "His lordship ain't never been there."

Mr. Hervey clears his throat. "What Jinks means is the fever scorched his lordship's skin and maimed his leg, but his mind was injured long ago. An accident as a lad, I've heard."

I cringe. That makes the way his family treats him even more hateful.

"He had buckets of coin, though." Jinks slathers sissy fruit jam over a thick slice of bread. "That's all that mattered to Bentalla when he come courting. Lady Greedy fixed it so she holds the purse strings, and the business strings. Only thing she don't have her dancing slipper on is that turd she calls her son."

I choke on my tea. What if Lady Forseti heard him say such a thing? If Taryn *ever* spoke of Mother like that, she'd be let go on the spot. What would be the punishment here?

Bridgie frowns. "Jinks, I told you, don't talk disrespectful of our betters."

"Why not? These missies gotta know what a stinker Juning is." Jinks eyes each of us in turn. "He plays games with all the gells. Gives you a bucket of compliments or does something nice for you. Brings you a pretty fob from town or offers respite from your chores."

Or takes the blame for a clumsy spill, sparing me a juicing.

"He don't do nothing unless he gets what he's after in return." Jinks's voice turns bitter. "That's the sport of it for him. Small favors turn to big favors. Anything to get a gell owing him. And he always collects on those debts."

Bridgie clucks in disapproval.

"Don't be cross. You know it's true," Mr. Hervey says. "And her ladyship turns a blind eye. S'pose I can't blame her, after everything." He pauses a tick. "My lady had four other sons. Lost them all to the fever fifteen seasons ago, when Lady Netti was a babe. The little missy got it first, and it spread through the family like a flame on dry timber."

I gasp. No wonder Lady Forseti treats her daughter like a poor relation. She blames her for the loss of her other sons.

"That's why Bentalla coddles him," Jinks says. "You'd think with this place and the mine operation, he'd learn how to manage things. But no, when he's not dragging me to the village to cause mischief, he lolls about here, amusing himself with the troci."

"Be still, Jinks," Bridgie snaps. "His lordship's a good lad. He's never hurt any of my gells."

"Not physically," Jinks snaps back. "But what about what he did to poor Wynnie—"

"I said, be still." Her voice turns to steel. "Stop banging your gums. I won't tolerate disrespect."

Jinks looks mulish, but he shuts his mouth. A gloomy cloud descends over the kitchen as we all fall silent. Varina pulls the sink stopper and the *glug-glug* of the water draining is the only sound.

"You missies are warned now," Mr. Hervey says after a bit. "Stay out of Sir Juning's way. *Don't* play his game. He'll win. He always does."

He sits back, fills his pipe with crushed klenda leaves and lights it. The smell is minty, not tangy like the tobacco in my father's pipe, but I think of Father all the same.

I stare into my empty teacup, heartsore and blue. The certainty that we'll be ransomed or rescued seems less likely with each passing day, and I despair of seeing my father or my home ever again.

I push the teacup away. I have to get out of here.

It's as simple as that. I can't live out my days in this horror of a life, running from Juning's grasping paws and his insidious games.

I don't want to escape the drudgery by drifting off to some fantasy world in my mind, like Mr. Hervey.

I want to escape for real.

The only question, the most daunting and insurmountable question is...

How?

CHAPTER 15

Kai

STITCH KISSES BETSY ON one of her floppy ears then takes up a position at her front left flank. I move to one side of her rump, the butcher's troci stands at the other. The butcher signals. He tugs the leash connected to the cattle's bridle and I shove as hard as I can. Betsy puts up a fight, like she knows she's headed for the slaughterhouse, and it takes a goodly amount of huffing and puffing to get her up the ramp and into the butcher's van.

I give the transport a good look-over before the doors slam shut and the vehicle rolls down the access road past the vehicle barn. It hitches around the corner to the front drive—and the gate to freedom.

My brain gets busy. I can likely figure a way to slip into the van when it returns with poor Betsy sliced into chops and T-bones, minus the butcher's cut. But I still can't figure a way out of my zati.

"How does the butcher's lad come and go with that thing around his neck?" I ask Stitch. "Don't he have to worry about getting zapped?"

Stitch watches the van vanish from view then turns to me, his eyes wet. "You ain't got one of them control boxes, like him. The watchers at the gate do something when the boy goes through. I hear he gets a jolt, but not as bad as what you'd get if you tried it."

"S'pose I'd get juiced?"

Stitch laughs, like I'm even dimmer than he thought I was. "You'd be dead, boy. Yer guts burned to cinders. Now, unless you got more fool questions, let's get back to work."

I help him feed and water the cattle then secure their stalls for the night. I leave him staring mournfully at Betsy's empty pen. I wash my barrow then clean myself with a sliver of soap Stitch gave me. I'm beyond aggravated to learn another possible escape route is closed. I scrub around my zati, wishing I could scrub this mother-humping thing right off.

Finished, I dry my hair and face with a towel Stitch had also given me. Soap and a towel are almost as precious as a spoon here. If I had some taters and bread to trade, I'd be doing well. If I had a stash of abyssa, I'd be king of the troci.

I take my usual route back to camp between the fields and the house. Something moves in the garden as I pass. It's Meili, bent over some greenery, still at work at sundown. I'm impressed. She works harder than any Habeni I've ever known. Harder than some Matalans, too.

I watch her at her task for days as I trek back and forth from the fields to the barn. An appealing view, the way her skirt clings to her bottom. She's taken some of the vines that grow wild all over this place and laid them in three lines. She lifts and crosses the vines back and forth, weaving the strands, the way Ma braided Ayva's hair until she got too weak from her sickness to lift her arms.

What in Dageth's crusty pocket is she doing?

After the fourth day, I figure it out. She's twining the vines into a rope. Two ropes, actually. My hope she's planning to use them to strangle the watchers fizzles when I go by the next day. She begins to secure the rope to the garden's crumbling posts.

Clever. She's making a fence.

She manages to hang the rope all the way around the garden in a neat rectangle but struggles to secure it to the final two posts. The rope's too taut. She needs another pair of hands.

I glance around. No watchers in sight for once. Now's my chance.

I push my barrow toward her. The shovel bounces and the rusty wheel squawks like an angry crow. Meili straightens at the sound and turns my way. I stop as close as I dare. She looks me over. I can't ken what she thinks, but I can imagine. Flies swarm around me and the empty barrow. I'm filthy and smell like death warmed over times ten. I wouldn't blame her if she held her nose.

"Do you need help?" I ask, studying her. She looks weary, but otherwise healthy. They must eat well in that fancy house. Her cheeks turn pink under my scrutiny and she looks down at the vine rope at her feet.

"Oh. I guess I do need help." Her eyes meet mine again. "What do you think? Am I loopy for hanging vines as a fence?"

I think she's brilliant. No way I'll admit that, though, and sound like a toadying Mucker. "It won't keep out the rachees, or even a determined peahen. Might stop the cattle, though. They're dumb as stumps."

That gets me a smile. It lights her up. Lights me up too. I have to clear my throat twice before I can speak. "How's Ayva? Is she well? Is she safe?"

A brief silence before she answers. "Yes, she's well, Kai."

I notice she doesn't say Ayva's safe and I know why. I glare toward the orchard, where I saw Juning on his rev cycle earlier, buzzing around the gells at their chores. I long to break that lecherous kutama in half. But I can't. I grind my teeth. I can't do anything.

"Why don't I see my sister outside? You seem free to come and go."

She gives a grim laugh. "Not like I have special privileges. I'm assigned to work in the garden. Otherwise, I'd be locked inside with Ayva and everyone else." Her brow furrows as she scans the tangled mess around her. "I must nurse this sad bit of green back to health or..."

My gut clenches. By the gods, would those heartless peigus punish her if she fails in this near impossible task? Would they brutalize my sister if she doesn't complete a chore to their liking? Or zap her for a minor infraction, as the watchers do with anyone who earns their displeasure? Have they hurt her already?

I frantically scan the fortress, now more anxious than ever to get to Ayva. "How can I get inside? How can I get her out?"

"No, don't." Meili's hands shoot up, as if to halt me from racing to attack the manor's front door. "You can't. I'm told the whole place is electrified. The housekeeper Bridgie says there was a revolt some seasons ago. A half dozen troci were killed. Afterward, the family electrified the entire house, and the courtyard walls. Even the door where I come and go is closely guarded. Entry is impossible without permission. If you try to force your way in, you'll be scorched to cinders—"

She cuts off, coloring, maybe remembering similar words she spat at me on the airbus. I don't know what to say. The silence between us stretches. I stare into those soft, golden eyes and my gut flips and twists, like a fish on a line. This was a bad idea, coming here.

"I'm sorry, Kai," she murmurs. "If it helps, I can carry a message to Ayva for you."

My mood brightens, only to darken a tick later when a voice shouts, "What goes on here?" It's the fat watcher, Dall, trotting toward us.

"Quick, act like I'm a slupa." I droop my shoulders and scratch my head.

Meili tenses but nods in understanding as Dall reaches us. He doubles over, palms on his thighs, trying to catch his breath. "Yer not s'posed to be here, troci." He glowers at me. "Explain yourself."

"I called him over," Meili says quickly. "I need help tying this vine to the post. I asked him to help." She glances at me and I see mischief in her eyes. "But he appears to be hopelessly dense. Doesn't ken my meaning at all. Perhaps you can get through to him?"

"He *is* a slow one," Dall says with a wheezy chuckle. "Needs to be reminded of what's what more 'n once in a day. Here, you, do as the missy asks. Hop to it, or..." Dall strokes the hilt of his holstered weapon, letting the threat hang. He turns to Meili. "Would Missy like another to help with yer chore?"

His manner's a far cry from the way the watchers treat us. Does her position working inside the manor earn her such regard, or is it her beauty that causes him to stammer and grovel? Whatever the reason, Meili plays along. She lifts her chin and looks down her nose at him, as if she's the highest status Habbie in the land, scolding the lowest Matalan.

"Yes, that will be acceptable," she says and dismisses him with a wave.

Dall hustles off and I snort in amusement. "Now that's a role you were born to play."

Her cheeks go pink again and I fear I've insulted her. I don't know why that bothers me. I hastily step over to the fence post and snatch up the vine rope.

"Mind the barbs," she says.

Too late. Several thorns pierce my fingers. The sting is sharp, and the burn ripples through my hands, making them tingle.

"The venom wears off," she says. "But not quickly."

"Good to know."

This time avoiding the thorns, I lift the rope and pull with all my strength until it's flush against the post. She steps close to me and bends, securing the rope with a thinner piece of vine, her slim fingers deftly tying the knot. Her scent is clean and as sweet as a losys at full bloom. I feel even more ashamed of my stench.

"What message would you like me to deliver to Ayva?" she asks, her gaze on her task.

Being near her has me so twitchy, I nearly forgot about my sister. And everything else.

"Tell Ayva..." I lower my voice, though there's no one close enough to hear. "Tell Ayva I'm going to get her out of here. Going to get *us* out of here."

Meili's eyes go as wide as Hephas' twin moons. "You mean... escape?" Excitement laces her voice. "Do you have a plan?"

Figures she'd ask that. I've got no answer. And if I did, would I tell her? Once a secret's spilled, it travels like a fast wind, Pa says. Probably travels twice as fast when it's shared with a Habeni. I don't know if I can trust her to keep her yap shut.

"I'm working on it. Tell Ayva to stay strong. I'm going to figure something out."

She finishes tying the vine and stands straight, facing me. "Like what? Getting into the house is nigh on impossible, breaking through the barrier doubly so. You know what we were told the first day. No one has ever escaped from here."

I ignore her doubts, and my own. "Meili..." My voice softens as I say her name. This is the first time I've said it to her face. "*I'm* not no one."

She directs her gaze at the body ink on my upper arm, a nascent bloom in a bed of thorns.

"I'm beginning to realize that," she says, a declaration that fires my blood. She's about to say something else, but stiffens, looking past me. "Frickle! The watcher's coming back."

I turn. Dall trots toward us, with Ullr in tow.

"Meili, I missed you," Ullr cries as he stumbles up to her and crushes her in a hug.

Irritated, I bend over the post and tie a second piece of vine around the rope.

"No lovey-dovey stuff." Dall yanks Ullr away by the collar. "Git to your task."

Meili sets us to work. Ullr and I lift the vine on either side of the post. Ullr moves as slow as the dead. The abyssa has him so pacified, he barely has the strength to pull the vine taut but we eventually get the job done.

"Alright, you worms. Back to yer chores." Dall groans as Ullr hunkers down on the grass and falls asleep. Dall prods him with his boot then hauls him up by the arm. Ullr's knees buckle and he's back on the ground.

Meili watches, her expression troubled. "My heart aches to see him like this." Her voice is full of distress. "He's so thin."

My mood turns black. Does she have a tender spot for him? "He's thin because the fool's been smoking the black leaf since we got here. He's weak-willed."

She winces, but I have no time to rue my harsh words as Dall, who has Ullr in a headlock, barks at me to be on my way.

"Wait," Meili calls. Dall halts and swings toward her. "I have need of this troci." She gestures haughtily at me. "Well, not *him*. I need his cattle droppings. I'd like him to come by each day and bring manure for the garden." The watcher looks skeptical so she hastily adds, "Her ladyship will be pleased to see her garden thrive."

Dall puffs up. "Well, if her ladyship wants it, don't see why not. You hear that, boy?"

He drags Ullr away and I give Meili a grateful grin as I follow. She returns a small smile and returns to work, squatting down and yanking at weeds.

By Dageth, she's smart, and quick thinking. She wrapped Dall around her finger with a few simple words. She's given me an excuse to come to the garden each day. I may not be able to see Ayva, but through Meili I'll have a connection to her.

For the first time since those stinking pirates rammed our ship, I feel a spark of hope.

I'll find a way to escape. I'll get Ayva away from Juning. Meili too. I'll get the three of us out of this shithole. Somehow. If I can't find a way to hitch a ride in the butcher's van, I'll think of something else.

I'm sure of it.

I arrive back at camp to a ruckus at the cookfire. Jeers and coarse laughter rise from the crowd gathered in a tight circle. A feminine shriek rises from the circle's center.

I plow to the front of the mob and grimace to see Petra at the middle of the uproar. Her bowl is at her feet, and stew spatters her dress and shoes. Her body's rigid. Her dark eyes snap in fury—at Agron. He towers over her, his face coated with sweat, his skin washed out and sickly in the glare of the floodlights.

"Here's your supper, slag." He holds out a tater. "Come and get it."

Petra lunges for it, but Agron tosses it over her head. It splats into Dipro's greedy hands. Agron lets loose a mocking laugh that's echoed by most of the onlookers.

How in pakao did Petra get into this mess? She usually disappears at the first sign of trouble.

I cuss. Agron hears it. He stiffens, snaps his head toward me. A cold smile curls his mouth. When Dipro hurls the tater back to him and Petra tries to grab it, Agron catches her instead. He crushes her to him in a one-arm hold.

"I got something tastier for you, love," he says. Another glance at me and he cups Petra's bottom, forcing her full against him. He grinds into her. Hoots and catcalls ripple through the crowd. The Dryan Agron's been bedding watches, her expression stony.

My blood turns to fire. Seems he's been taking lessons from that master predator Juning. I can't stop that culbana from molesting my sister or Meili, but I sure as shit can stop Agron.

I stomp up to that peigu and growl, "Let her go."

He does, shoving her so hard she thuds to the ground.

"Rachee humper," Petra spits and scurries away.

"I've been waiting for this." Agron ices me with a look that promises to destroy me. "Come on, Mucker. Let's go."

He cracks his knuckles. This is the fight he wanted on the ship. The fight he's wanted since the pirates grabbed us. Since he was booted from his top status throne into this dung pit of helplessness.

I don't back away. Guess I want this fight too.

In a flash, we're at it, fists flying. Agron's trained, skilled. Knows the right moves, the right places to punch and kick. But I have one thing he doesn't. Centuries of Matalan fury pulsing in my blood. Fueling my fists. Pa says we fight like cornered animals, dirty and deadly, because we have nothing to lose. I prove it in the ferocity of my attack.

The crowd eggs us on with frenzied cheers. I'm not sure who they're rooting for. I stab a thumb into my opponent's side, jabbing his kidney. He grunts and swings, trying to punch my throat. I feint left and bite his forearm, tasting sweat and Habeni flesh. He yowls, aiming a vicious kick at my leg. My kneecap explodes in pain. I whirl and plow my fist deep into his gut.

We dance our bitter dance until I bash him in the mouth. That sneering, superior mouth that slurred Meili and her questionable ancestry all these years. The mouth that taunted Petra. That disrespected my sister and every Matalan that ever had the misfortune to serve his vile hide.

Every ounce of anger and frustration and hatred boiling inside of me goes into that punch. His lip splits and blood spurts, spattering the cheering crowd. I think I've cracked his tooth.

Agron screeches and lurches back. Dipro and the other minions start to move on me, but Agron throws up a hand. "No." He wipes his mouth with the back of his wrist. "No more. I'm through."

I unclench my stinging fists. I think it's done.

I'm wrong.

Agron seizes one of the benches and swings it like a cuttleball bat. A quick move on my part keeps the bench from cracking my skull. Instead, the wood shatters across my back. A blast of pain dims my vision. The world spins and I land flat on my face in the dirt. Whoops and jeering laughter echo in my ringing ears. The cheering fades, feet shuffle, and the mob breaks up.

Now it's done.

I drift for a while in a twilight world. Someone's soft fingers feather through my hair and caress my cheek. I'm so dazed I think it's Meili. I smile.

Waking for real, I roll onto my side and open my eyes to see Petra sitting next to me. She brushes dirt and wood chips off my tunic. I wince as she touches a sore spot on my shoulder. Wince again as she touches another. I suspect my back and shoulder will be one giant bruise tomorrow.

"You gonna live?" she says.

"Dunno." It hurts to move my arm, but I push her hand away and sit up. My head throbs. I stiffen, suddenly alert. "The watchers? Did the noise bring them out?" All I need is a juicing to add to my misery.

"No. No sign of 'em."

Figures. The watchers don't care if we beat each other senseless as long as we show up to work in the morning.

I dig my towel out of my pocket and wipe blood and snot and dirt off my face. Only a few troci remain at the cookfire. Agron's found an unbroken bench to sit on. He's puffed up and preening, laughing with his minions over his defeat of the insolent Mucker. I hate him with all the heat of Dageth's fiery realm.

Petra's not fond of him either. She eyes him warily as she darts across the camp, retrieves her bowl and scoops her tater off the ground then hustles back to me. The tater's muddy, studded with pinum needles. She holds it out.

"Here, you eat it."

"Are you loopy? I don't want your supper."

"Then why'd you fight him?" she snaps. "What do you want from me?"

She thinks she owes me now. Thinks I'm as craven as the rest of them and I want something in return for sticking up for her. "I don't want a klacking thing, Petra. You were in trouble. I tried to help."

"I wasn't in trouble." She tears into her dirty tater like she's biting the head off a live vole. "I'm not one of those ninnies—" She gestures to Agron's Dryan, cozying up to him once again. "I don't beg or perform bedroom tricks for favors. I can take care of myself."

I lift an eyebrow. She's doing a great job of it. No way I'm saying that out loud. She's so angry I think she'll find her own bench to smack me with. I don't ken the female mind at all, not Meili, not

Petra, or even the Dryan, who still fluffs Agron though he casts his eye—and his attention—on others. Useless to even try.

I abandon the conversation and stand. After a struggle, anyway. My head spins, my back aches, and my legs feel like jelly. Petra watches me stonily and doesn't offer to help.

I shuffle to the cookfire to see if there's anything left to eat. The putter of Juning's rev cycle fills the night air and the females scatter.

I can't escape from this place fast enough.

Chapter 16

Meili

Bridgie slides her empty plate away and leans back in her chair. "Best gingerberry tart I ever tasted." She pats her round belly and nods at me. "My compliments on scrounging up those berries."

The others pipe up in agreement, except Jinks. He's gone with Sir Juning into the village, where they're sure to get into trouble. The rest of us gather around the table for our usual snack before bed. I accept their compliments with a cool nod, but inside I'm busting. I found some scraggly gingerberry bushes near the courtyard wall. Most of the berries had gone by, but I was able to salvage enough for tonight's dessert.

Varina collects our dishes, noisily scrapes the leavings into the bin, and dumps plates and cutlery into the sink with a clatter. Bridgie looks daggers at her then levels a much friendlier gaze on the rest of us.

"A gaggle of gowns come in on a lorry from her ladyship's dressmaker today," she says. "Gowns to try on for the ball. Such finery. Saw a delicious yellow gown perfect for Lady Netti. I hope she'll choose it."

I hope not. Netti would look dreadful in yellow.

"Her ladyship seemed partial to one particular frock," Ayva says. "It's... interesting."

Gwynn, seated next to Ayva, gazes at her with bright eyes. "What do you mean, interesting?"

Ayva describes a pink monstrosity adorned with ruffles and feathers. She has a musical voice, gentle like Gwynn's. She and Gwynn have become friends, something I couldn't have imagined back home.

Of course, back home I couldn't think of Kai as anything but our school's servant. Now here I am, delivering messages for him. If I ever get a moment to speak to Ayva alone, that is.

Varina sighs heavily. "I once wore such finery." She listlessly scrubs a plate, looking wistful. "Gowns of spun silk and satin. And shoes…" She stares down at her flimsy shoes with distaste. "Oh, I had so many beautiful shoes."

She goes on to talk about each pair as if they were her beloved children. Ignoring her, I cross the kitchen to sit on the window seat and gaze out through the bars. The rain began early tonight. It splatters against the windowpane, making the outside lights and the little houses by the fields where the troci live seem to ripple.

I picture Kai in one of those houses and my belly flip-flops. What's wrong with me? Why do a thousand flappermoths dance inside me whenever I see him or even think his name? Why did I tremble and blush every moment he was near me today, helping me with the fence? This isn't the time and place to indulge in a girlish crush. Especially for a Matalan who loathes and despises everything about me and my people.

Not to mention a Matalan with the loopy conviction he can escape from this cussed place.

Varina runs out of shoes and finery to natter on about. "I was a fine lady back home," she says with dejected finality.

"You're still a fine lady," Mr. Hervey says, like a father trying to convince his ugly duckling daughter she's a beauty. He sits in his chair near the cooling element, reading a book. Did he, or Bridgie, ever think of trying to escape, when they were new troci, like us? Did they find it as impossible then as it seems now?

"I'm not a fine anything. I'm a worthless cleek. A nothing." Varina glares down at Ellse, who squats on the floor near the sink, picking scraps out of the garbage bin. "Gods, does she *have* to do that? Get away, you filthy worm."

She kicks at Ellse, who twists like a pretzel, nimbly avoiding Varina's swinging foot.

"Leave her be," Ayva snaps. "She's not hurting anyone."

Varina turns a pout on Ayva. Amazing how much pouting and complaining Varina does now. I get why. When she's not up to her elbows in soapy water, she's stacking dishes, sweeping, and scrubbing floors. Tedious, unrelenting work, but I've grown heartily sick of her attitude.

"Poor Ellse." Bridgie sighs and pours herself another glass of dromé. "She wasn't always this way, just been here too long."

"We've all been here too long," Mr. Hervey murmurs, turning a page in his book.

The rain's beating against the roof as we toddle off to bed. I'm the last to wash up. I decide not to wash my frillies tonight. It's so humid they'll never dry. I don my nightgown and climb into my cot. Varina's already asleep. Gwynn's lying with her head propped on her fist, watching Ayva as she brushes her thick, silky hair with one of Lady Netti's castoff hairbrushes.

"When we get home, I'm going to buy you a proper hairbrush," Gwynn says. "One with a pearl handle."

Ayva smiles wistfully. "I'll settle for one with all its bristles."

"Face it, we're never getting home," Varina mutters. I guess she's not asleep after all.

"Not true. They'll come for us." Gwynn sounds more hopeful than sure. She turns to me. "Won't they, Meili?"

I shrug, loathe to admit Varina is most likely right. "I don't know. We've been here nearly three full moons."

"Yes. But it's simply taking a while." Gwynn's voice takes on a note of desperation. "The Councils have to debate and vote. And vote again. Setting a ransom is probably the sticky point. You know no one can dicker over a price like a Habeni."

Varina scoffs. "Sweet, sunny Gwynn. Don't you get it? We're trapped. Forever. The only way we'll ever get out of here is to die of that cursed fever. Or..." She sits up and her expression turns sly. "If I could slip away from Bridgie and get above stairs, I'd find Juning and strike a bargain with him. My virtue for my freedom."

"Why would you do that?" I ask, shocked. A Habeni lady's virtue is second only to status as an asset in a joining contract. "He won't hold up his end of the bargain. You heard Hervey and Jinks. It's a game to Juning. A game he always wins."

Varina adopts the most magnificent pout I've seen yet. "Well, if you know a better way to break free from this dungeon, I'd like to hear of it."

The subject apparently closed, she pulls her blanket up to her chin and orders Ayva to put out the light. Soon, everyone nods off. I stare at the ceiling, unable to sleep. I try to think of other things—the rachee howling in the night, the strange pentagon-shaped leaf I found today, Sir Juning and Varina, who's turning out to be far more calculating than I could ever imagine. But only one subject fills my mind.

Kai.

Kai and his certainty that he'll find a way to escape in particular. When everyone tells him it's impossible, he insists it isn't. I wish I possessed even a crumb of his confidence. Or his determination.

Ayva turns over and her eyes flutter open. "You still up, Meili?" she says, groggy, half awake. "Can't you sleep? Is there something wrong?"

"Um, yes. No. Well, sort of." This may not be the ideal time to deliver her brother's message, but when will I have another chance? "I spoke to Kai when I was in the garden today."

She's fully awake now. She sits up. "You did? How is he?"

What can I say? He's growing thin, like Ullr. Here in the house, we eat pretty well but I suspect that's not the case for the outside troci. Kai's hungry. I can do something about that. Tomorrow, I'll bring out some food for him. I bet he'll like that.

"He's grumpy as usual," I say, keeping my answer light and vague. "He works with the cattle, so he smells, but he's fine otherwise. He wants me to give you a message." Varina stirs, muttering sleepily. I lower my voice. "Come, let's speak where we won't disturb the others."

We slip out of bed and pad past Ellse, curled up in her nest of blankets by the door as if it's the height of luxury. All is quiet in the darkened kitchen, except for the hum of the electrical appliances and the splash of the nightly rain against the windows. Ayva sits next to me on the window seat and gives me an expectant look.

I keep my voice low. "Do you think it's possible to escape from here? Not by using Varina's scheme. I mean, some other way."

"I don't know. Perhaps. Probably not. But if you're thinking on trying, can you wait 'til morning?" Her levity evaporates. "What does this have to do with Kai? What is he up to?"

"Nothing yet. He said he's going to escape, and for you to have courage till he figures out how to do it."

Ayva stiffens. Light from the floodlights spills through the window, casting shadows of the rain running down the panes on her face. Her expression is both stunned and terrified. "Escape's impossible." She wrings her hands. "By all the gods, he's going to get himself killed."

"That's what I told him."

"Let me guess. He said to keep your Habbie opinions to yourself."

"Something like that."

"Kai's the most ornery Matalan that ever lived." She scowls, looking just like him. "You know what Ma called him? A mule with a thorn in his rump."

I can't help but smile. A ridiculous, but apt, image.

"If there's danger, or someone in trouble, my brother will rush in headfirst, leaving his brain behind. He's got no fear. No, that's not right. He lets fear drive him. He always, *always* pulls against the chain." Tenderness and frustration lace her voice. "Have you seen the body ink on his shoulder?"

Not a question I was expecting. "Yes, a nascent bloom. Quite artful, if illegal."

Her eyes widen. "Don't you know what the nascent bloom is?"

Her question is good natured, but I still feel like a slupa. "It's a beautiful flower and quite hardy. But... that's not what you're asking, is it? It has some kind of significance?"

Several ticks go by before she speaks again. "The nascent bloom is our symbol. It means defiance. Strength. Like us Matalans, it endures. Even caught in a bed of thorns, it endures. It's our way of saying we're here, we matter, and someday, we'll be free."

A host of memories flood my mind. I've seen that image at home many times. A nascent bloom surrounded by thorns, painted on a warehouse wall near the Sklon Bridge. Chalked on the pavement in the marketplace where Matalans line up to scrub for work. Some of the servants at the public dance hall wear a nascent bloom pinned to their uniforms. I never understood the significance, or at least never cared enough to ask.

"Does this mean Kai's a... Rowlanite?" I shiver, simply saying the name of the cold-blooded terrorist group I've feared—and been told to fear—all my life. After our argument on the low-grav, I suspected he was part of the resistance, but to think of him aligned with those ruffians leaves me cold.

Ayva shakes her head. "I never asked. I don't want to know. The way he talks and acts, I think he agrees with the cause." She laughs with little mirth. "Funny thing, it was schooling that done it. Ma didn't want him at a Matalan school where you don't learn anything but how to punch rivets. She wanted him to get proper schooling, to make something of himself. She begged the regents to let him into Velten. He was never as meek as sheep, but mixing with the Habbies made him see what you had, and what we didn't. Got him noticing how unfair things are and questioning why it's so. Ever since, he's been pulling against the chain."

"Pulling against the chain," I echo. "Escaping from here is a pretty big chain. We've got the barrier and these holding us back." I flick a finger against my zati—and freeze. An idea, a brilliant, amazing idea flashes into my mind. My heart slams against my ribs.

"What is it, Meili? What are you thinking?"

I stare out the window and grin. "Perhaps there *is* a way." I must get out to the garden early tomorrow so I can tell Kai.

Ayva's eyes widen. "Gods, you're as loopy as he is. I'm not saying escape's impossible, but... Please, think hard on this. You could both be hurt, or worse."

"Yeah, there's that. But what's our other choice? Bedding Sir Juning? No thanks. Ayva, you know there's no rescue coming." I take a breath. To finally admit that, to say what I've been thinking for several weeks out loud sounds deathly final. "We're on our own and we'll be stuck here forever unless we do something. Like it or not, your brother's planning to *do* something."

And I'm going to help.

Not long ago I stood in that troci pen at the auction market, dejected, full of despair, thinking I had no skills and nothing to offer. How wrong I was. The garden is thriving. I can out-dust and out-mop any of our maids back home. Tonight, Bridgie ate the most delicious dessert she's ever tasted because of me. I can do a lot of things.

Even escape.

How did I go from telling Kai exactly what his sister said—he'd get himself killed—to choosing to help him? It's the loopiest of all things, a Habeni working with a Matalan to escape a prison impossible to break out of.

But that's what I'm going to do.

If that opinionated Rowlanite will let me.

Chapter 17

Meili

It's late in the day, but it's still hot as pakao. I drag my hand across my dripping forehead then go back to pulling weeds that have already sprouted around the young plants.

The squeak I've been waiting for since post-noon announces Kai's arrival. Maddeningly late. I stand and signal to him to come to the front of the garden. The barrow's wheel squawks as he pushes it along my new snakevine fence to the open gate.

He's drenched in sweat, his hair soaked, his brow glistening with perspiration. He's tied his tunic around his waist, exposing his slick, muscled chest. He looks like the statue of a Matalan warrior I saw in a museum back home, lean and fierce. I fear I might swoon, and not from the heat.

I get a liberal whiff of cattle stink as he and his barrow enter the garden, trailed by a horde of buzzing flies. I spot an ugly bruise across his right shoulder and down his back.

"Rossa's pocketbook, Kai, your shoulder. What happened?"

"A fight. Nothing to worry you," he mutters, brushing me off.

Annoyance flares. Of course it's something to worry me. He looks to be in some pain. It stings that he won't tell me about it, but I'm not going to drag it out of him.

I reach into my gardening basket and pull out two gingerberry tarts I'd whisked out of the pantry when Bridgie wasn't looking. She won't punish me for taking an extra treat between meals but swiping food for Kai could be a different matter. Especially since Varina's constant pouting and Jinks's insolence have put her into a crabby mood.

Kai's face lights up and I decide the risk of Bridgie's ire was completely worth it. He liberates the tarts from my hand and pushes them into his mouth.

"Water," he says around a mouthful.

I dart to the rain barrel, lift the ladle from its hook and fill it with water from the spout. I hurry back and hand it to him. He drinks greedily. His zati bobs against his throat as he swallows. Water trickles through his beard and down to his chest, trailing through the dark hairs like a winding stream. My belly does a riotous dance and I flush as hot as coals in a blazing fire.

He finishes. "More. Please," he adds, almost as an afterthought.

I trek to the rain barrel and back to him once again. He hands me the ladle after he drinks, then snatches a towel draped over the barrow's handle and swipes it across his face. He wipes his chest, and I wonder what it would feel like to touch him there. To run my fingers along his skin and down to his hips, and further. I tear my gaze away and rush to refill the ladle, tempted to dump the water over my head to cool my heated blood.

The way my body is responding to him is shameful. He's a Matalan. We may be thousands of centumes from home but joining between our peoples is still wrong. My head knows that, but my racing heart and throbbing pulse clearly need a reminder.

I return to Kai, somewhat more composed. He's put his tunic back on. To my relief. And disappointment.

He drops to his knees and scoops dung from the barrow with a small wooden shovel, spreading it over some newly sprouted weeds. I don't tell him it's the wrong spot. He drinks, nods that he's satisfied, and I slip the ladle into my apron pocket.

I crouch beside him. The smell nearly overwhelms me. Again, I think I may swoon, but for an entirely different reason.

"I gave Ayva your message," I say after several ticks. "She says you'll get yourself killed. Said your plan is risky and foolish." He gives me a pout Varina would envy. I almost laugh. "But she didn't say don't try. She knows it's not futile, and so do I. There *is* a chance of escape. But you'll need help."

"Yeah? Who's gonna help me?" He tosses a scornful look toward the troci in the fields. "None of them will lift a finger. I'm still a lazy Mucker to them. Someone to blame for their comedown. I never seen a stupider lot of Habbies. Ever. How your people managed to control my people all these years I don't ken."

"Really Kai? Just when we were getting along so well."

That earns me a grunt. His version of an apology, I guess.

I study the ink on his left arm. The nascent bloom's many petals are vibrant purple, the yellow as bright as the noonday sun. The thorns twined around the flower look painfully real. A defiant symbol. A *proud* symbol. I chew my bottom lip. Will he be too proud to work with a Habeni in attempting to escape?

I won't know until I ask. "Listen, Kai. If you can stop being angry at every Habeni that ever lived, you might discover one of us wants to help you."

He stretches toward the barrow, moving stiffly, and scoops more dung, dumping it around the weeds. "Help me? Help me what?"

"Escape, you loon. When I said you'll need help, I wasn't talking about Agron or those other numb brains. I'm talking about *me*. You can't do it alone. Getting Ayva out of the house will be difficult enough. Finding a way to slip by the watchers and get through the barrier will be doubly so. You need help. From *me*."

He sits back on his heels and gazes at me in surprise. No, more like amazed disbelief, and a whole lot of suspicion.

"You? You'll help? A Habbie will help me escape?" He stabs his shovel into the muck. "Is this a trick? Are you plotting with the watchers to trap me?"

That hurts. Can't he put aside his mistrust and dislike for one tick?

"Well, if that's how you feel, forget it." I scramble to my feet. "I had an idea and a brilliant plan and everything, but I guess you're too proud to listen to someone like me. Goodbye. Thanks for the shit."

I turn on my heel and stomp to the rain barrel. I scoop a dipper full of water and settle on a small wooden bench I've reclaimed from the vines. I don't have to wait long before he comes over. The bench creaks ominously as he sits. I'd like to fling the water at him, but when he reaches for the ladle, I let him take it. His fingers brush mine and my skin seems to burn.

I watch him drink. Away from his barrow, I catch a different scent. Soap and clean, with only a little of the barnyard. He must've recently bathed. Can't blame him. I'd bathe ten times a day if I had his smelly chore.

"Thank you." He hands the water dipper back to me. He eyes meet mine, a steady gaze. "Meili…" A long pause. "Tell me why I should trust you. I've been burned by Habeni before. Too many times."

I concede with a nod. It strikes me he has as many negative notions about my people as I've had about the Matalans, most of them justified.

"I'm not a Habeni anymore. And you're not a Matalan. We're troci." The word is gloomy, hanging over us like an oppressive cloud. "We're stuck in this mess together. If we can't trust each other now, we'll never find a way to break free."

He scowls, his favorite expression.

"Ayva's right. You're as stubborn as a mule."

I'm still holding the ladle. A bead of water drips from the bowl and plops into my lap. If Kai won't take my word, perhaps I can show him he can trust me. I lift the ladle to my lips. He stills, watching me keenly. No Habeni would *ever* put her lips where a Matalan's lips have been.

I meet his eyes and drink it all.

He lets out his breath, a long, slow exhale, as if in shock.

My heart lifts. I won this round. "Now, would you like me to tell you how we're going to escape?"

Kai's scowl returns as I beckon for him and his barrow to follow me across the clipped lawn to the courtyard wall. It's constructed of a thick, heavy stone and is several times my height. The spiky snakevines I used to make my garden fence crisscross every inch of stone, twisting and climbing all the way to the top.

"Spread the manure here, troci," I say loudly, gesturing to the scraggly gingerberry bushes at the base of the wall. The plants are well past the need for fertilizer, but most likely the watchers don't know that and any of them passing by will assume we're working.

As Kai dutifully shovels shit at the mostly dead bushes, I continue in a softer voice. "Last night, when I spoke with Ayva, I started thinking about this." I touch a callused finger to my zati's smooth surface. "It's powered by something, right? So's the kitchen door, and the perimeter barrier. *Everything* keeping us penned in here gets power from somewhere."

He nods. I can't tell if that means he gets what I'm saying or not.

"Even *this* is juiced."

I step closer to the wall. The yellow budgies nesting in the snakevines peep in alarm and flap away. I hold out my hands and my zati begins to pulsate then heat up. My throat tightens. Growling, Kai hooks his arm around my waist and yanks me back, out of range. It's cool here in the wall's shadow, but such an intimate embrace makes me burn all over.

"I get it, there's juice everywhere." He hastily releases me. "You don't have to fry yourself to prove it."

"I was nowhere close to that." Time to get to the point. "The current flows everywhere, but what powers it is in just *one* place. I hear it hum, day and night. Even through the heavy rain. The sound comes from the other side of this wall. Do you hear it?"

Kai flings more manure at the gingerberry bushes then pauses, listening. The budgies alight nearby and attempt to drown out the sound with their merry chirping, but there it is, a steady drone from inside the courtyard.

His eyebrows shoot up. "A power station?"

"I don't know why I didn't think of it before. I've been in the courtyard a dozen times hanging linen and never gave it a thought. We have a power box at home that provides a current to just about everything. There's a larger one near school that powers the entire complex, if I remember Blix's lecture correctly. I'm sure you've seen it. Stands to reason that box in the courtyard connects to all electrical functions, in the house *and* outside."

His eyes glimmer with excitement. "And if it was turned off..."

"No juice. Not for the zati, not for the watchers' weapons, and hopefully not for the barrier. If we can kill the power, there'll be nothing to stop an escape. We just walk to freedom."

I smile at my own brilliance. Kai chokes, as if something's stuck in his throat. He quickly looks away.

"What's wrong?" I ask. "You don't think it's a good plan?"

"Yes, it's good. It's clever."

I beam in delight. No one's ever called me clever before.

"Will you stop doing that?"

"What?"

"Smiling. Being all... happy like that."

I imitate Kai's scowl. "Is this better?"

"Infinitely."

Really, he might as well walk around with a hundred rain clouds above his head. "So how do we do it?"

"What? Shut down the electricity? No idea. I need to get a look first. You know, do a recon. See what material the building's made of, check out the locking mechs and whether I can get in without getting jolted. I've got to get into the courtyard." He studies the wall, his eyes narrowing. "I'll have to go through the house." He turns to me. "Is the housekeeper armed?"

I've been tapping my foot in annoyance as he's been nattering on. "She's armed, not that it matters. *You* don't have to get inside. I'll do this... recon thing. I'll do it this very night."

His mouth gapes so wide a budgie could nest inside. "You?"

I cross my arms. "Where's it written that you have to do everything? Why not me? I have access, you don't."

He gestures to the cottage where the watchers eat and bunk when they're on duty. Connected to the courtyard wall at the opposite end from the manor, the house is a white, two story wooden structure that would look almost pleasant without the barred windows.

"I'll go inside that way." He sounds doubtful and a bit desperate.

"You could try. And probably get a jolt from the watchers. Face it, I'm the only one who can get to the power building."

He scowls again. Does he have *any* other expression? "Simple as that, eh? Don't you care about the risk?"

I bristle. "Of course I care. If you can think of a better plan I'd like to hear it."

"A better plan is me doing it."

"I know what this is about. You think I'll get scared and back out, like with... Lil." Saying her name, remembering what I did, fills me with shame.

"That's not it. It's just too dangerous."

"And it's not *more* dangerous for you?"

He spits a litany of Matalan cusses. "You're *not* doing it."

I put up my chin. "Who are you to tell me what to do?"

I expect him to snipe back, accusing me of being a snotty Habbie, but he doesn't. He just gazes at me. A long, long time. My belly dances again, and my knees go weak, but I can't look away.

"I'll make a deal with you," he says finally, his voice a deep rumble. "Give me one day to find some way in. If I fail, you can do the recon tomorrow. Agreed?"

I blink, convinced he's lying. In fact, what I've seen of him so far, the way he hurls himself into danger, I *know* he's lying. He'll never trust a pampered Habbie to do the job. He'll find a way in or die trying. But at least he's willing to compromise.

I run my gaze along the wall, then past the kitchen entrance, the main part of the manor, and the west wing beyond. The sun is lowering. I'm not serving tonight, but I'll have to go in soon to help prep dinner. Perhaps I can be a little late.

I look back at Kai. He cocks an eyebrow, waiting for my answer. An answer he's not going to like.

"I think I have a better idea."

Chapter 18

Kai

I CLEAN MYSELF UP as twilight falls but don't return to camp. I head for the manor house instead.

I keep my head on the swivel, checking for suspicious eyes watching me. On the east side of the property, the workers flood to the cookfire for our nightly slop. The guards are lumbering toward their cottage, looking to fill their bellies, too.

I take a chance and dash up the rise and across the lawn, with the west wing as my destination. There's only a short time until the security lights flash on. Only a few ticks to recon the property, to find some way into that klacking courtyard.

I reach my destination, a cluster of rosebushes near the ballroom. My aching shoulder twinges as I push into the tangled branches and out of sight. I've put on my tunic but the thorns tear at my arms.

I squat down next to Meili. "Does every scheme of yours have to involve thorns poking into me?"

"Hush. Do you want someone to hear you?"

"What I want is to do this myself, with you safe inside. How is this a *better* idea?"

She flashes a pretty pout that would cause my knees to weaken if I wasn't crouched down.

"We made a deal, Kai. If we can find a way inside, you'll need me to guide you. I know the house, you don't."

I'm regretting that deal. Regretted it the moment it was struck. How is it one little Habeni can convince me to do the loopiest things? More like *threaten* me into it. She vowed to stay outside and dog my heels while I searched the property if I didn't agree to work with her.

Her grit is admirable—and surprising from one of her people—but she's foolhardy. Now we're both at risk.

"Let's start with the balcony at the ballroom," she says.

I move to crawl out of the bushes when I hear a sound and pull back. Boots plod heavily across the grass nearby, a watcher ambling by. I hold my breath, hoping he can't see us through the thick leaves. Meili's so close to me I can feel her tremble. Why did I ever let her do this?

The watcher takes his time walking past. There must be plenty of grub waiting for him at the cottage and he doesn't have to rush. Roasted boar. I'm sure of it. The smell's been in the air since noonday, torturing me. Even now, the thought of it makes my belly grumble, though it's not as empty as usual thanks to those tarts Meili gave me.

That was a surprise. Or maybe not. My waistband has loosened up since we got caught. She must've noticed I've grown thin and took pity on me. I pull away from her as much as I can in this tight space. The last thing I want from her is pity.

After I'm sure the watcher's gone, I creep out of the bushes toward the ballroom. It's a massive space, taking up almost the entirety of the wing, with floor-to-ceiling windows shrouded by silky curtains. The balcony runs along a good length along the outside of the room, topped by stone posts and a wide handrail. The posts are too high for me to reach, the stone too smooth to climb, and even if I could find a foothold, the electricity that surges across the wall's surface like a steady wave would burn me all the way up.

I signal for Meili to hang back and aim for my only option. The wide steps at one end. I remember seeing the Forsetis come down those stairs our first day in this asylum, their noses in the air, coming to inspect us.

My zati begins to shimmy and heat up. I step closer and reach out my foot toward the bottom step. A ring of fire shoots into my neck, like someone's turned a cooker's burner up to high. Heat scorches my skin. My stomach lurches. Those tarts threaten to come up.

"Kai." Meili's harsh whisper yanks me awake and I jump back. My zati calms. Dageth's hairy balls, that hurt, and I don't need Meili's glare to tell me there's no way in here.

We move quickly until we reach the end of the wing. A dozen or more sissy fruit trees border the long gravel drive in a tidy row. I put Meili behind me—to a bleat of complaint—before stepping around the corner toward the front of the house. I haul up fast and she slams into me. A wall of electricity shrouds the air before us like a heavy curtain. I can smell it. It shoves against me, making my ears ring.

Shit. Stitch was right. If I hid in the butcher's wagon I would've been a smoldering pile of ashes before I reached the front drive. Meili's right, too. It's looking more and more like there's no way in for me. There's only one place left to try.

The watchers' house.

I signal and start to turn when a ground transport rumbles up to the entrance. We both freeze in a crouch. A small, stocky Adsullatan gets out, darts around the vehicle and opens the rear door.

"That's Jinks," Meili whispers. "He's Sir Juning's valet."

Juning himself lopes down the front steps and hops into the transport. He's dressed in a godsawful topcoat spattered with sparkling gems. Meili cringes beside me, as if trying to make herself invisible. Fury erupts and the only thing stopping me from murdering that lecherous twip is that curtain of juice that keeps us apart.

"Let's go," Meili says, as the transport rolls away. Her voice is urgent. "There's not much time."

I snap a nod. It's getting darker and the floodlights will be on any tick.

We turn back toward the east wing, moving swiftly, keeping to the shadows. We duck as we pass the kitchen windows. The soft lights from within shine through the bars. I wish I could slow down to glance inside, maybe get a glimpse of Ayva, but it's too risky.

We reach the courtyard wall and hunker down on the cool ground beside a large wooden toolbox with a moss-coated lid. The wood is rotting and smells bitter and wet. The toolbox barely hides my bulk.

I peer over the mossy lid at the watchers' quarters, a house three times the size of one of our crumbling hovels. It's painted white with green shutters framing barred windows. Several watchers loll about outside, smoking, eating, joshing one another. Hup leans against the wall, digging a finger into his nose.

I cringe and my zati seems to tighten against my throat. So far I've kept out of the way of those goons, kept my head down and done my work. Avoided a juicing for as long as I could. But now, I have to risk it. I have to find out if I can get inside.

I look back at Meili. "Stay here." I prep to move.

She puts a hand on my shoulder. It's the sore one, but her touch is gentle.

"No. Stop, Kai. Just stop," she says in an exasperated whisper. "You can't go over there. Even you aren't loopy enough to confront that lot. You'll get yourself fried. You *must* concede. You must agree that only I can recon the power station."

I turn to face her, ready to debate that point.

She shakes her head. "Don't argue. I know you think I'm a weak-kneed female, and maybe I am, but I'm more scared of being stuck here for the rest of my life than anything else." She gazes steadily into my eyes. "You *have* to trust that I can do the job. I'm frightened, but I promise I won't run away."

My shoulders sag. Her courage has never been in question. And if it was, all my doubts were obliterated when she drank from the same water dipper as me today. I'm sure she can stand up to anything. But it kills me to step back and let her take the risk.

I nod, feeling as if I'm agreeing to my own doom.

She beams an excited smile. "You won't regret this, Kai."

I already do. "You're going to have to be very, very careful."

"*Meili!*" a shrill voice calls out.

I jump. Meili winces and shoots a worried glance over her shoulder. The housekeeper pokes her head out of the kitchen door and calls Meili's name again.

"I've got to go," Meili says. "I'll sneak out to the courtyard tonight, after lights out, when everyone's asleep." She starts to stand. "I'll report tomorrow what I find—"

The snap of a twig seems to boom in the gathering darkness. I yank her back down and whip my head around. A watcher strides purposefully toward us. He must've heard us yapping.

Meili and I lock gazes. Should I run, to draw him off? Should Meili run, hoping the sudden movement won't startle him into pulling his weapon?

He draws closer. Too late for either of us to run. We'll have to hide.

I'm already sitting. I shift and huddle against the toolbox, feeling as big and awkward as a rachee. I put my arm around Meili and pull her close, shielding her as much as I can with my body. She nestles against me, hunched up as small as a bobnut. We're far too close to the wall and its deadly fire. The current hums against my back and stings my neck, promising more if we get any closer.

The housekeeper wails for Meili again. The watcher has almost reached us. We don't move. Barely breathe. I brace for a juicing, when suddenly...

I hear a trickle that turns to a flood, liquid splashing against the wall.

I chance a glance over the top of the toolbox. Dageth's armpits, the goon is taking a leak, not two lengths away from us. Meili claps her hands over her ears and gapes at me, her face scrunched in disgust. I almost laugh at her dismay. *Would've* laughed if the slightest sound didn't threaten to betray us.

Two ticks later, the watcher's done. He shambles back to join his friends outside the house as the housekeeper shrieks for Meili again.

"Go." I yank Meili to her feet and push her toward the kitchen. "Be careful," I add as if that will magically keep her safe.

Then she's gone and I'm running faster than a jackrabbit with a burr in his bottom toward camp. The security lights flash on. I look back to see Meili barrel into the house, with the housekeeper's scolding voice following her inside. The door slides shut with a forceful snap.

I reach the cookfire, pulling in huge gasps of air, my heart hammering, my neck muscles coiled. There's no grub left but I don't feel like eating, anyway.

I won't unwind, won't sleep or draw a normal breath until I see Meili again, safe and sound.

Chapter 19

Meili

I climb into my cot and stare at the ceiling, waiting for the others to fall asleep.

I talk myself out of this loopy plan ten times. Back into it eleven. I'm terrified, and I only have myself to blame. It isn't as if Kai silver-tongued me into doing this recon. He's grumpy at best and insulting at worst. He couldn't sweettalk anyone into anything.

I jumped head-first into this scheme.

When I'm convinced everyone's in dreamland, I fling off my blanket and get up. My body trembles like I've got a bad case of the Matalan shakes as I tiptoe from the room.

I can't back off now, no matter how scared I am. Only a few hours ago, Kai was willing to walk into a mob of watchers and their juicing guns, on the slight chance he could get through their cottage to the courtyard. Just so *I* wouldn't have to take the risk.

I want to prove to him I'm no shrinking flower. Prove that I'm as hardy as that nascent bloom inked on his shoulder. Prove to myself I can be as brave as he is. Okay, maybe half as brave, the way my knees are knocking. But still, I'm determined to see this plan through.

I pass through the darkened kitchen, and peer into the wide hallway, bathed in a dull yellow glow from the ceiling light over the stairs to the upper level. All's clear. I step into the corridor and turn right, toward the courtyard door at the end. It seems far, far away.

I pad swiftly along the cool tiles, my nightdress fluttering. The door to Jinks's small room is ajar and it's dark inside. He must still be out with Juning. Bridgie's room is next, then Mr. Hervey's. Both doors are closed.

Good. After the scolding I got from Bridgie today for coming in so late, I don't want to disturb her slumber. She seemed to accept my story about getting distracted looking for the minty herb klenda, but only just barely.

I don't want to push my luck.

I reach the door. It has no security shield or alarm, or even bars on the window. Not necessary. With that thick, electrified wall enclosing the courtyard on both sides and the watchers' cottage at the other end, who would dare attempt to escape this way?

A glance through the window shows the nightly rain has stopped, and the clouds have broken up enough for the waxing moon to peek through. I wish it were still raining. The steady patter would drown out the click of the latch as I open the door, which seems to boom like a cannon in the stillness.

Outside, the scents of wet grass and sissy fruit greet me. The rain-slicked stones are cool on my bare feet. The cottage at the far end is quiet, the windows dark, indicating the watchers inside are asleep. The floodlights atop the walls point toward the compound, casting the courtyard interior into muted darkness.

I move swiftly along the winding dirt path. This area is pleasant in the daytime, but at night, it's creepy. The back of my neck prickles, as if a hundred pair of eyes stare at me from the shadows. Tree branches creak ominously in the breeze, and the stone benches look like beasts crouched to attack. Something furry skitters across my toes and I swallow a shriek.

I'm relieved and almost surprised when I reach the center of the courtyard without incident.

The power station is a large boxy building constructed of concrete and a generous size, as large as our gardening shed at home, with a peaked metal roof. The door is metal too and has a keypad where the knob should be.

A steady thrum comes from within. I'm all but certain it's the facility that channels power from the central grid our low-grav flew over on our way here. The source of electricity for this whole compound. For the lights in the house and the workers' cabins. The cleaning devices I'm becoming too familiar with. The watchers' juicing guns they use with such abandon.

And the barrier penning us in.

I reach out and push on the door. It doesn't budge. Not a huge surprise, but I admit I hoped it would easily open and I could get a glimpse inside.

I examine the keypad, looking for greasy finger marks, dirt on the keys, anything to give me a clue to the code. Nothing. The clouds play hide-the-moon and block what little light there is. I cuss. Ample illumination would make things far too easy, and we can't have that.

An idea hits me. A loopy idea I can't resist trying. A glance left, then right. No sign anyone is stirring, but still my heart pounds as I punch in the code for my school storage bin.

Beep.

I nearly wet my frillies. A light on the keypad flashes red, as if saying, *wrong number, slupa.* A frantic giggle catches in my throat. What did I expect?

I circle the small shed, looking for any weak point, any gaps or holes where the concrete has flaked away. Nothing. Not even a sign of a burrowing animal trying to get in.

A light pops on in the watchers' cottage. I freeze. Muffled footsteps and faint voices mutter from inside. Growing louder, getting closer. Then, to my horror, a click and the door starts to open.

I'm cooked.

Frickle!

Why wasn't I more careful? They'll find me here and shock me to within an inch of my life. Worse, Kai will be disappointed. He'll say he knew I'd fail, knew I didn't have what it took to do a proper job. No Habeni does.

The hinges squeak as the cottage door opens wide. Figures silhouetted by the light inside fill the opening.

Stop thinking and hide, you dip.

I dive for cover behind a stubby rosebush. Apparently my favorite hiding place. Though I wasn't nearly this frightened hiding earlier today in the bushes with Kai. Funny how much safer I feel with him by my side.

Through the leaves, I see three people stagger out of the house. Or, rather, attempt to. The door keeps knocking back into the large figure in the front. He's supporting someone, propped between him and another, smaller person. Much cussing and door bumping later, the trio reels into the courtyard as one entity.

I tremble harder when I realize the big one is Hup, the most vicious watcher of all. His burly arm supports Sir Juning. On the other side is Jinks, doing his best not to collapse under the dead weight he and Hup struggle to hold up. Juning's head lolls, his fine boots scuff the stones, and he mutters drunkenly as they drag him down the path.

"What happened to you in town?" Hup asks, grunting. "Ya smell like a barbeque pit."

"Sir Drunkard happened." Jinks's voice sounds strained, as if his throat's been burned. "He nearly burned down the fancy house."

Hup snorts. "Probably won't remember come daylight. Never does. He'll cry for my lady to buy his way out of trouble, without giving a rachee's fart what misery he caused."

"She'll have to start with the lawkeeper that brung us back here." Jinks chuckles, far from amused. "Was gonna lock us both in the hole and throw away the key 'til he recognized this brat. He'll come by for his payoff soon as his shift ends."

"She's diggin' this place into a hole cuz of this waste o' flesh." Hup can barely disguise his loathing.

"Brat," Juning slurs. "Waste of flesh."

He's described himself exactly. I'd sneer, but he sounds so disgusted it takes me aback.

I must make a sound, because Hup cocks his head. He stops dead and slaps his free hand to his holster, squinting in my direction.

Great. He'll see me. How can he not? My nightgown is as white as a cloud, easy to spot through the leaves. *Slupa*. Why didn't I hide behind the power building? My body quivers, head to toe. My throat tingles, anticipating a blast of juice.

A bead of water splatters my forehead. Another plops onto my arm. *Raindrops*. Fat raindrops that rapidly pick up the tempo to a downpour. I'm quickly drenched, and so are the unhappy trio.

"Klacking waterworks," Hup grumps, adjusting his burden with a shrug. "Let's get this twerp to bed."

He and Jinks resume their trek and drag the muttering Juning to the door. They haul him up the stairs. The young lordship's boots bump up each step. The door latch clicks and then they're inside.

I let out my breath and turn my face up to the downpour, never so grateful for this blessed rain as I am now.

Doesn't take me long to get over it. I'm soaked to the skin, but I have to wait until I'm sure they've passed through our quarters and gone upstairs. I stare at the door, waiting. Probably the hardest thing of all to do. Taryn told me many times that I'm the most impatient child she's ever met. I close my eyes and count to ten in Matalan as she taught me. I count to ten twenty times, then twenty more before I creep toward the door and up the shallow steps.

Wringing out my drenched hair, I peep through the rain-splattered window. The hallway's dotted with puddles but it's empty. It seems Hup and Jinks have dragged their drunken package away without anyone waking.

I'm inside in a tick. The door latches a bit too loud, but it's not that sound that alarms me. It's the click to my right—Mr. Hervey's bedroom door creaks slowly open.

I brace for him to step out. He doesn't. He's not even out of bed. He's awake, though. I don't mean to look. I should scoot down the hall back to my cot, but soft sounds from within draw my attention. I know why the noisy trio staggering along the hallway didn't wake the butler and the housekeeper.

Through the slight opening, I see Mr. Hervey in bed. With Bridgie.

Light from a candle on the bedside table flickers over their naked bodies, coupling, joined as one, thrusting in rhythm. Bridgie moans. Her hair is loose and she looks young and beautiful, her scars mostly invisible in the candlelight. Hervey is... far, far away.

Shock and dismay shoot through me. He has a wife. He and Bridgie aren't legally joined. They're different people, from different worlds, sharing an intimacy I've always been taught is forbidden.

My mind flashes to Kai and the way my body responds whenever I'm near him. When he pulled me into his arms earlier to protect me from the approaching watcher, all I could think of in the face of danger was him holding me so close and safe. And how much I wanted to kiss him. Wanted him to kiss me. And more.

The thought burns me even now, inside and out. The feelings he's stirred in me are untoward, unwelcome. Against every rule, law, and custom drummed into me since the time I could walk. Taboo, shameful thoughts that would warrant severe punishment for both of us if we were home.

And yet... I can't stop thinking about him.

I hurry back to the kitchen, grinding my teeth. The *only* thing I should be thinking about is escape. There *must* be a way to crack that power station's door and get inside.

I creep by Ellse, curled up in her blankets, and past the others in their cots to the lav, where I strip off my sopping nightgown. I towel off my hair and slip into dry frillies. My bed creaks softly as I lie down and let out my breath.

"Where'd you go?"

I jump. *Varina.* She sits up and eyes me with suspicion. I think it's suspicion, anyway. It's too dark and our cots are too far apart to see for sure.

"I went to the lav," I whisper and don't even have to pretend yawn. I'm exhausted.

"I mean, before that. I saw you sneak in. Don't bother to lie. I know what you're up to."

"You do? You followed me?" And will she tattle on me? That'll put an end to the escape plan before it can even begin.

"I didn't have to. I heard Juning out there. You snuck out to meet him. You hope to use him to get out of here."

Oh. She has no idea. "Not true. I heard noises in the hall and went to see what was going on. That's all."

She mulls that over a tick. "That better be all. He's *my* transport out of the scullery, so you better stay away."

I should've known. Varina doesn't have a grain of good sense in her whole body. Or any sense at all.

I flop back and yank the blanket up to my chin. There are two temperatures in this backwater—humid and more humid—but I'm shivering.

"Go to bed, Varina."

I turn onto my side and show her my back. I can't help a satisfied smile as I drift off to sleep. I did it. And I didn't die.

And I can't wait to tell that grumpy Matalan all about it.

Chapter 20

Meili

THE TOOLBOX COVER DROPS with a thud and moss bounces off the lid as it flops shut. I've finished raking and return to the garden for my next chore, when a telltale squeak stops me at the gate.

Kai reaches me. He releases the barrow's handles and looks me over with an expression of supreme relief and a little bit of surprise. "So, you're still in one piece."

"As you can see. Does that disappoint you?"

"You don't have to look so pleased with yourself."

I reply with a shrug. He's shirtless again. His hair's wet and he smells of soap. Does he wash up before coming to see me? The thought brings a flush to my cheeks, followed by a mental scold. He barely likes me. He wouldn't be trying to impress me.

I hold out a sandwich of sissy fruit jam slathered between two slices of tater bread. He eyes me a long tick, then takes it, mumbling his thanks. The sandwich disappears into his mouth.

"You might as well tell me about it," he says, chewing with relish. "After you tell me where you want this shit."

He and his barrow follow me to toward the gingerberry bushes. The dung from yesterday is still piled high around the roots, but anyone watching won't know that. Kai swallows his food with an audible gulp then he seizes the shovel from the barrow and flings globs of manure at the bushes.

I tell him about my adventure in the courtyard last night, minus my knock-kneed terror. "Unless someone hands us the keypad code, there's no way to open that door. We'll have to find some other way in."

He frowns. "Probably need a candle."

"A candle?"

"A bomb."

I go wide-eyed. "A bomb?"

He shoots me a hard look. "Yes, a bomb. Getting inside and taking out the electrical grid won't be as easy as your recon."

Easy? His lack of gratitude, or praise, for my success aggravates me to no end. "Well, I'm sure we can find someone clever enough to make a candle or whatever."

He keeps focused on his work. "We won't be finding anyone. I will. You're not going anywhere near explosives. You got lucky last night. I don't want you to risk yourself again."

I fume. *Easy. Luck.* What about courage?

"All right," I say, trying not to let on how frustrated I am. "Shouldn't we make some kind of plan? A schedule?"

"Hold up. There's still much to figure out before moving forward. First thing, no one can know about our plan but us. You can't tell anyone, not even Ayva."

I'm about to ask why when the answer comes to me. In case I'm caught. And punished. And made to tell who else is involved. I swallow that fear and nod.

"I mean it, Meili." He stabs his shovel into the barrow and scoops up more dung. "I've seen how you gells yabber. Can't keep a secret for anything. You *have* to stay quiet."

Why am I surprised by this criticism? He's swept and mopped and fixed things at school for years. It makes sense he would hear us chatter and gossip, oblivious to his presence.

My cheeks flush again, this time with anger. Not at him. At myself. The silly, and sometimes downright mean, things he must've heard me say. And what he must have thought of me. Two words come to mind, *light brain*. It's no wonder he grumps at me all the time, worried about trusting me.

"This is one secret I assure you I'll keep," I say. He grunts doubtfully. "Please, Kai. I know the Habeni haven't given your people much reason to trust us, but I promise you can trust *this* Habeni."

He stops shoveling and straightens, eyeing me. A range of emotions plays over his face, uncertainty, doubt, and a few others I can't even begin to name.

"I want to trust you," he says. "I hope I can. You've shown you're not like the others. Shown you're willing to break from their rigid rules." His gaze touches on my hair. "Though I can't ken why you did it. Let your hair go red, I mean. You could have hidden that secret all your life. Or at least until you were joined and had a protector to stand up for you."

I flinch. My answer is blunt. I stopped bleaching my hair to irritate Mother. She's been embarrassed by me since I was born, ashamed of the daughter she sees as a stain on her Habeni heritage. How better to needle her than to let my hair go back to its natural shade? But I can't tell Kai that. He would think me petty and callous.

And he'd be right.

"I don't know why," I say instead. "I guess I was tired of bleaching it all the time. Wasn't trying to make a point, if that's what you mean."

"You made a point to *us*." He leans the shovel against the barrow and steps closer. His chin's thrust out, his shoulders squared. I feel his warmth, breathe in his scent, soap mixed with the earthy smells of the barnyard. "You, your red hair, the fact that you would so freely flaunt a connection to our people, however slight. We thought it took a lot of spine to do that."

The Matalans at school talked about me? They admired me? "Oh. I didn't realize that simple act was such a big deal."

"Big deal? You showed a fire I've never seen in a Habbie. Never hoped to see." His voice deepens and his eyes glimmer. "The day you come into school with your red hair spilling down your back, I thought you were the bravest, most beaut—" He cuts off and looks away, his cheeks darkening. "I thought you were brave," he finishes with a snarl.

My breath catches. The Matalans looking up to me is one thing. *Kai* being impressed is another. Despite all the bickering and mistrust and his gloomy words and general attitude of doom when he's with me...

He thinks I'm brave.

The angry whine of Juning's rev cycle suddenly cuts through the air. The vehicle shoots around the corner of the watchers' house a tick later. The revver's engine buzzes like a hive of angry wasps as the cycle speeds up, heading for us.

Kai's expression turns to terror. "Get out of here, Meili."

Before I can do just that, Juning is on us. Aiming for *me*. Kai swings the barrow and shoves it between me and the cycle. A feeble barrier, but it works. Juning squeezes the handbrake and the revver scrubs out. The steel wheels bite into the soil, showering us with dirt and grass. The engine mutters to a stop.

"Hello, Red. Isn't my revver a beauty?" Sir Juning slides back and pats the empty space on the cycle's leather seat. "Come for a spin. Nothing would give me more pleasure than to see the wind in your hair."

His hungry gaze prowls over me. His face is sallow, his eyes red-rimmed and bloodshot, a stark reminder of his debauched condition last night. I hope his head throbs and his stomach spins, too.

Kai jumps in before I can speak, forgetting his slupa act. "She's busy."

Juning's eyes narrow. "You do not have permission to speak, troci. Get this reeking thing out of my way. And get back to work."

Kai's close by my side. I feel rage radiate off him like heat off pavement. "Piss off. I'll go back to work when you're gone."

Juning's weapon is out of his coat pocket and aimed at Kai in a flash.

"Wait. Please don't hurt him," I cry.

Juning smirks. "I see. I saved you from punishment at dinner the other night. Now you want another favor. Yet you offer nothing in return." His finger curls around the weapon's trigger. "What's your pleasure, Red? A ride with me, or the troci gets the blasting he's asking for?"

Acid burns my belly. Do I even have a choice? Go with him, or watch Kai get juiced. Juning licks his lips. He knows I'm crumbling. Kai moves before I can. He grabs the shovel, scoops up a pile of manure and herks the whole mess at Juning. Dung spatters Juning's coat. More lands in his hair. A wet glob splats onto his nose.

Juning's retaliation is swift. A surge of electricity that smells like roasting metal crackles from the weapon. My neck scalds as the bolt shoots by. A thousand white hot pins stab my flesh. A tickle compared to what must jolt Kai. His body jerks and convulses as if he's a marionette in a gruesome puppet show. His shovel clunks to the ground. His eyes roll back and he folds like a paper chain, hitting the ground with a thud.

"You hateful kutama," I spit.

"Temper, gell. You forget who you're talking to." Juning shoves the punisher into his pocket and swipes a gloved hand over his face. He looks down at his filthy coat then back at me, his expression deceptively mild. "Next time, remember what he got and do as I bid. Makes no difference to me to give a troci pain or pleasure. Think about what you prefer."

He twists the handlebar controls, the motor whines, and the cycle shoots away.

I kneel beside Kai. Ugly purple burns bubble around his zati. The stench of roasted flesh turns my stomach. I touch his neck with trembling fingers. His skin is as hot as fire.

"Kai. Are you alright?" My voice trembles. Emotion lumps in my throat. He attacked Juning *knowing* he'd get burned. He did it to protect *me*.

"I'm fine," he croaks, then clamps his teeth, as if fighting a new wave of pain. He pants. "You... weren't gonna... go with him."

I watch the cycle race across the meadow. The cattle scatter in terror. The truth? I don't know. But to Kai I say, "Of course not."

He sits up. His breathing is returning to normal. *He's* returning to normal, the way he scowls at me.

"Well," I huff. "Why'd you ask if you weren't going to believe me?"

"Why'd it take you so long to answer?" His voice is better too, but still rough. And angry.

He struggles to stand. I try to help him but he pushes me away. His legs shudder and he almost falls. I catch him and he gives in, leaning on me for support. I try to ignore the sensation of my breast pressing against his bare chest and fail miserably.

Our gazes catch. His breath is warm on my face. His eyes blaze with an emerald fire. I melt inside. He'd taken a brutal punishment to protect me. Rash and dangerous, but also braver than brave.

I kiss him.

I don't know why I do it, I just *do*. Perhaps the adrenaline of fear still sizzling through me triggers such a daring move. Or I've gone completely loopy. Whatever the cause, I lift onto my toes and press my lips against his.

He flinches. Then, to my surprise, he kisses me back.

I'd always imagined what my first kiss would be like, but I never thought it would be so... intimate. His lips against mine are soft and warm, his taste as sweet as honeydots. His beard tickles my chin. He slips his arms around me, a tentative, uncertain move that becomes more assertive as he tightens his hold, bringing me against him. An unfamiliar sweetness floods my nethers. Heat flames over every part of my body and I shoot right up to the sky, so over the moons it's a wonder we both don't float away.

A door clunks shut in the watchers' cottage. We leap apart like children caught doing something wrong.

If we were at home, our kiss *would* be wrong. Forbidden. A Habeni female kissing a Matalan would be a scandal of the highest order, not to mention illegal. Mother would disown me. I'd be shunned, called a thousand vile names and banished to the Matalan sector, never welcomed in polite society again. Worse, they'd jail Kai and likely sentence him to the fire pits. A gruesome death.

For a simple kiss.

That thought startles me to the core. I gape at Kai in shock, even a little fear. "I'm sorry. I didn't think... Ah, I mean, thank you. For what you did. With Sir Juning."

Kai's posture goes rigid. His gaze turns equally stony. "You don't owe me a thing," he growls.

He snatches up his shovel and flings it into the barrow. The wheel squeaks madly as he grips the handles and hurries away without a backward glance.

Chapter 21

Kai

I barely manage to make it back to the barn, and it's not the sting of the juicing slowing me down. It's my jumbled thoughts.

I kissed her. I kissed Meili Bengough.

And I wanted to do a whole lot more.

What in pakao was I thinking, kissing her? Letting her kiss me? The thing I wanted most, the thing I've wanted for a long time, Meili in my arms, holding her, my lips claiming hers, tasting her sweetness. For a searing moment, I thought her kiss meant a true feeling, some tenderness for me.

Then we broke apart and I knew what that kiss truly meant—I'm the most gullible slupa in all the worlds.

Her expression and her cloying words told me that. *Thank you.* For standing up to Juning for her. Gratitude for getting myself zapped. The kiss her payment for services rendered. A transaction like everything else in this stinking place.

Why did I fall for that? How could I believe for even half a tick she wanted a shit-stinking Mucker like me?

I shove the barrow and smack it against the rain barrel. Humiliated, furious with myself for letting her get to me. For letting down my defenses. I slam the barrow into the barrel again. And once more for good measure. The thud of wood on wood fills the air but does little to ease my frustration.

"Here, boy, what's this ruckus?" the watcher Cresp calls. He staggers out of the barn, followed by Stitch, bringing the licorice scent of burning abyssa with them.

I stutter something subservient and supremely apologetic. I'm tempted to add a bow. Anything to stave off another brutal blast of fire.

Cresp releases a phlegm-filled laugh. "Don't sorry us, lad. Go grovel to the one that juiced ya."

Stitch piles on. "And stop beatin' up on your barrow. Ain't another one in stock and you know our ladyship won't open her pocketbook to buy another."

They chortle again at their mighty wit then stumble back into the barn and their black leaf social hour.

I get about my chores. I do a slipshod job washing out my barrow then quickly clean myself up. I scrub my face but hesitate at my mouth. I can still feel her silky lips against mine. Still taste them, like fresh buckleberries dipped in cream. I still feel the way the stars seemed to explode in my chest when I held her in my arms.

Get a grip on yourself, Kai.

No use mooning over a bossy Habbie who doesn't give two snaps about me beyond what I can do for her. We're partners in a futile and most likely fatal plan to escape this dung hole. Nothing more.

I scrub her taste off my lips with a vengeance, determined to remember that.

The nightly chaos is in full swing back at camp.

Agron and his underlings have decided tonight is bully Blix night. Agron snatches the book from the lad's hands, then rips out a bunch of pages while his minions laugh and jeer. Blix looks like he wants to cry.

I don't help him. I turn away and get my grub then huddle on the ground by the cookfire, wincing in pain from my many injuries. The ache in my back and in my throat remind me I can't be in the helping business. Not anymore. I have one goal and one goal only and it doesn't involve caring about other people's troubles or fighting their battles.

Or kissing.

I've got to keep everyone at arm's length from now on. And that goes double for Meili.

Petra comes over and holds out her tater without a word. I turn her down. Maybe some night I'll take the klacking thing, so she'll feel she's paid her debt. But not tonight. She stalks off, leaving me alone.

It's a torture to eat. The taters hurt as they slide down my throat, even though I mash them up in the stew juice. But I swallow every bite.

Later, in the free moments before curfew, I wander over toward the watchers' cottage, getting as close as I dare. I *need* to get in there. If we're going to need a candle to take out that power station, it's my only hope of getting inside and doing the job myself. The only way to keep Meili from taking any more risks.

The question dogging me now is how? We aren't allowed to get within spitting distance of that house. There's not a shrub or bit of greenery anywhere nearby, so I can't even use shit-shoveling as a reason to wheel my barrow close and do a proper recon.

The watchers' meals are cooked and served in their cottage, but the veggies for their supper are prepped by the gell assigned to kitchen duty. They're the only troci I've ever seen walk through that cottage door, delivering the bags of taters they've peeled and the greenies they've chopped. Maybe I can cozy up to one of them, offer to help with their chores and tote the bag inside for them.

Yeah, help them. Or use them? I must be getting desperate, to sink as low as Agron and the others. There's got to be a better way.

The door to the cottage squawks open and I turn away before a watcher catches me gawking and asks what I'm up to.

To allay suspicion, I stroll with slow, deliberate steps toward the troci graveyard as if going to pay my respects. A fenced area just beyond the watchers' house, the patch of dirt is studded with grave markers and bathed in a sickly gray light by the floodlights. It's so close to the barrier, I can smell the electricity. A cruel joke, to bury a troci so near to freedom.

In the distance, a rachee howls. I peer into the darkness beyond the graveyard and the wide orange line painted on the grass along the perimeter to mark the barrier, a warning to go no further. I can just make out the rachee's silhouette, a hulking form the size of a boulder. The beast stomps through the forest, yowling and crashing into tree trunks as if trying to shove them out of its path.

The barrier may pen us all in, but it does squat to keep one of those creatures out, so I turn back toward camp. My brain flips and twists over ideas and schemes and worries but always comes back to the one thing I don't want to think about.

Meili.

Keeping her safe. Protecting her from Juning. Getting her out of here. And our kiss. Especially that kiss.

I give up after a while. Meili will be in my mind whether I want her there or not.

A few ticks later, the watcher Dall makes his way through the camp, swinging his stinging stick and counting down to lights out. I hit the privies to clean myself up. I'm exhausted, and in considerable pain. I'll be glad of my ratty bed tonight.

Afterward, I spot Blix sitting on the stoop of his palatial living quarters as I head toward my own bunk in the hovel next door. Normally I'd stroll by without a word, but he lifts his chin in greeting.

"Hey, Kai."

It's odd to hear him say my name. Then again, everything about this day's been odd. "Hey." I slow, then stop. "What're you doing out here?"

"Too tight and hot inside. Can't stand the smell—"

He chokes off his words, as if suddenly realizing who he's talking to. I'm the king of smells around here.

"Sorry about your book," I say, surprised to realize I mean it. So much for trying to stay detached and keeping everyone at arm's length.

He shrugs. "It was in Adsullatan. I couldn't read it anyway. It gave Lord Agron and his friends something to do, so they'd leave off me for a while." He studies me a tick, assessing the burns on my neck, I think. "Leave off you too. Looks like you've got enough troubles of your own."

Clever lad. Clever enough to figure out how to make a bomb. Maybe smart enough to find a way into the watchers' house that doesn't involve seducing the cooking staff or getting myself zapped into oblivion.

But will he keep his mouth shut about what Meili and I are scheming? Can I trust him? I gaze at his earnest face, his tousled yellow curls. Meili would say I've *got* to trust him, if I want to escape.

"Listen, Blix, I got a proposition for you."

His eyebrows pop up and I drop down on the stoop next to him.

He's about to become my new best friend.

Chapter 22

Meili

"My lady says the second planting's going well," Mr. Hervey says. "She's beside herself with the abundance of the first harvest. Not to mention the haul from the mines this quarter."

We're gathered once again in the kitchen, talking about the day. Mr. Hervey's in his rocker. Varina collects our dessert dishes. She edges around Ellse, who squats near the sink, licking gingerberry jam off her sticky fingers. Gwynn sips cold tea next to Ayva, who's darning Lady Forseti's stockings.

Only Jinks is missing. He's out with Sir Juning again. I guess scaring the cattle with his rev cycle and juicing Kai today weren't enough mischief for Sir Troublemaker, and he must go raise pakao in the village once more.

"Her ladyship says we've got more taters and greenie stalks put by than ever before. They should last the winter." Mr. Hervey is whittling a branch he's cut from the sissy fruit tree in the courtyard. The branch is too green for whittling, even if his knife wasn't as dull as my gardening spade. I make a mental note to find him a proper piece of wood.

"That's news to celebrate." Bridgie takes a hearty sip of her dromé. "I'll make lots of tater pie to keep us warm in the cold weather. And with the herbs Meili's bringing in, lots of tasty soups too."

I jump when I hear my name. I'm at the counter, grinding dorette leaves into a paste, with a sole recipient in mind. Kai, to soothe his burned neck. It won't heal his wounds completely but will take away the worst of the sting. At least, that's what dorette did for me as a child when Taryn applied a liberal amount to my perpetually skinned knees and elbows.

I try to focus on my task, nearly impossible when my thoughts swirl and spin and come back around to only one thing.

That kiss.

Those dratted flappermoths roar in my belly, thinking of the heat of Kai's mouth on mine. A riot quickly quelled as I recall the way he gazed at me after we broke apart. A storm raged in his expression. Unsettled, frustrated, and... disappointed.

Well, why shouldn't he be? I initiated that kiss, like a shameless, teasing cleek. Thoughtless, too. He knows the risk of kissing a Habeni. Even so far away from home he can't forget. I'd selfishly put him in a precarious position. And he despised me for it.

"I think I'll make jocakes to celebrate the harvest," Bridgie says, her gaze on Ayva. "Would you like that, love?"

Ayva pulls a needle trailing silver thread through a silk stocking. "Oh, yes. I love jocakes, 'specially with butter frosting on top. Ma always made jocake for harvest festival. When she could beg, borrow, or steal the flour, I mean. And the butter."

Bridgie presses her fingertips to her lips to stifle a belch. "Your ma sounds like an enterprising sort. The way you talk, I'm guessing she's gone to the gods?"

"Last season," Ayva says. "She got the Matalan flu. Kai took it hard, but Pa took it worse. He couldn't get meds, so I think he blamed himself. They cost too dear. We tried to get her over the bridge to the med center. But it was too late."

Tears glint in her eyes. Gwynn touches her shoulder. My heart wrings for Ayva, and for Kai. Maybe losing his mother is what makes him so stern and protective. And angry.

"I wonder if my ma's still alive." Bridgie reaches for the dromé decanter, then stops when she sees her glass is still mostly full. "She loved harvest season. Would bake dozens of jocakes. Gods, I'd eat so many, I thought I'd pop. The festival was so jolly. Presents, food, dancing. Had my first kiss behind a neighbor's barn one year. Ma found us and whupped me good. What was the lad's name? Rubal? Funny. I remember the stars, the smell of sweet hay. His lips against mine." She touches her mouth with a scarred hand. "But I can't recall his name."

"Missy Bridgie, you scamp," Mr. Hervey says, brushing wood shavings off his lap.

"I had my first kiss under the bleachers at school." Varina dumps the dishes into the sink and turns on the water. "We were supposed to be at physical training, when he drew me away and said, 'How about some private physical training?'"

"Was it Agron?" I ask. Sounds like him. Cliché, and with a decided lack of cleverness.

"I'll tell you, if you tell me who your first kiss was," she says coyly.

A smile trembles on my lips before I can stop it.

"Ooh, Meili, it must've been the kiss of a lifetime." Varina squirts soap into the dishwater. "Who was it could make you blush like that?"

Now I quake. If she knew, she'd be horrified. "Never you mind," I manage.

"Never you mind," she mocks and turns to Gwynn. "What about you? You have so many admirers, I can't begin to guess who stole your first kiss."

I'm relieved she's moved on but startled at Gwynn's reaction. She doesn't blush. She stiffens and turns as pale as a corpse. Strange, we've been friends forever, yet this is a subject we've never talked about. And surely, she *has* been kissed. She's so lovely, she must have a lot of kisses to her credit.

Ayva speaks up instead. "I had my first kiss in the library at school. No one saw, but I was scared all the same."

"Who with?" Varina asks. "It was that big gallumph Rost, wasn't it?"

"No." Her expression turns defiant. "I kissed a Habeni, and it was the sweetest thing ever."

I stiffen. Ayva and a Habeni? What would Kai think about that? My heart twists. After the way he reacted to my kiss today, I doubt he'd welcome that news.

"By all the gods." Bridgie's eyes pop as round as a jocake. "Have things changed so much at home since I left that such illicit behavior is now the thing?"

"It most certainly is not." Varina vigorously scrubs a plate. "It's forbidden and always shall be. It's been our way for generations to keep Habeni and Matalan separate. Ayva knows that. Everyone knows that."

I scrape the dorette off the cutting board and into a small tin, frowning, feeling glum. Everyone knows it, including Kai. Especially Kai.

"It shouldn't be that way," Gwynn bursts out. "Why should two people who love and care for each other be kept apart, just because of who they are? Why make people live in misery based on some old customs and laws? Why shun a gell and deny her a dowry for falling in love with someone different? It's a ridiculous rule, and simply wrong."

Time for my eyes to pop in surprise. I had no idea Gwynn felt that way. Then again, she has always been so quiet and reserved back home, and even now. I have no idea what she thinks about a lot of things.

"None of that matters here, anyway," she goes on. "There's no reason to cling to the old ways. No one to scold us if we step out of our cages and do as we please. We're a million clicks from Hephas and we aren't... we aren't going home anytime soon."

She chokes up but doesn't cry. Ayva takes hold of her hand.

"You don't have to remind me." Varina shoves a plate into the strainer. "I can't forget for a single tick where we are."

Silence falls, quiet except for the patter of rain on the roof. Mr. Hervey skims the knife along the branch as he whittles, his expression vague, oblivious to the ruckus. He manages to forget where he is quite handily. I wish I could shut out my troubles as easily.

"Brighten up, missies, things ain't so bad." Bridgie downs the remainder of her drink. "We got her ladyship's harvest ball to look forward to in a few weeks. It'll be a gala the likes of which you never seen. There'll be folks from all along the ridge, decked out in their finery. We'll have flowers trucked in from the north. And pastries. What a sight to see. It'll be *the* ball of the season."

Varina laughs, a mocking sound. "You're such a country mouse. *I've* been to many balls. I've danced and drank champagne. I didn't watch from afar like an envious bumpkin. *I've* worn finery someone like you can never imagine. S-so many beautiful gowns."

She seizes a bowl and cracks it against the edge of the sink. It shatters, pieces flying everywhere. A shard lands in Ellse's tangled hair. Ellse plucks it out as if porcelain chips fall into her hair every day.

Bridgie flies out of her chair and snatches the juicer from her apron pocket. "I told you before, have care with the crockery." She aims the punisher at Varina, her arm trembling.

Varina gapes in horror. I hold my breath, terrified of the crackle of electricity to come. The twitching, and the smell. Like Kai.

Mr. Hervey is on his feet. He takes Bridgie's hand, his voice gentle. "No need to lose our tempers. Varina didn't mean it, did you dearie?"

"No. I'm sorry. I'm so sorry." She drops to her knees and sweeps the broken pieces into a pile with her hand. "I won't do it again, I promise."

"You see?" Hervey's tone is mild. "She just misses home like you do. Like we all do. She'll tidy up, and everything will be peaceful and calm once more."

He holds Bridgie's gaze for several anxious moments until her expression softens. She even smiles. I don't think I've ever seen her smile. She fumbles the weapon back into her pocket. The tension in the room fizzles like a dying fire, and I finally exhale.

Mr. Hervey stretches his arms and lets out a fake yawn. "I believe it's time to retire, gells."

We shuffle off to our room. Varina stays behind to finish cleaning up, snapping at Ellse to get out of her way.

I brush my teeth and wash my face and hands, my mind whirling with everything that happened today. Mr. Hervey is wrong. Nothing is calm and peaceful here, least of all my heart. I wash around my zati with a soapy cloth, scrubbing away the grime and sweat, hating the thing with a passion. Me, Kai, Varina, all of us, are at the mercy of these horrible collars. And at the whim of any kutama with a juicing gun. Even Bridgie.

Gwynn's wrong too. The rules still matter here. They have to, if there's ever a whisper of a chance that this loopy plan of ours will succeed. Kai and I may work together now, but if we somehow escape and find our way back home, we'll have to go our separate ways.

They'll make us.

I climb into my cot and huddle under the covers, vowing never to kiss Kai again. I swear I'll stay away from him and his tempting lips from now on.

Liking Kai, and kissing him, can't happen here—because it can't happen *there*.

Chapter 23

Kai

"Come. Sit over there," Meili says as soon as I push my barrow into the garden.

She closes the gate and tips her head toward the bench. I narrow my eyes, suspicious, but do as she bids. The flimsy bench creaks in complaint as I sit down.

It's the end of the day. My chores have kept me from her until now. The sun is sinking and the shadows of dusk are lengthening. We don't have time for bench sitting or conversation. I need to deliver my message and go. Need to get away from her as quickly as I can, before the madness that led to me kissing her yesterday sweeps over me again.

She steps up next me. *Close* beside me. I feel her warmth and inhale her sweet scent. She uncaps a small tin she's taken from her apron pocket. She scoops a generous glop of a pasty gray substance from the tin onto her fingers.

Then she touches my neck.

I wrench away and shoot to my feet. Or try to. She clamps my shoulder with her free hand in a surprisingly strong grip, pushing me back down.

"Be still, Kai. It's dorette balm. It'll soothe your injuries."

My injuries are not what I'm worried about. She massages the paste into the raw wounds around my zati. The substance is grainy and cold and stings like pakao, but all I can feel, all I can think about is her fingers on my skin, so warm and gentle. Caring. Helping me. In return for helping her.

"Rossa's pocketbook," she chides. "You're as stiff as stone. Relax. I'm not going to slice an artery."

"Would that I could be certain." My voice is deep, husky, threatening to betray my desire.

"Must you always be such a grump?" She taps my neck in a playful slap then massages with more vigor, working the paste deeply into the burns. "How does that feel?" she murmurs. "Any better?"

I answer with a grunt.

"I'll take that as a resounding yes."

"How is Ayva?"

"She is well. She... it's odd, Kai, but we've become friends. Especially Ayva and Gwynn."

I grunt again, highly skeptical.

"It's true. We've grown fond of one another. We support one another." She sounds mystified. "So unthinkable at home."

"Yeah, unthinkable." Impossible is more like. If the law and restrictions and status don't keep us apart, the Habeni's ingrained sense of superiority does the job. The only Habbie who'd befriend a Mucker does so to fleece us of our precious coin. But here, I guess we're all one and the same.

She gives my neck a few more vigorous swipes then steps back. "There. Let the potion sit until it dries." She caps the tin and slips it back into her apron.

I stand and touch my neck gingerly. "Thank you." The word seems to squeeze from my mouth with bitter reluctance, though I have to admit, the sting of the burns has already lessened.

I step to my barrow. She directs me and my shovel to some greenish plants with spiky orange petals she calls scucca plants, and I get to work.

She watches me a moment, then, "What progress do you have to report? Have you found someone who can make a bomb... er, candle?"

"I have. Blix. He says we'll need not one candle, but two of 'em."

"Blix? Of course. Why didn't I think of him?"

"He says he can build what we need as easy as rachee pie." I dump a pile of manure around the plants and tamp it into the soil. "But there's a catch."

"A catch? He wants something in return?"

I scowl. "Who in this godsforsaken stink hole doesn't want something?" Or eagerly give something in exchange for a favor? Like her kiss.

"Well, what is it? Must be valuable to make you sound so miserable. Correction, you always sound that way, but Blix's demand must be considerable or you would've already struck a deal."

I stab the shovel into the mound of muck in the barrow and meet her gaze full on. "He wants you."

"What?"

"Blix thinks he can make what we want but he won't lift a finger till he hears from you that it's a true plan and not a trick from me." I sigh again. "That kutama will sit and pass time with me, sup with me, and share a lav, but by Dageth, he won't trust a Mucker."

She chuckles, a soft, almost merry sound that tickles me inside and out. "I'm inclined to think the whole trust problem is the other way around." Stepping closer, she wipes her shiny hands on her apron. "If Blix needs to see me, then make haste and bring him to me. I'll put his doubts to rest."

I gust a sigh and shift position, putting some space between us.. "That's the rub. He can't come here. Not without great risk. You have to go..." I look toward the camp. The setting sun paints the small shacks in a pinkish glow, making them appear almost livable.

The workers are streaming out of the fields, heading home after a long day.

"And that's a problem because…?"

She knows why. It's in her expression and her tone but I voice my concerns anyway. "Because the workers' village is a rough and treacherous place. Ten times more dangerous for an outsider like you. Far more dangerous than when I let you do that recon—"

"You *let* me? Only after I argued until I ran out of breath. I survived the recon, and I'll make it through this. If Blix won't come here, I'll go there. Come. Let's go tell him to make that bomb."

"Wait."

I grab her wrist before she can race away. She stills and our gazes lock. I should abandon this scheme entirely, find some other way to convince Blix to help me. I almost didn't tell her about her friend's cockeyed demand, so she wouldn't have to risk traipsing into troci land. But my selfish need to escape won out. I fear it's beginning to outweigh all other concerns.

I stare deep into her eyes. Except my need to keep her safe.

I release my hold on her arm. "I mean, you can't just rush off with your skirts and hair flying willy-nilly." I sigh again, like a persistent windstorm that shows no sign of stopping. I suppose it won't stop. The fear and worry never will, as long as I'm working with this far too alluring Habbie. "I'll take you to Blix, but we must proceed with care. You can't just stroll into camp like you've been invited to a garden party."

She sniffs. "I can be stealthy."

I answer her sniff with a snort. "No Habeni I ever met knows how to be stealthy. You'll be caught in an instant. Your hair alone is a beacon sure to attract watchers or troci with mischief on their mind. We must proceed cautiously. And for Dageth's sake, keep your voice down. Why do you Habbies have to be so loud? You shout out every secret, every move you're going to make with no care who overhears."

"I know you don't like me, Kai, but must you perpetually insult me?"

That sobers me. The problem is, I like her too much. That's why I snap at her and lash out. I'm being hard on her to protect my own feelings. Perhaps I need to lighten up.

I offer a mumbled apology. She takes no notice as she snatches a kerchief from her seemingly bottomless apron pocket and ties it around her head with angry movements, hiding her beautiful hair under a cloth the color of dirt.

"There. Done. Now, can we proceed while there's still a sliver of daylight? I must go into the house soon and I don't want to risk a scolding for being late like last time."

That sobers me some more. I've worried so much about what could happen if she's discovered in the workers camp, I hadn't thought about what she might face if she's late to return to the house. Though the dorette has eased the burn, my neck still stings and it took hours for my eyes to uncross after my juicing. I wouldn't wish that agony on anyone. Okay, maybe Agron, but certainly not Meili.

I don't get a chance to answer—she storms off, heading for the gate.

With one more aggravated sigh, I leave my barrow behind and follow.

We move swiftly across the lawn from the garden toward the fields and the building beyond. I focus on putting one foot in front of the other. Focus on watching for suspicious guards. Focus on *anything* but the beauty hurrying beside me and the danger I'm dragging her into.

At the greenies field, I tug her arm, steering her to the left. She glances around as we hurry toward the camp. Looking for Ullr, no doubt. We pass the first of the shacks and a gang of troci lounging on the stoop. They inspect her with greedy interest. I pull her along faster. I'm not in the mood to fight tonight, especially three on one.

We reach Blix's hovel and meet up with him at the corner near the rain barrel. A bittersweet look lights his face when he sees Meili, and I swear I see tears glimmering in his eyes in the fading light. I always knew the Habeni had emotions, they're just cunning at hiding them.

"Meili." Blix pulls her to him and they hug. I itch to bust them apart, so I stick my hands in the rain barrel's tepid water and busy myself scrubbing off the remnants of dung and dirt that cling to my skin. The hug goes on for a long time. I hope Ullr doesn't stumble by or we could have a hugging party all night.

Meili finally breaks away from her friend's embrace. "Rossa's pocketbook, Blix." Her voice is tender, full of sorrow. "You've grown so thin."

Gaunt, more like. But he takes her criticism with a lopsided grin.

"I hate taters," he says. "Hate greenies and anything else leafy, too. I'm so hungry, I'm about ready to eat one of those rachees if I can catch one."

Water flies as I shake my hands dry. "Hate to bust up such a fine reunion, but can we get to the point?" Blix eyes me like he forgot the point entirely. "The candle? You can build one?"

"Wait. Ears are listening." Meili jerks her chin and I glance back to see Petra lingering by the edge of the field. She picks up stones and hucks them into the greenies, scaring black birds with scarlet-tipped wings out of the stalks.

"She's too far away. She can't hear us," I say, though not fully sure of that. "She... Look, I trust her, you ken?"

Meili eyes me a hot tick. "Oh." Not sure what she means by that small word, but whatever it is makes my face burn.

She turns back to Blix and we speak in low voices. Meili quickly describes the escape plan and the building at the center of the courtyard. Blix brightens.

"Well done, Meili. A place like this needs a lot of juice, and I've not seen a structure on site that would provide it. Makes sense it'd be hidden, protected. From the size and dimensions you describe, we'll need a lot of wick in the bomb to—"

I growl and he claps his mouth shut. I *told* him not to use the B-word.

"But how will I attach the... candle to the building?" Meili's gaze bounces between me and Blix. "There's no place to hang it on the door. It can't go underneath. Even a teakslug couldn't slither under there. I suppose I could put it on the roof, but someone might see me."

"Let *me* worry about that," I snap.

Dageth's toenails, she speaks as if she sets off explosives every day. She may have figured out the plan, and I'll credit her with more fortitude than any Habbie I ever met, but the sooner she understands I'm not handing her a bomb and letting her blow herself to bits the better. *How* I'll get in there and set the charge, I still don't know, but I'll find a way.

I turn to Blix. "First *you* gotta get these klacking things built."

Blix nods. "It's not impossible. I can scrounge the tools I'll need. There's plenty of Mollystone grease, wiring, metal bits, and sundry in the tool shed. Those mechanized farming devices are always in need of repair, especially the hoers. These Adsullatans may be handy with those stinging weapons, but they don't know a whit about proper equipment maintenance or..."

I clear my throat. Loudly. Meili shoots me a smirk. I swear she revels in my annoyance.

"Sorry," Blix says. "So, with those bits and some of the Mucker's shit, I should be able to build an effective bom... er, candle. Two of them. One to pop the door, a larger one to disable the grid and neutralize the electric flow."

Meili nods, though I suspect she understands as much as I do. No matter, his words get my blood pumping all the same. Escape, once impossible, now seems closer to possible. I wait for Blix to demand his price, but he just gazes at us with a self-satisfied grin on his puss. Maybe he's not as smart as I thought. I name his price for him, offering to take him with us when we break out.

"That'll be fine," he says, almost surprised. "If the plan works."

"Big if," I mutter.

Meili's chin goes up and she spears me with her gaze. "It will. I'll make sure of it."

Not if I can help it. "Hold on, my lady. We're a long way from fireworks. We gotta make a plan that's got no seams first. How do we get past the watchers when the power goes down? If all goes as planned, the juicers won't work, but those goons could still crack our heads with 'em."

"Might help to have a map, or an atlas," Blix puts in. "We don't know where we are. Be nice to have a direction to point in."

Smart. I kick myself for not thinking of that.

"I bet there's an atlas or something in the library," Meili says. "My father has lots of maps and star charts in our library at home. He pores over them all the time."

I snort. "Surveying property. Looking for Matalan land to steal and build on, I bet."

"That again, Kai?" she says with a frown. I can't decide if she's more beautiful when she's angry or when she's happy or even when she's gleeful at the thought of setting off a bomb.

Maybe all three.

"Kai... Watchers," Petra warns. She jerks her thumb toward the end of the row of cottages and I cuss. It's Dall. He strolls down past the stoops, poking troci with his punisher.

"Get to yer vittles," he barks. "Afore they're gone."

Dall is the densest, dimmest watcher on the payroll, but even a slupa like him will remember Meili from the garden. And he'll wonder what she's doing here with us grubby mother-humpers. I don't want to imagine what he might do to her. Meili grimaces. She's thinking the same thing.

"Time to go." Blix laughs with no mirth. "See you, Meili."

He slips into the passageway between two of the buildings. I grab Meili's arm and pull her along after him. It's dark and the sun rarely warms this narrow alley. The ground is slick and muddy. She slips. I catch her, circling her waist with my arm. She's warm and soft against me.

Blix races up the alley and pops out at the other end, heading toward the cookfire. A hulking figure steps into the opening. It's Hup, standing with his back to us, on the lookout for trouble. Or looking to make trouble. Whatever, he's a solid roadblock to our exit. Behind us, Dall's footsteps thump closer.

With nowhere to go, I haul us to a stop and push Meili into the shadows against the wall. I put a finger to my lips. She nods, her eyes wide. Dall reaches the passageway and cranes his neck, peering into the darkness. I press as close to Meili as I dare, shielding her.

"Hey, shit eater," rings out and Dall spins toward the sound. Petra flashes into view and hurls a stone at him then darts away. Dall cusses and gives chase. A tick later, Hup moves on.

A glimmer of light cuts down the passage and touches on Meili's face. She gazes up at me, her eyes shining, her breathing fast and shallow. Her pulse throbs wildly in her neck above her zati. She's trembling. So am I. In fear, sure, but also sudden need.

"Are you alright?" I ask, my voice gruff.

I search her face, as if to confirm the answer to my question. A lock of her hair has slipped free of her scarf. I lift my hand and catch it, an automatic, unbidden movement. My fingers brush her cheek and skim along her smooth skin to her temple as I tuck the silky strand under the cloth.

She trembles. A small, yearning sound escapes her mouth. My gaze centers there. She tips her head back. Her lips part. An invitation? I don't wait to find out. I long to kiss her. More than anything.

My lips close over hers.

This kiss is as different from yesterday's as winter is from summer. That had been a prologue, an introduction, brief and sweet. This is a searing exploration, a connection blazing with desire, pulsing with need.

I shift and wrap her in a tight embrace, kissing her more fully. She moans softly and lifts her arms, digging her fingers into my shoulders, pulling me closer, closer until I'm pressing her against the wall. I tilt my head and open my mouth. Our tongues touch and my head spins.

We break apart for a moment. She meets my eyes, her cheeks flushed, her breath coming in sharp gasps. I reach up and slip off her scarf. Her hair tumbles down, shimmering like fire in the low light. I pull in a ragged breath and slide my fingers through her hair, reveling in the feel of those silky locks.

"Meili," I murmur and seize her lips again.

My blood rushes through my veins like the Osch River in springtime. I tumble into the stream and let myself get swept away. Swept away from this stinking place, far from Hup and Dall, the juicers and the zati ringing my neck. All I can think and feel and taste is *her* and the sweetness and joy of her lips on mine.

Something hard and sharp pings the back of my head. I yank away from Meili with an outraged yelp and swivel to see Petra standing there, hands on hips and as angry as a stormy night. She'd chucked a stone at me.

Meili gasps and I swing back to her. Her gaze pops back and forth from me to Petra, her eyes as round as teatime saucers. Her expression darkens. A hard-eyed expression I can't begin to ken. It sure isn't the bliss I felt kissing her.

"Meili, I—"

She balls her fists—and socks me in the gut.

Then she tears down the alley and around the corner, her skirts flapping. I grip my stomach and watch her flee with a frustrated frown. Then I swing on Petra. She'd hurled that klacking stone and made me jump away from Meili. If she hadn't done that, we might still be kissing.

"Why'd you do that?"

She glowers, a look that says I'm the biggest slupa in the land. "Watchers, you ninny. They mighta come back. You mighta got zapped. Not that you wouldn't deserve it." She stoops and grabs Meili's scarf out of the muck. "She was so hot to get away, she forgot this."

I snatch the cloth from her hand and the stark truth penetrates my kiss-addled mind. Hot to get away from me, Petra means. Dageth's balls, could there be a bigger fool anywhere? Meili ran away from *me*, the Mucker who foisted himself on her.

That's the only explanation. That first kiss between us Meili had instigated, her way of thanking me for standing up for her. This kiss… Was me. All me. My selfish need to feel her lips against mine drove me to do it, with no permission and no thought of her. Or what that kiss meant to her.

I cuss, loud and long. How many times do I have to remind myself she's kissing me, and letting me kiss her, out of obligation? Because she feels she owes me. Because she sees her kisses as some sort of reward.

No wonder she ran off the moment she could break free.

Petra folds her arms across her chest, glaring at me. "We gonna go eat, or you gonna spend all night cussing over that wench?"

I don't answer. What I want to do is kick myself from here until next noonday. What I *have* to do is make sure Meili gets back to the house unscathed. I dragged her down here, I'm responsible for her safety.

"You go, Petra. I'll catch up with you."

She glares some more but turns away. I take off toward the garden. I get there in time to see Meili disappear into the house. My shoulders droop as the door snaps shut, cutting her from my view.

Maybe for the best. We should keep apart. Kissing her brought me gut wrenchingly close to something I don't want to feel for her. Something aching and terrifying and utterly unwelcome.

I don't want to feel that for a Habeni.

I carefully fold Meili's now-filthy scarf and slip it into my pocket, then go retrieve my barrow, ignoring what's shouting in my brain, and in my heart.

She's not a Habeni. She's Meili. Just Meili.

And I want her to be mine.

Chapter 24

Meili

My stomach flutters as I approach the library. Convincing Ellse to agree to split our chores today instead of cleaning each room together was the easy part. Convincing myself to open the door and go inside is the hard part. Yesterday I was full of ginger when I promised Kai and Blix I'd pop into the library and find a map or an atlas. Today, I'm a knock-kneed mess, certain I'll be found out.

But it's now or never.

I take a deep breath and slip inside. I put down my bucket, switch on the light, and go to the sole window to draw the shade. The library's adjacent to the ballroom. Even though it's the smallest room on the main floor and little-used, we must dust and clean it all the same. Dark paneled bookcases line the walls, two plump armchairs sit in the center of the room, and a small desk stands at the window.

I circle the room, scanning each shelf, searching for a bound volume big enough to be an atlas. I try to focus on my task, but bewildering, painful thoughts chase each other around my head, centering on that exquisite moment yesterday when Kai and I kissed—and the heartbreak that followed.

I don't know how it happened. One moment, Kai and I were hiding from the watchers. The next moment, we were kissing. Did he reach for me, or did I sink into his arms uninvited? I couldn't be sure. I only knew our lips joined in a heated rush, a blistering kiss that sent pinpricks of pleasure skittering across my skin and igniting a burning desire to feel his mouth on mine for all of time.

Desire and longing bloom anew as I remember how he gazed at me, his eyes glittering, piercing, and the way he murmured my name, both tender and desperate, before he tightened his hold and kissed me with greater demand. Our tongues touched in a wanton dance no proper Habeni female would even think to indulge in.

Yet, I couldn't stop myself. The sweet heat in my nethers became a blazing fire, wanting his lips on mine and more, yearning for him to touch me, to join with me, becoming one. Not Habeni, not Matalan, not troci. Just two people, equals, sharing the most intimate moment together as one.

And then...

Kai yanked away. Broke the spell and brought me back.

I'd blinked open my eyes, confused, until I saw the Adsullatan he called Petra standing there, watching us. Kai's gaze had flicked from me to her, his expression filled with regret and more than a little guilt. She looked furious, hurt. And jealous.

That's when I ran. He'd called to me, but I didn't stop. I had to get away. It was a good thing the floodlights came on, lighting my way up the path to the house, because tears clouded my eyes.

Kissing Kai, something I've never felt before flooded through me. Desire, yes, but something more, something deeper I can't even bear to give a name to. Something Petra feels for him too. I saw it on her face.

Who is she? Who is this curvy Adsullatan with the soulful brown eyes? Someone close to Kai. Very close. *I trust her*, he'd said. The Matalan who's suspicious of everyone. Who claims to trust no one, least of all me, but he trusts this Petra. Someone he's only just barely met.

Are they together? Does Kai love her? And if he does love her...

Then why had he kissed me?

Stop it, you fool. I'd torn my brain to shreds, going round and round, asking that question again and again and coming up with no answer.

I blink away new tears and force myself to focus on my task, on our escape, instead of what's making my heart hurt so much.

I scan the shelves and run my fingers along the coarse bindings of dozens of books, inhaling the musty scent of the old paper. For a moment, homesickness edges out the other emotions in my chest. How many times did I sneak into Father's library, searching for a book to take to my room and read under the covers? A vidpad's all well and good, but to see the words spill across the paper, to hear the crinkle of a turning page, brings the story so vividly to life.

A clatter in the hall pushes away my pining and accelerates my jitters. Ellse? Is she finished cleaning the parlor already? I hope she goes straight downstairs and doesn't decide to come help me, but I grab my bucket just in case and speed up my search.

Many ticks later, I find what might be what I'm looking for—three thick, folio-sized books with leather bindings stacked on the bottom shelf of the bookcase closest to the window. I pull them out and lay them on the floor, quickly flipping through each folio. Two look to be technical tomes, with equations filling the pages. I shove them aside and open the third.

Aha. Pages and pages of maps. Maps of Adsullata, I hope. I remember Blix saying we traveled southwest to get to Mollystone Ridge, so I look for a symbol representing directions. I let out a soft cheer when I find a topographical map with a picture of what I think is a mollystone over some hills, which must indicate the mines.

The atlas is too big to fit into my work bucket, so there's only one thing I can do, though it hurts like pakao. I tear the map from the book with a decisive *rip*. The edges are jagged, and a chunk of the page remains caught in the binding, but I've got most of it.

I fold the map and look around for a smaller book to stuff it into. A poetry book? Kai would like that. Time ticks away. Tension coils my muscles and I repeatedly glance toward the door as I pluck book after book off the shelves, skimming the pages for poems. How I wish the translator in my neck had a visual component. The letters make no sense.

And why am I wasting precious time in such a loopy hunt? Kai can't read Adsullatan any more than I can. Besides, why would he care about a gift from me? Let his Adsullatan with the soulful eyes find him a poetry book.

I snatch a random book from a shelf, open it to stuff the map inside, and laugh. The sentences are laid out like poems on the pages.

Kneeling again, I tear out two more maps, fold them, and tuck them all into the book. I'm ripping out a fourth page when the door opens. *Frickle!* My bucket sits forgotten on the hardwood, too far away for me to grab. I'm cooked for sure.

Lady Netti steps into the room, but she doesn't see me. She's looking back over her shoulder. That gives me time to stuff the map into the book and snap it shut. She carefully closes the door. She notices me then, and she freezes.

"I didn't think anyone was in here," she says, dismayed.

Still kneeling, I stare up at her like a fool. A frightened fool. "Forgive me, my lady."

Her gaze goes over me, from the book in my hand to the larger books strewn across the floor. She steps closer. The gold starbursts that speckle the bust of her green day dress twinkle in the light from the window as she moves.

Her thick black eyebrows draw down. "What's happened here?"

"Uh..." is the most intelligent thing I can manage.

"Did you drop these?"

I tuck the poetry book under my arm and shove the atlases back on the shelf. "Oh no, I was... dusting." I scramble to my feet, sure she can hear the lie. "I've finished now."

She looks skeptical. Her dark eyes touch on the book under my arm. "What's that?"

Oh, gods, I'm in for a juicing. She'll accuse me of stealing. Or notice the edges of the folded maps sticking out from between the pages. Before I can stutter an explanation, she snatches the book from me. She examines the binding and the title, then her curious gaze settles on me.

"You were reading?" She sounds beyond surprised. "You can read Adsullatan?"

I stiffen. Never mind stealing a book, a troci reading is probably a worse offense. "No, my lady. As I said, I was dusting." I long to tear the book out of her hands and dash from the room.

"You're lying."

My stomach clenches and I brace for her weapon's sting. But she doesn't reach for it. She studies the book a tick longer, then hands it back to me.

"Cliftee's good, but if you want to read a truly amazing poet when you're done with this, try Holmes. Top shelf, over there." She points to the bookcase near the desk. "His work is romantic and passionate without being cloying." She steps aside. "You may go."

She doesn't have to tell me twice. I seize my bucket and rush by her to the door.

"Oh, gell," she calls.

I have my hand on the doorknob, almost free. Is she toying with me? Playing a game, like her brother?

"Please don't tell anyone you saw me in here. Her ladyship in particular."

I bob a curtsey and bolt from the room. I close the door and lean against it, releasing my breath in a whoosh. That was close. I slip the book into my bucket, arranging a dust cloth over it. It looks like I'm hiding a book, but it'll do until I can find somewhere more secretive to stow it. I dash down the hallway to the servants' door under the stairs, immensely pleased with myself.

The door stands slightly ajar, which surprises me. Ellse is usually more careful when she comes and goes. I realize my mistake as soon as I reach the door and peep into the narrow opening.

Mother of a Mucker.

Ellse hasn't left the door open. Sir Juning has. He's there on the landing.

With Varina in his arms.

Juning gropes Varina like a ten-armed sea monster enveloping its prey. She reciprocates with a healthy amount of groping of her own. My stomach turns.

"You know what I like," he says as she nibbles on his neck.

"Mm. And I know what you want." She slides her hand down the front of his trousers. He gasps.

Now my stomach heaves, and I fear I'll upchuck right there in the hall.

"Let's retreat to the library," he says urgently. "No one will disturb us there."

Oh? I think he's in for a big surprise.

"I want to, but I can't," Varina says coyly. "Not until you promise to give me what I asked for."

"You'll get it, gell."

He slides off her scarf and fists his hand in her thick yellow hair. He wrenches her head back, exposing her neck. I remember Kai stroking my hair yesterday, and the gasp of pleasure that slipped past my lips. Varina's gasp is nothing like that. It's a squeak of terror.

Juning kisses her neck around her zati. "This ugly thing will be gone, I promise. But I can't wait. I've got to have you *now*."

I've had enough. I yank the door fully open. They disentangle, and after a moment of surprise, Varina glowers at me.

Juning gives me a haughty grin. "Jealous, Red? Wish it was you?"

Not for a tick. Before I can snap a retort, Bridgie huffs out of the gloom from below.

"There you are. I been looking for you." She grabs Varina by the ear, eliciting an indignant howl. Juning bleats a laugh, and Bridgie swings on him. "Go on, boy, git about your business."

He pouts like a child whose toy is snatched away. "Aw, Bridgie, why do you always ruin my fun?"

"Diddling my troci ain't fun, love. You should know better. Now, go away. Hear me?"

"I'm going," he mutters.

I goggle at the way she speaks to him, and the way he complies. If only he'd take Bridgie to the village with him instead of Jinks then maybe he wouldn't get into so much trouble. Of course, that culbana hasn't learned his lesson. He slaps my bottom as he passes, earning my fiercest glower.

Bridgie drags her wayward, and shrieking, scullery maid down the stairs. I scoop Varina's scarf off the landing—which needs sweeping, I notice—and skitter downward after them.

In the kitchen, Gwynn's washing pillow slips in the soak-sink. Ayva's nearby, vigorously scrubbing one of Lady Forseti's blouses with a small brush. Ellse is sweeping. Mr. Hervey looks up from his book and gawps at the spectacle of the three of us bursting into the room like a sudden storm.

"How *dare* you go upstairs without permission." Bridgie shoves Varina toward the sink.

"How dare *you* touch me," Varina retorts. "Don't *ever* lay hands on me again, Mucker."

Bridgie sniffs. "You're the stupidest gell I ever known. That boy ain't gonna set you free, no matter what you do."

"He will. He said he'd get me out of this dungeon, and by Dageth, that's what's going to happen." Ellse creeps over and pats her shoulder. Varina shrieks. "Get. Away." She snatches the broom from Ellse and bats her with it. Ellse scurries away.

Bridgie's eyes narrow ominously. "Leave her be. Don't blame her for your mistakes."

"You can't talk to me like that. *I'm* top status."

Varina's voice hikes in pitch to a frenzied fury. So does Bridgie's. "You ain't nothing but a caterwauling harpy and you better shut your mouth. *Now.*"

"I *won't* be quiet. I won't do *anything* you say. I'll do what I want. I'm getting out of here and you can't stop me, you old crone. He made me a promise—"

Quick as lightning, the punisher's in Bridgie's hand. A hot current sizzles across the room. The hairs on my arms crackle. Varina hunches over and screeches, clawing at her zati. Gwynn and Ayva cry out. I watch in horror as Bridgie squeezes the trigger again.

"Shut. *Up.*" Bridgie's entire body shakes. "Why must you *always* make trouble? Why can't you behave?"

She stabs the trigger again. Varina makes no noise now. Her mouth's open in a soundless scream. She buckles and hits the floor with a bang, twitching in agony, still gripping the broom.

Gwynn and Ayva clutch one another, weeping, trembling. I snap out of my daze and lunge for Bridgie, but Mr. Hervey gets to her first.

"Enough." He slaps her across the face so hard she staggers.

Bridgie stills. Touches her cheek. Her scars blaze with red finger marks. She looks down at the juicer as if she has no idea how it got into her hand. It drops to the floor with a clatter.

"Are you better now?" Mr. Hervey asks her, gentle but stern.

She nods, tears filling her eyes. Hervey picks up the punisher and tucks it into her pocket. He leads her to the counter where a mound of dough awaits, what she must've been doing before she went looking for Varina. Bridgie begins to knead the dough as if nothing happened.

Ellse cowers under the sink while Gwynn and Ayva help Varina stand and drag her to our quarters. She's drooling. The stench of burnt flesh overpowers the kitchen's usually pleasant smells. I glare at Bridgie. *She* did that to Varina. The motherly housekeeper who calls us love as if she truly means it. I can't even begin to digest that. I just want to cry.

And I want to get out of here *now*.

Mr. Hervey takes his seat and beckons me to his side. I stow my work bucket in the cupboard under my gardening basket, hiding the poetry book and the maps, and pad across the room to his rocker.

"She's hurting," he says in a low voice. "Her heart's been broke over and over by that wild lad. She raised him, you know, since the day she got here. He was a spoilt tyke. After her ladyship lost the others to the fever, she never dared say no to him. No one did. Except Bridgie. She did her best, but it didn't stick."

I watch Bridgie roll the dough into a pan and slide it into the oven, thinking of Taryn. She raised me, more so than Mother and Father. I never realized that before.

Would Taryn be disappointed if I grew up to be as selfish and carnal as Juning, or as willful as Varina? When I decided to let my hair go red, she found a dye close to my natural shade in a Matalan shop and helped me do the deed, but she never uttered a critical word. Did she think I did the right thing? Did she think me brave, as Kai claims he and the others did? Does she miss me?

One thing I do know, Taryn would never hurt me. Never take out her anger at someone else on me. Because she's kind, as opposite from Bridgie as a person can be. The opposite of all the hateful people in this horrible place.

"Will Juning ever have to answer for his wicked ways?" I ask.

"Will his lordship regain his senses? Will I ever see my wife again?" Mr. Hervey's voice holds no rancor or bitterness. It also holds no hope.

When Bridgie steps into the pantry and out of earshot, his voice turns urgent. "Warn Varina to take care. A gell thinks Sir Juning will honor his word, if only she will... Well, you understand. He gets what he wants, but he never pays what he owes. And he doesn't care about the wreckage. I've seen it before. He didn't care one whit for poor Wynnie and look what happened."

"Wynnie? The troci who tended the garden before me? I thought Molly fever got her."

"If only. That lovely gell threw herself into the barrier. Burned herself till it was over. A terrible thing."

"She... she killed herself?" Such desperation. I shudder to think any of us could get so low. But maybe we could. We've been troci just over four turns of the moon, and it feels like a lifetime.

"Wynnie fancied herself in love with that stain on his father's name. He laughed in her face to hear of it. She couldn't take it."

"She lost her mind."

"Had to, to walk into that wall of fire." He eyes me for several ticks. "I'm telling you this because I suspect you'll make it. You've got guts. I saw you jump to halt Bridgie just now. You had no fear she'd turn the punisher on you."

I gulp. I didn't think of that. I just wanted to make it stop.

"As seasons pass, you'll need that strength, Meili, if you want to escape the darkness. Wynnie didn't have it. Varina doesn't." He lets out a bitter laugh. "I don't either."

"That's not true. You're pretty tough."

"Me? I'm just marking time." He touches the book on his lap then gestures toward Bridgie, bustling around inside the pantry. "*She's* tough. She's been here more than twenty seasons. Takes a will of steel not to go stark, raving loopy after all that time."

I have my doubts. The vicious way she attacked Varina doesn't bespeak a healthy mind.

He takes my hand. "Help Varina. She needs you, needs her friends. Don't let her slip away like Wynnie."

Tears well and it takes a lot to hold them back. Maybe that's strength. "I'll try. I'll help her, if I can."

I'll help him too. I'm determined now to take him with us when we escape. And Ellse and Jinks and even that Adsullatan with the soulful eyes. Bridgie comes out of the pantry, carrying a flask of cooking oil. Even her, despite everything.

Kai's not going to like me inviting a mob of people to run with us, but too bad. I may not be as gutsy as Mr. Hervey thinks, but I have enough ginger to tell one bullheaded Matalan that everyone deserves a chance to break out of here. Whatever the risk.

It's probably not a good idea to pester Bridgie to let me out to the garden today. Kai and Blix will have to wait until tomorrow for the maps.

I head to the pantry. It's filled with delicious aromas, dried sissy fruit, the butterscotch scent of spencer's boot, and a variety of meats in the larder. I open the herb cupboard and take out the dorette paste to soothe Varina's burns. I grab the abyssa tin, too. It's almost empty, but there's enough to mix in Varina's tea to help her sleep. I'd dearly love more abyssa, but I haven't found even one leaf in the garden. I close the cupboard door, wondering how Ullr gets his hands on it.

Oh. A new idea begins to take shape. Something to aid in our escape. It's so obvious, I should've thought of it before. I'll need to tell Kai about it.

I hurry across the kitchen, suddenly more hopeful.

In our quarters, Varina shivers on her cot while Gwynn rubs her back soothingly. "I want to go home," Varina whimpers, her voice hoarse, barely audible.

We will go home. All of us. There's no question now *if* we can escape.

It's when.

CHAPTER 25

Meili

I DON'T GET OUT to the garden the next day, or the next. Lady Forseti is the reason why. She has us as busy as bees building a hive, preparing for the harvest ball, ten days away. We dust, scrub, vacuum, sweep, and polish every inch of the manor. I carry my work bucket with me everywhere and only return to the kitchen for a quick meal before I'm back upstairs again.

I try to keep my spirits up but I grow more frustrated with each day I'm stuck inside. I think Kai's frustrated too. I've seen him through the window, pushing his barrow past the garden, searching, as if he thinks I'm hiding in the weeds that must be growing like mad again. His shoulders slump and he moves on.

The fourth day, Gwynn and I tackle the ballroom, which comprises the entirety of the west wing. We scrub the hardwood on hands and knees, arrange a dozen potted palms ordered from the village, and dust the crystal chandeliers suspended from the high ceiling with rags attached to wooden poles. Then we turn to the heavy drapes framing the balcony doors.

"My mother would be envious of these curtains," Gwynn says, running the hand-held vacuum along the shimmering blue fabric.

My vacuum whirrs, sucking dirt off the curtain, and probably an army of spiders, too. "These drapes would make a more tasteful gown than anything I've seen her ladyship wearing."

Gwynn glances back to check for eavesdroppers before she laughs.

When the drapery is complete, we exchange the hand vacs for brooms, and step through the doors onto the balcony. Once we sweep here, our ballroom chores will be complete.

The balcony is a wide space, paved with polished mollystone and bordered by a thick supporting wall that's waist high on our side and twice as tall as Kai on the other. It's also quite lengthy, so we split up and sweep in opposite directions. Dirt and leaves have blown across the floor, snagged on the legs of the three small tables and their uncomfortable-looking chairs, and gotten wedged against the base of the wall.

I sweep toward the stairs at the far end, outside the library. The sweet scent of roses blooming in the bushes clustered several paces from the balcony's wall carries on the breeze. The memory of hiding within their branches with Kai several nights ago flashes into my mind and I go hot all over.

Why must I always burn like an overheated boiler when I think of him?

I sweep the debris down the steps and sweep Kai from my thoughts as best as I can, then turn to join Gwynn at the other end. I peep through the library's curtained windows as I pass, seeing Lady Netti curled on a chair, her nose in a book. Her mother's gone to town, but, nonetheless, I hope she locked the door.

Gwynn's finished her task and leans against the wall. I come up beside her. We gaze out at the view of the meadow, the sloping front lawn, and the majestic main drive. A worker pushes a quietly humming grass-cutting machine, trimming a lawn that doesn't really need it. Watchers are keeping an eye on the troci picking sissy fruit.

"Look, there's Halia."

Gwynn gestures to a petite figure clinging to a ladder with one hand, plucking fruit with the other. Dipro approaches with a bushel box and holds it up for her to drop the fruit into. He puts down the box and helps Halia down the ladder, then takes her into his arms. They kiss.

Gwynn gasps. "Remember how heartbroken she was when Yorath was taken away? How easily she's forgotten him."

At least it's not Sir Juning she's kissing. I suppose he's put off chasing Halia around the orchard now that he's found more willing prey in Varina. "Don't be hard on her. Kai says it's rough living in the workers' camp. Perhaps Dipro offers her protection."

Gwynn flushes a pretty pink. "I didn't think of that. How unkind of me."

I didn't think of that either. Perhaps Kai gives Petra protection. Perhaps that's the only thing between them. I brighten. Kai's protective by nature. It stands to reason he'd take a helpless friend under his wing. I willfully ignore Petra's less-than-helpless taunting of the watcher that drew him away from Kai and me.

"I suppose I understand *why* Halia's turned her affections to Dipro," Gwynn says. "But I don't think I'd get over someone I loved as quickly as Halia seems to."

"No, you wouldn't. You couldn't. I believe it'd take an eon to ease your grief. I suppose that's why you rejected so many contract offers. You haven't met a lad worthy of your love." She blushes again, looking uncomfortable, so I change the subject. "And who says Halia's given up on Yorath? Inside she may be hurting, but she needs someone to keep her safe. Dipro's willing to help."

"Willing to take advantage of her, you mean. Like Sir Juning with Varina."

A watcher stomps over to the couple, waving his juicer, bellowing, threatening. Halia and Dipro leap apart.

"Reminds me of Mr. Kirl." Gwynn's voice turns wistful. "Remember how he'd break up couples who danced too close at school dances? Or the way he chased after people sneaking into corners to nuzzle?" She sighs. "Remember how excited we were to go to Aine? Who would've thought we'd end up here?"

I turn to face her. I promised Kai I wouldn't breathe a word of our plan and I don't want to be yet another Habeni who broke a promise to a Matalan. But she seems so blue I fear she's slipping into the despair and darkness Mr. Hervey warned me about. And, Rossa help me, I will *not* let that happen to my dearest friend.

"Gwynn, listen, it won't end here, not for any of us. We're going to get out of here. All of us. We're going home."

"Sure, Meili. And I'll be the belle of her ladyship's ball."

"I mean it. We're going to escape. We've come up with a plan, Kai and I."

I've done it. And now that I've done it, I spill the details as quickly and as quietly as I can. Her reaction is unexpectedly underwhelmed. She stares off across the meadow, her brow furrowed.

"Then what, Meili? Don't get me wrong. I want to go home. Desperately. But what will happen to us? We'll be back where we started. Everything we do will be monitored, where we go, who we're with. We'll be told what to do and who to join with." She shifts her gaze to me. "You'll have to join with Ullr, if we all make it back. You'll have no choice."

Her words echo the doubts I've had from the moment I first entertained the thought of escape. Doubts I don't want to think about now. "We can try to change things when we get home. But we have to get out of here first. We must take one step at a time if we want to get anywhere, as my minna says. We'll deal with the other problems when we get to them." She still looks skeptical and

I lose patience. "Well, would you rather stay here and be a troci forever? Far away from everyone you love?"

She frowns. "Of course not."

"I know the plan's dangerous, but I think it'll work. Kai thinks so too."

She studies me as if she hasn't seen me in a long time. "Do you trust Kai? No, not trust, he's Ayva's brother, he must be trustworthy. What I mean is, are you sure he's not taking advantage of you? Like Dipro with Halia?"

I consider that. Kai started coming to the garden because he wanted something. But I proposed the escape plan, promising to help him only if I can escape too. "I think we're both sort of taking advantage of each other." Me coming to like him wasn't part of the plan.

"Well then." She brightens. Or pretends to. "I'd like to help. If there's anything I can do— *Shh!*"

She stiffens, listening. A tick later I hear what she hears. Muffled, strident voices in the hall.

"That's Ayva," she cries.

Gwynn races off. I sprint after her through the ballroom and into the hallway to see Ayva at the servants' door. Sir Juning thrusts an arm across the doorway, blocking her way. He's wearing a flowing green coat with tails and looks like a toad in people clothes.

"Excuse me, Sir Juning. I have work to do." Ayva clutches a wad of clothing to her breast and tries to duck by him.

He laughs, a falsely benign chuckle. "Come, gell, there's no chore more important than pleasing me."

She backs up. "Please, let me pass—" He grabs her arms and snatches her to him. A rainbow of clothing tumbles to the floor.

Gwynn, sweet, timid Gwynn is on him in a tick, her fists flying. Juning's eyes bulge in surprise. He shoves Ayva away then seizes Gwynn's forearms and flings her to the ground. She bangs to the carpet. Ayva kicks him in the shins while I attack from his left. Forgetting every blessed thing I learned in defensive arts, I throw a wild punch to the jaw, stinging my knuckles. Caught off guard, he totters but doesn't fall.

His juicer's in his hand in a flash. The air crackles with electricity. I'm unlucky enough to be in the line of fire. My zati shudders. Fiery pinpricks radiate from my throat and rush through me like a raging tide. The pain builds in intensity until a thousand scalding knives stab into my skin. My eyes cross, and I see two Junings. Both laughing. The tinny echo of my friends begging him to stop penetrates my brain. I scream. No sound comes out.

Then, the world darkens.

I gradually come around. I'm sprawled on the carpet, panting, struggling to breathe. Clouds fill my brain, my ears buzz, my eyes are sticky and unfocused. Through the haze, I see Juning cringing against the wall, arms shielding his face as Gwynn and Ayva pummel him.

"She devils. Get off me," he squawks.

"What in the worlds is going on here?"

That's Bridgie, her voice cutting through the chaos. Juning's expression turns to fear. He ducks away from the beating fists and skitters off. I think Gwynn would've given chase if Bridgie didn't grab her.

"Stop, gell. He can't harm ya now. Let's get poor, dear Meili below stairs afore her ladyship comes along."

She helps me to stand but I sink right back down. My bones seem to have taken a vacation from my legs. Finally, with Gwynn's help, she gets me up and they half-carry me through the door and down the stairs. Ayva scoops up the clothes she dropped and follows.

"He's a beast," I say, my voice raw and sounding far away. "He doesn't deserve to live."

"There, now, love, watch your tongue," Bridgie chides.

Why should I? Juning nearly burned my tongue out of my head. Gods, how could Kai stand it? How could Varina? The shock I felt at the kitchen door and at the courtyard wall were tickles compared to the agony of a full-on juicing.

Mr. Hervey drops the pot he's polishing as they drag me into the kitchen. "What happened?"

No one answers and no one has to. He knows what happened. So does Varina. She watches from the sink as the others guide me to a chair.

"Good," she says with a smirk. "Now you know what it feels like. I hope the rest of you get scorched too."

Chapter 26

Meili

THE DAYS PASS. WE scrub and clean and watch out for Sir Juning, running away whenever he looms, no matter what we're doing. It'd be comical if the threat to our safety weren't so dire. I haven't gotten out to the garden for more than a week. I'm sure weeds have swallowed it completely.

The day before the ball, Ellse and I roll up the rug in the ballroom's foyer, drag it downstairs, and out to the courtyard. We drape it over one of the benches and I bang on it with a flared wooden pole, raising clouds of dust and getting out some of my many frustrations.

Mr. Hervey sits on the bench under a sissy fruit tree. He coughs, probably from the dust, and looks up from his book at me. "The burns on your neck are healing nicely. I trust there's no other serious effects of the punishment?"

I shrug. He's the only one who calls a juicing "punishment." As if that makes shooting a thousand volts through my body any less vicious. As if deserved. I glance at Varina, on the grass near the rosebush I hid behind the night of my recon. Juning's attack on me was tame in comparison to what she suffered at Bridgie's hands. That's what it was and what it is, an attack, plain and simple.

I give the rug a hard thwack and scowl at the power station building. The key to our escape. The components inside hum steadily, as if taunting me. If I don't get outside to see Kai, we can't move our plan along.

Gwynn comes out of the house carrying a basket heaped with sheets and towels, sparkling clean and smelling of essence of lilac.

"Good timing," I say. Ellse and I pull the rug off the bench and spread it on the grass to roll it up. "A tick earlier and those linens would be covered with rug dust."

"The dust will cling anyway. They're still damp. It's so humid the dryer must spin for hours to get them dry." She drops the basket on the grass with a thump and sits on the bench. "This is only the first load today. Her ladyship had me strip every bed and wash those sheets too." She folds a pillowslip with Lady Netti's monogram stitched in hooped yellow letters. "I don't know why. There are no overnight guests expected for the ball."

I pluck a towel from the basket, give it a brisk snap and fold it. The corners don't meet exactly so I fold it again. "Perhaps she simply wanted to give us more work."

Excited shouts sound from beyond the wall, followed by the rumble of several transports crossing the compound.

"The Molly miners." Gwynn tosses the pillowslip back into the basket and jumps up.

I help her carry the bench to the wall and we both climb onto it. Varina and Ellse move the other bench and climb up too. Ellse is too short to see anything and even I have to stand on tiptoe to peer over the top of the wall. Sparks zing from the metal spikes only inches from my nose. It smells hot and sharp. My throat constricts unpleasantly, so close to the current.

Two transports waddle along the patch of grass from the fields to the workers' cottages. Everyone abandons their chores to run and greet the vans. Their shouting turns to cheers as the vehicles' doors burst open and the Molly miners spill out. The workers and miners embrace and clap one another on the back. Agron shakes Brote's hand vigorously.

Ullr's there too, watching, but I don't think he knows what's happening. My chest tightens. If things were different, we would've been joined by now. Kai lopes over from the barn. My breath catches, seeing him, even at such a distance. If I were joined to Ullr, I'd be desperately unhappy. Ullr could never make my pulse zing like that. Never make me burn the way I do when Kai looks at me. Never turn my insides upside down with a simple kiss.

Petra joins Kai and they speak. I can't make out his expression, or hers. Jealousy pricks me, that she gets to be with him, when I'm trapped in here. I wish I could vault over this klacking wall and run to him.

"Is that Tew?" Gwynn shifts, trying to see between the spikes.

"Yes, and that's Loyd," Varina says, then shouts, "Halloo there!"

Everyone swivels at the sound of her voice, but they can't see us through the spikes and the snakevines. I shoot my arm up and wave furiously, mindful of the current. Gwynn and Varina wave too. Cheers ring out again, followed by clapping and fists pumping the air. Even Kai joins in. How I wish Ayva was out here to see him, to be as happy and giddy as I am. We're all in one place again. Most of us, anyway.

The excitement is short lived. Hup stalks over and orders the troci back to work. The group disperses. The miners troop toward the workers' dwellings, the others return to the fields. Kai lingers, staring toward the wall, searching for Ayva I think. Then he moves away, with Petra at his heels. Much to my annoyance.

"Get down. You wanna fry yourselves silly?" Bridgie calls, opening the door and poking her head out. Her scolding expression turns to a playful grin. "You best come inside, missies. Your new gowns are on the way from the village."

Varina jumps down off the bench. "New gowns?" she gurgles, more animated than she's been in weeks.

"Indeed. My lady wants you to look smart at the ball, so she ordered new gowns." Bridgie motions us inside. "Come along, they'll be delivered soon."

The rest of us leap off the benches and spill into the hallway behind Bridgie, but I stop at the door and turn back to Mr. Hervey. "Are you coming?"

"Soon," he says with a weary sigh. "Just want to rest a moment more. Go, enjoy yourself."

"New gowns," Varina's crowing when I reach the kitchen. "We're going to a ball!"

"We're *serving* at a ball," Gwynn scolds.

"I don't care. There'll be music and dancing and gossiping, and I shall have a new gown."

Varina grabs my hands and twirls me around the kitchen. I'm already bouncy from the miners' return, so it's easy to be infected by her giddy humor. Ellse joins in, doing a jig. Gwynn pulls Ayva out of the chair where she's repairing a tear in one of Lady Netti's blouses, and they dance too. After a while, Mr. Hervey comes in and sits in his chair, smiling at us like a doting father.

Bridgie's at the window, peering out. "Ah, here they come," she says, and even she seems excited.

A lad carrying a pile of boxes passes by the barred windows. Bridgie taps in the code, and the door swooshes open to a chorus of delighted squeals. Bridgie calls Ellse, and she seizes the stack of boxes from an Adsullatan with spider web streaks on his face. He tips his cap and leans into the doorway, trying to get a look at us. A mistake. His curious noggin is nearly separated from his body when Bridgie hits the keypad and the door snaps shut.

I learn something new about Ellse—she can read. She calls out the names on the label on each box. The stack gets smaller as we snatch our treasure away.

"Ayva. My-ee. Winn. And Esse." She hiccups with pleasure at seeing her own name on the bottom box.

Varina waits eagerly as Ellse gives out the boxes. Then she stands empty-handed. "Where's my gown?"

"I'm sorry, love, you don't get one," Bridgie says.

Varina's face falls, all disbelief and hurt. "Why not? I've been good. I haven't misbehaved a single time since..." She trails off.

"I know." Bridgie goes to the stove and stirs a pot of stew, avoiding Varina's accusing eyes. "You'll not be servin' with the others. You'll be down here with me, washing glasses and filling trays. My lady didn't see the need to pay for a gown if you don't need one."

Varina's wounded expression hardens. "I see. I'm to be up to my eyebrows in dishwater, while they get to listen to music and look at the dancers and the sparklers and everything." She turns to the sink and flicks the water. "I can't tell you how *not* fair that is."

Bridgie bangs the lid onto the stewpot. "Oh, no, do tell, we can't hear it often enough."

"You're against me. You're *all* against me. It's not fair."

"No, it isn't." Mr. Hervey coughs into his fist. "You're a troci, child. There's nothing fair about that. You need to accept it."

"Accept it? Like *you* have?" Varina's voice cracks. "You live for nothing more than to fawn over those people. You'll die here, bowing and scraping like a spineless fool. That's not me, brother tree bark. That's not me."

She's being mean, though there's truth in her words. The skin around Hervey's zati is smooth. No scars, no sign of a juicing, ever. But she has no call to speak to him like that.

I take the cover off the garment box and run my hand along the soft black fabric within. "You can have my dress after the ball." I give Varina a smile. A sincere offer. I mean, what will I need a party dress for when I dig in the dirt all day?

She glowers, clearly determined to be unhappy. "I don't want *your* gown. I want my own. I want what's due to me as a pure Habeni, not a castoff from a mewling neb like you."

"Varina!" Gwynn cries.

"Oh, don't pretend to be shocked. You know it's true. Back home, all she ever did was grovel, desperate to be part of our crowd." Varina stabs a finger at me. "You were never one of us. We knew you were a neb even before you stopped coloring your hair. We all laughed at you. The social climbing twip who thought she could fool us into thinking she was like us."

I sink into a chair. "That's not true," I say dully, though I know it likely is.

Mother fed into that perception since the day I was born. Ensuring I was enrolled in the most exclusive schools and registered at the most expensive fitness clubs. Forcing me to bleach my hair. Cautioning me to be agreeable and deferential to those of higher status. How could Varina and her hangers-on not see me as anything but a desperate social climber caught between two worlds?

Varina titters. "Of course it's true. No one in our circle ever liked you."

Gwynn rushes over and squeezes my hands. "Don't listen to her. She's just angry. Frustrated and taking it out on you. I'm your friend. Your true friend. Always have been."

"Oh, please. You'll be friends with anyone." Varina glares at Ayva, who glares back at her from across the kitchen.

Bridgie groans in exasperation. "Close your mouth, Missy, or I'll give you a reason to close it."

Varina snorts. "Do you think I care? Go ahead. I'm sick of it. Sick of you and your rules. Sick of *all* of you. I don't care one tiny whit."

But she does care. Tears flood down her cheeks as she turns to the sink and plunges her hands into the water once again.

The clouds reflect the violet hues of the setting sun by the time we complete our chores and begin to prepare for dinner. I'm at the table crushing scucca root, still fuming from the fight with Varina earlier. I glower at her back as she stacks plates at the sideboard.

She's such a pill, and that's nothing new. She's always been a high-nosed priss. At school, she mercilessly mocks those of lower status. Out in society, at balls and teas and social gatherings, she teases anyone who might think or dress or behave in the slightest manner different from her, her words filled with venom, aiming to induce tears. And regularly succeeding.

The kitchen doorbell rings, knocking me out of my mental mutterings.

"Who in the worlds could that be?" Bridgie taps the wooden spoon against the pot she's stirring and sets it down. "Not expectin' any more deliveries today."

She wipes her hands on her apron and pads to the door. Humid air rolls in as it shunts open. Kai stands on the step. His tunic is clean, as if newly washed. His hair is wet and even looks as if he's run a comb through it.

My anger instantly vanishes. Flappermoths crowd my belly and begin their giddy dance. He gives Bridgie a low, respectful bow, a measure of deference I've never seen him display with anyone, then he tries to come inside.

She holds up her hand. "Ho there, son. You know you're not allowed in the house."

He sure does, but I suspect he's trying to see how far he can get.

"Yes, Missy. I ken." He cranes to see over her shoulder. My heart thuds to think he's straining for a glimpse of me, but of course he's searching for Ayva. He longs to see his sister. But she's engaged upstairs, where her ladyship needs her stitching skills for the final fit of her ballgown.

Bridgie's gaze sweeps over Kai then centers on his right hand. "What're you holding there?"

"What? This?" He holds up an oblong lump crusted with dried soil. A scatch tuber that still has spiny roots attached to it. "I got a question for your gardener about this plant. Wanna know if it's ripe."

He tries to push his way in again. Bridgie plants a palm on his chest, shoving him back.

"Behave yourself, lad." She eyes him with a brittle expression and I tense, willing him to go away. She's in a juicing mood today and I don't want him to be her target.

Kai swallows, shifts from foot to foot, uncertain. I suppose he just expected to walk right in with no resistance. How many times do I have to tell him he can't get in the house, whether through charm or force?

"Uh, then how'm I gonna know if this veggie's ripe?" he says quickly. "Me and the others want to toss it into the cook pot, to spice our grub, you know? Taters all the time can be awful bland. But I'm thinking I better find out if it's okay to eat. It might make us croak. Or worse."

Bridgie lifts an eyebrow, softening a bit. "What's worse than croaking, son?"

"Well, Missy, the watchers sometimes steal food from us. If this root is sick making, then they might take ill." He taps his zati and adds a rueful smile for good measure. "I wager you know what a watcher with a volcano in his belly can do to a poor troci."

"Oh? Is that your story?" She titters. "You're blessed with a smooth tongue, lad. And a mighty heap of cunning. But you don't fool me, not for a tick."

His eyes widen. I stifle a gasp. Does she know what Kai's really up to? Is she on to us and our daring scheme?

"You don't wanna know about the plant. You're sweet on our Meili. I seen you two out there in the garden." Bridgie swings toward me and chuckles like a sly old granny. I want to sink right through the floor. "She ain't been out in many days. So you come here, bolder than a Mucker has a right to be, with a piddling excuse, hoping I'll let you in so's you two can indulge in some kissing and cuddling."

He stammers uncomfortably and, if I'm not mistaken, his cheeks flush. I tap my foot, annoyed. Is the thought of being with me so repellant he can't even *pretend* to be over the moons for me?

He takes a breath and gets control. He nods. "That's it, missy. You caught me. So, can I come in?"

She plumps a fist on her hip. "And have her ladyship give me pakao for letting a ruffian like you muddy her floors? Not on your life." Kai's expression tightens and she clucks. "But tell you what, I'll let Meili out for a short piece."

She steps out of the doorway and gestures to me.

"Go on, love, tell this pert one all about his fascinatin' veggie." She gives Kai a wink. "Don't keep her out too long, and no funny business. I mean it. You think a watcher with the shits is a mean bird, you don't wanna find out what they'll do if they catch you messing around with one of my gells."

Kai lowers his head sheepishly. A good thing. He can't see the way my cheeks flame. The thought of messing around with him tickles my mind constantly now, but the last thing I want is for him to see the truth of my desire on my face.

I ignore Gwynn's curious gaze, and Varina's disgusted glare, and head for the door. I don't have time to grab something for Kai to eat, and I'm so flustered I nearly forget my gardening basket.

I don't regain my composure until we pass through the garden gate. My first look in over a week at what once were neat rows of plants sends my heart plummeting to my toes. As I feared, the weeds have made an aggressive comeback.

I long to get to work and set the garden aright, but first things first. I grab the scatch tuber from Kai and fling it away. "Unless you really want to croak, I wouldn't put that in the cookpot. You don't know the first thing about plants, do you?"

"I know they have roots." He scowls at my neck. "You've been juiced." He reaches out to touch me, seems to think better of it and drops his hand. "What happened?"

I stroke my blistered throat. There's no dorette left to help heal the burns, so my skin is still red and puckered. I'll probably have scars. Scars I got fighting to protect a Matalan. That news would twist Mother's frillies in a knot to hear, but I'm kind of proud of it. Would Kai be proud too?

Not that we have time for me to explain, especially the part about Juning pawing Ayva. "It's not important right now."

"Like pakao it isn't." Kai's scowl turns explosive. "Juning hurt you, didn't he?" He directs his furious glare at the house, his fists clenched. "That kutama. I'll break his neck."

My pulse quickens. Odd how his protective anger generates such a sensation. "Please, Kai." Without thinking, I put a hand on his chest, as if trying to still a raging beast. "I'm touched. Truly. But I'm all right. The problem's been dealt with."

He looks down at my hand and his anger deflates like a cuttleball losing air. I feel his heartbeat, hard and fast, under my palm. I long to kiss him. I want him to like me. For real, not just pretend when he comes calling at the kitchen door. I want him to like me and to want me and to kiss me again and again.

Oh gods, what's wrong with me? If he could read my thoughts, he'd think me as wanton as a street hoyden the way I yearn to throw myself into his arms. Arms I'm certain he'd rather put around that Adsullatan with the soulful eyes.

I snatch my hand away.

"Let's sit," I say, forcing my voice to a neutral tone. We settle side by side on the creaky bench. "I have what you and Blix wanted from the atlas."

I look around to see if we have an audience. Daylight has all but faded. The workers are streaming past their little houses to where Kai says the cookfire and their dinner awaits. A watcher leans against a stile smoking a pipe. Behind us, I see Bridgie in the window, her nose pressed against the pane, her gaze on us. When I catch her eye, she vanishes, and the curtain swishes back into place.

Careful to keep my back to the house, I reach into my basket and uncover the book. I take it out and hand it to Kai. He eyes it curiously.

"You'll find three maps tucked inside. It's a poetry book." That comes out in a strange way, as if a poetry book is the most impressive thing ever. He doesn't respond, just looks down and flips through the pages. Feeling like a slupa, times ten, I let out an awkward laugh. "I hope they're the right kind of maps. With any luck, Blix can find our location from the illustrations and match it to the stars. He knows all about the stars."

"He knows all about everything." Kai closes the book and puts it between us on the bench. "Never knew anyone could be that smart."

I stretch out my legs and tap my toes together, staring at my shoes. Does he think I'm smart? Does he think of me at all, beyond a convenient ally? Beyond the shameless Habeni who tempts him with her kisses?

"Kai, I've got another idea. When I knock out the power—"

"You mean when *I* knock out the power."

I scoff. One thing he *does* think about me is that I'm inept. I'm setting off that bomb, whether he likes it or not. But now's not the time to argue about it. "Yeah, sure. Well, when we manage to knock out the power, we'll still have the watchers to worry about. I have an idea how to slow them down."

He straightens, intrigued. "How?"

"We knock them out, too. Please don't grin. I don't mean bashing them over the head like I know you long to do." Come to think of it, I'd like to do that too. "I mean, we drug them."

Another grin, less sarcastic this time. "Keep talking."

He sounds almost affectionate. That brightens me up. A lot. "Mr. Hervey says abyssa grows wild near the mines and both the troci and the watchers are hooked on it. It's the only way they can tolerate the work, and that's why there're so many accidents in the mines. It's terribly inefficient from a business perspective, but that's neither here nor there. Mr. Hervey says the miners bring big bags full of abyssa with them when they return. Your camp must be rife with the stuff now."

"It is." He tugs on his bottom lip. "So, you suggest getting the watchers dopey on abyssa? That's good. That'll slow them down."

"Not just abyssa. Yes, it calms and slows a body down, but we need something more. Something stronger that when mixed with abyssa will put the watchers to sleep, good and deep."

He whistles softly. "And you have something in your magical garden basket that will do the trick?"

"Not exactly."

I stand and pluck several reddish-green leaves off a squat stalk. Sitting back down, I poke a vein in the leaf with my thumbnail and shake a few of the tiny, blood-red flakes out onto my palm. I hold my hand under Kai's nose to let him sniff the powdery substance's syrup smell.

"This plant looks a lot like carteria from back home. It's used as a sleeping draught. If this is anything like its sister plant on Hephas, a dose of this will send our victim into cloudland. But I haven't found much of it here. So, I'm thinking if we can somehow mix a little of this with abyssa, it'll be the perfect potion for knocking out the watchers. Juning, his family, and everyone else too. It'll make the escape easier and give us more time to get away before they even know we're gone."

He gapes at me for several ticks, then, "I'm sorry."

I flinch. "What do you mean? It's a sound plan."

"No." He shifts, facing me. "I mean, I'm sorry for every unkind word I ever said to you. You're brilliant. The plan is brilliant."

I puff up. I guess he does think I'm smart. No, brilliant. I feel as if I could walk on air and maybe I would if I wasn't sitting down.

"How did you ever learn such things?"

"You mean how does a spoiled Habbie like me know gardening?" That comes out waspish, but I'm so unsettled I'm surprised I can even speak. "I learned from my minna."

"You learned well."

I did. It occurs to me that I've learned more from Taryn than I have from my parents and all my schoolteachers combined.

"All we need is some black leaf, and some of that..." Kai nods at the plant in my hand. "Carteria, right? And we're set?"

"Well, I'll need to test my theory first. I need a willing, or unwilling, test subject." Varina immediately comes to mind, but I reject the idea almost as fast. I'm not as petty as that. "This plant may not hold the same properties as carteria and may not work at all. Or it may work too well, and we could have a dead body on our hands."

"In that case, I volunteer Agron as tester."

I laugh, and he smiles at his own joke. He looks young and carefree, but only for a flash before sober Kai clicks back into place. "Blix says the candles are almost ready. Everything is nearly in place. We'll go when the moon's full. We'll have its light to guide our way."

That's more than a week away. I scan the fields, the barn, the rough little buildings where the workers live, and the watchers' cottage, bathed in shades of red and purple from the setting sun. Tomorrow will be another sweltering day. The ballroom's cooling element will be working overtime. Sweat dots my forehead and trickles down my back.

One more week. Can I stand the heat and this awful place for one more week? Can we evade Juning until then? Can I avoid my feelings for Kai for that long?

"There's something else, Kai. Unless we want to drug the other troci, they'll hear the explosion. They'll know what's going on. Shouldn't we warn them? Shouldn't we give them a chance to gather supplies, some way to survive on the run? *If* we get out, I mean."

"No. We can't tell anyone. No one can know, until the power's down."

I look at him full on. I have to ask, though I'm loathe to hear his answer. "What about Petra? Surely you'll want to tell her. You'll want her with you when we escape, won't you?"

He scowls. "Petra? What's she got to— What in pakao is that?"

Kai leaps from the bench. I follow his alarmed gaze and gasp. Jinks shoots around the corner of the watchers' house and sprints across the grass. He's wearing a vest adorned with red and blue blinking lights. He's screaming.

I shoot to my feet and seize Kai's arm. "Gods, it's Jinks. Is that a...?"

An immense, six-legged beast with a horned snout and quivering, leathery shanks pounds around the corner. The creature snarls and snaps and chases Jinks as if he's stolen its cubs.

"It's a rachee," Kai says, stunned, horrified. "Look, Jinks is harnessed to it."

I see the rope now. It stretches from the back of Jinks's vest to the rachee, looped around the beast's thick neck like a noose. A blink later, Juning's rev cycle skids around the corner. The engine whines as it picks up speed, driving the beast—and the terrified Jinks—straight toward the garden.

Alerted by the noise, the workers abandon their dinner and race over from behind the cottages to gape at the gruesome spectacle. Jinks sails over the garden's makeshift fence like a champion hurdler and the spectators cheer. He hits the ground running. The rachee barrels after him. It smashes into the fence headfirst. The braided snakevines snap as if they're made of gossamer thread, the posts splinter like toothpicks, and the entire structure collapses.

"My garden!"

I don't think. I act. I snatch up the nearly toothless rake, on the ground nearby, and run toward the beast, determined to beat it senseless. With a strangled cry, Kai locks his arms around my middle and yanks me back. I drop the rake and watch helplessly as the rachee flattens losys and scucca and a dozen other precious plants.

Jinks sees us. "Meili, help," he shrieks, arcing toward us. The rachee thunders after him. Juning follows them both into the garden. The revver's wheels dig into the soil, spitting up weeds and killing more plants.

Kai tugs me toward the gate at a fast clip. His arm around my waist propels me along, away from danger. I can't help looking back, terrified to see the beast snap at Jinks's heels as it closes the distance between them. The rachee obliterates the wooden bench, sending the book with the maps flying. We reach the gate. It's toppled over, covered with snapped snakevines. Kai releases me, and we scramble over the vines. My skirt catches on thorns. I'm stuck.

"Dageth's elbows." Kai tears at the fabric, his eyes wild. He looks toward the house. Bridgie and the others press against the windows, mouths agape. "Open the klacking door!" he shouts, but Bridgie doesn't move.

I push Kai's fumbling fingers aside and wrench my skirt free. Jinks flies up to us. He stumbles over his own feet, flails, and splats face first on the ground. The beast behind him skids to a stop, a whisker from my face.

My blood stills. The rachee paws the ground and looks at me, its red eyes full of fury. Heat pulses off its mountainous black hide like waves from hot coals. Its head is a bulbous mass, its coarse skin festered with pimples. I gag at the creature's stench, as rancid as a garbage pit under a scorching sun.

The beast snorts, coating my face with a slimy spray. Its jaws crack as it opens its huge mouth. Saliva drips from teeth like sharpened spikes.

"Run, Meili," Kai roars, in a voice fraught with fear.

I want to. I'm desperate to. But my legs won't work.

I've been frightened since the moment those pirates took our ship. Scared to pieces. But I've never felt such bone-deep terror as I do now. Paralyzed, unable to move, I can only brace for those powerful jaws to snap me in two.

It lunges.

Chapter 27

Kai

I HURL MYSELF AGAINST the rachee's big body. Futile and desperate, but what else can I do? I'm not going to stand here and watch those sharp teeth rip into Meili's tender flesh and crack her bones.

The rachee's a solid wall. It doesn't budge.

"Meili, run," I shout again and throw myself at the beast once more.

The rachee snaps toward me. The poor kutama tethered to the rachee springs up from the ground. He yanks the rope connecting him to the animal, tightening the noose around the beast's throat. It chokes but still strains to lock its jaws around me. I beat at its side with my fists.

Meili breaks out of her trance but, by the gods, she doesn't run to safety. She grabs a fence post and swings it like a club. The post cracks against the rachee's skull and disintegrates into bits. The animal barely staggers. The blow merely provokes it to rage harder.

"Will you *run*?" I snarl at Meili and snatch up the broken gate. It's heavy, a strain to lift, but adrenalin propels me. I swing it upward then down—and bash it over the rachee's back. The wood breaks into a dozen pieces. The rachee staggers, wounded, but still fights.

Jinks grips the rope and pulls, doubling his efforts to strangle the beast. Its head swings left and right, jaw snapping, trying to get its teeth into me or Jinks or Meili. Any of us will do. I scrabble around for another weapon.

A buzz penetrates my brain and I glance back. Juning. The architect of this chaos rides back and forth on his rev cycle, taking in the mayhem with a demented grin.

"Do something," Meili screeches at him. "*Please*. It'll kill us."

That mother-humper laughs, and I think for a hot tick that's what he'll let happen, until, with deliberate slowness, he stops the cycle and reaches into a pouch on the revver's side. He pulls out a weapon I've never seen before, long, with a double barrel. He squints through a scope then presses the trigger. Twin lightning bolts burst from the weapon. The gust of electricity blows me back and knocks Jinks off his feet. Meili yelps. My skin blisters, the hairs on my arms burn.

The rachee rears back. A roar, an aching, bone-chilling howl I hope I never hear again, tears from the creature's mouth. Two more bolts rip from the weapon. The beast convulses, all six legs going stiff. I leap out of the way as the animal topples like a felled tree and hits the ground with a crash.

Dead silence.

Then, Juning. "Is it dead?"

I gaze at the body. Smoke pours from the animal's ears, its snout, and every orifice. It's been cooked from the inside. Smells like it too.

"Yes, it's dead," Meili says, nodding dumbly.

"You're welcome." Juning tucks the weapon away with a satisfied smirk. "You really owe me now, Red, and I mean to collect."

The cycle's buzz becomes a whine and Juning disappears into the sunset before I can rush him and beat him brainless.

I dash over to Meili and snatch her to me in a choking hug. Hard and fast and filled with every bit of relief that spills through me.

"I thought you were a goner," I growl, releasing her. I can't keep the fury from my voice. "Dageth's breath, Meili, why didn't you run?"

"Why didn't you?"

I snort. As if I'd run when she's in danger.

I'm about to pull her into another hug and maybe something more when Jinks groans, getting our attention. He sinks to the ground and we rush over. Meili kneels by his side. The shock is catching up to him. He trembles from head to foot. He starts to bawl, and I see that he's soiled himself.

I might've done the same in his shoes. That rachee could've stomped him to death. Could've bitten Meili's head off. I toss her a glare, wanting to yell at her again for not running.

We help Jinks get out of the still-blinking vest and then to stand. He leans on me and moves on rubbery legs as I guide him toward the house.

"What happened?" Meili asks.

Jinks is still weeping, unable to form words.

"I can answer for him," I say. "That shit stain harnessed Jinks to that." I jerk my chin toward the dead rachee. "Then he went hunting. Is that about right?"

Jinks blubbers some more. I take it as a yes.

"What a vile thing to do," Meili spits. "How can anyone be so cruel?"

I scowl. "Do you still not get it? He did it because he *can*. Because the privileged take advantage of those they deem beneath them. The wealthy crush the poor, the strong prey on the weak, no matter what world we're on."

I cut off the lecture and help Jinks to climb up onto the doorstep. The housekeeper's waiting in the doorway. He falls into her open arms, bawling. She rubs his back and murmurs baby talk. Ayva peeks out from behind the both of them and latches her worried gaze onto me. My heart catapults, to see her face after all this time.

I offer her a reassuring smile. "I'm alright, melysette." I have trouble getting out that endearment, the Matalan word for sweetheart. There's a big lump blocking my throat. Meili's watching me, her eyes shining, and I have to wonder what's going on inside her busy brain.

"Come inside, Missy," Bridgie says to Meili. "You've had a fright."

"Just a moment?"

Bridgie's gazes slips from Meili to me. "Make it quick." She hits the keypad, and the door zips shut. My shoulders slump as Ayva disappears from view.

Meili's eyeing me. "Would you like to see Ayva?" she asks. "Maybe even talk to her for a few minutes?"

This is unexpected. And something I want above all. "You know I do."

"She'll be serving at the ball tomorrow. We're all serving, which means we'll be upstairs all evening. If you come hide in the rosebushes near the balcony, I'll try to get Ayva outside at some point. I can't promise anything. We'll be busy, but I'll try my best. Agreed?"

"Agreed." Every ounce of excitement surging through me is in that word.

"Oh, what about the book?" she cries, as if that's more important than nearly getting bitten in half two ticks ago.

I follow as she picks through the thorny vines in the garden to the shattered bench. "Here it is." It's been stomped into the ground, a giant rachee footprint all around it. I dig it out of the muck. "It's fine. The binding's broken but the maps are still here."

She puffs in relief then scans the garden with a pained expression. It's dark and the floodlights have come on, giving us a good look at the broken fence, the trampled plants, and the hulking rachee corpse by the gate, flattening a bed of red flowers.

"After all my hard work," she mutters. "I hope some of the carteria survived."

"I'll look for it. First thing tomorrow."

"Pick as much as you can find. I don't know when I'll get outside next. And you *must* get hold of some abyssa, threefold as much as the carteria."

I touch her hand and she stills. A hot current seems to flow between us. "Don't worry. I'll take care of it."

She nods and pats her apron. "I have enough carteria and abyssa to make a test. I'll test it tomorrow. At the ball."

"On...?"

"On him." She glares across the floodlit fields, where that rotting excuse for an Adsullatan and his revver have ridden off.

She scoops up her basket, which somehow made it through the rachee's stampede unscathed, and we head for the house. She shudders and tosses an anxious look at the beast's smoldering carcass as we make a wide berth around it.

She turns at the door and locks her gaze on me. I swallow, hard. She's so beautiful, even in the harsh light. Even with muck and rachee goo on her face. Even still pale and terrified from our ordeal.

"Thank you, Kai," she says, her voice trembling. "You saved my life."

She kisses me. I taste sweetness, salty tears and a goodly amount of rachee snot. I don't pull away. I welcome her kiss, a supple, prolonged blending of our lips that gets my head spinning and dangerous thoughts racing through my mind. I can no longer deny my feelings for this feisty Habeni. I ache to feel her lips against mine forever. To hold her in my arms for always.

Because I love her.

And Meili...? Can her feelings for me be equal to mine for her? Could her kisses be willing and real, a sign of her true emotion and not prompted by some warped sense of gratitude? Could she actually have a tenderness for me?

The thought should shoot me over the stars, but I sink lower than the bottom rung of Dageth's realm. The one thing I want more than anything will be the one thing that splits us apart. If we succeed, if we somehow escape and find a way home, we won't be allowed to be together. We'll be busted up, separated, punished.

If she feels something for me.

And if she does, better to nip such emotions in the bud than let them flower.

Though it hurts like pakao to do so, I break off our kiss. I grip her by the shoulders and push her back. Confusion flashes across her face and her cheeks turn scarlet red.

I drop my gaze. I can't bear to see her pain, or for her to see mine. I know my expression betrays how much I care for her.

And how shattered I am to turn away.

Chapter 28

Meili

THE DAY OF THE ball dawns as I expected, sticky, hazy, swelteringly hot. I'm already dripping with perspiration as I pick up my work bucket and hurry across the kitchen, about to head up to the ballroom for some last-minute dusting, when I nearly slam into Lady Forseti coming in from the hallway.

She squeaks in fright and jerks back, as if she's thinks I'll stick a knife in her breast.

"Get out of her ladyship's way, gell," Bridgie snaps, glaring at me from her spot at the cooker.

I move. Slowly. I'm cussed if I'll scurry out of her way like an obsequious mouse.

She wafts past me into the kitchen. She's wearing an orange polka-dot morning gown and smells of lilac oil and pit stink. Everyone stops what they're doing and stands at attention. Jinks struggles to rise from his seat at the table, still shaky and hurting from yesterday's rachee horror. Gwynn races over to help him.

"My lady." Bridgie drops a curtsey so deep her knees crack. I put down my bucket and follow suit, minus the joint popping. Mr. Hervey executes a perfect bow. Jinks, less so. Lady Forseti accepts our curtsies with a nod worthy of the queen of Adsullata, if there is one.

"What brings you below stairs, your ladyship?" Bridgie asks, her brow squinching in confusion. "Do you have late changes to arrangements for the ball?"

"The ball? The *ball*? Will we have a ball at all?" Lady Forseti claps her bejeweled hands over her bosom. "The florist is late with his delivery. My footman's limping like a new gelding." She glowers at Jinks then swivels to Mr. Hervey. "And now I hear my butler's ailing. Today of all days. Tonight is supposed to be my triumph. This is *unacceptable.*"

Bridgie retreats behind the center island, as if fearing she'll get a zap. I wouldn't be surprised. Her ladyship's cheeks are flushed, her chin quivers violently, and she fumes at Bridgie as if it's all her fault.

"My lady, all will be well, you'll see," Bridgie says, twittering nervously. "Jinks will be in fine form by nightfall. He'll attend to your guests, as smart and quick as can be. As for Mr. Hervey..." Her gaze slides toward the butler, standing near the table.

"I'm fine, my lady, truly." He touches his throat then pats his chest. "My discomfort is small. Only a tickle."

"It's not... Molly fever?" Her voice dips to a whisper, as if saying the name aloud will summon the dreaded disease. I admit I'm worried about the same thing. He doesn't appear as well as he claims.

He lets out a wheezy chuckle. "No, my lady. I suffer from nothing more than a touch of the Dryan kiffle."

She mulls this over then gives a brusque, reluctant nod and turns to Bridgie with a question about the caterer. As reluctantly reassured as Lady Forseti, I skitter out of the kitchen to get to work, followed by Gwynn and Ayva.

We're in a flurry all day, polishing, sweeping, wiping water spots off fluted glasses. Surface vans come and go, delivering ice and food and pastries from the village. The flowers finally arrive and

Bridgie breathes a sigh of relief. So many things to do. I had no idea this much preparation went into holding a ball.

My most pressing concern—the sleeping potion. I've barely had time to think about the concoction, let alone prep it.

Late in the day, I steal a moment and combine the carteria with the small amount of abyssa I have on hand, crushing them both into a fine powder. I pour the mixture into a teabag. It won't completely dissolve in liquid. It would work better cooked in stew or some other food, where the powder's grittiness wouldn't be noticed. But, with the ball catered, it'd be impossible to make certain Juning will eat the drugged food. And I don't want to sicken, or gods forbid, kill an innocent by mistake.

I decide to spike a glass of malmsey and serve it to Juning myself. I'll have to make sure he's so well-oiled he wouldn't notice if I poured a bag of sand into his drink.

Finally, it's time to dress. Perhaps thinking we'll overshadow the Adsullatan ladies in their sparkles and garish patterns, her ladyship has chosen solid black for our gowns. A flattering fit, with cap sleeves and a floor-length skirt that hugs the limbs. After being clad in a scratchy wool tunic dress for so long, the feel of the gown's soft, smooth fabric against my skin brings a delighted smile to my lips.

I take a moment to brush and style my hair. It's completely grown out now, with no trace of the dye left. It's taken a while to get used to my natural color, a pinkish red with a touch of gold. I scoop the thick tresses into a loose coil and secure it with an ornately carved wooden comb Lady Forseti tossed because it has a broken tooth.

A glance in the lav mirror tells me I don't look half bad, if a bit tired and gaunt. I guess staring into the gaping maw of a hungry rachee will do that. I'd spent half the night shuddering at the memory of that beast's attack, the other half fretting over my inability to keep myself from kissing Kai.

And his bitter reaction to it.

"The gown makes your bottom look enormous," Varina mutters when I come out of the lav. She refuses to help us get ready and sits on her cot, sneering with resentment.

"Thank you." I twirl and laugh, which only makes her sneer more.

Gwynn is gorgeous as always, her thick golden hair neatly braided, and even Ellse looks good, thanks to vigorous washing and combing of her normally tangled hair. But it's Ayva who's undergone the most amazing transformation. Her hair's tied back with a red ribbon Bridgie gave her and she wears a clinging gown that accentuates her long legs and graceful figure. She's as elegant as a queen.

Gwynn gazes at her with shining eyes. "You look... beautiful."

A delicate pink blush colors Ayva's cheeks and she casts her eyes downward. "Do you really think so?"

She seems touched and sounds overwhelmed. I'd wager she's never worn anything so lovely in all her life. Varina snorts and scoffs at the same time. I glare, fresh out of sympathy for her, then turn back to Ayva with a significantly friendlier expression.

"You look superb. Except..." I pluck a losys from a vase I'd put on the windowsill days ago and tuck it behind her ear. "There. Perfect." The red petals are somewhat wilted with age, but the flower looks lovely against her russet-colored hair.

Bridgie shouts for Varina to come and help her. Varina unspools from her cot with a gloomy sigh and drags her feet as she leaves our quarters. We follow, spilling into the kitchen to see Bridgie in a frenzy, opening the cooker doors and rearranging the trays the caterer has delivered.

"Go," she says without looking up. "Ellse will bring up the yummies directly. Drinks are your first priority."

We carry trays of empty glasses up the stairs and rest them on the long shelf on the landing, then go back for more. Mr. Hervey and Jinks hauled dozens of bottles of malmsey up here earlier and stuck them in two ice-filled barrels by the door. Ayva shows Gwynn how to pull the corks, and they pour the crimson liquid into the glasses.

I peek through the door crack into the hallway. Jinks is at the front door, looking wan and stiff, ushering the guests inside. At the ballroom entrance, Mr. Hervey stands tall in his new black suit with white gloves and a starched neckcloth.

He announces each arrival. The guests then move inside and greet the lord and lady in a swirl of clashing colors and gaudy zig-zag patterns that hurt my eyes. Confirming my suspicion that the Adsullatans have the worst fashion sense of all the peoples on all the worlds.

The parade of arriving guests subsides, and Mr. Hervey uses the lull to break away. He slips through the servants' door and joins us on the landing, where we're almost done filling the malmsey glasses. He plops onto the stairs leading to the upper level.

"Are you feeling alright?" I ask, though it's clear he's not. His face is as green as a hillside in summer, his brow dotted with perspiration, his breathing ragged. Gwynn and I exchange worried glances.

"I'm fine." He sounds wheezy and annoyed by my question. He hauls himself up, mops his brow with a handkerchief, and straightens his coat. "Are those glasses ready? Good. Now, in you go."

He takes a breath, bumps the door open with his shoulder, and sails out into the hall as if he's good as new. We follow him, carefully balancing full trays on our fingertips.

Music swells as we enter the ballroom. My feet tap in time with the music, and I understand why Varina's so angry. We can't dance, we aren't guests, and we'll have to clean up once the party is over, but *oh...* to be at a ball after so much time lifts my heart and spirits.

The electrified chandeliers twinkle, casting a butterscotch glow over the packed room. Scents mingle—flowers, a variety of perfume fragrances, pipe smoke, the sweet aroma of roses, sissy fruit, and the night air rippling in from the doors open to the balcony. The floor we scrubbed and polished until it gleams like glass reflects the dazzling, if discordant, array of colors adorning the dancers twirling around the room.

I can't help a smile as I wade into the crowd.

In an instant, it's clear we're the most popular people at the party. The guests swarm and pluck glasses of malmsey from my tray as if they're beyond parched. My tray's empty in a tick. I rush back for more, repeating this process a number of times. I target Juning, making sure he gets plenty of refills.

I'm on my fifth malmsey run when I catch Varina peeping around the servants' door, watching with wide eyes, trying to catch a glimpse of the partygoers through the ballroom's open door. We exchange trays. She takes the dirty glasses to be washed and hands me a platter of puff pastries stuffed with roasted greenies.

"What's it like in there?" she asks longingly.

"No time," I say and rush back to the ballroom, feeling bad for cutting her off without satisfying her curiosity, but only a little. The pastries disappear from my tray almost as fast as the malmsey. A male in a pair of argyle patterned bloomers pops one into his mouth like a snake devouring a gigg's egg whole.

Gwynn comes up beside me. "I can't get over how lovely she looks."

I follow her gaze across the ballroom. "Lady Forseti? She looks like she crashed into a paint factory in that wrap."

"Meili." Gwynn lifts an eyebrow. "I'm not speaking about her."

I smile. "I know. Yes, she's lovely."

She means Ayva, whose sole duty seems to be shadowing her ladyship wherever she goes, at her beck and call for any tasks or errands needing attention. That poses a problem. It's going to be difficult to separate Ayva from Lady Forseti and get her outside to see Kai.

The night proceeds. My initial excitement fades as I'm consumed with work. I run back and forth to the landing and alternate between trays of food and drink. Back in the ballroom, I feed and water the voracious Adsullatans, one eye on Ayva, the other on Sir Juning. I make sure he always has a drink in his hand and no food in his belly. I want him drunk when I slip the potion into his malmsey.

"Bentalla must be serious to find someone for her son this time," a lady in an orange hat says as she plucks a roasted beef skewer from my tray. "Every eligible female from the ridge and beyond is here."

"She *is* serious. I heard she wants that good-for-nothing contracted by the end of the season," says her companion, who has white streaks crisscrossing her face and arms. "If she thinks a spouse will cure Juning's wildness, she's sadly mistaken. Once a cad, always a cad. There's no guarantee getting spliced will keep him in check."

I'm amazed she speaks so bluntly, with me standing there. I suppose I'm invisible. How many balls have I attended where I barely noticed the help? Gossiped and made cutting comments about others while looking right through the servant holding the tray?

"None of that matters to those ninnies," Orange Hat says. "The only thing that matters is the coin and property he brings to the arrangement."

She gestures with her beef skewer to the female mob swarming around Juning, hanging on his every word. He looks wobbly. I hide a smile. The time is just about right to test my potion.

"He does have a considerable amount of coin," the companion says. "And here you are, with a houseful of sons and not a daughter to spare."

"There's always the gell." Orange Hat directs her gaze at Lady Netti, who's spent the evening in a corner with her equally plain friend, goggling at gowns and gentlemales. "She's a dog in a fancy frock. And, from what I hear, she's... *bookish*." Her voice hikes up in pitch, scandalized. "However, she'll have a nice dowry, and that counts for something."

"My dear, that counts for *everything*," the companion says and the ladies titter.

Fuming, offended for poor Netti, I move on. As soon as my tray's empty, I head back for more, and the sleeping mixture.

I come upon Mr. Hervey in the hall, coughing with great, wrenching hacks. My eyes widen in horror. He can barely stand. Afraid he'll fall, I search for Jinks. He's nowhere in sight, possibly assisting a departing guest to their transport.

"Please, rest, Mr. Hervey." I take his arm and steer him to a chair. Even through his coat sleeve, I can feel he's burning up. "It'll do you no good to collapse on the ballroom floor. Think of how rumpled your fine suit would get."

He flops down and dabs at his sweaty forehead. The handkerchief is instantly wet through. "Can't... imagine what Bridgie will say if..." A coughing spasm cuts him off.

My heart twists. He says he's got a cold. Bridgie insists it's a cold. They've both seen the Molly fever before, they know its symptoms and how it progresses, so I must believe them.

The spasm subsides and he struggles to get up. "I must... Tray..."

"I'll take your tray this round." I don't wait for his response and hurry to my task. My need to be alone long enough to spike Juning's drink eclipses my concern for Mr. Hervey. Shameful, I know, but this is my only opportunity.

I quickly fill a dozen glasses sitting on a tray. I shove the empty malmsey bottle back into the ice bucket and glance around. Ellse is coming out of the ballroom so I have only two ticks. I shut the door, reach into a handy pocket in my frillies under my dress, and pull out the teabag. I shake the contents into the closest glass.

It foams.

Frickle! My heart thuds. Ellse must be almost to the door by now. What's worse, Varina's coming up the stairs with clean glasses. Purplish froth foams over the lip of the glass. Varina's almost here. The door begins to open. I blow on the liquid. Ridiculous, but I don't know what else to do.

"Get out of the way," Varina snaps behind me.

Glasses rattle as I snatch up the tray. I clap my hand over the top of the foaming glass as Ellse opens the door. The bubbling froth tickles my palm.

"How I wish this night would end." Varina shoves a platter of sweet-tart cookies into Ellse's hands and takes her tray of empty glasses.

I murmur something sympathetic and slip out as quick as I can. I pause outside the ballroom and slowly lift my hand off the glass. The foam has subsided. I wipe away flaky residue with my thumb and glance at Mr. Hervey. He's slumped in the chair, eyes closed, breathing heavily. I don't have time to worry about him now. I have to keep focused on my task.

I set my mouth in a grim line and enter the ballroom.

Every raging malmsey addict in the county is at this ball, apparently. Keeping the guests from grabbing all the drinks from the tray before I can reach Juning is a challenge. My victim is near the open doors to the balcony. He's hard to miss in his shimmering gold and ruby coat. He's surrounded by admiring ladies, as he has been all evening. He says something, a joke, I think, from the way he throws back his head and whinnies. The ladies dutifully laugh.

"Another drink, Sir Juning?"

He blinks at me with bloodshot eyes and reaches without a word. I twist the tray so he can pluck the right glass. Easy. Surprisingly easy. I watch him put the glass to his lips and can't help a satisfied smile as I turn to hustle away.

"Wait, gell."

I freeze at his command and nearly drop the tray. Even his twittering admirers freeze. Not so easy after all. I turn. He studies me, his lips curved in a sly smirk. Does he know about his drink? Has he figured it out?

"Come here, troci," he demands.

Oh, I'm dead.

Chapter 29

Meili

"Is there something else you need, Sir Juning?" I force myself to sound calm. Force myself to gaze at him steadily. And force myself not to run.

He snickers. "Turn around."

"What?" My stomach squeezes. My heart pounds against my ribs.

"I said, turn around. Let me see you."

I do a slow pirouette. What's his game?

"I need your opinion, ladies," he says, slurring a bit. "What do you think of Mother's new troci?" He thrusts out his glass to gesture at me. Liquid sloshes out and I itch to catch it in my cupped hands. "She's a Habeni, you know, a rare catch. Is she up to standards?"

His admirers rake me up and down with brittle gazes, as if they're studying a laboratory specimen. My panic he's discovered my plot turns to mortification. I feel like I'm at the troci market again, facing judgmental Adsullatan eyes.

"She's awfully... *big*," one of the ladies says. "Too many muscles, like one of Papa's miners."

"I've heard the Habeni are dim-witted, and as ugly as rachees," another snipes. "Now I see the rumor is true."

A third crinkles her nose. "Do they *all* smell like that?"

Bychen. I feel about two feet tall. "May I go, my lord?"

He snickers. "You may. For now. Remember, you owe me. I mean to collect."

He lifts his glass in a mocking toast. He puts it to his lips again, and I'm satisfied to see him take a hearty gulp as he turns back to his fawning entourage.

I let myself relax a little and melt into the crowd, out of his sight.

Several ticks later, I see Lord Forseti pushing his lady around the dance floor. That means Ayva's free for a few precious moments. I drop my tray on a table, grab Ayva, and hustle her out onto the balcony without a word.

"Meili, what're you doing?" she hisses when we're outside. "We'll get into trouble."

"Not if we're quick. And quiet."

"I don't understand."

I shush her and scan the floodlit grounds. I see several watchers on patrol near the front drive and on the west lawn. Too far away to see us, I think, but I steer Ayva to the dimmest corner of the balcony just in case. Our movement disturbs a canoodling couple. They start guiltily and skitter back into the ballroom.

"One of them's joined to someone else, I'll bet," Ayva says, watching them go.

"I think they both are," a voice says from below. "You should've heard the mush they were saying."

We dash to the wall and look down. Kai emerges from the tangled rosebushes into the light.

My pulse jumps, but I wish it wouldn't. I wish my heart wouldn't race in such an alarming fashion, just seeing him. How could I allow myself to get so wrapped up and giddy over someone who's not interested in me in the slightest? He made that clear yesterday after we tangled with that rachee. I kissed him and he pushed me away, his message cool and final. He holds no tenderness for me.

It's Petra he wants.

Kai reaches the wall and gazes up at us. My belly twists at the aching look he gives his sister.

"Hello, melysette," he murmurs.

Melysette. A Matalan word meaning sweet one. A word any minna worth the title lavishes affectionately on her female charges. It was my second word. Taryn was my first.

"Hello, Kai." Ayva leans as far over the wall as she dares and reaches out, though they can't touch without risking a shock of electricity.

Tears drip from her eyes. I can't see Kai's face clearly, but I think he's crying too.

And now I am.

Ayva points to his zati. "That thing looks terrible on you."

"You know me, never in fashion."

She lets out a tremulous laugh. "Oh, Kai, I miss you."

"I miss you too."

Really, if this keeps up, I'll be floating away on a sea of tears.

"You look nice," he says.

"That's what everyone seems to think." She turns to me. "What about Meili? She looks beautiful, doesn't she?"

He grunts and I scowl. *Ladies and gentlemales, may I present Kai ObDen, king of flattery.*

"You can do better than that," she chides. "Everyone here thinks she's gorgeous. They've been admiring her all night."

That's not true. Every pair of eyes in that ballroom has been fixed on her, but she has a kind heart and wants him to say something nice even if she has to goad him into it. He doesn't take the bait.

"Moving on," I say. If he doesn't want to lie about how I look, I'm certainly not going to force him to. "Let's talk about more important things." I turn to Ayva. "You should know, Kai and I have set the plan. We esca—" Kai hisses and I bite back the word. "We'll, you know, do the thing on the full moon."

"So soon?" Ayva looks down at Kai. "What if we fail? What'll they do to us if we get caught?"

He growls, both dismissive and frustrated. "We won't get caught."

"Your brother has more guts than sense," I hear myself say. I don't know why I can't resist a dig at him.

He digs right back. "*You're* the one with no sense. I *told* you to run from that rachee."

"Oh and I'm simply supposed to do whatever you tell me to?"

"If you want to live long enough to break out of here, maybe you should."

Ayva's gaze pings back and forth between us and she laughs. "You two bicker like an old joined couple."

Kai's tone darkens. "A good reason to get us out of here."

I bristle and would've shot back another insult, but Ayva holds up her hand. "Peace. Save the arguments for when we escape."

"For Dageth's sake, Ayva, stop saying that word. And keep your voice down. We'll be cooked before we start."

Ayva's saucy amusement sobers. "I'm sorry—"

"What're you doing out here?"

Ayva freezes and I swivel around, swallowing a gasp. Sir Juning staggers toward us, weaving wildly. Is that the potion taking effect or a result of all the malmsey he's imbibed tonight?

"Who's that?" Kai asks darkly.

I think he already knows, but I lean over the wall and whisper, "It's Juning."

"That leering son of a spunhound. Let me get my hands on him."

I wave Kai away. "Shoo, before he catches you. Go. *Now.*"

Juning lurches up to us. "You slags oughta be working, 'stead of out here."

"Yes, my lord." Ayva curtseys and arcs around him to head back inside. I do the same, but he grabs my arms and yanks me to him.

"Go on," he snaps at Ayva, who eyes me in panic. "Mother needs you. She spilled... something... on her... whatever." She doesn't budge. He glares at her. "I said git, gell, or you're in for it."

I nod for her to leave. I don't want both of us to face his wrath. She goes reluctantly.

"Well, Red, here we are." He squeezes my upper arms and leers comically. "All alone."

Not entirely. Out of the corner of my eye, I see Kai below. He paces back and forth like a caged lion, staring up at us. What part of *shoo* didn't he understand?

"You better let me go." I try to break out of Sir Juning's hold, but his hands are like grasping talons, pinching my arms so tight he cuts off the flow of blood.

"Let you go? Did you forget your debt?" He leans in, his hot, malmsey-scented breath on my face. "I saved you and your friends from the rachee. I think that's worth a kiss."

I don't. I jerk my knee, aiming for that vulnerable place between his legs, but he anticipates. He shoves me against the balcony wall and pins me with his body.

"That mouth..." he murmurs. "Made for so much dirty business." His slimy lips fall onto mine. I taste malmsey and my own bile.

"I'm gonna rip him in two," I hear from below.

Big help. Kai will be fried as crisp as a timpfowl if he tries to climb up that wall.

Juning presses against me, slobbering all over my face. I gather my wits and clench my fist, swinging upward with all my might. His eyes roll northward, into his head. He collapses. Like a house of cards, straight down. An unappetizing *crack* echoes in the night as his chin strikes the mollystone floor.

I stare down at Juning's still figure. My record as the worst student in self-defense class still stands. My fist didn't even brush his whiskers. The sleeping mixture has finally kicked in.

"Is he dead?" Kai asks.

I kneel, touch Juning's chest, and pop back up. I lean over the wall. "Out cold. Not dead."

"You sound disappointed."

"I am. Am I a terrible person to want him dead?"

"You're asking *me*?"

"Right." I prod Juning with my toe. He doesn't stir. "Do you know what this means?" I call down to Kai. "The potion works. We can dose everyone, the watchers too."

"Now you sound excited. You're the most bloodthirsty Habbie I ever met."

I don't know why that insult makes my pulse pound so hard, but it does. "And you're the most willful Matalan I ever met. I thought you wanted to get out of here."

He grimaces. "You know I do."

"I have to go. I'll try to get out to the garden tomorrow. Did you gather the carteria? What about abyssa? We'll need every bit you can lay your hands on. You also need to get Blix to finish the you-know-what and—"

"Juning?" Lady Forseti's shrill cry pierces ears in and out of the ballroom. I hear Ayva's voice then her ladyship's again, drawing closer. "Junie, are you out here?"

"Ayva's bringing the rescue party," I call down. "Time for you to go."

"And miss all that fun?"

"Go, before one of the watchers finds you."

"You are the bossiest female on all the planets."

I think he's teasing, but he's not smiling. And that's when I know. That's when the truth bursts up from the deep well inside me where I've been hiding it.

I'm in love with him.

I'm in love with every grumpy, scowling bit of him. My heart seems to flip end over end. My knees weaken and all the heated, unbidden emotions I've ever felt for him burst through me like fireworks.

By all the gods and goddesses and Rossa's precocious nephew. I've fallen completely in love with Kai ObDen.

"You do look nice," he mutters then disappears into the night.

Chapter 30

Kai

I DIVE INTO THE rosebushes and out of sight. My gut's tight with fury, frustration, and so much else.

Meili's safe, for the moment. Ayva too. I don't want to think about what can happen to either of them when that imbecile wakes up and puts the puzzle pieces together. Even he's not that stupid.

Thorns scratch my arms and catch on my tunic as I push through the rosebushes to the other side. I bust out into the clear and stop cold. A figure's lingering in the shadows close by.

It's Petra. She could teach the Rowlanite resistance fighters back home a thing or two about sneaking up on someone.

I narrow my eyes. Or spying on them.

Has she followed me? Was she close enough to listen to my conversation with Meili and my sister? We kept our voices low, and the music from the ballroom is loud enough to wake the dead, but still, she might have overheard enough to catch onto our plans.

I told Meili I trust Petra. I hope I'm right.

"What're you doing here?" I demand.

She shrugs. "Too much havoc in camp."

I'll buy that piddling excuse for now. I can hear the ruckus from here.

She falls into step beside me and we head to the cookfire. The night is hot and steamy. The noise grows louder as we draw closer to camp. We walk single-file down one of the alleys between the cottages and come out in the middle of the chaos.

Except, chaos is a mild word to describe the place. It's been like a Mucker fight club here since the miners got back, but tonight the revelry is out of control. Our captors have rewarded us for a good harvest from both the fields and the mines with a keg of liquor called dromé. Most everyone is drunk or high on the black leaf.

People dance and embrace and crash about. Agron and an Adsullatan I don't recognize are scuffling. One of the gells strips off her clothes, while several wide-eyed miners watch. She begs them to reward her show with abyssa. Jervis smashes up one of the few remaining benches and sets it ablaze.

Some enterprising sorts have managed to hack off a piece of the dead rachee's rump and it simmers in the cauldron. It smells greasy and salty, and a touch rancid. I make a note to avoid sampling that delicacy.

I hunker down on the ground next to Petra on the perimeter of the mayhem. The grass is cool and damp against my bottom. I watch the gruesome party, my thoughts turbulent.

Halia's nearby, leaning against Dipro. He snakes his arms around her and holds her tight. Claiming her. Like a possession. She grips a tin cup. She brings it to her lips and sips, staring at the fire, her gaze unfocused.

"Dipro," she says, her voice thick from drink. "Do you think I'm a rutting slag, for... you know, with Juning?"

A long pause. Halia's no friend of mine, no friend of Meili's either, the way she always needled her at school, but I want Dipro to say no. I want him to tell her Juning is the lowest form of vermin on any planet in the galaxy. That she did what she had to do.

He doesn't. The lout doesn't say a word, just gives a disinterested grunt.

Her eyes glisten. Then she begins to bawl. I look away. I don't want to feel for her, or any of the Habbies. I don't want to feel for anyone.

Someone shoves a battered tin cup filled with dromé into my hands. I sniff it suspiciously, my gaze on Agron. Meili isn't the only one here who'd consider drugging someone. I take a swig. It tastes like feet. I pass the cup on.

A black leaf cigar comes my way next. A leaf peeled from a greenie stalk is rolled around a wad of abyssa's coal-black leaves. The smoke coiling from one end smells like licorice. The burning abyssa crackles as I take a hard pull. It scorches my throat and has the flavor of spicy dust.

Could be what licorice tastes like. Never had any of the candy to know. Never had any candy. Ma hoarded coin like a miser, and every bit of that she spent on proper food.

My muscles relax and uncoil from that one puff, so I hand the cigar to Petra. I don't want to relax any more than I want to feel. I want to be aware and angry and detached. On alert.

A soft rain begins to fall. It does nothing to dull the revelry. Blix has wisely removed himself from this insanity. I hope that means he's holed up somewhere, working on finishing those mother-humping candles.

And what am I doing?

Not much beyond grumping and grinding my teeth and worrying about Ayva and Meili.

Meili especially. She's in danger every moment we're stuck here, with Juning on the prowl, pawing her and yowling about how she "owes" him. I know that scum juiced her, though she hemmed and hawed about it.

The stripper completes her disrobing dance and turns away from the goggling miners. She clutches her garments to her naked breasts with one hand, while holding a fistful of abyssa in the other.

Abyssa.

That's what I have to focus on. Meili has her plants and potions. Blix has his candles to build. My job is to gather every scrap of abyssa I can find. Not an easy task. Though there's a lot of it here in camp, those lucky enough to hold a stash guard their supply as carefully as the Habbie physicians guard their meds. And they charge equally steep prices.

I have nothing to trade, nothing to offer, no way to get my paws on what we need without murdering someone or debasing myself.

Except...

I glance at Agron, pummeling his Adsullatan opponent to the rabid cheers of a dozen onlookers. An idea pops into my mind. Dageth's crispy toenails, it's a terrible idea, but it's the only option I have.

I scramble to my feet and tug off my tunic. Warm raindrops spatter my shoulders and chest.

"Listen to me," I call out. No one does, so I shout this time. "Listen up, you brainless cleeks." That works. The hubbub drops to a dull roar and a goodly number of eyes turn toward me. "I'll fight any one of you culbanas to a throw down. Loser stays down to a count of three. A finger of black leaf's my price for each fight."

Agron abruptly stops fighting and swings my way. An excited buzz passes through the rest of the bloodthirsty mob.

Except Petra. She sputters an objection. "Kai. What're you doin'? You'll get pounded, whether you win or not. Have you gone stark, raving loopy?"

"Maybe I have."

I definitely have. But it's the only way. Meili's proved her sleeping potion works. The abyssa is the last ingredient, the final piece in the puzzle of our escape. We need it, and I'll get it the only way I know how.

With my fists.

I lace my fingers together, stretching my arms until my knuckles crack. I strafe the crowd with a challenging glare.

"I'm ready to fight, you cretins." I pin my gaze on Agron. "Who's in?"

I move with slow, aching steps to my dormitory and creep inside.

Raindrops fall through the holes in my dormitory's roof, spattering the floor and the cots unfortunately placed directly under the leaks. I strip off my muddy trousers. Gingerly. Every part of me aches. Every part of me is bruised. I change into dry underdrawers and stretch out on my bunk against the wall and out of the rain.

My bones creak. My jaw throbs. I think I dislocated a finger. Agron took great pleasure in pummeling me. I demanded twice the price for the pleasure of letting him beat the shit out of me. It was worth every punch. I've got a sack full of abyssa, wrapped in Meili's head scarf, to use as my pillow.

The party still rages outside. I suspect sleep for most won't come until dawn. The door squawks open on ancient hinges. I pop open one eye to see a shadow moving swiftly across the room. Tensing, I flex my sore fists and prep for another round of pain.

It's Petra.

"Are you well?" she asks, kneeling beside my cot.

"As well as can be expected. What're you doing in here? Is someone bothering you?"

"No. I don't want to be out there." She sounds afraid and I don't blame her. She touches my bruised and bloodied nose. None too gently. "Told you you'd get banged up. Why'd you do it? You don't smoke the black leaf."

I grunt.

"Because of her. 'Cuz she wanted you to?"

I tense again. Should I be suspicious of this visit, and her questions? Is there more than my well-being on her mind? Had I been right earlier that she'd been lurking near the rosebushes, eavesdropping?

She sighs at my silence and climbs into the narrow bed, laying down beside me. I tense for a third time, for a different reason.

"Petra..."

"I thought you might want to... you know. Everyone's... celebrating."

"I hurt too much to celebrate."

"Is that it? Or something more?" She turns on her side, facing me. We're nose to nose. "You're a sap, Kai, pining for one who don't deserve you." She puts my hand on her breast. It's full. Soft. I feel the warmth of her skin beneath her tunic. "I'm not her, but you can pretend I am."

I skim my gaze over her face. She has a tempting mouth. Her lips are full. Her scent is honey-sweet, slightly earthy. Her eyes shine in the dim light. She's desirable. And willing. I don't know what this is, gratitude, loneliness, a need for comfort. Whatever it is, it's not love.

And it's not what I want.

I pull my hand away. "I can't pretend, Petra," I say gently. "And I don't think you want me to."

She nods and starts to get up, but I pull her down and fold her into my arms. Protectively. Like a brother. To keep her safe, and maybe to keep her close, too. Until I can figure out if I have cause to mistrust her.

She nestles against me and sighs again, seeming content. Soon, she drifts off to sleep.

I'm far from content, and far from sleep. I want Meili here in my arms. Not just because I desire her, or because of her beauty. Because she's smart and clever. Because of her smiles, and her frowns. The way she sticks out her chin when we argue and the way she speaks her mind. I want to be near her, day and night, to hold her and protect her. To feel her lips on mine, to kiss her now and forever.

I don't want to pretend with anyone else.

I want the real thing.

Chapter 31

Meili

Mr. Hervey brushes me out of the way and he and Jinks lift the unconscious Juning. Grunting, they lug his dead weight through the doors and into the ballroom.

The party guests whisper and snicker as they watch the trio pass by. Lady Forseti follows them across the room, her eye paint trickling down her cheeks, washed away in a flood of tears. She explains feebly to anyone who will listen that her darling Junie has been taken ill.

I barely watch the spectacle, barely gloat over my success with the sleeping potion. My mind whirls around one thought. One monumental thought.

I've fallen in love with Kai.

How can that be? How can I be in love with a Matalan? A Matalan who makes no secret how much he despises my people. And me. I don't have a hope that he could love me back.

Or do I?

The kisses we've shared... He may have grumbled and turned cold afterward, but when his lips were on mine, he didn't kiss me like someone who hates me. The fire in his touch, the way he held me and murmured my name has me thinking entirely the opposite.

I'm tempted to stamp my foot. I wish I had more experience in matters of the heart, so I could know for sure what he feels. I must ask Gwynn. Surely she can give me some guidance. Or maybe Ayva, since she admits to having kissed a Habeni.

No, you slupa, not Ayva. What gell wants to talk about her brother kissing anyone, Matalan or Habeni?

The ballroom door closes on Sir Juning and his beleaguered pallbearers. I return to my serving duties. The guests linger, buzzing with speculation and amusement, but eventually the musicians pack up their instruments and the party wanes as the evening rain begins.

Back from depositing the unconscious young lord in his bedroom, Mr. Hervey bows as the partygoers leave, while Jinks follows them to their transports, holding an umbrella over their heads. Ayva, Gwynn, Ellse, and I gather up glasses left on tables or tossed into the potted plants. We sweep up crumbs and turn out the lights. Time enough tomorrow to finish the clean-up job, and then after that...

My heart pounds. This time next week, we'll be gone. If all goes well.

We come out to the hall as Mr. Hervey closes the door on Jinks, escorting out the last guests. Our butler shows no outward signs of illness as he bids Lord and Lady Forseti good night, but after they climb the stairs, he folds. It's as if he's been holding it back through sheer force of will. He slumps against the wall, coughing and wheezing like a slewdog with a hairball caught in its throat.

The front door swings open and Jinks comes back in. After much wheezy objection on Mr. Hervey's part, Jinks and I get him to drape his arms over our shoulders. Sweat drenches his fine suit all the way through. We help him down the steps. Ayva and Gwynn run ahead, calling frantically to Bridgie. Ellse follows, whimpering, patting Mr. Hervey on the back.

Bridgie meets us at the bottom of the stairs. Her eyes grow as big as twin moons when she sees the butler's sweat-drenched face. "Get him to his room, loves."

We practically have to carry him down the hallway. I'm grateful for Jinks's strength. By the time we reach his room, Mr. Hervey's no longer coughing. His head lolls.

"He's really sick," I say, my voice unsteady.

Bridgie flings open the door. "He'll be fine. He just needs rest." Her flat tone doesn't convince me.

"Is there anything I can give him? Sweet tea perhaps?"

"Yes, tea. That's a good idea." She takes Mr. Hervey from us as delicately as removing an egg from a nest. "Go now, all of you. You too, Ellse. Go help Meili."

I'm sure she's trying to get rid of us, but I do as she says. I boil water and mix the tea and sugar as quickly as I can. Ellse places two biscuits on the tray.

"He be hungry," she says, sniffling.

I doubt he has an appetite but thank her and carry the tray to his room. The door's ajar and I peep inside. Mr. Hervey lies on the bed, stretched out as stiff and straight as a plank. His breath comes in heaving rasps and he shivers violently, though he's piled under many blankets. Bridgie sits beside him, holding his hand.

A distressed mewl escapes my lips. Bridgie stiffens, then gets up and pads quickly to the door. She takes the tray from me.

"Will he be well?" I ask.

Her eyes are sad, her shoulders stooped as if all the worlds rest on them. "We shall see." Her voice is so soft I can barely hear her.

Back in the kitchen, Jinks drops into Mr. Hervey's rocker as if his legs will no longer hold him up. I'm equally exhausted. We head to bed. No one speaks. The night's events fade away. Even Kai is pushed from my thoughts. I can think of only one thing. I stare up at the ceiling and beg the gods and goddesses to make Mr. Hervey well.

Eventually, I fall asleep. Dark dreams batter me. I run from a rachee that snaps at my heels. A tree with bare, gnarled branches screams like a person as it topples. Juning runs his rev cycle over Kai, slicing him in two.

I wake with a pounding headache. It's morning, but the room is dim and rain ticks against the roof. I sit up, my body sore all over. My temples throb. Am I ill? Do I have what Mr. Hervey has? Ayva stirs, then Gwynn. She covers a yawn with her hand. Varina's still snoring.

I blink fully awake. Bridgie hasn't come to rouse us as she usually does.

I scramble out of bed. I bolt past Ellse, crouched on her mat, fingers tangled in her hair. In the kitchen, I stiffen. Bridgie's slumped at the table.

"How is Mr. Hervey?" I ask hesitantly.

She gazes up at me with red-rimmed eyes. "He's dead."

Bare feet pound as Ayva and Gwynn rush up behind me, followed by Ellse.

"No. It's not true," Gwynn cries, her voice a mix of anguish and disbelief. She turns to Ayva and falls into her arms, sobbing against her shoulder.

A gaping hole seems to open before me, dark, ominous, like the fire pits back home before the coals are set ablaze. I sink into a seat. The tray I brought to Bridgie last night is on the table. I stare at it. The tea and biscuits are untouched.

"So, it wasn't a cold," I say when I can finally speak.

Bridgie looks at me as if I'm a simpleton. "No, love. It never was."

"It was the Molly fever," I say. "You knew all along."

She nods. "He didn't want to ruin her ladyship's party." She says that as if it explains everything. "She planned the ball for so long.

How could she go on without a butler? It woulda disappointed her so."

"Do you hear yourself? He basically killed himself so he wouldn't disappoint *her*. That's horrible. That's intolerable."

She shrugs. "We're troci. We gotta do as is expected of us. Hervey himself would say there's nothing else we can do."

I go cold all over. Didn't I say something similar to Kai once about the Matalans? Didn't I use the same reasoning when agreeing to an alliance with Ullr? Do what's expected, even if it means joining with someone you barely know. Do as you're told, even if it means working yourself to death.

I step to the window and stare out at the rain through the bars. Water trickles like tears down the windowpanes. It rarely rains during the day, but it seems appropriate today.

I've never known anyone who died. The Habeni are strong and fit, and it's the reason we live such long lives. If a Habeni does get sick, there's meds to fix it. Mr. Hervey didn't have any meds. I shift my gaze to the troci houses, where Kai is. His mother didn't have meds either. I look back at Bridgie, sitting listless at the table, eyes moist. She had to watch Mr. Hervey suffer through the night and breathe his last. Did Kai and Ayva watch their mother suffer, too? I feel sick.

The sounds of sorrow fill the kitchen. Gwynn and Ayva cling to one another, sobbing. Ellse squats by Mr. Hervey's chair, rocking back and forth, keening. Even Varina has joined us, still in her nightdress, tears streaming down her face.

Everyone cries except me. I don't know why. I'm devastated, but the tears won't come. I just stand at the window, staring at nothing, thinking of nothing, feeling nothing. Except a hard, black stab of hopelessness.

"I suppose her ladyship will want her breakfast soon," I hear Bridgie say, as if from far away. "I'll wake Jinks, so he can serve."

She plumps her fists on the table and pushes herself up with a heavy sigh.

"You missies should get about your chores. There'll be much to clean up today."

We lay Mr. Hervey to rest early the next morning in the troci graveyard.

Morning mist shrouds our small band of mourners. All of us from the house have been permitted to attend the service, with a handful of outside workers joining us to assist in the burial. We walk in slow, somber steps behind our butler's shrouded body as Kai and Agron wheel it on a cart from the house. The watchers Hup and Dall follow at a discreet distance.

The cemetery is beyond the watchers' house, uncomfortably close to the barrier. We pass through the wooden gate and gather by the grave. Jinks leads a simple ceremony. Bridgie has insisted Mr. Hervey be interred according to Dryan custom, his body wrapped in a shroud of moss-speckled bark peeled from the sissy fruit trees.

As Jinks speaks, I scan the surroundings. I've never been permitted in this area. It's a grassy space. Peaceful, quiet, save the steady hum of electricity powering the barrier. Even the usually raucous budgies keep a respectful silence.

Beyond the graveyard and the orange line that marks the barrier lies a dense forest, stretching as far north as the eye can see. Pinum, Mr. Hervey called those towering, wide-trunked trees, with their long, grasping branches and thick needles. It nicks at me to have our butler rest here, with the trees he loved so close, yet unreachable.

When Jinks finishes, Agron and Dipro lower the body into the ground as gently as those two oafs can manage. Kai shovels dirt on top with more grace. The soil patters against Mr. Hervey's bark shroud like a soft rain. Afterwards, everyone but Bridgie and Ellse drifts away. I start to go too then turn back and touch Bridgie's hand.

She stares down at the freshly tamped soil. "Hervey was a good one." She dabs at her eyes with ragged piece of cloth. "A rare one."

I don't know what to say, so I nod. I think she loved him in a way, and perhaps he loved her. Or maybe they clung to each other because there was no one else. Whatever, they had a union of sorts, and now she's lost him. I hand her a small bouquet of losys that survived the rachee's stampede. She drops the flowers one by one onto his grave.

Out of the corner of my eye, I see Varina and Gwynn talking with the other Habeni, including Ullr. Ayva and Kai stand off to the side. His arm is around his sister and she rests her head on his shoulder. If I squint I can almost imagine we're home, on the grounds at school, with the Habeni and Matalans separate as usual. That division seems out of kilter now.

Or maybe I'm out of kilter.

"I suppose this is the beginning." Bridgie releases a teary sigh. "The fever will spread faster than fire in a dry field." She gestures to the many mounds with narrow wooden markers bearing a name and date of death. Ellse is hunkered down by one of the mounds, tracing the letters of a name carved into the wood with her forefinger. "We'll soon see many more of these."

Including one with my name on it. And Gwynn's. And one for Ayva, Varina, and… Kai. I try to swallow but can't. There's a lump in my throat the size of a boulder.

I leave Bridgie to her sorrow and wander through the cemetery gate toward the others, but I don't join the Habeni group. I walk straight to Kai and Ayva. Varina whispers something as I pass. I'm sure it isn't nice.

"I'm sorry," Kai says, his expression as gloomy as an endless night.

I cringe to see he's been fighting again. He sports a purple shiner under his left eye and several new bruises on his face.

"I'm sorry too," I murmur. "He was... good. Kind. He didn't deserve this end."

Now the tears come. Not yesterday, nor last night, or even as I walked behind the cart carrying Mr. Hervey's body. The tears begin as a trickle then become a flood. I don't want Kai to see me being so weak, but I can't hold back.

And as suddenly as the tears fall, I'm wrapped in his embrace. Clutching him, bawling like a baby. He holds me close and I don't think about how inappropriate it is. Don't think about anyone seeing us. All I think is how much I need this.

Need *him*.

And how much better being in his arms makes me feel.

"Ullr, look. Your intended's fawning over a Mucker," I hear Varina say. "Next, they'll be humping in the dirt."

Ullr doesn't respond, doesn't even seem to hear her. The others turn and stare at us with expressions ranging from shock to disgust.

And... I don't care. Not one tiny whit.

I sniffle and let that sink in. After all this time struggling to fit in and be someone I'm not, after trying to be part of their crowd for so long, only to be mocked and rejected at every turn, facing snubs and noses lifted in contempt and snotty high status cleeks like Varina and Agron calling me a neb day after day...

I don't give a flying frickle what any of them think.

I gaze up at Kai, still holding me safely in his embrace. And if I want to hug a Matalan when I'm grieving, I will. I'll let him hug me back, too. If I want to kiss him I'll do that as well, and to pakao with the law or tradition and all of those strictures keeping both Habeni and Matalans in our constrained and unhappy little boxes for centuries.

I love Kai, and that's all that matters.

To me, anyway.

To Kai? I'm still unsure. He gives me one last squeeze, then his hold on me slackens, his scowl firmly in place. And completely unreadable. Does he feel even the least tenderness for me? If he does, would it be fair for me to ask him to risk everything to act on those feelings?

Varina moves on, demanding gossip and news of the other Habeni in the workers' camp who've returned from the mines. Gwynn breaks away and comes to join us.

"Ignore Varina," she says, offering me a supportive smile. "She's back with her snobby friends and she's just showing off."

Ayva barks a laugh. "When doesn't she show off?"

Hup interrupts to announce the time for grieving is over and we must return to our chores. We troop across the lawn toward the house. Varina and her gang lead the way. The rest of us hang back. Kai's next to me.

"We can't wait a tick longer," I whisper, leaning close to him. "The fever is here and it'll sweep through the ranch. We must flee *now*. Tonight if we can. If we don't, it will surely be too late."

I feel him stiffen beside me. He clearly disagrees. He looks to Ayva, then to Gwynn. Both of them nod. Three of us, a united front against one doubtful Matalan.

He grunts, giving in.

At the edge of the garden, Kai stops and turns to me. "See if you can get outside this afternoon. I'll light a fire under Blix to get those candles finished and bring them here."

"Thank you."

"Thank me when we're gone from this dung hole."

On that gloomy note, we go our separate ways.

I do a terrible job with my chores. I'm so preoccupied with thoughts of Mr. Hervey and with our imminent escape, I can't focus. I swab the ballroom floor haphazardly, missing several sticky spots where malmsey was spilled the other night. Later, Bridgie lets me out to the garden without a question. She's far, far away.

I climb over the ruined fence, making a wide arc around the rachee's reeking and fly-speckled corpse. Or, what's left of it. The carcass has been hacked and torn, as if someone went at it with blunt instruments.

I pick through the destroyed plants, hunting for carteria. I don't find more than a smattering, but they'll have to do. I hope Kai's managed to pick some and I double hope he's gotten his hands on abyssa to mix with it. Knocking out the watchers is *the* most crucial part of our plan's success.

I go on the hunt for as many medicinal plants and roots I can find and don't look up until I hear that familiar squeak. Kai stops his barrow at the back of the garden. I pick up my basket and hurry over to him, heat flooding me as usual.

How would he react if I tell him how I feel? Maybe I will tell him, but not now. When the deed is done and we're far from Mollystone Manor, I'll tell him everything.

We don't speak. He shovels manure onto some plants that are beyond help until he uncovers a rectangle of cloth at the bottom of the barrow. He lifts the filthy rag and I see two implements—a small gear box studded with wires and what looks like a juicer without its metal shell, its electronic innards exposed. He glances around, motions for me to dump out the contents of my basket, then, as swift as a thief in the night, he tucks both devices inside.

"The smaller one, the juicer, Blix says put it against the keypad and hold the buttons for five ticks. He says it'll short out the lock." Kai wipes his hands on his towel, watching me arrange the plants and roots back in the basket, covering the devices. "The big one, that's the killer. Set the timer then run like pakao." He pins me with his gaze. "Blix says you'll have only twenty ticks before it blows. Give or take a tick."

I have to nod because I can't speak. I can barely breathe.

He pulls a bit of cloth the size of a teabag out of his pocket and hands it to me. The bag is stuffed full. "Here's all the abyssa I can spare. I need the rest to dose the watchers and I can't get any more. Everyone in camp's fighting over the stuff."

Including him, if the bruises and cuts on his face are any indication. I'm torn between admiration for his determination and dismay over his headstrong ferocity. Someday, leading with his chin could get him killed.

"That should be enough to knock the family out." I drop the bag into my apron. "Did you find any carteria?"

"A little. I ventured to pick through your garden at sunrise but a watcher chased me off."

I give him as much as I can. The leaves disappear into his pocket. Then it's my turn to give instructions.

"You must mix one part carteria to three parts abyssa. Crush it together to a powder and stir the mix in some stew if you can. Alcohol makes it work faster, but it's easier to taste. Judging from Juning's response, it'll take about an hour for full effect, so if you dose the watchers with the evening meal, I can set the charge at ten. The whole vile crew should be deep in dreamland by then."

That's more of a question than a statement, but he nods like he thinks my timetable is simply dandy. I realize he's as nervous as I am. Somehow that makes me feel more confident.

"Don't make a move until I'm sure the watchers are out," he says. "I'll signal you somehow. I'll..." His gaze sweeps the troci houses, the fields, the barn, and the meadow beyond, then back to the garden. He looks down at his barrow. "I'll set this klacking thing on fire. If all's well, I'll put the barrow here and torch it."

That prompts me to smile. "With glee, seems like." A long pause. All the things we have to do, and all the things that could go wrong tumble through my brain. Probably Kai's too. "Well, I'd better go in."

He lifts my basket and hands it to me. "This is heavy. What is all that stuff?"

"Leaves and plants and roots we might need on our journey. I'm packing a bag too."

"Good idea." He looks toward the courtyard wall. "I wish we could wait a day or two. Buy more time."

"Buy time? For what?"

"For me to figure how to place the bomb myself."

Again? "Kai, we've been over this. Bridgie will never let you in. There's no way to force the door. End of argument. Why should you get to do all the fun stuff?"

"This isn't a joke. It's dangerous."

"Do you think I'll blow myself up? Don't you have any confidence in me at all?"

"Dageth's nostrils, Meili, will you stop? I'm worried about you. Afraid you'll get caught or hurt. And, yeah, I'm terrified you'll blow yourself up."

His voice is gruff, intense. He shoots me the mother of all scowls and for the first time ever, I don't think it means he's angry with me.

"Well… that's quite… nice," I manage. "But I think you'll find I can do a lot more than you give me credit for."

"I'm reminded of that every day," he says, with an odd smile.

He takes my free hand in both of his. He lifts it and turns it over and kisses my palm. His lips linger, gentle and like silk against my skin. My insides turn to jelly.

"Be careful," he murmurs, gazing into my eyes. "By the gods, Meili, be careful."

And then he's gone, the barrow squeaking into the afternoon.

It takes a long time to catch my breath.

I shift my basket from one hand to the other and scan my garden one last time. I won't miss it. I won't miss anything about Mollystone Manor, but I feel a deep sense of satisfaction at all I've done here. Or *did*, before Lord Rachee came for a visit. I've grown more plants than Taryn herself could identify. I've built a fence from a thorny vine. I've cooked up an elaborate escape plan.

I gaze at my hand. The sensation of Kai's warm lips against my palm still tingles. I've kissed a Matalan. Fallen in love with a Matalan. I've fallen completely, breathlessly, head-over-bottom in love with Kai ObDen.

I feel as if I can do anything.

And now I'm going to blow up a building.

Chapter 32

Kai

I DITCH MY BARROW and trudge back to camp, my thoughts as dark as pitch, my gut twisted into knots. I wish we could've waited, but Meili's right. We need to make our move and we have to do it now. *She* has to do it now. But that doesn't mean I won't worry about that feisty redhead every tick until the deed is done.

I go straight to my dorm and set about mixing the sleeping herbs together. I spread Meili's scarf on my cot and dig the carteria out of my pocket, sprinkling what I hope is the right amount over the abyssa. Then I fold the scarf, shake it up and crush the leaves inside to bits using a stone I found near the greenies field. I don't stop until the substance becomes a fine reddish-black powder.

I try to keep my mind from dipping into gloom as I work. It'd be a lot easier if it were Varina or Agron about to blow themselves to bits. Their open contempt toward Meili today at the graveyard scorched me. Holding her in my arms as she cried through her pain scorched me in a different way. I felt helpless to ease her grief, and now I'm helpless to keep her safe.

A shiver crawls along my spine, as if someone's watching me. The miners are still here, creating havoc, and the watchers have been busy chasing them around. Why would one of the guards waste their time sniffing around to see what a shit-shoveling slupa like me is up to?

I glance over my shoulder. The door's closed tight. There's no one outside, peeping in on me through the tiny windows, though it's hard to see anything through those grubby plastic panes.

I cram the scarf filled with the sleeping powder into my pocket, then follow Meili's lead and pack a bag. I grab an old tunic off the floor, tying the cloth into a lopsided pouch, then shove the few pieces of clothing I have inside, along with my spoon, some tin bowls I've been able to scrounge, and a small torchlight Blix liberated from the tool shed. I admit to a grudging respect for the lad. He's turned into quite the sneak thief.

Taking my tunic carry-bag, I leave my quarters for the last time. I'm not coming back. This time tomorrow, I'll either be dead or on my way home.

With Ayva—and Meili—at my side.

I slip down the alley and make a wide berth around the rowdy crowds milling about the camp. Keeping a lookout for watchers, I tote my bag of provisions past their cottage and the graveyard to the northeast corner of the compound. If the plan works, if the power goes down, this is where we'll run. Into the forest, heading to the north, to the city where the pirates dumped us. Hoping to find a way home.

The orange line that marks the invisible wall of electricity ringing the property is just ahead. No troci has the guts to push the mechanized lawnmower close to the barrier, so the grass from here to the line is ragged and overgrown. I know I'm getting too close even without the tangled grass. My zati hums like it's filled with a thousand angry bees trying to get out.

My arms still ache from my fights the other night, so it's a chore to lift my bag. I hurl it past the barrier, aiming for the woods beyond, when something flashes to my left. My arm seizes and my throw arcs too high. The bag flops to the ground in the grass just inside the perimeter.

I spin around, bracing for a juicing, but there's not a watcher in sight. No one's in sight. I shake it off. I'm so wound up about Meili and what we're about to do, I guess I'm jumping at shadows.

Struggling for calm, I set to work on my next chore in the plan, getting the sleeping mix into the watchers' food.

The sun is lowering into the west as I head to the station near the cookfire, where the troci on kitchen duty peels the taters and preps the greenies for the watchers' meals. She then brings them to their cottage, where they're given to another troci, who adds them to a stew or a beef roast. I've trailed the troci with her bag of taters and greenies a dozen times and never once has she been invited into the cottage.

My plan to change that. My plan is to get hold of the bag, get inside the watchers' house, and somehow mix the sleeping potion into their meal.

A task as easy as jocakes.

Halia's on kitchen duty today. She sits on a bench, a slop bucket between her feet, peeling taters like the amateur she is. My sister Raymie's only seven and she can peel any legume as fast as a switch. Halia's knife isn't very sharp, but that doesn't stop her from cutting up her fingers. I hope the watchers don't mind a little troci blood mixed in with their meal.

"Hey, Halia." I amble toward her at the fire. I try on a smile, going for charm, even though Meili says I don't possess a whit of it. "How's it going?"

She spares me a quick glance. Her expression turns extra sour. "What do you want, Mucker?"

So, charm's out. She clearly still resents me not sticking my neck out for her all those months ago. Time for my other plan.

"I don't want nothing. I'm done with my chores and thought I'd come say hello." I dig into my pocket and pull out a black leaf cigar. I hung onto some of the abyssa for emergencies like this. "And to see if you're interested in sharing one of these."

Her eyes light up.

Ten minutes later, I sling the bag of taters and greenies over my shoulder and leave Halia giggling in the dirt. I barely took a puff, but she smoked that thing down to the nub end and is feeling no pain. That'll come later, if the watchers find her. I don't care if she's punished. Maybe I'll care someday, but not now.

I keep my focus on the cottage as I close in, shoulders back, trying to look as if I belong there. At the door, instead of knocking like a polite troci, I make a bold move and turn the doorknob. To my surprise, it opens easily. I hesitate, swallowing hard. Could be a lapse of security on the watchers' part. Could be a trap.

No turning back. Gut clenched, I step inside a sizeable kitchen, painted a warm and cozy yellow. The room smells of fresh baked bread and beef on the boil. Makes my mouth water. Makes me lonely for home.

A quick recon shows a small table in the center of the room, where a wispy Adsullatan with a pinched mouth and fever scars over every bit of her exposed skin sits. She's mighty relaxed for a troci, lounging with her feet up on a chair and sipping a purple liquid like she's the lady of the manor. Behind her by the back windows is a sink and a counter for chopping, a cot in a corner where the servant must sleep, and a closed door to my left.

I pin my gaze on the door. I'm sure it leads to the courtyard between this house and the manor beyond. An idea flashes into my mind. Another of my terrible ideas, but worth a try. Once I complete my task, I'll take a stab at getting through that door, into the courtyard, where I'll wrest the explosives from Meili and set them off myself.

A plan with little chance of success. But I'm determined to give it a shot.

The troci at the table notices me and she jumps. "Where's Halia?"

"Sick." At the last tick I remember to speak real slow, playing the slupa. "Got the shivers."

Her suspicion vanishes. "Come down with the fever, has she?" She starts to get up. "All right, hand over the bag."

"Sit, Missy. I'll dump 'em in the pot, if you like."

She puts her feet back up. "I like very much."

My mood soars. Luck's been with me and I've gotten this far. Now to do the deed. I cross to the stove. Chunks of beef swim in a thick gravy in the pot. I'm tempted to snatch a piece and swallow it whole.

The servant watches me, her eyes bright. She licks her lips. "Ain't you a big, strappin' fellow. What's your name, troci?"

My eyebrows shoot up. She's twice my age. "Agron, Missy. Agron Osch."

I hope she remembers the name well tomorrow, when the watchers wake and demand to know who put them into their stupor. *If* I can get this klacking potion mixed in with her eyeing me. I turn away from her and ease Meili's sleeping powder-filled scarf from my pocket.

"Been here long, Missy? Where you from?" I ask, hoping she's a chatterer.

The door bangs open and I nearly drop both scarf and tater bag. Cresp pushes in. The servant leaps to her feet, clears up her dishes and darts to the sink. I think she's lucky. Cresp's the least bloodthirsty of the watchers. Had Hup caught her lounging, she'd get a zap for sure.

Cresp grabs a water flask from the larder and downs it in a noisy gulp. He lets loose a belch that shakes the windows. "What's that there?" he asks, narrowing his eyes at me.

"Yer dinner, you big oaf, what does it look like?" the servant snaps.

Cresp swings on her. "Quit yer wailing, Cece. Don't you ever shut your yap?"

She crashes the dishes into the sink. "What can I do *but* complain, when you give me so much to wail about."

My eyes pop at the way they bicker. Like they've been joined for years and can't wait for death to come and part them.

Cresp turns his back to me and I see my chance. My heart slams into my throat as I dump everything into the pot. Taters and greenies and Meili's special poison plop into the stew. Broth splashes up, scalding my hand and arm. But I don't care. It's done.

The two are still arguing. Time to try that door. I adopt the most confused expression I can muster and move across the kitchen. My blood pumps in a terrified rush and I want to run but I force myself to shamble stupidly.

Heat stabs me under my zati like tiny knives, stabbing harder the closer to the door I get. I reach out, my fingertips hovering over the doorlatch. Electricity crackles up my palm and the hair on my arm stands on end. I grind my teeth but it's not the juice that pains me. I don't have to touch the door to know there's no way I'm getting in there.

"Hey!"

I nearly leap through the roof at Cresp's bellow. He's behind me, his wheezy breath hot on my neck.

"Where you going, fool?"

I give him a dopey look. "Out. I done my chore. I'm goin' to the cookfire for grub."

Cresp's eyes narrow. He's not buying it. "That ain't the way out."

His punisher's suddenly in my face, sparks shooting from the weapon's barrel. I pull in a hard breath and brace myself.

"Aw, leave him alone, Cresp," Cece says, grabbing my arm with both hands. "Can't you see the lad's a bigger dimwit than you?"

She tugs me back across the kitchen, squeezing my muscles with abandon as she steers me to the door. "Go on, boy. Git."

The door bangs shut behind me as I'm pushed outside. My shoulders sag and my knees quake. That was my last hope. My last chance to take charge of those candles. My gaze skims the courtyard wall.

It's up to Meili now.

CHAPTER 33

Meili

I wrap the candles in my blanket, set it on the floor, then gently slide the package under my cot, careful not to move too fast or jostle the deadly devices. What a joke on me if the dratted things explode in a ball of fire and put an end to all our plans before the final step can even begin.

Not to mention put an end to me.

I move on to more mundane chores. I strip the case off my thin pillow and stuff my meager belongings inside, followed by the herbs and roots I gathered in the garden earlier. The plants should probably be chopped and crushed or dried before they spoil, but there's no time to do a proper job, so in they go.

"I can always tell when you've been with my brother," Ayva says, coming into our room. She waves her hand in front of her nose.

I'm confused for a tick then remember Kai's stinky hiding place for the explosives. "I barely notice it anymore. I'll wager he'll be glad to leave the smell behind."

I pick up the dress and shoes I wore for the ball.

"You're not taking that gown, are you?" Ayva folds her spare frillies and nightgown and tucks them inside her own pillowcase. "The shoes are sturdy, but the gown's so thin, it'll be no good against the elements."

"I know." I hold the dress against me, admiring its style, recalling the way Kai said *you look nice* that night. Funny how one reluctant compliment from him can turn my insides to pudding. "I admire your practicality, Ayva, but…" I stuff the dress into my pillowcase. "I just can't leave it behind."

She digs her own gown out from under her cot and examines it fondly. "It *is* pretty." She tucks it in her sack, too. "You should take more useful things though." She lowers her voice. "I stole scissors and needle and thread from her ladyship's sewing box."

"Smart. That will come in handy for repairing our clothing."

"I'm not thinking about sewing rips and tears as much as I am stitching a wound. The scissors can be useful in many ways. For hunting or as a weapon, you see?"

"Oh." I hadn't considered the need for weapons, or the possibility of wounds. I haven't thought about anything beyond my task tonight.

"You're nervous," she says. "I've had my doubts, but now I'm sure the plan will work."

"And you know that how?"

"Because I used to think Kai was the smartest, bravest person I knew. Until I met you."

Her words hold no guile or false flattery. I believe she means it. "I don't know what to say, Ayva."

"Say you'll let me help you."

"No way. Kai will *kill* me if we both get blown up."

She thrusts her pillowcase under her cot and laughs. "You're so ridiculous. I never knew Habbies could be so… Whimsical? Is that the word? You Habeni are always so stern."

"Because we're endlessly having to scold you Muckers to get to work."

That's Varina. She leans with arms crossed against the door jamb, frowning at us. I return a frown of my own. How long has she been there? How much has she overheard?

Ayva shuts down, her easy manner evaporating.

"Lay off," I say.

"Was somebody speaking? Somebody worth listening to? All I see here is a Mucker and a toadying neb not worthy to polish my shoes."

Anger flares. I haven't even breathed the word *escape* to her, and I have a strong urge to leave her behind. "I'm glad to see you in such a pleasant mood today."

She sneers and flounces into the room, smacking her shoulder against Ayva's as she passes. "Watch yourself, you cleek."

"Excuse me," Ayva mumbles, her gaze on the floor. "I need to find Gwynn."

Ayva hurries away and Varina glares at her as she passes.

"Why do you persist in sticking up for that feeble twip?" Varina drops down onto my cot. The slats groan and sag under the sudden assault and I suck in a terrified breath, expecting the worst. "You know she'd stab you in the back the moment you turn away, just like the rest of them."

I take hold of my temper as best as I can. It's a struggle, what with Varina demonstrating Habeni prejudice at its finest while bouncing on top of a dangerous amount of explosives.

"What do you want, Varina?"

She sighs the most self-pitying sigh ever heard in all the worlds. "I'm bored. And I'm heartily sick of this place." She yanks at the plastic ring around her neck and sighs again. "Wait. What's that? What're you doing? What's in the pillowcase?"

"Nothing." I quickly shove the bulky bag under my cot. "It's... my ballgown. I'm putting it away. I suspect there won't be another ball for a long time."

"Not until the fever passes, you mean. Do you think Lady Ghoul will wait until we're all dead, or will she start planning now for the next shipment of troci?" She coughs, then laughs when I gasp in horror. "Got you, didn't I?" She laughs again, a totally mirthless sound, and I believe she's gone completely loopy.

Bridgie is slumped at the table with a glass of dromé when I come out to the kitchen, with Varina on my heels.

"Dinner will be late," Bridgie says. "Having trouble getting myself to move." She gestures for me to join her, but not Varina. She sips her drink and gazes at me over the rim of the glass. "You ever been to the Purple Mountain?"

"Mount Fioled? No. I've only seen digipix."

"Fioled's named for the mountain god. It's the most beautiful spot in all Hephas. It ain't all flat, like your fancy cities. The hills slope up and down like one of them rides in a Habbie fun park. The grass is as soft as a gigg's feathers. Pools of icy blue water. Air so pure..." She closes her eyes and inhales deeply. "Of all the sights, the most pleasing are the nascent blooms. Thousands of them, spread across the slopes like a purple army, pushed by the wind but never bending. I never smelled anything so sweet, nor saw a place as lovely. Hervey woulda liked it there."

She blots a tear on her cheek with her thumb.

My heart wrenches. "Would you go back if you could?"

She puts down her glass. "Oh, I don't dwell on thoughts like that, love. That can never be."

Varina's at the sink. She catches my eye and points to her temple, making wide circles with her finger. I disagree. I don't think Bridgie's gone mad. I think she's given up. I'm more determined than ever to take her with us.

I get up to retrieve my basket and go about my tasks. My portion of the abyssa and carteria are still in my apron. I haven't had a free moment to blend them together, but when I do, I'll put a light dose in Bridgie's nightly glass of dromé, enough so she'll be too drowsy to ask questions when the chaos begins. When we escape, she'll be groggy, but able to run.

She'll see her home again and stroll in that field of nascent blooms.

I'm sure of it.

The day wanes and dusk arrives. So does the first step in our escape plan.

I'm with Gwynn on the landing of the servants' stairs, getting ready to help serve dinner. Jinks has gone ahead with the first course, ruck soup. Gwynn is to follow with a pan of skillet-fried timpfowl. I'll bring up the rear with glasses of malmsey, as soon as I make one important addition. I shake the last of the sleeping potion into Juning's drink and stir the liquid with a spoon.

"There's already some of that in the soup," Gwynn says. "Couldn't the extra dose kill him?"

I put the glass next to the others on my tray. "Perhaps. At this point, do you care?"

She lets out a distressed moan. "I hardly recognize you, Meili."

I respond with a shrug. Earlier, I got Gwynn to distract Bridgie and stirred enough mix into the soup to send the whole family to dreamland. But I'm taking no chances with Juning. I want him beyond unconscious when I make my move later.

"Please don't nag, Gwynn. You want to escape from here, don't you?"

"Yes, of course I do. But the cost seems almost too dear."

Hefting her tray, she pushes the door open with her foot. I follow her down the hallway and into the dining room. The electrified candelabra at the center of the table is dimmed, casting a ghostly glow over the four Forsetis. Jinks is removing the soup bowls. Their *empty* soup bowls, I'm happy to see.

Gwynn puts down the pan and moves the timpfowl to a serving platter with a pair of tongs. I head for the table with the drinks.

"It's about time, Red." Juning watches me keenly as I place the glass next to him.

My shaking hands betray my nervousness. I fear I'll spill and lose the last precious bit of sleeping potion. Juning tries to grab my bottom and I almost do spill as I leap out of reach. I glare at him hard, wishing I'd had triple the dose to put in his malmsey.

I move on. Jinks takes the platter from Gwynn and follows me around the table, placing several pieces of timpfowl on each plate.

His lordship gazes down at his plate and rubs his hands together. "This looks delish, Hervey."

After an awkward silence, Juning jumps in. "That's not Hervey, Father, it's the other one, what's-his-name."

Jinks grimaces and Lord Forseti squints. "How's that, son?"

"I said, that's not our butler. Hervey's gone."

"Gone? Where'd he go?" He gapes at her ladyship. "My dear, did you hear this? Hervey's run off."

"No, Father, he's dead," Lady Netti says loudly, as if this will help him understand. "The fever got him, sad to say."

"What d'ya expect of a Dryan?" Juning says. "They're weak. If he was Adsullatan, maybe he'd have stood a chance."

His sister's stare oozes every bit of resentment she feels toward her unmarred, favored brother.

He returns her gaze with a smirk then swivels toward his father. "Hervey was the first, Father. In a day or two, the rest of 'em downstairs will get it. You'll be needing more troci when this lot croaks."

Lord Forseti smiles vacantly. "I'll speak to Deke. He'll know what to do."

"Ask him to look for gells with a decent disposition. This bunch have such sour faces they could curdle milk."

Her ladyship titters. "Oh, Junie, stop. The fever may not be so bad this go-round. Perhaps we'll lose just Hervey and some others, and we won't take as big a hit to our pocketbook as last time."

Gwynn and I exchange glances. Nice to know we're no more than figures in a plus or minus column to these monsters.

"You could be right, Mother. Maybe this batch will make it, but they'll lose their looks, like ol' Bridgie." Juning eyes me and runs a finger over his tongue. "You slags won't be so standoffish then, eh?"

Fury flares inside me. I stare at his still-untouched glass of malmsey, willing him to drink down every drop. Hoping he chokes on the liquid. Hoping it turns out I gave him too large a dose. For Netti's sake, for every female he's ever played fitch-and-mouse with, and for poor, dear Wynnie, I hope it does kill him.

Jinks shoos us out of the room with a command to return with dessert. At the door, I turn back for a last loathing look at Sir Juning and I can't stop myself from saying, "Drink up, my lord."

He lifts the glass to me in a mock toast and puts it to his lips.

Chapter 34

Kai

Dageth's hairy knuckles—it works.

It takes a klacking long time, long after the floodlights come on, but Meili's sleeping herbs have done the job. The watchers usually take a spin around the compound a couple of times at night, harassing troci still awake, their weapons at the ready.

Not tonight. Most of them sprawl on the ground where they dropped when the potion kicked in. The ones still up stumble around in a daze, glassy-eyed, mumbling and giggling like slupas. Hup didn't even come out of the cottage.

I allow myself a satisfied smile. She did it.

I finish my last meal here and bring my bowl to the wash bucket. My excitement dims. I'm eager to get on with my final task but terrified of what will happen after I light the signal fire. Of what Meili's going to do and what I can't control.

Seems as if everyone's picked up on my mood. The cookfire's usual debauchery is subdued tonight, and even the miners are quiet. With the watchers knocked out, gloom hangs over the gathering, like the uneasy calm before a big storm blows in.

"Thanks for nothing, Mucker," Halia snarls when I hand her my bowl.

I'm stung by remorse seeing the raw burns on her neck. I quiet my guilt by telling myself she'll thank me later, if she has the brains to run when the power fails.

Petra tries to follow me as I leave, but I wave her off. I'm about to slip down the alley between two cottages when Dipro pops out. I herk to a stop. Someone's cold hands splay on my back and shove me hard. I spin around to see Agron. A couple of Habbies who went to the mines, Jervis and Tew, loom up on either side, penning me in.

I'm caught.

"Four on one?" I bite off, frustrated. Am I going to have to punch my way out? My fists are still bruised from my last brawl. I lift my chin and give Agron a cold stare. "Guess that's the only way a Habbie can win a fight."

But Agron's not the troublemaker this time. It's Dipro. He smacks his fist into his hand, his piggy eyes on me. "Halia says you got her juiced."

I wince. It may be the first time a Habeni accusing a Matalan of wrongdoing is true, but there's no time for this. How long will the watchers sleep? I've got to get that signal fire lit before they wake up.

"Speak up, Mucker," Agron snaps. "What'd you do to her?"

His eyes glitter in the pale light. The others close in, and I know speaking up won't help. They'll thrash me no matter what I say.

I curl my fists and ready for the fight.

"You're wrong," a nervous voice pipes up. Everyone swivels to see Blix, standing nearby, rigid and terrified. "I... I did it. I'm responsible, not Kai. It was me. If you're going to beat up anyone, beat me up."

Those last words tumble from his mouth in a terrified squeak, but it does the trick. The Habbies swarm around him like flappermoths on a bright light. Dipro starts barking questions. Blix catches my eye and jerks his head toward the alley. I nod my thanks and disappear, vowing to get my revenge on those bullies later.

I race across the grass between the garden and the fields toward the barn, casting a glance toward the house. The windows are lit. I imagine Meili sitting there, watching, waiting for my signal. Ayva's probably watching too, chewing her fingernails as she always does when she's nervous.

At the barn, Stitch is asleep in the hayloft above, snoring. I try not to make a sound as I remove the barrow, my shoulders hunched, moving inch by inch. The mother-humping wheel squeaks. Stitch snorts and cusses sleepily. I freeze, certain I'm cooked. A long tick passes, with no sound but the planthoppers in the meadow chirping in the night. Then, a booming snore that threatens to wake the cattle.

I can breathe once more. Stitch has dropped off again.

I'm not taking another chance. I lift the barrow up over my head and carry the klacking thing out of the barn. My aching arms strain against its weight. I make it to the orchard when I can't hold on any longer and the barrow drops with a thud.

I push it toward the garden at a teakslug's pace, cringing the whole way. The wheel keens low and slow, like a widow at a funeral. I won't miss this barrow, or the shit. Or even Stitch. I won't miss this squeaky wheel for anything. The cattle I'll miss. They're too dumb to get out of their own way, but they're sweet and trusting.

It seems to take days to reach the garden, but I finally get there. I scoop up the remains of some shattered end posts and dump them in the barrow with a clatter.

I look toward the kitchen, wondering if Meili can see me. She's really going to do this thing. I'd beseech the gods to keep her safe if I didn't have a solid feeling the gods don't give two humps what happens to us mere mortals.

We're on our own.

She's on her own.

I bend down and strike two stones together over the pile of wood, aiming for a spark, hoping for a flame. I bang the stones against each other until sweat beads on my forehead, with no luck. I grind my teeth, beyond aggravated.

"What're ya doing?"

I jerk up, dropping one of the stones. "Dageth's balls, Petra. Must you always be sneaking up on me?"

"Must you always be crabbing at me?" She puts on a mighty pout. "Don't think I don't know what yer at, Kai. Yer plotting a way out." She jerks her head toward the house. "With her."

I stiffen at the bitter way she says *her*. And the hard way she gazes at me.

Petra's been near whenever the subject of escape came up. She must've figured out our plan long ago. Has she alerted the watchers? Is Meili walking into a trap? Is that why I haven't seen Hup? My heart slams into my ribs. Is he waiting in the courtyard for Meili to come out?

Fury rolls through me like a raging tide. "What's your game, Petra?"

"No, Kai. It ain't like that." She steps back and holds up her hands. "Ever occur to you I might be of some help with what yer doing? The job might go faster if you let me give a hand."

I scowl. It's not in my nature to ask for help. Or to trust Petra or Blix or anyone else enough to let them help. To believe that Meili would help a piss-and-vinegar fueled slupa like me without wanting something in return. All my life I've focused on going it alone, never relying on anyone, never trusting anyone.

Maybe it's time I did.

I gust a heavy breath, surrendering. I hope I won't live to regret it. "Okay, you can help. But if this is a trick, if a single hair on Meili's head is harmed because of you, I promise you, I will not be kind. You get me?"

She swallows and nods.

"Good. In a few ticks, the power's going to drop. We can run. Escape. We're going north to where the pirates first brung us, trying to find a way home. You can go home, too, or wherever you want. You'll be free."

"Free." Her expression lights up with excitement and I regret my suspicions.

"Yeah, free." I fish in the pile of wood, trying to find the striking stone I dropped. "If I can get this klacking signal fire lit."

"That the only thing stopping us?" She holds up something silver. It's a pocket torch. "Liberated this from one of the watchers. Figured it'd come in handy someday." She flicks the wheel and blue flame dances. She touches it to the kindling and a fire bursts to life with a resounding *poof*. "Told you I could help."

I let out my breath. "By all the gods, Petra, you are amazing."

She closes the torch's lid with a snap and grins. "About time you figured that out."

Chapter 35

Meili

Waiting is the worst part.

Time seems to crawl by. I sit on the window seat, shucking the last of the season's ruck beans and willing the clock hands to move faster. Ayva darns stockings I think she's stitched before. Gwynn's at the table, watching Jinks play a card game. Bridgie shuffled off to bed a half hour ago. Varina takes advantage of her absence by resting in the rocker, her face turned to the frosty air pulsing from the temperature element.

The family should all be asleep by now. I peep out the window. The watchers should be asleep, too, and Kai's signal fire should be lit. Unless... Unless he's been caught. My stomach squeezes. I'm sure he's been caught, and the watchers are juicing him with no mercy, and it's all my fault.

"Meili, what *are* you doing?" Varina asks and I jump. "You've been pressing your nose to that windowpane all night."

"I have? I'm just... wondering if it'll rain. The rachee flattened everything in my garden. The plants need water to come back." I'm no longer surprised at how easily I lie.

"Of course it'll rain. It rains every blinking night." Varina turns back to the cool air.

Ellse comes over and tugs on my sleeve. I'm reluctant to leave the window but follow her to our sleeping chamber. A raggedy ball of cloth sits on her mat, stuffed full, the ends knotted together.

"Take Esse?" She clutches the makeshift bag to her chest.

An anvil of guilt presses down on me for not warning her of our scheme, but I'm impressed she figured it out. "Yes, of course," I say softly. "I wouldn't leave you behind. We're taking you, Bridgie and everyone."

"Vrina too?"

"Varina too." She frowns at that and I chuckle. "Listen, you can't say a word. Soon, there's going to be a big bang. I'll come get you and then we run, okay?"

She nods rapidly, like an excited bird pecking at a treat. "Then we run."

She reminds me so much of Lil that I choke up. Where is that little Matalan now? Are she and her brother Pyrr safe? I can't even bear to think of someone juicing Lil, her tiny body convulsing from the current. I shove the image away. One thing at a time. Get out of here first, then think about finding and freeing Lil and Pyrr.

I return to the window. Forgetting all about the ruck beans, I stare out, aching to see Kai's signal. A long while later, a fire ignites beyond the garden. A flicker at first then a flame that shoots sky high. Kai's barrow, going up in a literal blaze of glory.

I'm instantly on the move. I hurry to my cot and slide the blanket-wrapped incendiaries out from underneath. Fear shoots through me and I hold the blanket in hands so shaky I'm afraid I'll drop the package, proving Kai right by blowing myself to bits. Along with everyone else.

I can't let that happen. Won't let it. I pull in a breath and force myself calm.

"What's that?" Varina eyes me suspiciously as I speed through the kitchen. "Where are you going?"

"None of your business," I toss off and race into the hallway. Ayva and Gwynn rush up behind me.

"Wait," Ayva says. "We want to help."

I stare at them a precious few ticks. Ayva appears eager. Gwynn, terrified. I hold the deadly package gingerly, excuses tumbling through my mind. I definitely don't want their help, particularly Ayva. Kai will never forgive me if anything happens to her. I need some way to get rid of them.

"Okay, here's the plan. Go upstairs and drag something heavy across the door to block the way. If anyone's still awake up there, they're sure as sugar going to come downstairs to investigate when this thing goes off. You two have to make certain that doesn't happen. Got it?"

They nod and tear off down the hall and I don't waste another tick.

The air outside is oppressive, sticky. I'm instantly wet even though it isn't raining. It's as silent as the grave, except for the soft drone that comes from the power station. Frightened prickles crawl up my spine as I rush across the courtyard. Lights burn in the windows of the watchers' house, though no one seems to be stirring.

Kai's done it. He's knocked them all out.

I reach the shed and carefully set the package on the ground in front of the door. I unfold the blanket. The lovely stench of manure wafts upward. I guess I *do* still notice the smell. I hold my breath and pick up the modified juicer in my sweaty hands.

Kai's instructions were simple. Hold the device against the keypad and press the buttons for five ticks. I crouch and do as instructed, pressing one of the buttons. It beeps so loud it echoes off the courtyard walls.

Frickle. I have to press *both* buttons at the same time.

I hit reset, hold the device against the keypad and... The buttons are too far apart. My fingers can't stretch that way. Blix must've designed this for Kai's monstrous hands, not my annoyingly dainty little fingers. I'll have to use two hands. Perhaps I can hold it against the keypad with my elbow, then—

"Need help?" a voice whispers behind me.

I nearly jump out of my skin. I bite my lip to keep from crying out. "Ayva, I told you to stay inside."

"Don't give me that Habbie attitude. You need me."

"What about helping Gwynn?"

"She's okay. We both know you were trying to get rid of us. So, what can I do?"

I grumble. Kai will murder me, but the job will go easier and take less time if I have another pair of hands. I hand her the juicer, and she holds it against the keypad. She looks around for suspicious eyes as I press and hold the buttons then count five ticks.

"Duck," I cry and we both cringe, bracing for a bang.

Nothing happens. No pop, no boom or puff of smoke, just a whirr and a hiss and the door lock releases with a satisfying click. Ayva gurgles in delight and tucks the device into her apron string like a lawkeeper holstering his weapon.

"Thank the gods for Blix and his love of science," I say and pull the door open. The hinges object with a prolonged moan I'm sure can be heard two clicks away. Ayva puts her finger to her lips as if that will quiet the squeak.

I tug the door just wide enough for us to slip through. Ayva shoves the blanket aside and tries to pick up the incendiary but I push her away.

"Nothing doing. You don't touch a thing." I remove the device, leaving the blanket on the ground, and we slip inside.

Electricity buzzes everywhere, as if we've stepped into a honeycomb. The current tingles along my skin like a living thing. My zati vibrates.

On each side of a narrow aisle are rectangular metal boxes standing floor to ceiling. The boxes are comprised of grids, copper coils, rotors, knobs, and other devices that must take in the electricity from the central power plant and pump it throughout the compound. A temperature element chuffs out frosty air, keeping the machines from overheating. The metal floor is cold and slippery through the soles of my thin shoes.

Kai wasn't clear where to put the charge, so I circle the room, hunting for a likely spot.

"What's this?" Ayva points to a small plaque bolted to the wall. It appears to be an illustration of the power station, with each component labeled. A black line comes off the main illustration to another, smaller grid.

My heart sinks. "I think it means there's a backup system. You know, in case the main one goes down." I try not to panic. "We have one at home. Father had one put in two years ago, after the Rowlanites attacked the central grid." I trail my finger along the line. "It looks like it's buried not far from here. We'll have to hope the boomer's big enough to take that out too."

"Let's hope." The doubt in her voice echoes my own.

"This looks like a good place." I set the incendiary on the floor, dead center of the small room. "Now to find out if Blix knows what he's doing. This little device better turn everything off. There'll be pakao to pay if the power goes only *half* out. Okay, I'm going to set it." I look at Ayva. "You, out."

She opens her mouth to argue then snaps it shut. She leaves, but hovers in the doorway, watching. I turn the knob and press the switch. The number twenty flashes in the timer window, then nineteen, eighteen, seventeen...

I stare dumbly as the numbers count down. Is that it? It seems too easy. Seems like I'm forgetting something.

"Come on, Meili," Ayva yells, not even trying to keep her voice down.

That snaps me out of it. I run. Ayva's halfway to the house before I clear the building. I forgot the blanket outside the door and my feet get tangled in its folds. I trip and sprawl on the ground. My knees scrape, my palms slap against the mollystone walkway. Ayva stops, turns to come back and help.

"No. Go inside," I shout.

She does, watching me struggle with the blanket through the door's window. She looks terrified. I *am* terrified. I count down in my head... ten, nine, eight. Finally free, I scramble up and run. My feet seem not to hit the ground I move so fast. Ayva opens the door, hauls me inside, and slams it shut.

Not a tick too soon.

A violent, splintering *boom* rips through the night.

The entire east wing shudders, perhaps the whole house. As I duck, I see the power building's metal roof shoot into the sky. One wall bulges out, then crumbles. The door blasts across the courtyard and over the wall. The lights in the watchers' house and in the hallway behind us flicker, then go dark. The security floodlights wink out.

"Holy pakao," Ayva cries when we dare to raise our heads and look out through the shattered window.

My jaw drops. It worked. The power building is decimated. Fire licks out of the rubble. Black smoke coils upward like a snakevine come alive. The sissy fruit trees and the rosebush I hid behind weeks ago are also burning.

An alarm suddenly blares. Emergency lights pop on. A disembodied voice calmly announces, *Systems experiencing fatal error. All gates breached. Emergency system booting up. Power restored in twelve minutes.*

Twelve minutes? Ayva and I exchange alarmed glances. We've got to go.

Now.

Chapter 36

Meili

"What'd you do?" Jinks demands when we race back to the kitchen.

"We killed the juice. The fence is down. The watchers are asleep," I blurt excitedly. "We're running."

Varina leaps from the rocking chair, looking like a ghost in the harsh white of the emergency lights. "What? Why didn't you tell me?"

I ignore her and head for the door, snatching up Bridgie's heavy meat tenderizer on the way. Ayva races to our sleeping quarters, shouting for Gwynn to grab their bags. I swing the mallet at the door lock and it smashes to bits. The seal pops with a gasp. That's the easy part. The door slides open a fraction, then stops, as if there's something impeding it.

"Open this klacking thing," Kai growls from the other side.

I'm relieved to hear his voice, though not pleased at the way he bellyaches. "I'm trying." I thrust the mallet's handle into the crack and use it as a wedge. It snaps. Kai jams his fingers through the opening, grips the door's edge, and pulls to the side. I toss the mallet and pull too.

"Together," he yells through the small space. "Ready? Go."

I pull with all my might. The door gives a little but fights to close. It must be on some kind of spring. We yank again. The door slides open another fraction. There's a lot of cussing from Kai's side and a healthy amount from mine as well.

The warning claxon revs up again at a volume that nearly splits our eardrums. *Emergency systems booting up. Security gates restored in eleven minutes.*

"Pull. *Harder*," Kai shouts.

"This thing's as stubborn as you," I shout back, doubling my effort.

Someone shoves me aside. It's Jinks. He braces a foot against the jamb, grabs the door, and pulls. The door creeps open a bit more. I see Kai's mud-caked shoe against the outside jamb. His hands and fingers turn white from the strain of pulling.

"*Hurry.* Open it, you weak-livered imbeciles," Varina shrieks.

Ayva runs up, holding two bags, a blanket draped across her shoulders. "Gwynn's not here. She should be back by now. Something's wrong."

Behind her, Ellse clutches her own bag, quivering in distress, her eyes wide.

"Ayva, go find her. Be careful. Ellse, go and wake Bridgie. Tell her we're leaving. Varina, shut up."

Everyone moves. Varina shuts up. I swing back to the door. Kai's flashes me a grin through the small gap in the doorway.

The door jerks open, bit by bit. A hydraulic hiss marks every stubborn inch until, finally, it slides all the way open. Jinks and Kai clasp hands and cheer their success. Brief harmony, as Jinks pushes Kai aside and sprints out the door toward freedom.

Kai spares him a scowl before snapping back to me. His gaze sweeps over me as if tallying each part, making sure I'm all in one piece. I blush. Actually blush. After everything I just went through, I can be completely undone by one look from him.

I shove my missish flustering aside. "Kai. We don't have a lot of time."

"You don't say?" He steps inside and his gaze sweeps the kitchen. "Where's Ayva?"

"She went to look for Gw—"

A pop and the spring or latch snaps into place. The door shudders and begins to slide shut. Kai leaps into the doorway. Planting his feet firmly, he shoves his broad back against the door and reaches out, his arms rigid and straight, his hands pressed against the jamb on the opposite side, holding the klacking thing open like a human wedge.

"This thing's angry. Can't hold for long. Meili, get Ayva, get your stuff—"

His eyes widen. I pivot to follow his gaze. Ayva's backing into the kitchen. The bags she's holding hang limply by her sides. Something shambles in from the hallway. I gasp. *Two* somethings. Juning has his arm wrapped around Gwynn's middle—and he presses the sharp edge of a sword to her throat.

Emergency systems booting up. Security gates restored in ten minutes.

"Look what I found wandering upstairs." Juning grins like a demented demon. "A troci out of place. No, don't move, any of you. I might get nervous and cut her throat."

Ayva releases a strangled moan. I'm too terrified to move. Varina stares, a goggle-eyed statue near the sink. Kai cusses helplessly behind me. If he moves, the door snaps shut.

"Gotta say, I'm impressed," Juning says. "A shit-shoveler and a bunch of worthless females. You've done the impossible. Killed the power, knocked out the gates. Now you can walk away." He blinks and stifles a yawn. He must have some of the sleeping potion in his blood, but not enough. "Tell you what, I'll let you go. No hard feelings, no punishment. *If* you agree to my price."

I spot a paring knife Gwynn used earlier on the table. Its blade is duller than dull, but it's a weapon. If only I can grab it. "What do you mean, price?" I ask, trying to buy time.

"I'll let you all go, but I keep *her*." Juning shoves his fist into Gwynn's belly. She yelps in pain. "A fair price for your freedom, I think."

"No way, kutama." Ayva flings down her bags and balls her fists, ready to attack.

"Don't be stupid. You try to fight me and..." Juning slides the sword along Gwynn's neck, just above her zati. Ayva freezes. "That's better. Now, take my offer, all of you. Leave this beauty with me and run." He smirks. "Before the power's back and you're caught again."

"Go," Gwynn urges, tears in her eyes. "Just go, Ayva. Meili, you too."

"No, wait." I risk a step forward, creeping closer to the knife. "Sir Juning, please. Let her go, let them go. I'll stay."

A sound like a rachee's howl erupts from Kai behind me, straining mightily to keep the door open.

Juning's eyes narrow. "You'll trade yourself for her? Why should I trust you? After you drugged me at the ball? Tried to drug me tonight?" I must look surprised, because he scoffs. "I'm not as dense as you think. Drink up, you said. So pleased with yourself, I knew something was in my drink. Just like a female, you couldn't resist getting the final word."

"I'm a slupa that way." The knife's within reach. "What's your answer? Do we have a bargain? Me for Gwynn."

Bridgie stumbles into the kitchen, blinking sleepily, Ellse clinging to her skirt. "What—? Sir Juning! What *are* you doing?"

All pakao breaks loose. I dive for the knife. Kai shouts and Bridgie screams. Ayva lunges at Juning. A sudden, sickening *crack* cuts through the chaos. The sword clatters to the floor. Juning sprawls next to it, moaning and clutching his head. Blood spurts from his temple, trickling down the side of his face like a crescent moon.

No one moves, but we all gape in stunned silence. At Varina. She'd smacked Juning in the head with a frying pan.

Emergency systems powering up. Security gates restored in nine minutes.

Varina throws the bloody pan to the floor with a clang. She straightens her skirt and lifts her chin. "I'm leaving," she declares then ducks under Kai's outstretched arms and disappears into the night.

Kai and I exchange a brief, somewhat hysterical look. Ayva snatches Gwynn into a tight, breath-stealing hug, then she gathers up their bags, and together they hurry to the door.

"Go with Petra," Kai says as they slip past. I see his Adsullatan friend hovering outside. "Head for the forest beyond the graveyard." He looks at me. "Meili, let's go."

"Wait. My bag."

"Hurry." The door shoves against him. His arms tremble with the strain of keeping it open.

I grab my bag and rush back to the kitchen, then over to Bridgie where she kneels on the floor next to Juning.

"Meili, *move*." Kai's voice isn't the least bit friendly.

"Bridgie, come with us." I help her to stand. "We'll go back to Hephas. You can see your folks. Climb the Purple Mountain again."

She looks at me with glazed eyes, her pupils huge. I think I gave her too much sleeping powder. "There's nothing here for you now. Run with us."

Kai shouts at me again. Ellse plucks at my skirt. I signal for her to go.

"You'd better run, Red," Juning says from the floor. Blood pulses down his face onto his spangled coat. "Time's running out."

"Bridgie?" I hold out my hand. "Don't you want to go home?"

She nods and reaches for me—then snaps me into a crushing hold.

Emergency systems powering up. Security gates restored in eight minutes.

Bridgie shakes me like a rag doll. I lose my grip on the knife. It tings to the floor. "Watchers, watchers," she shrieks against my ear. "Stop this troci!"

I kick her and claw her arms and squirm and twist and struggle. A futile fight. Bridgie's strong from years of kneading dough and lifting heavy pans. She has me pinned. She lifts me off the floor and drags me back toward the hallway.

Ellse tugs on her arm, wailing for her to stop. Bridgie flings her off and she spanks hard against the wall.

Kai's not cussing anymore. He watches in hopeless agony. He's losing his fight with the door. He's got to go, or he'll be trapped too.

"Go," I mouth to him. He shakes his head. "Go, you stubborn Mucker," I yell.

His eyes spit fire. I blink, and the last thing I see before Bridgie pulls me around the corner into the hallway is the door snap shut.

Kai's gone.

Emergency systems booting up. Security gates restored in seven minutes.

Chapter 37

Kai

THE DOOR NEARLY SLICES my head off, but I skit out of the way in time.

Dageth's hairy elbows on a cracker, why won't that redhead ever do what I tell her? Why did she waste precious ticks trying to get the housekeeper to run with us? She's soft-hearted, always has been. That's her weakness. And it's proven to be her undoing.

I must be soft-hearted too. Soft-headed, more like, to jump *inside* the kitchen, with freedom so close at hand. I could've gone. I got what I wanted. Ayva is free. I could've run with her, made our way to safety, eventually seek out a way home.

But I couldn't abandon Meili. After all we went through, all the risks we took, all the risks *she* took, there's no power in the galaxy that could get me to leave without Meili Bengough by my side. It would break me.

I hear Juning's voice. That prince among pigs has managed to regain his footing and has followed Meili and the housekeeper around the corner.

"The Matalan could've fought for you," he says with a cackle. "But the coward ran, wouldn't risk a whisker to save you."

Surely Meili doesn't believe that kutama. After all this time, she should know I'd never do that. At least, I hope.

I bolt across the kitchen, skirting the blood that slicks the floor. I skid to a stop at the hall opening to peer around the corner.

Horror fills me to the core. Bridgie squeezes her arms around Meili's waist and drags her up the hallway. Juning advances on them, past the little troci, Ellse I think her name is. She's curled up against the wall, moaning. Juning's sword glints in the emergency lights as he waves it menacingly. His fine coat is torn and spattered with blood. More blood cakes on his face and mats his hair. His mouth stretches in a ghoulish grin, enjoying the pursuit.

Meili fights her captor, I'm proud to see. She howls and spits and calls the housekeeper vile names I'm shocked to hear spill from a proper Habeni's lips. She digs her nails into Bridgie's arms, gouging her face, her teeth snapping, trying to bite any bit of flesh she can reach.

"Give the wench to me, Bridgie." Juning beckons with his sword. The housekeeper mewls an objection, and he snarls, "Do as you're bid."

His sword slashes the air, too close to Meili's face. I'm on him in a tick. I race up from behind and curl my arm around his throat, squeezing with all my might. He gurgles in surprise and the sword slips from his grasp. It clatters to the floor. Meili busts free of the housekeeper's hold and kicks it away. Bridgie wails.

Juning rallies. He elbows me in the side, repeatedly and hard, shoving me back, struggling to break my hold on his neck. He drops down and wrenches free. He spins, choking, gasping for air. He dives for the sword. His mistake. My fist meets his nose as he lunges and it's all over. He lurches back and falls on his ass with a crashing thump.

"You didn't run," Meili cries, flying up to me. "You were free. Why didn't you run?"

"You pick now to nag me? For all the gods, Meili. Of course I didn't run—"

She shuts me up with a kiss. A kiss as bright and fresh as the dawn. I want to wrap myself in that kiss, sink into her lips forever.

Juning has other ideas. He rolls over, snatches his sword, and rises like a beast of the underworld, roaring mad and with murder on his mind.

We've got to go.

Emergency systems powering up. Security gates restored in six minutes.

I yank the little troci to her feet. She's shaking but seems okay. I turn to Meili. "Which way?"

"Uh." She tosses a frantic glance toward the door beyond Juning and Bridgie, at the end of the hall. The small window looks out onto the courtyard and the fire that blazes within. "They're blocking that way. This way."

She scoops up a bulky cloth bag, swings around and runs. I'm hot on her heels, squeezing Ellse's hand and tugging her behind me.

"Wait." Meili slows and picks up a piece of metal glinting in the light—a small knife—and drops it into her apron. Then she runs faster.

"Where're we going?" I ask.

"Upstairs. Through the house."

We race upward and reach the first floor landing, popping out into a grand hallway. Old man Forseti, the lord of the manor, slumps like a sack of taters in a plush chair, snoring happily. Ellse's fist pounds my shoulder. I glance back. Juning flies up the stairs behind us.

"Culbana." I slam the door and push my bulk against it. Juning cusses loudly on the other side. The knob jiggles furiously, followed by thumps as he tries to shove it open.

"Wait." Meili drops her bag and darts to a thick-legged sideboard against the opposite wall. "Ellse, quick. Help me."

Ellse doesn't hesitate. It's a struggle but they scrape the table across the hall, knickknacks toppling and lampshade fringe dancing. When they're close enough, I reach and grab the table's end. In a tick, we shove it against the door.

"That'll slow him down," Meili says. "But he knows his way around troci territory. He'll find another exit." She snatches up her bag again and points to a door down the hall. "The library. It's the fastest route to the rear of the house, where the others are waiting for us."

Nodding, I grab her arm, she grabs Ellse's, and we're off again.

I yank open the library door and lead the way inside. A single emergency light shines in here, blanketing the furniture and bookshelves in a pale glow.

I dart to the sole window and fling the desk aside like it's kindling. It tips and crashes to the floor, scattering paper and writing implements. I wrench open the window and bash out the screen. I give Ellse a boost and she hurtles through.

Meili's turn. I swing around and growl.

She's stopped dead.

Emergency systems powering up. Security gates restored in five minutes.

<h1 style="text-align:center">CHAPTER 38</h1>

<h2 style="text-align:center">Meili</h2>

"WAIT," I CRY.

"Will you stop saying that and move?"

Kai's voice has gone past annoyed into raging fury territory, but I have to stop when I spot Lady Netti slumped on one of the chairs. I rush over. Netti's book is open and face down on her chest. It slowly rises and falls as she takes sluggish breaths.

Her eyelids flutter open. I think she recognizes me. "Am I going to die?" she asks, her voice slurred.

My heart wrenches. She's the only person I regret doing this to. The only one of this awful family I have even a hint of feeling for. Pity yes, who wouldn't feel sorry for Netti, having to face her mother's accusing grief every waking minute? But I also feel empathy. We have a sort of kinship, both of us the sore thumb on a healthy hand in our mothers' eyes.

I touch her shoulder. "You'll be fine. You'll simply have a good sleep."

A gentle smile curves her lips, and she drifts off again. I hope she dreams of the worlds she finds in her books.

"Meili, move," Kai commands and this time I listen.

In a flash, we're on the balcony. The stones are warm and damp with humidity, the air heavy. It'll rain soon. We race toward the steps then I stop with a gasp. Is the power really off? Everywhere?

I reach out gingerly, feeling for the invisible barrier, bracing for a blast of juice.

"It's off," Kai says. "You succeeded." He proves it by running down the steps, then back up. He holds out his hand. "My lady?"

A crash as Juning flings open the ballroom doors and lurches onto the balcony. No more hesitation. I take Kai's hand and we flee. My hair flies behind me, my bag bounces, the delicate plants inside getting jostled and probably squashed. We round the corner to the back of the house. We skid to a stop. I let out a shriek.

It's as if a fireworks display has gone horribly wrong. The entire compound is burning.

Emergency systems powering up. Security gates restored in four minutes.

All the buildings are ablaze. Part of the barn's roof has collapsed and flames roar through the gaping hole straight up to the sky. The outbuildings burn, and even the sissy fruit trees are on fire. The fruit still hanging on the branches roasts from the heat. Black smoke billows everywhere, making me choke.

I'll claim credit only for the fire in the power station. This carnage must be the doing of the now free workers, inspired by anger, or a parting gift to his lordship before they run toward freedom. It says something that no one's dared to set fire to the manor house.

"The cattle," Kai cries and suddenly dashes toward the blazing barn.

I chase after him, Ellse in tow, calling for him to stop. I catch up and grab his arm. "They're okay. Look. Stitch, or someone, saved them."

Saved them from the fire, anyway. Not from their own panic. Spooked by the flames and the noise, the cattle crash about willy-nilly. Some dash across the meadow. Some stampede through the fields, crushing greenie stalks and young plants. Some have stumbled over the remains of my fence into the garden and can't get out again. They cry out in terror and confusion.

Kai looks stricken. I fear he'll try to round up each and every one of them. I suppose he's grown close to the funny-looking beasts, tending them and shoveling their shit all these months, but Juning is behind us, and the clock is counting down. We don't have the time.

As if to remind us, the claxon clangs another warning. *Emergency systems powering up. Security gates restored in three minutes.*

We're off again, aiming toward the troci graveyard and the forest beyond. Easier to disappear among the thick forest of pinum trees than escaping through the meadow or into the hills, Kai says.

We close in on the garden. We have to slow not to stumble over the debris scattered everywhere, including the power shed's roof, hurtled this far in the explosion.

A dark figure I think is Cresp staggers out of the watchers' house and into the smoke. He lunges for a troci carrying a burning stick. Cresp misses and the troci hurls the stick onto the roof of the cottage before darting away.

I gasp. I hope the roof doesn't catch. There might be some watchers in there and I don't want them hurt. I just want to escape, not kill anyone. Or *anything*, I think, as one of the terrified cattle thunders by us.

We pass the blazing troci houses and have to slow even more. The smoke is so thick and heavy we can barely breathe. The heat from the fires is searing. I see the graveyard in the distance, lit by the flicker of the flames, but the woods beyond that is dark. Hopefully, Gwynn and Ayva made it past the chaos and are waiting for us there.

Kai crouches, as if seeking fresher air closer to the ground. I follow his lead and creep behind him, seized by a coughing fit. Ellse's hand in mine is slippery with sweat, but I hold tight.

A hulking figure bursts out of the smoke, as if ejected by the bonfire.

It's Hup.

Emergency systems powering up. Security gates restored in two minutes.

Hup's tunic is singed and his expression twisted in fury. He howls, a scream of rage like a feral beast. He lurches toward us, pointing his useless juicer and stabbing the controls.

I tug Kai's arm. "The potion didn't take. He must need a double dose."

Kai grimaces. "Noted for next time. Come on, we'll go around the buildings."

We turn back but jolt to a stop to see Juning racing toward us. Hup draws closer. Ellse wails. My heart sinks in defeat. We're cooked. This is how it ends. The power will be back on soon. We'll be caught once more. They'll juice us till smoke pours out of our ears. If they don't kill us.

I meet Kai's gaze, wracked with guilt and regret. It's my fault he's trapped here too. "I'm sorry, Kai. I wish you had run."

"Dageth's breath, Meili. Don't you know by now I'd *never* run? I'd never leave you." His eyes blaze at me, as intense as the fire. "I'm in love with you."

My heart soars and all the flappermoths in creation dance in my belly. Even at a time like this. "Oh, Kai. I lo—"

"Isn't this a pretty scene?"

Juning's voice, too close behind me. I spin around to face him. He gasps for breath, his face bloody, smoke-stained, and furious, as grotesque as the masks the pirates wore when we were caught all those months ago.

He licks his grimy lips. "A pity I'm going to cut this drama short."

Hup chuckles. Juning jabs the air with his sword, taunting us.

"Fight, Meili," Kai says. He moves so we're back to back, with Ellse protected between us. "If you have even a lick of fondness for me, then don't let my death be easy. Dig deep. There's a Matalan warrior somewhere in your blood. Find her and *fight*."

By all the gods, the pirate captain was right. Kai's got a heart as fierce as a lion's. His bravery inspires me. I snatch the paring knife out of my apron pocket and brace for battle. Firelight glints off the stubby blade.

Juning sneers at my pitiful weapon. He raises his sword and charges at me, just as Hup's huge paws close around Kai's neck.

Emergency systems powering. Security gates restored in one minute.

Chapter 39

Meili

It's over in a tick.

Hup's chokehold on Kai suddenly loosens. He wavers, like a tree buffeted by hurricane winds. His eyes roll back in his head, and he collapses. The earth seems to tremble as his mountainous body hits the ground.

The sleeping potion worked, it just took longer to tame this big beast.

At the same instant, I duck and Sir Juning's sword slashes past my ear. He teeters, and I put my physical training to good use for a change. I loop my foot around his leg, jerk hard, and we both fall. Juning hits the dirt. I bounce on top of him. Ellse stomps on his wrist then kicks the sword out of reach.

Kai's there in a flash. He yanks me off Juning, sets me on my feet, and crushes me to him, enveloping me in his strong arms, holding me tight. But only for a moment. He releases me with a strangled cuss.

I follow his startled gaze to see the paring knife—sticking out of Sir Juning's gut. I somehow stabbed him when I fell. He doesn't move. Blood soaks his spangled coat.

Gods and goddesses. I've killed him.

Emergency systems powering up. Security gates restored in thirty ticks... Twenty-nine... Twenty-eight...

"Get back here, slag. I'll murder you!"

Or perhaps I haven't. Juning's enraged bellows follow us as we link hands and, with Kai in the lead propelling us forward, we race past the graveyard toward our goal.

Twenty... Nineteen...

Ahead, people flee into the forest. I see Ayva, Gwynn, Varina, and Ullr beyond the barrier, illuminated by the fire. They wave and shout at us to hurry.

Sixteen... Fifteen...

My feet pound the ground. My lungs burn. I have no air left, but I barrel forward. Ellse clings to my hand, keening. Will we make it? I glance at Kai's sweat-streaked and oh-so-kissable face. We *have* to make it.

Eleven... Ten... Nine...

I leap over some tall grass and the orange line marking the barrier like a hurdler in a race for her life. I'm engulfed by Gwynn and Ayva in a bone-crunching hug. I pull in great gulps of air, then stop breathing altogether when I see Kai dash back *inside* the perimeter. He aims toward a lump on the ground some twenty feet away.

"Kai, what're you doing?" Ayva shrieks.

I want to shriek too but can't even do that. I can only watch as the ticks slip by.

Five... Four... Three... Two...

Kai snatches up a cloth carry pouch. It bulges with provisions. He arcs around without even slowing, running back so fast he's a blur. The countdown reaches *one*. The claxon strikes a last, solemn peal.

Then, *Systems restored.*

The current swells up from the ground like an angry wave. We're knocked back by the surge. My zati clamps, squeezing my throat. Security lights pop on all over the compound and I'm nearly blinded. The electrical sting fades. My vision clears. Ellse and

Gwynn help Ayva up from the ground. Blix crouches by Varina, who coughs and moans in pain but is very much alive.

And free.

My blood seems to still in my veins. Are we all free? One person is missing. I scan frantically for Kai. Please, gods, tell me he made it in time.

"Over here," a voice calls.

I rush toward the sound and find him, on his back on the ground like an upended turtle. His hair's tangled, his expression dazed, and smoke curls up from the soles of his shoes, burned by the electrical surge as he jumped through the rebooting fence.

He leaps up, giving me the widest, most welcome grin I've ever seen.

"Kai ObDen," I say, my voice filled with every bit of joy and happiness I feel. "How could I ever have fallen in love with such a loopy Matalan?"

I get my answer as he pulls me into his arms and kisses me.

CHAPTER 40

Kai

THE NIGHTLY RAIN BEGINS as soon as we enter the forest.

The downpour doesn't slow us down. We all know we need to put as much distance between us and Mollystone Manor as we can before morning. The lights of the Forsetis' compound fade and even the flames licking the sky are swallowed by the night and the clouds as we hustle away.

The trees form a leaky curtain over our heads, blocking some of the rain and all trace of light. Our surroundings become as dark as ink. I shift the bag I risked my life for and pull out the torch Blix found. The beam's a pinprick in the darkness, but good enough to guide our way.

Meili and I take the lead of our ragtag group. Ayva and Gwynn are behind us. Blix and the others trudge along after them. Ullr's at the rear, shepherded by Ellse. I don't know what happened to Petra. I hope she's on her way home, or somewhere folks will be kind to her.

"It's not as bad as all that, is it?" Meili says. "We're free. We escaped. Why are you frowning?"

I turn my gaze on her. Raindrops dribble down her cheeks and off her nose. I lighten up, looking at her. She loves me. Something I didn't dare hope and now it's fact. She loves me.

"Sure, we got out, but we've got new troubles to face. The rachee. The other troci that swarm the forest now. We have provisions, they likely don't. They're a threat. We gotta find a way to ditch these zatis. We've been exposed to that klacking fever. And don't forget the Forsetis. We're valuable to them, they'll send people looking for us. Sir Juning might come looking for *you*."

I let that hang. In the distance, a rachee roars, and Meili shudders.

"You really know how to sweet talk a gell," she says. "I didn't mean to stab him, you know."

I laugh softly. "If you meant to stab him, I think you would've got closer to his heart."

"He doesn't have a heart."

I laugh again and take her hand. "I'm not trying to scare you. I just want you to remember what we're up against. But we're gonna face this together. We'll all get through this, even that whiny one." I jerk my head to Varina behind us. She's been crabbing since we set out. "We all get through, or none of us do."

She looks down at my hand and squeezes. "Is that a promise?"

"I promise. A Matalan is as good as his word."

We walk on, holding hands in the rain. Matalan and Habeni joined in common purpose.

Author's Note

Thanks for reading THE NASCENT BLOOM Book1: Caught. I hope you enjoyed Kai and Meili's adventure. If you did, please help others find this story by spreading the word and by leaving a review. You can find more about me and my books at www.eviekelley.com.

Kai and Meili will be back in THE NASCENT BLOOM Book 2: Running. Now free, Kai, Meili, and their friends take a perilous trek across an unforgiving landscape, facing new challenges and old enemies in their quest to return home.

https://www.eviekelley.com/

Acknowledgements

THE NASCENT BLOOM series came to life through many sessions at my kitchen table, numerous cups of tea, and the dedication, diligence, and gentle prodding of my friend Jenny Applegate. The story took on a less gelatinous shape thanks to the numerous contest judges who read the early versions of Kai and Meili's journey and provided valuable feedback, as well as the stellar support of my first readers Katherine Decker, Jess Collette, and the inimitable Suzanne Turner.

Thanks also to my family, my author friends Jean M. Grant, Sharon Healy-Yang, Kari Lemor, and Barbara Wallace for keeping me on track, to Cori Deyoe for her cheerful cheerleading for this book, and to Alice Jerman for those crucial two words of advice she gave me that I took to heart—more kissing.

Books by Janet Raye Stevens

The Beryl Blue Adventures in Time
Beryl Blue, Time Cop
It's Been A Long, Long Time
Every Time We Say Goodbye
The Suitcase: A Beryl Blue Time Travel Short
also available in audiobook
Time Travel Suspense
The Titanic Time Heist
WWII Historical Suspense
A Moment After Dark
Romantic Suspense with a Supernatural Twist
The Fateful Knight
Mystery & Suspense
Clues & Chills: New England Stories of Mystery & Murder
The Vanishing Volume: An Emily Applegate Spinster Librarian
Mystery
Coming Soon
Indiana Jones meets Romancing the Stone—in space!
Kilroy Was Here: Adventure on Abergin
a romantic sci-fi adventure

About the Author

If she can't live in the 1970s or a galaxy far, far away, Evie Kelley figures she might as well write about them. Evie scribbles angsty Young Adult Sci-Fi and stories set in the era of mood rings, platform shoes and the eternal debate of who's cuter, Starsky or Hutch.

Evie also writes WWII-set historical mysteries, suspense, and romantic time travel adventures as Janet Raye Stevens. Visit Janet at www.janetrayestevens.com.